THE KILLING BAY

Also by Chris Ould and available from Titan Books

The Blood Strand
The Fire Pit (February 2018)

THE KILLING BAY

A FAROES NOVEL

CHRIS OULD

TITAN BOOKS

The Killing Bay
Print edition ISBN: 9781783297061
E-book edition ISBN: 9781783297078

Published by Titan Books
A division of Titan Publishing Group Ltd
144 Southwark Street, London SE1 0UP

First edition: February 2017
10 9 8 7 6 5 4 3 2 1

A CIP catalogue record for this title is available from the British Library.

Printed in the USA.

For me mam,
At last, and with love

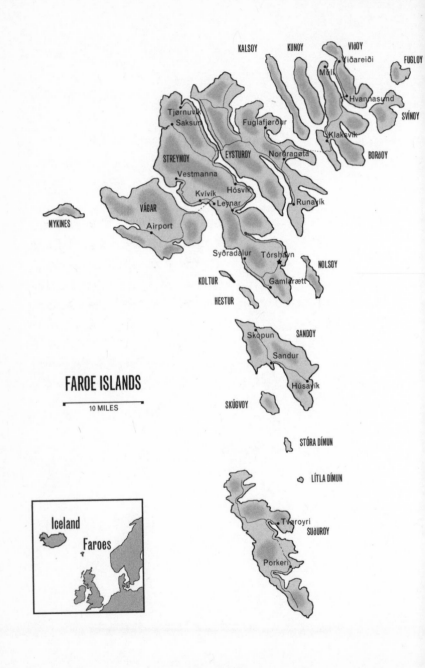

FAROE ISLANDS

10 MILES

FAROESE PRONUNCIATION

THE FAROESE LANGUAGE IS RELATED TO OLD NORSE AND Icelandic and is spoken by fewer than eighty thousand people worldwide. Its grammar is complicated and many words are pronounced far differently to the way they appear to an English-speaker. As a general rule *ø* is a "uh" sound; *v* is pronounced as w; *j* as a y, and the *Ð* or *ð* is usually silent, so Fríða would be pronounced Free-a. Hjalti is pronounced "Yalti".

The word *grind* (pronounced "grinned") is Faroese for a school of pilot whales, but is also used generically to refer to the whale drive and associated activities.

PRELUDE

HE WORKED ON HIS KNEES NOW, AS IF PRAYING. DARKNESS and rain; darkness and pain – from his back, from his fingers, from all over. Sweating and hot, working blind: as good as blind. The yellow light from the torch was so feeble it lit only the grass a hand's length in front of it.

The rocks were heavy: rough basalt, flecked with green. Abrading his fingers and nails as he scrabbled them free then heaved them aside. It was harder now that he had reached the lowermost stones. Over years – decades – they had grown into the earth; or the earth had grown into them, unwilling to give them up. He should have brought tools. But he had only a torch and the vodka.

Coming here in darkness had been instinctive. Something held silent and hidden this long couldn't be exposed in the light. It still demanded the ritual of secrecy, even in its uncovering. He needed the darkness and the vodka to cover his fear.

Another stone broke free. He rocked back with the shock of its release and let it fall to the side and roll down the slope. He panted, half sobbing. How much more could there be?

How much more could he do? He was weak, he knew that. Weak-willed and weak of body – more now than ever. It was only his fear that kept him going. Fear was all he had left.

For a minute, then longer, he didn't have the strength to raise his chin from his chest. He felt sick and hollow: a shell, eaten up from the inside. Eaten up, eaten away.

How much more?

He reached for the torch; brought it up, shook it, and was rewarded, he thought, by a faintly brighter light.

Thrusting it forward he played the glow over the rocks, into a hollow, tried to make sense of the shadows it made.

And then he recoiled with an exclamation of shock. Fumbled the torch, dropped it; felt his heart racing. Smooth roundness, mottled with dirt. Not rock. Bone.

She was there.

At the grave there was stillness and nothing to see within the circle of family black. The pastor's voice fluctuated on the wind, but he was twenty yards away and even if the sound had carried clearly all I'd have understood was the tone.

On the far side of Skálafjørður patches of sunlight came and went, daubing and shifting over the distant hillsides. My eye was drawn by the movement, following the light as it picked out the scattered dots of houses in a place I couldn't name; then drawn again by the distant movement of a car on the shoreline road, glinting. It was that kind of day: one of the bright ones when the rain has passed and you can have a fresh start.

Before I'd left England I'd said that I wouldn't come here to stand by a graveside. It hadn't been my intention, but there again I was pretty sure that dying hadn't been Signar Ravnsfjall's intention either – not if he'd been aware enough to think about it after his penultimate stroke.

Even if intention and result are two different things, I'd stayed true to my word: I was not by the graveside. That was for family. He'd been my father in name only – not even that – and to remain at this distance seemed about right.

And then the breeze shifted and it was all done. Signar Ravnsfjall was in the ground and beside the grave the mourners were released from their stillness. I cast a last look and then moved away.

The church at Glyvrar stood above a slope that ran down to the waters of the fjord, choppy and restless. The building wasn't one of the traditional Faroese churches, with tarred clapboard walls and grass on the roof. Instead it had the look of architectural thinking – solid white walls, with a square tower and steep-angled roofs nested together. The car park beside it put me in mind of an out-of-town shopping centre. It was full now. The great and the good had turned out in force to send Signar Ravnsfjall on his way.

My half-brother Magnus Ravnsfjall found me about ten minutes later as I stood by the car. It must have taken some determination to do that, given the number of people still clustered round the church. They were in no hurry to leave until news and views had been passed and chewed over: it's the Faroese way. No hurry at all.

I watched Magnus exchange a few words with a cluster of smartly dressed men near the gates of the churchyard, but he clearly didn't want to linger. After nods and a few words he moved on.

I'd bummed a cigarette from one of the same men a few minutes earlier, but now I trod it out and went forward to meet my half-brother. And for a moment it struck me as odd that he could still have such a resemblance to the man they'd just buried, as if Signar's death should have lessened the physical similarity between father and son. It hadn't though, and I guessed that Magnus had probably inherited the mantle of Signar's business concerns, to go with his genes.

"Will you come with us now to the house?" Magnus asked when he stopped in front of me. "It will be only family and close friends. My mother doesn't want more, but she would like to meet you."

I shook my head. "*Nei, men takk fyri*. I don't think it's the best day for introductions, do you? Besides, if Kristian's there…"

Whatever Sofia Ravnsfjall's reasons for wanting to meet me, I couldn't see Kristian being thrilled by my presence. He was my half-brother, too, but I knew him much better and because of that I doubted he'd want me around. His wounds would still be too raw.

Magnus understood what I meant, but for a moment he seemed undecided, as if still under some imperative. In the end, though, he nodded. "Perhaps in a day or two, then. You're not leaving yet?"

"No, not yet."

"Okay." It seemed to satisfy him. "There are also some details from our father's testament – the will – that we should discuss."

I couldn't guess what sort of details those could be. "Sure, if you need to," I said. "Give me a call."

"Thank you." He said it as if I'd granted a favour. Then, for a moment, he was distracted by the view across the sound.

"It's a good place to be, isn't it?" he said.

Better if you were above ground, instead of below it. But I didn't say that. He'd lost his father and I knew they'd been close.

"Yeah, a good spot," I said.

He drew himself back to the moment. "Okay then," he said. "I will call you. Thank you for coming."

We shook hands and he moved back towards the church passing Fríða, my cousin and, for the last week, also the provider of a roof over my head. She knew where I'd be and didn't have to search. Today was the first time I'd seen her wearing a skirt and heels – all formal black – and they suited her. With her blonde hair up in some kind of knot she looked effortlessly stylish and when she arrived at my side she put her arm lightly through mine.

"Will you come to the house?" she asked. "My father will take us."

I liked Jens Sólsker, her father, but I shook my head. "Magnus just asked, but I don't think so."

She assessed that for a moment, then said, "Okay, I understand. You had better take the car then. My father will give me a lift later."

"Are you sure?"

"Yeh, of course." Ever the pragmatist. She held out the keys and looked at me as if assessing the damage, or lack of it. "You'll be okay?"

I nodded. "I'll go for a walk," I said.

"Okay," she said, then she gave me a small hug before extracting her arm. "Safe home, then."

"You, too."

A little before nine and still a couple of hours from the end of the late shift, Officer Annika Mortensen passed the multi-coloured lights in the Norðoyatunnilin – the grotto, as she always thought of it. Red, green and blue floodlights shone up the rock walls and across the roof of the road tunnel to mark the deepest point under the sea, halfway between Eysturoy and Borðoy.

Annika was heading for Klaksvík to meet up with Heri Kalsø for a coffee and hotdog at the Magn petrol station: hardly the most glamorous of locations, but convenient enough. A bit like their relationship, she thought, and then immediately chastised herself. It was an unkind assessment, especially because she knew it wasn't one Heri would share.

There was little traffic in the tunnel and Annika kept her speed at a steady eighty up the incline, half listening to an REM song on the radio. Then the tunnel ended and she emerged into the night. Up ahead she saw three or four cars on the shoulder of the opposite lane, just past the first curve of the road. A couple of people were looking into a car that was pressed up against the embankment just beyond the junction with Mækjuvegur.

Annika assessed the situation, then slowed. She let an oncoming car go past, then switched on the blue roof bar lights and crossed the carriageway, pulling up in front of the first car; a VW Polo with its nearside front tyre down in the mud. Beside it a man in a Föroyar Bjór bomber jacket had opened the driver's door and was leaning inside; an older man was peering over his shoulder.

"Hey," Annika said as she approached. "What's happened?"

"Don't know," the older man said. "I was following him about fifty metres behind and he just drove off the road."

"How fast was he going?"

"Not very. About forty maybe. I had to slow down."

The man in the Föroyar Bjór jacket stood away from the door now to let Annika see. She moved forward and bent down to the driver, but the smell of alcohol and unwashed body told her as much as his lolling head. He was well into his sixties, greying hair down over his collar and a face grizzled with a grey beard where it wasn't streaked with dirt.

"Hey, hey, can you hear me?" she asked, putting a hand on the shoulder of the man's greasy tweed jacket. "Are you okay?"

No response. His clothes were muddy and wet, especially the knees of his trousers, Annika noticed, and there was a bottle of vodka on the passenger seat, uncapped and empty.

Annika considered, then pinched the man's earlobe, hard, between her thumb and index fingernail.

It did the trick. The old man roused with a snort and a swatting motion from his hands, as if trying to fend off a fly.

"Wha— Where's this? I don... Where?"

"Talk to me, please." Annika's tone was insistent. "Are you hurt?"

For a moment the man tried to focus. "She... she wa' dead... I need to... Not me to..."

He trailed off into incomprehensible mumbling and his head lolled again. Annika frowned. As drunk as a halibut, as her gran used to say. Not an ambulance job though. She straightened up from the car.

"He's pissed again, right?" the man in the Föroyar Bjór jacket said.

"Again? Do you know him?"

"Sure, that's old Boas," the man said. "Boas Justesen. He lives near my sister in Fuglafjørður. He took to the bottle when he lost his job in the 1980s – hasn't put it down since."

The name seemed vaguely familiar to Annika, which wasn't saying a lot: it was harder *not* to know people around here. Something about his wife dying? Maybe. It didn't matter.

"Will you give me a hand to move him?" she asked the man. "Just as far as my car."

By the time Annika had secured Boas Justesen's car, turning off the lights and locking the doors, the man himself was slumped across the back seat of her patrol car snoring. There was also a powerful smell of urine. Annika opened her window and switched on the fan.

There was no point driving Justesen to Tórshavn to be charged: he was too drunk. Instead Annika called the station and arranged to take him directly to the holding cells in Klaksvík; something she would have had to do anyway now that Tórshavn's own cells had been closed. Even arrestees from the capital ended up being driven the seventy-five kilometres to Klaksvík for holding. It made no sense and wasted everyone's time, but there it was. At least this time she was only five minutes away.

When Annika drew up in the parking lot outside the station Heri Kalsø was waiting. He'd heard her call to control and was pleased to have the opportunity to come and lend a hand, manhandling Boas Justesen out of the car and as far as the cells.

Ever since the incident at Kollafjørður when Sámal Mohr had been decapitated, Annika seemed to have put aside the fact that she had ever been mad with Heri; at least, she hadn't mentioned it again, and it had been more than a week since the incident. Heri wasn't sure if this was because of the way he'd reacted at the accident scene – by taking over and getting Annika away – or whether Annika's forgiveness would have come anyway. He wasn't foolish enough to ask, though. The burnt child fears the fire, and he'd learned his lesson. No, things were back to normal, and it was better to leave it at that. He'd even started to think again about asking Annika to move in with him. It fell short of a proposal of marriage, but that might be too much, he'd decided. The first thing was to gauge her reaction. They'd been together for over a year. Time for a change of gear, surely.

* * *

Once Boas Justesen had been booked and deposited in a cell Annika decided to put off cleaning the back of her car until they'd had coffee and something to eat. They took Heri's car for the short drive to the Magn station and Annika sat in the passenger seat.

"I've applied to join CID," she said as Heri negotiated the parking lot to the road. The words just came out. She had no why. Perhaps because it was dark.

"Yeh? That's great," Heri said, glancing at her. "You should. You'll do well at it, especially if Hjalti takes you under his wing. Which he will."

Annika shook her head. "I don't mean here: I've applied to Copenhagen."

"Copenhagen? Why?"

"Because they have a wider variety of cases. That's what I want, so I can see which area really interests me. I've been thinking about the homicide squad."

"You just worked on a homicide case: Tummas Gramm."

"Yeh, I know," Annika acknowledged. "But how long till the next one comes along here?" She sensed Heri stiffen in his seat but he didn't reply, instead turning the car on to Biskupsstøð gøta.

"I'm not saying I want to stay there for good," Annika went on, filling the silence. "I think two or three years to get experience, then it might be good to come back."

"Sure, yeh," Heri said. "That makes sense."

"So you'd be okay with it?"

"Sure, of course. It's not like it's so far away, is it?" Heri flicked the indicator and turned in at the petrol station. "An hour and a half on the plane. That's only the same as driving out to Viðareiði."

"Yeh, well that's true," Annika said. "When you put it like that."

1

Friday/fríggjadagur

"JAN?"

It came after the knock on the back door. Fríða's voice.

"*Hey. Koma í,*" I called.

A moment or two later she came into the sitting room. I'd known she hadn't gone to the clinic because her car was still parked outside, but I'd assumed she was working from home so I'd left her alone instead of crossing the six feet between the guest house where I was staying and the main house. She was wearing jeans and trainers beneath a chunky-knit sweater, her reading glasses pushed back into her hair.

"Do you feel like an expedition?" she asked. I saw her spot the large, buff envelope on the table and the empty coffee mug near it.

"To do what?" I asked, partly to redirect her attention.

"A trip to Sandoy. Finn – my brother – has sent me a text from his boat. They have found a pod of whales so there will be a *grind* at Sandur, unless they escape." She checked her watch. "We'll have to leave in a few minutes, but if we're lucky I think we can catch the next ferry from Gamlarætt and be at Sandur by the time they arrive – but only if you want to," she added. "If you want to see it."

"Are you going anyway, or would it just be for my benefit?" I asked. I had a suspicion that Fríða thought I needed more exposure to my cultural roots. At various times she'd brought me books she thought I should look at – collections of old photographs of the Faroes and novels by Heinesen, Brú and others. I wasn't sure I agreed with her diagnosis, but I appreciated the thought.

"No, I'll go anyway," Fríða said. "I haven't seen Finn for a while and it's a nice day."

A nice day to kill whales.

"Okay, sure," I said. "Do I need to bring anything? Harpoon? A big knife?"

She gave me a look, slightly beady, but she was getting used to me by now. "No, I don't think you need anything like that," she said. "You don't want any more injuries, I think."

She could be very sardonic, which I liked.

When she'd gone I went to find boots and waterproofs. Essentials, even for a nice day on the Faroes. At least I was that much in touch with life here.

So where was I?

Mending/mended. Suspended. Putting things off: decisions; movement; leaving; asking. I supposed I was waiting for something: to take a hint. I *can* take a hint. But there was none, and I had no imperative until one came along.

Fríða had still given no sign of wanting to kick me out of the guest house and a few days ago when I'd told her I thought it might be time I went back to a hotel she dismissed the idea as if I'd suggested something illogical. "Why? There's no need. It would be a waste of money."

I didn't want to impose on her hospitality or outstay my welcome – I was still English enough for that – but if I read it right, she viewed my presence as a pragmatic solution to my situation: first injured, then – after the news of Signar's death – awaiting his funeral. I also knew her well enough not to argue when she'd made up her mind.

So I stayed.

I'd also emailed Kirkland, my superintendent back in England, and told him I was unavailable to be interviewed by the Directorate of Professional Standards on the dates he'd requested. I used the word *request* deliberately because it hadn't been one. There had been a family bereavement, I told him; on top of the fact I was recovering from injuries sustained while assisting the Faroese police. I even offered to provide medical notes and testimonials if he required them. Not necessary as it turned out. I hadn't thought so. He knew what he could do.

And I walked.

Not to outdistance or shake off the black dog, but because I wanted to. Because, by and large, I hadn't walked for the sake of the walk for a long time and if I tired myself out I hoped it might bring my sleep back to normal.

Ever since the concussion and painkillers had scrambled a couple of my days I'd been waking in the small hours, vaguely conscious that in my dreams I'd been inhabiting a place I didn't like. It was a sensation I remembered, like *déjà vu*, from almost a lifetime away: a primal thing, almost childlike in its simplicity. Maybe not surprising because I had *been* a child when I'd last felt it: waking up and not knowing where I'd been.

So I walked, and after the first day when I'd underestimated the terrain, I remembered the addictive muscle-aching satisfaction of accomplishment it gave. This was something I could do, and while I was doing it there was nothing else I could do at the same time: just be preoccupied by the next step and the one after that.

So, that's where I was: abstracted from reality, I guess. As much in limbo as Signar Ravnsfjall had been when I'd seen him that one time in his hospital bed, between his first stroke and his last. Unresolved. Unanswered. Unfinished.

2

BEHIND THE BOAT THE WATER WAS CHOPPY AND DISTURBED BY the wakes of the pursuing craft; half a dozen, strung out in a loose, ragged line, engines throbbing. Ahead, though, the water was calm, almost unbroken even by the smoothly arcing dorsal fins as the pilot whale pod sliced the water with apparently effortless ease.

Did they even realise they were being herded? At the wheel of the *Kári Edith* Finn Sólsker had wondered about this before. They were supposed to be smart, these whales. So why didn't they just turn, dive beneath the boats and head for open water instead of the mouth of the bay? But they just didn't. That was the way of it.

In the bow of the boat Høgni Joensen stood by the rail, leaning forward slightly into the light breeze. He was a short, square man with coarse hair under a woollen hat and a stubbled, round face which bore a broad smile. He was caught up in the sight of the whales and the thrilling uncertainty about whether or not things would go to plan. Everything else was forgotten until the regular beat of the engine faltered for a moment, then picked up again.

Even though the interruption was brief, Høgni cast a glance back at the engine hatch, then towards Finn Sólsker in the wheelhouse. Høgni had cleaned and reinstalled the fuel pump a couple of days ago, so if it started to play up again now it would be his fault. And to choose this moment, that would just make it worse. Høgni always wanted Finn to know that he could rely on him and trust him to do a good job. But as often as not the world conspired to undermine him in front of his friend and employer.

By now the *Kári Edith* and the other boats were drawing level with the point at Boðatangi and the vessels on the outermost, easterly end of the line began to speed up a little, bringing them round to make a large, shallow semi-circle. The intention was to force the whale pod to bear around to the left and head for the broad beach at Sandur.

Off the port side Høgni saw a flotilla of smaller boats, waiting close to the shore for the pod to pass before coming in to join the drive. It was still too far away to see how many people were on the beach, but Høgni could guess that there would be a fair few. In the two hours since the whales had first been spotted there had been plenty of time to put out the news.

Then the engine faltered again – slightly longer this time – before picking up once more. Høgni debated for a moment, but then decided it would be better to face Finn now, rather than wait until – if – the pump packed up for good. He left his place in the bow and went back to the wheelhouse.

Finn was on the radio, talking to Birgir Kallsberg, the whaling foreman, who was on the *Ebba*. He didn't look away from the window when Høgni opened the wheelhouse so

Høgni just stood there and waited, then dug out his tobacco tin and started to roll up, so it didn't look like he was standing there like a moron.

"Okay," Finn said into the radio's handset. "Once the others are in line I'll drop back and head in to the harbour."

"*Understood,*" Birgir Kallsberg's voice came back through the speaker. "*Don't worry, you'll still get the finder's whale.*"

"Yeh, yeh, I trust you," Finn said with a laugh.

He hung up the handset as the boat's engine spluttered and misfired again. This time there was a definite drop in speed before it picked up.

"I reckon it's that fuel pump again," Høgni said. He realised it was a stupid thing to say as soon as it was out of his mouth.

Finn nodded. "I hope that's *all* it is."

"Yeh, yeh, it is, I'm sure of it," Høgni said, trying to be reassuring. "We should probably have got a new one instead of trying to fix it again."

"Yeh, maybe." Finn allowed. "Too late now, though. At least we're not fifty kilometres out: that's one thing."

Seeming to take this as an indication that Finn wasn't going to blame him for the fault, Høgni stepped into the wheelhouse. "I'll have a look at it as soon as we're back at the quay," he said. "I'm not bothered about the kill."

The affected nonchalance wasn't lost on Finn. Høgni loved the *grindarakstur*. He took the roll-up from Høgni's stubby fingers and put it to his lips. "Don't worry, I'll do it later," he said. "No need to miss out."

Høgni passed him his lighter. "Do you think those

Alliance people will turn up and try to spoil things?"

Finn chuckled. Høgni was like a little boy, everything seen in black and white: good or spoiled; liked or disliked; friend or enemy. Except that Høgni had no enemies: he was too good-natured for that.

"What?" Høgni said, reacting to Finn's laugh.

"Nothing," Finn told him, waving him out of the wheelhouse. "Go on, go back and watch. The protesters are probably all still in bed."

At the eastern end of the broadly curved bay, Erla Sivertsen panned her camera along the line of people standing on the grass-covered sand dunes above the beach. More were arriving – men, women and children – coming from the road and a line of parked cars. Some of the men carried ropes and hooks, striding purposefully until they reached the edge of the grey sand, then halting to look and assess. No one went further. That was the way of it. You waited until the whales came to the beach.

At each end of the bay there were groups of AWCA volunteers, easy to pick out through the viewfinder because of the light blue sweatshirt they all wore. AWCA, pronounced as "Orca" by its members, was the Atlantic Wildlife Conservation Alliance. They had been on the islands for nearly two months, but this was the first time they had been scrambled, ready to take action, and it seemed that only a dozen or so had made it here in time. Now, like everyone else, they stood with their attention trained on the sea, watching the line of disparate boats ploughing closer and straining for sight of the whales.

Erla shifted the camera again, adjusting the focus on the telephoto lens. There were nearly two dozen police officers stationed at intervals along the line of the sand dunes, all dressed in tactical gear. Some had been brought in by a naval helicopter – clearly a show of strength by the authorities – and Erla knew that when her footage was edited the dark uniforms and bulky equipment of the police would look truly ominous in contrast to the unarmed AWCA protesters.

Having captured the scene down the length of the beach, Erla stopped filming for a moment and checked the progress of the boats out at sea. She'd witnessed four other *grinds* in her life – the first when she'd been six or seven years old – and knowing the way things would go now, she'd already planned the footage she wanted to get. Video was not her favourite medium, but she knew it would have the most impact when showing the actual drive. Then she'd use stills for the aftermath of the kill.

The whales were still more than three hundred metres from shore but now there was a growing desperation in their movements. They had sped up and broke the surface of the water more often. Their slick, arching bodies were more tightly grouped, as if they sensed that they were running out of room to manoeuvre. And still the boats came on behind them, grouping them tighter, pushing them in.

Finally the larger boats slowed and stopped to let the smaller craft take over and Erla knew it was time. She moved the camera and refocused on the Alliance protesters at the nearest end of the beach, waiting.

And then it started. At a signal the protesters moved into action, each taking a length of scaffolding pipe from the ground and then running quickly down towards the water. No one pursued them, but there were shouts of protest and gestures of resentment from the locals on the dunes.

The protesters paid no heed. They waded straight into the water, using their metal poles like walking sticks to test the bottom, moving out further through the low, rolling swell until they were thigh deep, spacing themselves out at intervals. And then, in a ragged line, they produced hammers and crow bars from pockets and waistbands and started to bang their submerged scaffolding poles as hard as they could, adding to the noise with shouts and whistles.

It was a tactic no one had anticipated and for a moment the onlookers weren't sure how to respond. The police shifted uncertainly, but then they seemed to receive an order over their radios and left their positions to jog quickly across the sand and into the water. They were followed by several men from the crowd and when the protesters saw them wading into the shallows they redoubled their noise-making and moved further out into the water.

Because the water hampered everyone's movements equally it produced the strange effect of a slow-motion game of tag in which no one could outdistance anyone else. Whenever the police made headway towards them, the protesters waded deeper or moved left or right, all the while keeping up their hammering and whistling, which became ever more urgent as the whales got closer to shore.

Erla kept the camera trained on this cat-and-mouse game

for a few seconds more, then zoomed out and panned round to the open sea. The whales were concentrated together now and behind them the bullying boats had increased their speed. It almost seemed that the whales and boats were racing each other to be first to the land, but then – a few metres from shore – the whales hesitated, as if realising their mistake. A few made to turn back, but the imperative of the boats prevented it, and then, as the creatures finally reached the shallows, the people on the dunes swarmed forward. They ran across the sand and plunged into the water amidst the thrashing of fins and black bodies and Erla held the shot, zooming in slowly on the churned waters and the first men to seize their prey.

Through the lens Erla spotted an AWCA sweatshirt, adjusted the focus and managed to zoom in close on an American woman she recognised, just as she was finally corralled between two burly cops. They were all up to their chests in the water and seeing the whales already thrashing in the shallows, the woman appeared to realise she'd failed. When the police officers took her by the arms she just stood there, and as Erla zoomed in closer she was pleased to capture the look of abject misery on the woman's face. Even at this distance you could see that she was crying with grief. It was a good picture.

Finally lifting her eye from the viewfinder, Erla glanced around. There were a few spectators nearby but everyone's attention was focused on the whales and no one took any notice of her as she quickly unclipped the camera from its monopod and started down from her vantage point. Her AWCA sweatshirt was well covered by her red waterproof jacket and there was nothing to tell her apart from the other Faroe islanders.

3

WE'D MISSED MOST OF THE KILLING, BUT I WAS AMBIVALENT about that. Besides, there was plenty to show what we'd missed, and it was bloody. A deep crimson stain spread the width of the beach, out through the water and a good thirty yards away from the sand. It looked like someone had emptied a tanker of chemical dye into the sea.

By the time I reached the far end of the beach I couldn't see Fríða. She'd been waylaid by an angular, insistent woman in the throng of spectators, someone she obviously knew, and I'd wandered on without her, between the onlookers at the wave line, taking the scene in until I was at the end of the beach. I chose a relatively dry spot on the sand and sat on my coat, braving the breeze in only a fleece. It was a decent day and as good a place as any to wait and observe.

There was something of a holiday mood on the beach, but now that most of the excitement was over, the people standing along the waterline had turned their attention to neighbours and fellow onlookers, gossiping and comparing impressions. While the adults talked, local kids came and went between them, daring each other to splash in the red waves, or standing intently as they watched the men still at work in the shallows.

Up to their thighs in the water, and sometimes beyond, the men worked with the concentration and focus of knowing they still had a long job to do. This was a serious business, done with the pulling of ropes, shouted instructions and the manoeuvring of boats. There was no jubilation as far as I could see, and no distaste either; just pragmatic resolve. You could debate the whys and wherefores of the whole thing, but I doubted that anyone here would think them questions worth asking. I was watching a thousand years of tradition and it ran just as deep as the blood in the water.

Twenty yards from where I was sitting there were three or four whale carcasses moving gently with the waves, separated from the main part of the kill. I wondered if they'd been forgotten or overlooked, but then a couple of small boats with outboard motors came to secure them: two lads in their late teens and an older hand who gave instructions.

I wasn't the only one looking on while this was done. Standing off to one side was a stocky middle-aged guy in a brown sweater and waders. We'd exchanged nods a few minutes ago, but now he wandered across to me, as if the new activity warranted comment.

"*Hey.*"

"*Góðan dag,*" I said, which made him cock his head slightly. My accent still wasn't that good.

"English?" he asked.

I nodded.

"You've seen the *grindadráp* before?"

"No, my first time."

"It's something to see, yeh?" he said after a pause. "Not one to forget."

"No," I agreed. And then, for the sake of something to say, "So what happens now?"

He gestured at the boats. "They pull the bodies to the harbour so they can be lifted out to be measured. It's done with a special stick – the *grindamál* – and afterwards there is a calculation of how the catch will be divided. Then tickets are given out for the shares in the meat and the blubber. It's a complicated business to be fair with everyone."

"So everyone here gets a share?" I asked, indicating the spectators further away.

"*Ja*, if they live on Sandoy. Each home is on a list, but you can be taken off if you like – if you don't want a share."

"Do many people do that?"

He shrugged. "Perhaps more now, but still not so many."

"Have the protesters made any difference?"

He shrugged. "Only to themselves. Now they will all go home with a criminal record for interfering with the *grind*. That's the law."

He said it flatly, as if things were as they should be, and then – as if he'd reached the end of his conversational reservoir – he shifted.

"So, have a good day," he said in that abrupt way the Faroese sometimes have of taking their leave.

"*Takk*. You too."

He headed off and I watched the men in the water for a few minutes longer, until I started to feel cold. Then my mobile rang. It was Fríða, who said she was heading for the harbour to find Finn. I told her I'd meet her there and stood up to shake sand off my coat.

Instead of walking back along the beach, I opted for the easier route via the road. It was lined with parked cars and at the far end I saw a knot of bedraggled and handcuffed protesters being held beside police vehicles. As I got closer I recognised a couple of the uniform cops, but they were preoccupied with the task in hand so I gave them a wide berth as they started to load the protesters into a van.

Most of what I knew about the Alliance – as the Faroese usually called them – came from dinner-table conversations, but it was a slightly vexed subject and one many people preferred to avoid. From what I could tell, though, the AWCA volunteers had publicised their campaign well since their arrival about two months ago. They'd stirred up a flurry of interest and concern in the international media, especially on the internet, with pictures of bloodstained seas and dead whales featuring heavily.

As a result the Faroese had suddenly and unexpectedly found themselves being vilified as barbarians and murderers for their traditional whale killings, while the AWCA protesters presented a well-managed image of themselves as the would-be saviours of defenceless wildlife. Whenever and wherever there was a whale drive, the Alliance had vowed they'd be there in force to stop it. The whole thing had promised to be very dramatic – and then it wasn't, because no *grinds* had taken place.

As far as I could tell it was unusual for there to have been no whale sightings at all during the summer, but if the islanders had missed out on their catch at least it meant there were no protests. The only real conflict had consisted of a few drunken confrontations in bars and some petty vandalism to the protesters' boats, and I got the feeling that most of the phlegmatic Faroese had rather hoped that would be all that happened. If so then when the Alliance left in October the whole chapter could be written off as what the Faroese call "a storm in a glass".

There didn't seem to be much chance of that now, though. When I reached the road junction and turned towards the harbour, a police van passed me with several bedraggled and downcast protesters inside. Still, I supposed the locals could count themselves one up over the activists. The *grindadráp* hadn't been disrupted in any significant way and, despite all their big talk, the Alliance had only been able to field minimal opposition, rather than the promised massed ranks.

The village of Sandur seemed deserted as I made my way through it to the neighbouring harbour: even the Eldhús shop and the bakery were closed and the only sign of life were a few passing cars. It was a different story at the harbour, though. Here it was noisy and crowded as boats came in with whale carcasses and men on the quayside directed operations to bring them ashore. I stood and watched from the corner of the dock for a while, keeping an eye out for Fríða, but when I couldn't spot her I wandered out past the fish-processing sheds towards the far end of the harbour where a couple of decent-sized boats were tied up.

Near the end of the dock half a dozen whales were already laid out on the tarmac and a man in his late fifties was using a wickedly sharp knife to cut rectangular openings about a yard long in their bellies. He'd already done this to some and their intestines spilled out in pale pink coils through the incongruously angular holes.

A few yards ahead of me a tall, dark-haired woman in a red storm jacket was taking photographs of the guy's handiwork with a long-lensed professional-looking camera. It wasn't until he finished sawing away and straightened up that the man realised he was being photographed. When he did he clearly didn't like the discovery and he barked out a couple of words at the woman.

Even though it was in Faroese I could interpret his tone – first annoyed and then demanding – as he stepped away from the carcass. The woman lowered her camera and said something I couldn't hear, but it had no effect. The man became more insistent and started towards her, pressing his point.

It was none of my business, but a copper's instinct and the fact that the man still had the knife in his hand made me change direction and quicken my step. I reached them just as the man came to a halt in front of the woman and gestured at her camera, making a demand: hand it over. That much was clear.

"Hey," I said, leaving it somewhere between the Faroese greeting and a caution. I looked to the woman. "Everything okay? *Hvussu hevur tú tað?*"

The expression on her face was set somewhere between determination and uneasiness. She was gripping her camera firmly to her side but when she turned towards me I sensed her relief at having someone else there.

"Yeh, thank you," she said.

The guy shot me a black look then said something in Faroese – a repeated demand – and gestured at her camera with his knife. I tensed a little and weighed up the threat. Fifty-fifty.

"Listen—" I started to say, but was cut short by a short, stolid man in a yellow sou'wester who came towards us all at a brisk trot. He was in his early thirties, unshaven, with a woollen hat on his head and he might have cut a vaguely comical figure if it hadn't been for the fact that he was built like a bulldozer. From the way he swung his arms you knew there was a lot of muscle under his coat.

This guy said something to the one with the knife, then planted himself firmly in front of him, apparently undaunted by the knife or the man's grievance.

Now the older man turned his resentment and grievance on the newcomer. He spoke and gestured indignantly for several seconds, as if he'd been wronged, but none of it cut any ice with the bulldozer. He wasn't here to debate and he wasn't moving. Instead he just shook his head and said something final: take it or leave it.

Outnumbered now, the older guy took it. With some well-chosen words aimed at the woman he turned on his heel and stalked back to his whale.

We none of us moved for a couple of seconds, just to be sure, then the woman shifted and spoke Faroese to our bulldozer friend. I got the sense that she knew him, but her thanks seemed to embarrass him and after a short, mumbled reply he started to lumber away. She looked after him for a moment – seemingly slightly amused – then at me.

"Thanks for your help," she said. There was a faint trace of American overlaying the natural Scandinavian in her accent.

I shrugged it off. "You're welcome, but I think your friend had more effect than me."

That amused her again. "Høgni? Yeh, he's a sweet guy." Then she held out her hand. "Erla Sivertsen."

"Jan Reyna." We shook hands. She was about thirty, I guessed; a heart-shaped face lightly tanned, as if she spent time outdoors.

"Maybe we should move on," I said, glancing at the whales.

"Yeh, I think so."

As we walked along the quay she finally released her hold on her camera and let its strap take the weight.

"So what was the problem?" I said, gesturing back.

"Oh, nothing much," she said as if it wasn't an entirely unusual occurence. "He just didn't like having his photograph taken."

"That was all?" I asked.

By way of explanation she briefly opened her jacket to show me a blue AWCA sweatshirt beneath.

"Oh. Right," I said.

"He thought I'd post his picture on the internet to show 'the whale murderers' at work."

"Will you?"

"Sure, maybe," she said. "But not with that caption. I'm usually more subtle than that." She smiled and changed tack. "Are you English?"

I nodded. "More or less. I was born here but I left when

I was small: too young to remember it." It had become something of a litany over the last couple of weeks. Enough that I was considering having cards printed to save myself having to repeat it whenever the question came up.

"So are you local or…?" I left it open.

"Faroese, yeh," she confirmed. "I've been away for a while, too, though."

"Are there many Faroese with the Alliance?"

"No, I'm unique." She said it with a slightly self-deprecating smile. "The only one 'betraying my country'."

There was a slight undertone to that, but I couldn't quite read it.

"So are you here to visit family?" she asked.

I nodded. "My cousin on Streymoy."

"Ah. Okay. Who is that? I might know them."

"Fríða Sólsker."

"Yes, yeh, I know Fríða," she said, surprised but pleased to make the connection. "But I haven't seen her for a long time. How is she?"

"Fine. She's around somewhere. I'm supposed to meet her at her brother's boat, but…" I gestured at the size of the task. There were at least two dozen boats of varying sizes in the harbour now. I had no idea which was Finn Sólsker's.

"It's called the *Kári Edith*," Erla told me. "Over there." She gestured towards the end of the quay where a black-hulled boat with a white wheelhouse was tied up, slightly apart from the others that were towing whale carcasses in. Erla didn't seem to want to take any more photographs, so we strolled around the harbour together in the direction of Finn

Sólsker's boat, chatting a little, watching the activity. On the quayside a JCB was being put to use as a crane, raising the whale bodies suspended on straps and ropes from their dorsal fins, then manoeuvring them round and lowering them down on the tarmac.

What struck me most was the scale of it all: the size of the whales, and their number. There was a strange incongruity and fascination in seeing these bodies out of their element – incised and dissected, then measured and recorded. The knots of people who stood around to watch accepted the whole thing matter-of-factly, as they might assess the meat counter at the Miklagarður supermarket, and after a time even my own sense of the event's strangeness began to fade. There's only so much you can take in.

Finally we turned the corner on to the quay on the seaward side of the harbour and as we approached the *Kári Edith* I spotted Fríða standing with a man and a woman. I took a guess based on what Fríða had already told me and reckoned they were probably her brother, Finn, and his wife, Martha.

I was proved right when Fríða spotted us. She came over to greet Erla warmly in Faroese and exchange kisses, then turned to me and said, "Okay, come and meet Finn and Martha now."

I still wasn't entirely used to the interconnectedness of family that the Faroese take for granted, but I sensed that introducing me to her brother and sister-in-law was another part of Fríða's plan to reconnect me to my roots. By now I knew better than to resist, so I put on my best sociable front.

Finn Sólsker was about six feet tall, dressed in work

jeans and a traditional sweater, with a roughly trimmed beard. He shook my hand but kept his greeting to a nod and a neutral "Hey."

Martha was warmer. She was a full head shorter than her husband, with a ready smile and animated features.

"You know my father," she told me after we'd worked our way through some general pleasantries. Her English was slightly stilted, but still way more impressive than my mangled and mispronounced Faroese.

"Do I?" I queried.

"*Ja*, sure. Hjalti Hentze. He told me you worked with him to find out who killed the man at Tjørnuvík."

Like I said, there's an interconnectedness in the Faroes, so I shouldn't have been too surprised. And it was typical of Hentze that he hadn't mentioned it. He wasn't that sort of man.

"He said you knew a lot about murders," Martha went on.

"Yeah, well, in England we have a few more than you do, that's all," I told her.

"Maybe. But he says you have a good police eye."

I laughed. That sounded like Hentze, but I didn't need to say anything more because Finn shifted beside her and had another subject in mind.

"So, I hear you also had to be a police officer with Arne Haraldsen," he said.

"Sorry, who?"

"At the whales over there. Høgni told us. He said Arne had a knife."

"Oh, yeah," I said, getting it now. Then I shook my head. "I didn't have to do very much. When your friend Høgni

41

came along the guy changed his mind."

"Yeh, Høgni's useful like that," Finn agreed. Then he gestured across the harbour. "So, what do you think of this now you see it – the *grind*? Are you for it or against it?"

"Finn," Martha cut in, slightly reproachful, as if he'd been impolite. He hadn't, but I also knew why he was asking.

"I'm neutral," I told him. "But I thought I should see it."

"And now you don't like it?"

I could tell from his tone that he wasn't satisfied with my fence-sitting, so I shrugged. "To be honest, not much," I said. "I wouldn't go to an abattoir for fun either, but that doesn't mean I won't eat a steak."

"*Abattoir* is the slaughterhouse?"

"Yeah."

He nodded. "Okay, I see. It's a fair comment."

I wasn't sure I liked the slightly patronising tone, but I was prepared to put some of it down to translation. As it was, Martha took the opportunity to cut in. She said something in Faroese to Finn, then turned to Fríða.

"Will you and Jan come back to the house? The children will want to see you and you can stay to dinner."

Fríða sounded apologetic. "Sorry, we can't. Jan's arranged to collect a car from Tórshavn, so I think we should catch the next ferry back."

I shook my head. "Don't worry about that. You should stay if you want to. Just give me a lift to the ferry and I'll catch the bus into Tórshavn."

It was a convenient way out. I didn't want to stop Fríða spending time with her family, but I didn't really feel like several hours of small talk and perhaps Fríða knew me well enough to intuit my feelings because she didn't demur.

"Okay," she said. "If you're sure."

Erla had been keeping a slight distance, checking photos on the screen of her camera, but now, like me, she appeared to see a convenient exit strategy.

"I can give you a lift if you like," she said. "I need to go back to Tórshavn, also."

"Okay, thanks," I said. "If you're sure it's not out of your way."

4

IN THE CONTINGENCY-PLANNING ROOM OF TÓRSHAVN'S police headquarters, Hjalti Hentze surveyed the list of the arrested Alliance protesters that Hans Lassen, the uniform inspector, had just handed to him. He listened, too, while Lassen described the protesters' unexpected tactic of wading into the water in an attempt to drive the whales away from the beach.

"They'll need dry clothes, then, I suppose," Hentze said when Lassen had finished. "If they're to be locked up for the night."

"Yeh, it's arranged," Lassen confirmed. "We have forensic suits they can change into until their own clothes are dry. We'll also have to arrange for food: hotdogs, at least."

"Are you sure? A lot of them are probably vegetarian."

"Vegetarian? Dammit, yeh, you're right. It better be pizza then: plain cheese. Bloody hell."

While Lassen searched through the phonebook for a pizza delivery service, Hentze scanned the list of names again. Three Americans, four French, two German, two Spanish and a Pole. It was a very mixed bag, but they'd always known that it probably would be if it came to arrests.

Plans for how they would deal with the Alliance protesters had been drawn up soon after they'd announced their intention to come to the islands back in May. At press conferences and on their website the Alliance had claimed that three hundred volunteers would come to take part in direct action at every *grind* and it was a threat that had caused ripples up through the government and as far as Denmark. If true it would be nothing less than an invasion – or so people thought: a threat to peace and order and God knew what else.

So plans had been made at high-level meetings. A special task force of SWAT-trained police officers was formed, extra vehicles were sent over from Denmark and a naval frigate had been on permanent patrol around the islands for weeks. The ship was rumoured to have two or three dozen special forces personnel aboard, although Hentze had seen nothing to support that.

And even when the number of protesters arriving on the islands had proved to be far fewer than the Alliance had originally claimed, the contingency plans had remained in place. There was no telling what tricks the Alliance might have, and no one wanted to be caught out, least of all the politicians.

The way Hentze saw it, though, the politicians had already been caught out – by smart propaganda and effective PR from the Alliance. And until today the absence of any whale drives had made the whole thing moot anyway. He just wished it had stayed that way: not because he was required to do very much, but just because life would have been simpler if it had. Now everyone had been stirred up all over again and he seemed to be the only one who didn't find this new drama even a little exciting.

A few minutes later Remi Syderbø, the CID chief, came into the office while Hentze was still transcribing names into the computer. Remi had been closeted in a meeting with Andrias Berg, the Commander; a couple of prosecutors and an unnamed official – a Dane – for the last half an hour and now it seemed that he'd come to hand down their decisions.

"The Prosecutor's office has agreed that all the Alliance people from Sandoy can be charged with disturbing the peace and failing to comply with the police," Remi told Hentze.

"Not with obstructing the whale drive?" Lassen asked. He'd just managed to organise the delivery of a dozen margherita pizzas.

"No," Remi said. "They thought it would be more difficult to prove – more open to arguments about what is and isn't obstruction. The other charges are straightforward. We'll put them through court in the morning and if they're found guilty they'll be served with notices of deportation, so they'll be banned from returning for a year. With luck any fines will be kept small so there'll be no problem with non-payment. It's a token gesture. The main thing is to get them out of our hair."

It seemed like a typically political decision to Hentze. "Where are they now?" he asked.

"As we'd planned, the navy helicopter is taking half of them straight to Klaksvík, the rest are being taken to Runavík by van. Which leaves us two cells before we're at full capacity."

"I *said* the old holding cells shouldn't have been closed,"

Hans Lassen said. It was an old saw. "At least, not until we had something else in place."

"Okay, Hans," Remi said. "Let's not get into that again now."

"Yeh, well, we'll just have to hope it keeps raining for the next few hours," Lassen said. "That way we won't have to make room for the Friday-night drunks as well. I'll put out an advisory for the night shift to say that they should only make arrests if absolutely necessary."

"Fine," Remi Syderbø said, clearly not wanting to rise to that debate. "Whatever you think."

Hentze accompanied Remi out into the corridor, taking the list of protesters with him. His allotted task in the contingency plan was checking that the arrestees' details were correct and whether there were any outstanding warrants against them.

"Don't look too hard," Remi advised as they walked. "European arrest warrants, sure, but anything minor in their own countries isn't our problem."

"You want to get them gone as soon as possible?"

"That's the idea."

"And are they happy – upstairs?" Hentze made a gesture to heaven.

"Yeh, I think so," Remi said. "There were no injuries, no damage to property and the drive was a success."

"How many whales?"

"About sixty, I think."

"Not too bad," Hentze said. "A shame it had to happen, all the same."

Remi tipped his head to look at Hentze through the

upper part of his glasses. "Are you thinking of joining the Alliance, Hjalti?"

Hentze shrugged. "I just mean that now that it's happened the Alliance can say they were justified in being here – and keep coming back. Still, it's done now, so I guess we just make the best of it. What do the security service people think?"

"Security service?" Remi shot him a sharp look.

"Well I assume that's what they are, the Danes – security or intelligence. They're not completely invisible, even if they do only visit the fifth floor."

Remi considered that, then said, "You're too sharp for your own good, you know that?"

Hentze cocked an eyebrow. "How is that possible?"

"You know what I mean," Remi said, but without any kind of edge. "Some things are better left alone, though, eh?"

"Okay," Hentze said with a shrug. "As long as everyone's happy."

"They are."

"Good then. I'll get this list sorted out."

He moved off along the corridor, satisfied that Remi Syderbø's non-denial could be taken as a confirmation of his suspicion. A small victory, but Hentze always appreciated them the most.

It was less than a ten-minute drive to Skopun once we got back to Erla Sivertsen's car and we made the ferry with time to spare, just as it started to rain. On board we went up to the cabin on the top deck and took a couple of seats near the snack bar. I got coffees from the machine and came back as Erla took off her coat. I noticed several of the other passengers cast looks our way and then comment between themselves when they saw Erla's AWCA sweatshirt, but she seemed untroubled. She was probably used to it by now.

"So, you haven't asked if I'm pro or anti," I said, tipping a sachet of sugar into my plastic cup. It seemed as good a time as any to point to the elephant.

She shook her head. "I heard you talking to Finn. Anyway, it's none of my business. Like your religion, or sexuality."

"Atheist and straight," I said.

"So we only differ on whales then."

"I expect we could find something more if we tried."

"Do you want to?"

"Not particularly."

She considered that for a moment, then changed the subject. "So, what do you do?" she asked. "I mean, your job."

"I'm a police officer. Homicide." And when I saw a flicker of reaction I added: "See, I told you there'd be more differences."

"You think I don't like the police?"

I shrugged. "I don't know. I wouldn't have thought the Alliance are their greatest fans, though."

"No, well, that's true," she acknowledged. "Even so, it's not personal. The police do their job, we do ours."

"But you believe in the cause – I mean, it's not *just* another job to you, is it?"

She shook her head. "No, I think we need to make people aware of the issues. The whole Atlantic environment is under threat. It's a serious problem."

"So AWCA doesn't just do anti-whaling protests?"

"No, we're concerned for all Atlantic wildlife. Last year we ran campaigns about the effects of long-line fishing on the South Atlantic albatross, and about plastics in the environment. The Alliance gives smaller organisations the chance to be involved in campaigns that they couldn't mount on their own."

"So how long have you been with them?"

"About eighteen months. Before that I was living in Canada and Greenland for a few years, taking pictures for *National Geographic*, Sierra Club, people like that. Most of it had an environmental aspect, so when AWCA advertised for a staff photographer it seemed like a logical step, at least for a while."

"You don't think you'll stay with them?"

"I might not have the choice," she said, but as soon as she'd said it she waved it away, as if it was something she'd thought better of. "It's not so good to do the same thing for too long. I like a change."

I took the hint and didn't pursue it. Instead the conversation drifted into more generalised talk about the Faroes and family and coming back to your roots. It passed the time pleasantly enough until the *Teistin* docked at Gamlarætt and we returned to Erla's car.

After we'd clanked over the steel plates to the quay we followed the other cars on the road to Tórshavn and by the time we got there it was raining harder. Although it was only six thirty it was starting to get dark.

Erla pulled up by the pavement outside the Hotel Streym

where the manager had let me hire one of their cars.

"*Ger so væl*," Erla said.

I unclipped my seat belt. "*Takk*. I appreciate it."

"No problem," she said. "And in case you want to hear more about AWCA there is a debate on the whaling at the Nordic House on Monday evening. After today it should be an interesting meeting."

"Do you think you'll get any new converts?"

She shrugged. "Probably not, but even if it makes a few people consider the need for it to go on, that will be something. Anyway, come if you can. Ask Fríða too, if you like."

The afterthought could have been designed to remove any other implication I might have seen in the invitation. Or not, given that she'd left it to me.

"Okay, I'll tell her," I said. "Thanks again."

"*Sjálv takk*. It was good to meet you."

I got out of the car and fastened my coat against the rain as she drove away. I wasn't sure what to make of her. There seemed to be more under the surface than showed above, but that was a horoscope statement: not so profound.

As I walked round to the hotel entrance I glanced up at the grey-fronted police station next door. The ground-floor offices were in darkness but I wasn't surprised to see lights on the other floors. I wondered how much of a headache the arrest of the Alliance protesters was proving to be. Half a dozen detainees at the same time would normally be a big deal in the islands, so having to process twice that or more was probably giving them some grief. I was glad it wasn't my headache.

5

Sunday/sunnudagur

"ARE YOU AWAKE?" HENTZE ASKED.

Given that I'd answered the phone it seemed fairly self-evident that I was. It was six thirty.

"Yeah, just."

"That's a pity. We're put off until ten o'clock so you can go back to sleep if you like."

"What's the problem?"

"There is *mjørki* – mist – on the mountain so we can't see the sheep. We'll have to wait to see if it clears."

I cast a look out of the window. There was no mist over Leynar but that didn't mean much. A few miles and a couple of mountains can make a big difference between one side of an island and the other. The weather had already been responsible for cancelling the sheep herding yesterday, so instead I'd spent the day fixing a wooden railing on the guest house veranda for Fríða, earning my keep.

"Are you there now?" I asked Hentze.

"*Ja*, to see how it looks, but there's no need for you to

hurry. By ten will be soon enough, I think, if you still want to come."

"Yeah, sure," I said. "I'll see you then."

I still wasn't entirely clear what connection Hjalti Hentze had to a flock of sheep on the mountain, but he was full of little puzzles like that – facets that only came to light by accident. The best I could work out was that the sheep were some sort of communal thing and the people from two or three villages pitched in to maintain the flock; shearing, cutting hay and rounding them up when necessary. It was all well outside my own experience, which was partly why I'd accepted Hentze's invitation to help bring them in. Also, I was curious to get a better look at him away from police work.

It was mildly tempting to go back to bed, but I was awake now so I made a cup of coffee and went to sit at the table with a view out over the beach. I switched on my iPad and then slid out the contents from the manila envelope: my mother Lýdia's medical records. There wasn't much left to translate but I knew the combination of the doctor's handwriting and the Faroese – full of unfamiliar ðs, øs as well as sundry accents – would still take a while. Enough to fill the time before a drive to a mountain.

Just before ten I pulled in on the verge beside a single track road on the eastern side of Steymoy. Although Hentze had given me directions I probably wouldn't have found the place if there hadn't already been three or four cars and a pickup parked there. Beyond them, a hundred yards from the verge, there were a couple of dilapidated sheds of the sort that dot the Faroes landscape almost at random; built of concrete, with tin roofs and bare wooden doors. Most of them look as if they've been there for decades.

I parked behind the other cars and followed a rough track to the buildings to find Hentze standing with a group of jovial men near the open door of a shed. In a flimsy-looking wire mesh pen nearby there were about fifty sheep, bleating disconsolately. With shaggy fleeces and horns they looked decidedly more feral than anything you'd see in England, but I assumed that was normal for here.

"*Morgun*," Hentze said cheerily when I approached. He had a plastic cup in his hand. Coffee for sure.

"*Morgun*." I gestured at the sheep. "You've done it already?"

He shook his head. "*Nei*, there was a small break in the mist so we brought in these few. They were the closest, but the rest are still out there."

The mist hung heavy down to the lower slopes of the mountain so I had no idea how difficult it would be to locate the others, but it didn't seem as if it would be that easy.

I accepted the offer of coffee from a Thermos and Hentze introduced me to the other men, all dressed in work clothes and seemingly happy enough just to stand around and chat. Apparently we were waiting for someone to come down off the mountain with a decision about whether to press on or not, and no one seemed unduly perturbed by the delay. These things happen, especially on the Faroes: the weather changes, a mist drops or a storm blows in and you have to change your plans. In the old days they had a phrase for it: *You never know in the morning where you may sleep at night.* And even if modern tunnels and roads made it harder to be stranded by the weather, there were still times – like now – when it couldn't be ignored.

My arrival had prompted a new round of speculation and reassessment of the weather, but several of the men obviously found talking in English a strain, so when there was a natural break in the conversation Hentze suggested we took a look at the sheep in the pen. As we walked he cast a look at the mountain mist.

"I think you may have come out for nothing after all," he said. "Sorry about that."

I shrugged. "It's fine. I wasn't doing anything else."

"You still have no plans to go home yet?"

His tone was conversational but it was still a leading question.

"I'm getting to like it here," I told him. But I knew he'd see the deflection, so I said, "Besides, there's nothing at home that won't wait. When they've had enough they'll let me know, but I don't feel like going back just so they can keep me hanging around."

"This is your superintendent Kirkland you're talking about?" Hentze asked.

I nodded. After our first and only direct conversation about the fact that I'd been suspended from duty, Hentze hadn't asked any more about it. I knew that didn't mean he'd forgotten, but I took it as an expression of faith or of friendship that he'd never tried to satisfy his curiosity any further. And I knew he *was* curious, even if his own abstruse ethics wouldn't allow him to pursue it.

"Kirkland likes to play power games," I said, leaning on a wooden gate in the fence. "If I go back he'll decide it wasn't so urgent after all."

"So you push him to the last minute?"

"If I can."

From Hentze's look I could tell he thought that might be imprudent. "Is that a good strategy? If he knows what you're doing – if there is no goodwill…"

"There was no goodwill to start with," I told him. "He wants to get rid of me, but the inquiry is independent – or should be – so in the end it'll be up to them."

"So you're confident?"

I shook my head. "I'm a realist. Politics always wins one way or the other. Even if I'm cleared there are other ways for Kirkland to push me out. I just have to decide how much shit I'm prepared to take. I don't know yet – listen, let's change the subject. I met Martha and Finn the other day."

"*Ja?*" He seemed mildly surprised. "You went to Sandoy?"

"Yeah, on Friday. Fríða took me to see the *grind*."

"Ah, okay." He nodded, as if that new element needed to be assessed properly before making a reaction.

I said, "So, given that your daughter's married to my cousin, I was trying to work out if I should call you Uncle Hjalti." I gave him a deadpan look. "I don't think it suits you, though."

"Good, thank you," he said, finally cracking a smile. "I feel old enough already when Martha's children call me *abbi* – grandpa."

While we'd been talking a thin-faced man in a hat with earflaps had approached us and now spoke Faroese to Hentze. From his gestures at the invisible mountain I guessed what was coming. Hentze nodded a couple of times, then turned to me as the other man went off towards the sheds.

"We have to cancel again for today," Hentze told me. "Heini says the mist will not break."

"What about these?" I gestured to the sheep already in the pen.

"Oh, they can be kept nearby to wait for the others. They'll encourage them closer."

"Then what happens?"

He shrugged. "The old ones are taken out for slaughter, the rest go back on the hill."

"It's a good job you're with the shepherds and not with the sheep then, eh, *Abbi*?"

He gave me a wry look and chuckled. "For *both* of us maybe, I think."

We strolled back to the shed, said a round of *farvæls*, then headed to the cars. While we were on the move I took the opportunity to ask Hentze a question I'd had in mind since I'd arrived.

"Have you heard of a doctor called Lindberg?" I said. "He worked on Suðuroy in the 1970s so he'll probably be retired by now, if he's still alive."

Hentze thought. I could almost hear the Rolodex turning. "No, I don't know him," he said in the end. "Lindberg is a Danish name, although there are a few here. Why?"

"He was my mother's doctor," I said. "Fríða gave me her

medical records. You don't know that, though," I added. I wasn't sure if Fríða had broken any rules by doing that for me.

"No, of course." Hentze nodded as if it went without saying. Then: "Are they useful?"

"I'm not sure yet," I said, because I wasn't. "But if Lindberg's still around I'd like to talk to him."

"Okay, I'll see if I can find him." He cast me a look. "You're thinking that maybe you can find the reason for your mother's suicide, is that it?"

I shrugged. "I don't know. Maybe," I said. "From her records I think there may have been an underlying problem: something that started before she left here, so if I can find out…"

"Yes, I see."

Apart from Fríða, he was the only one to whom I'd told more than the basic facts – what few there were. After forty years, give or take, all it really came down to was the fact that Lýdia had killed herself and I didn't know why. I didn't know why she'd taken me away from the Faroes, or how we'd come to be in a Copenhagen flat when she took her own life.

What had happened after that *was* known, of course: I'd been taken in by Lýdia's sister and raised in the UK; that was all part of who and how I was now. And maybe that should have been enough. It had been until I'd come back, so why didn't I just leave it: go back to the way things had been? It was a good question, and yet another I couldn't answer. I just hadn't.

Hentze was looking at me speculatively, and I thought I sensed misgiving.

"You think I'm on a hiding to nothing?" I asked. "You think I should leave it alone?"

He shook his head, but only to negate the premise of the question. "No, I think you *should* look. There may be nothing to find now, but if you don't try to find out, how will you know?"

That was one of the reasons I liked Hentze: if he thought something was simple he saw no reason to embellish it further, just for something to say.

We reached the cars, but as Hentze dug out his keys his phone rang. He looked at the screen and I saw a shift on his face as he answered. Before he rang off I already knew it was a work call.

6

AFTER CHURCH — WHICH HAD NOT BEEN WELL ENOUGH
attended, she thought – Maria Hammer went home to collect
the dogs as she usually did. She left Erik to make his own way
when he stopped to gossip with the other men on the road.

Still spritely at seventy, Maria covered the distance to
her red-roofed house above Húsavík in five minutes and let
herself in through the back door. Unlocked, of course.

There was a pleasant smell from the oven, and after
checking the casserole Maria changed her coat for a work-
a-day waterproof, and her good shoes for a pair of short
wellingtons. Then she clipped the Labradors to their leads,
their claws impatiently scratching on the wooden floor, and
headed out again, taking the footpath along the slope of the
hillside towards the beach.

Of course it was no great surprise that church attendance
was not as great as it had been, Maria recognised that. These
days people had other distractions, other concerns. These
days people didn't feel the need for God's care as much
as they used to. It was different when people's lives were
governed by the land and the sea – either of which could

take a life without warning – and when God's grace, or the lack of it, could be the difference between enough and too little. These days people had comfort and warmth and more than enough food. It was taken for granted, as if God had no part. "These days" was a phrase more often than not at the forefront of Maria's thoughts.

Beyond the last house Maria checked she had her whistle before letting the dogs off their leads, glad to be free of their tugging. They sprinted away across the hillside, intent on the scent of hares, real or imagined, and Maria surveyed the landscape. There was a wispy-edged veil of mist hanging halfway down the slopes of Heiðafjall, and when she looked inland the shallow V of the valley was foreshortened by the cloud.

Walking down towards the beach, Maria located the white church but couldn't see the road. There was no way to tell whether Erik had started for home yet. Quite possibly not. He was a gregarious man and people liked his company. Strange then, that when he stood behind the lectern in church as the reader, people visibly sagged. It wasn't that he lacked belief in the words or didn't choose his texts well, but that he wasn't *inspired*. He had a dull reading voice, which became a monotonous drone no matter how hard you tried to concentrate on the words. Perhaps now that he was approaching his seventy-first year, Maria might be able to persuade him to stand down. *Let someone else take up the reins*, she could say; *encourage someone younger to become more involved*.

At the narrow gap in the dry stone wall Maria looked back for the dogs and gave two short toots on her whistle, calling them closer. The dogs were well enough trained that they responded almost immediately, running to catch up and then pushing through the space to race out on the other side towards the beach.

Maria followed on to the open ground where the rough grass levelled out near the foreshore. She walked at her own pace, knowing from experience how far to go before heading back in time to turn off the oven and to put the potatoes on to boil.

Where the grass gave way to rocks above the beach Maria stopped. On the horizon she saw the distant white shape of the ferry, *Smyril*, heading south for Suðuroy. She watched it for a while, then turned back and started inland. Time to head home.

It was the light blue of the bundle that caught her eye, standing out against the natural colours of stone and grass. It was on the ground, so it seemed – perhaps wrapped around something – in a small alcove formed by the stone walls of the three old storage huts. These days people would leave their rubbish anywhere, Maria thought with instinctive disapproval: they'd let someone else pick it up.

Maria changed direction and made towards the huts. Their walls were irregular stone, put together without mortar, and on their low roofs there was uneven grass turf. No one used them these days, but they were maintained because they were old: maybe hundreds of years. Which was why, when she saw them, the words someone had scrawled on a wooden beam shocked Maria. Not just because of the words themselves, but because of the vandalism. Written in English, the words said "Fuck the Whales".

Was nothing safe these days?

Maria lowered her eyes from the graffiti and looked further in to the alcove, gaze drawn to the light blue of the rubbish she had been seeking. Only now she saw that it wasn't a discarded plastic bag or bundle of litter, but a sweatshirt on the body of a woman.

The woman's face was partly obscured by dark hair and a clump of weeds growing in the corner of the walls. What Maria Hammer did see, though – what drew her unwilling eyes – were the woman's bare thighs, almost impossibly pale. Bare because her jeans and red lace panties had been pulled down to just above the knees, leaving her private parts exposed. Even more exposed because the woman had almost no hair there.

"Oh, Lord," Maria said, beseechingly, when she finally realised what she was looking at. "Oh, dear Lord."

And then the dogs came bounding in. They rushed up to the body, tails waving, sniffing interestedly at the exposed flesh.

"Oh no, come away!" Maria shouted. "Come away!"

Forced into movement, she took a couple of steps forward and grabbed first one dog and then the other by the collar, dragging them back several metres until she could fasten their leads again and get them under control.

Only then did Maria cast another look at the place where the body lay. She had an urge to go closer again, to take off her coat so she could cover the poor woman's legs and make her decent, rather than exposed like that to the world. But there was nowhere to secure the dogs, so she just held them, panting and tugging at their leads.

And then, for no reason she could later satisfactorily explain to anyone, including herself, Maria blew her whistle. She blew it again, then again, in short, regular blasts. She just kept on blowing – *peep* – *peep* – *peep* – until, at last, somebody came to investigate.

There was no patrol car on Sandoy when the call had come in to say a body had been found. Fortunately Rosa Olsen on the control desk had had the sense to ring Martin Hjelm on his mobile. Martin lived in Sandur, where his wife ran a small hardware and general goods store, and although he was off duty he left immediately to drive the eight kilometres to Húsavík as fast as he could. He hadn't bothered to change into uniform; everyone knew he was a police officer. For the next hour and a half he would be the only one at the scene.

Hentze spoke to Martin Hjelm from the car, en route back to Tórshavn from the sheep pens. Martin had the area around the body secured, he assured Hentze, and yes he had made sure that life was extinct. It was pretty obvious. Okay, then; no rush. Hentze would be there in an hour or so, depending on the ferry.

"There's one other thing," Martin said.

"What's that?"

"I think she could be one of the Alliance people. She's wearing a blue sweatshirt that looks like one of theirs – I mean, it's the right colour – but I didn't want to disturb anything by trying to look for their logo on the back to be sure."

"No, you did the right thing," Hentze assured him. "But

do me a favour and keep that idea to yourself, okay?"

"Sure."

Hentze rang off. It would set the cat amongst the pigeons if she *was* one of the Alliance, he thought unhappily.

He considered for a moment, but already knew that as inspector, Ári Niclasen would expect to be informed, so he put in the call.

Ári answered on the sixth ring. He was up north on Kalsoy for a family gathering, he told Hentze – his wife's family, he added quickly, as if he didn't want Hentze to get the idea that his own family would live somewhere like Mikladalur.

"Do we have an identity for the body?" Ári asked.

"Not at the moment."

"All right, well you'd better go ahead and see what it looks like," Ári told him, and Hentze heard a trace of annoyance in his voice: he wouldn't like missing out. "Once you've assessed it we can go from there. I'll start back as soon as I can, but it's bound to take a while."

"Okay, no problem," Hentze said, momentarily grateful that Ári had married a woman from the north.

Hentze called in briefly at his home in Hvítanes to tell his wife, Sóleyg, what was happening and to quickly change clothes. It was a matter of professionalism and also respect not to turn up to a dead body in sheep-herding jeans.

By the time Hentze got to the station in Tórshavn, Dánjal Michelsen was already there. Dánjal had worked in CID long enough to know what they'd need and he was already getting forensic cases out of storage. Then it was just a matter of organising half a dozen uniform officers to go with them and driving in convoy to Gamlarætt to wait for the ferry, ten minutes away.

Someone had suggested using the Search and Rescue boat to get to Sandoy, and if Ári Niclasen had been there Hentze knew that was probably what they'd have done. But it seemed unnecessarily flamboyant to Hentze, and probably no faster once you took into account that they'd arrive without transport at the other end. No, some things dictated their own pace and couldn't be hurried. The dead woman wasn't going anywhere.

An hour and a half after he'd first got the call, Hentze was on the road beside Húsavík's newly re-clad community hall, in a breeze spitting rain. Someone had had the foresight to open the hall, which was both good and bad. Good in the sense that it kept the concerned and curious villagers in one place and away from the scene; bad because it meant they had shelter and somewhere to sit and so were not inclined to go home.

Hentze had stationed three uniformed officers at the access points to the flat promontory of grass beyond the football pitch just in case more sightseers turned up, then he'd gone over the basic facts again with Martin Hjelm. A woman called Maria Hammer had found the body and she had been taken home by her husband, suffering from shock. Martin was unsure precisely how many people had been to look at the body before he'd arrived, but he was pretty sure that no one had interfered with it. One man had used experience gleaned from TV cop shows and kept people away

– once he'd looked for himself, of course.

With that sorted out, Hentze sent an officer to Maria Hammer's house to take a statement and then decided he might as well take advantage of the fact that a good number of villagers were gathered in the hall.

"Let's find out if anyone saw anything odd or suspicious around here in the last twenty-four to forty-eight hours," Hentze told Dánjal. "Especially vehicles coming or going." He fastened up his forensic oversuit and leaned on the car while he placed plastic overshoes on his boots.

"Shall I send them away when we've done that?" Dánjal asked. With his short-cropped hair and tough-guy looks he was someone who could get rid of even the most determined busybody.

"*Ask* them to go home, yeh," Hentze said. "We'll be here for a while so we'll use the hall as a base. It will be good to have a place for breaks, especially if it starts to rain harder."

"Okay. I'll see if there's any tea or coffee in the kitchen." Dánjal turned to go inside.

"Dánjal?"

"Yeh?" Dánjal looked back.

"Find out if anyone took pictures on their phones. If they did, confiscate them as evidence."

"Evidence?"

"We don't need anyone putting photos up on the internet."

Especially if she *was* one of the Alliance people, Hentze thought.

With a camera round his neck and a forensic case in his hand, Hentze set off towards the stone huts near the foreshore, deliberately taking the longest and least direct path. Two hundred metres, he estimated, *if* you took the shortest route, which you would if you were going there for any other purpose than his own. He assessed the ground as he walked. The rough grass was unlikely to hold any tracks but dogs might be useful. Later.

He walked without hurry, scanning the ground. Saw nothing, but stuck to the mantra he'd had dinned into him in training: there is nothing to be gained from speed and many things that can be lost. Stop often, look all ways. What you see won't harm the case, but what you miss will. Put everything else aside and just *look*.

He paused to orientate himself again; changed direction slightly to go around the huts from the far side, still seeing nothing that didn't belong there. The sea was to his left now and he could see the place as it had been described, where three stone huts formed an alcove.

Just look.

From this angle, this distance, he couldn't see very much. A shape: a bundle of clothes perhaps. He took a photograph, looked again to be sure he'd missed nothing, then he went closer.

He stopped again, three metres distant, looking at the ground around him first.

There?

A cigarette butt, fairly fresh. It was too soon to start picking up every scrap he came across until he had a better idea of the whole. Instead he opened the case, took out a marker flag and planted it in the ground near the butt.

When he straightened up he let himself look ahead.

Now, because he knew it was a body, that was what he saw. He couldn't help that. But if you *didn't* know – if you came across this scene when a body was the last thing you'd expect – well then, you still might not recognise it. Clothes, weeds, grass. He took another photograph and moved forward, watching where he stepped.

Finally he was at the entrance to the square niche formed by the stone walls. Facing him, at head height on the wooden beam were the words "Fuck the Whales". He put down the forensic case and photographed the graffiti first, although it was impossible to know whether it was relevant or not. Then he shot a dozen photographs of the body: a couple wide-angled to establish the scene, then close-ups, to make up a mosaic, capturing the situation exactly as he found it.

When he'd done that he lowered the camera, took a couple of steps forward and simply looked. He noticed how the weeds were flattened near her feet, which were clad in leather boots: urban wear, not for hiking. Jeans, crumpled up where the waistband had been dragged down to her knees along with her panties. Lace, not utilitarian cotton.

Her exposed skin showed no obvious signs of bruising or scratches and he noted that her blue sweatshirt was zipped up at the bottom, just a few centimetres, then open to show a black tee shirt beneath. There was a short tear in the black cotton and a dark stain around it about the size of a five kroner coin – blood almost certainly. Hentze assessed that for a few seconds, then examined her neck – what he could see of it above the rumpled hood of the sweatshirt. There were no marks there, just part of a gold chain visible against the skin.

Her head was tilted to one side with long black hair across her face, some of it tangled in the weeds, probably by the wind. Hentze reached down and moved the hair back from her face, teasing it gently away from the plants. Her eyes were closed – defined by a little make-up, not much – and her skin had the waxy semi-translucence of death. Still no sign of injury. She was in her early thirties, Hentze guessed.

After a moment he raised the camera again.

"I'm sorry," he said. "It's my job."

7

AFTER FIVE MINUTES WITH THE BODY HENTZE STEPPED OUT OF
the stone alcove and called Remi Syderbø on his mobile.

"Have you spoken to Ári?" Hentze asked.

"About the body? Yes, of course. Are you there now?"

"Yes, I'm with her."

A pause and then a measured, "How does it look?"

"To be blunt, not good. That's why I'm calling. I'm not
sure when Ári will be here, but I thought you should know.
There's a stab wound in her chest and there are indications
of possible sexual assault."

At the other end he heard an intake of breath.

"Jesus," Remi said.

"That isn't all," Hentze said. "She's wearing an AWCA
sweatshirt and someone has written 'Fuck the Whales' on the
beam near her body."

"What? Are you kidding?"

"No."

"Jesus." A moment's thought. "Is there any ID?"

"No. I've been through her pockets and they're all
empty. Not even a tissue. The thing is, several people from

71

the village have already seen the body and presumably the sweatshirt. The logo is on the back, so it can't be seen, but it's a distinctive colour so it might not take long for someone to put two and two together and make a connection to the Alliance. And in light of everything else…"

"Yeh, yeh, I understand," Remi said. "We need to identify her as soon as possible then."

"I've taken a photo on my phone – just head and shoulders. I'll email it across."

"Yes, do that." In the background Hentze heard Remi moving. "I'll put a team together here and go to the Alliance headquarters to see if anyone knows her. What are you doing now?"

"I have to finish securing the body, then wait for the doctor. After he's been I want to reassess. It's a question of whether it's better to move her, or wait for a full technical team." He looked at his watch. "There might still be time to get them here today. If we could I'd feel better about leaving things as they are."

"I'll call them now and see what I can do," Remi said. "I'll let you know."

"Okay, thanks. Do you want me to call Ári again and update him?"

"No, I'll speak to him. Just concentrate on what you have there."

"Okay. I'll send the photo now. Bye."

Hentze called Dánjal at the village hall and was told that the doctor had arrived. It was a formality to have life declared extinct, but necessary before anything else could be done.

"Shall I send him out?" Dánjal asked.

"Is he suited up?"

"Yeh, but I had to insist."

"Good. Okay, leave Rani in charge there and come with him – I'd like a second pair of eyes, a second opinion."

"You know I haven't had forensic training, right?" Dánjal said.

"That doesn't matter, just come."

The doctor was a middle-aged man called Hansen, a local GP who clearly didn't like the fact that he'd been called out on Sunday, or that Dánjal had required him to put on a forensic suit. He had to be asked again to put the hood up before going to the body, which he did grudgingly. His whole demeanour was that of a man who thought he was being asked to do something beyond the call of duty.

While the doctor examined the body Hentze stood back with Dánjal. "Anything from the local residents?" he asked.

Dánjal shook his head. "So far no one has reported anything suspicious and no one seems to have taken photos. I've sent them home with instructions – a request – not to talk about it. Not that it'll do any good. The whole island probably knows by now."

"Anything else?" Hentze asked. "What about the woman who found her?"

"She told Karin she was just taking her dogs for their usual walk when she saw what she thought was old clothes or rubbish."

"When she says their 'usual walk', does that mean she would have come the same way yesterday or earlier today?"

"I don't know."

"Okay, we'll need to find out. It might help establish how long the body's been there."

The doctor emerged from between the walls of the huts. He had taken less than two minutes.

"I can say that life is extinct," he told them, pointedly pushing his hood back and removing his surgical gloves.

Hentze nodded. "Thank you. Can I ask you about the wound in her chest? You saw it?"

"Yes."

"To me it appeared to be a stab wound. Would you agree?"

"I couldn't say. That would be for the pathologist."

"Yes, I understand." Hentze said. "But for the sake of argument, if it *was* a stab wound, would you not expect there to be a lot of blood from it?"

"Yes, I suppose so," the doctor conceded reluctantly. "Although it is also possible for bleeding to be mostly internal. As I said, I would leave that for a pathologist to determine."

"Okay, thank you," Hentze said. "If you wouldn't mind going back by the same route you came. And, of course, please don't speak about what you've seen here."

"Naturally."

The doctor departed and Hentze and Dánjal walked towards the huts.

Hentze had already fastened plastic bags over the woman's hands and feet to preserve any evidence there. Now that the doctor had pronounced death he could do the same

74

to her head. But not yet. He gave Dánjal time to take in the scene, then stepped carefully over the body.

"There's only a single wound that I can find." He showed Dánjal the hole in the tee shirt. "Here. But see the amount of blood? Almost nothing. And none on the ground."

"Maybe it was like the doctor said: internal bleeding."

"Maybe. What do you think about the weeds? Have a look. They're only broken where she's lying."

Dánjal assessed this. "You think if there had been a struggle – say if the attacker had forced her to the ground to rape her – there would be more flattened plants?"

"Do you?"

"Probably," Dánjal conceded. "But plants straighten up if they're bent, don't they? I mean, over a few hours."

"Yes, but these are old and dried out. They'd snap wouldn't they?"

"Yes, I suppose."

"So?" Hentze pressed.

Dánjal shifted uncertainly. "So maybe she wasn't attacked here – is that what you mean? Maybe the body was brought here."

"If she was, how did the killer get her body out here? Could one person have carried her so far? It's two hundred metres from the road if you go in a straight line."

"Someone might do it if they were strong."

"Could you?"

"I don't know. Maybe. Or she could also have walked out here with him: either voluntarily or because he forced her – with a knife or something. Then maybe he raped and killed her out in the open and dragged her body in here."

"Yes, that's possible," Hentze agreed. "But to attack her in the open, where he might be seen? More likely at night, then, but in that case you'd have to know the area well enough to find your way out here."

"Or use a torch."

"Which could give you away."

"I suppose." Dánjal was obviously unsure where any of this was getting them – or rather, getting Hentze – but he was saved from further back-and-forth when Hentze's phone rang. It was Remi Syderbø.

"I've spoken to Copenhagen," he told Hentze. "A technical team will be on the 19:00 flight tonight. They won't get to the scene until well after dark, but as long as we're prepared for that I think we should leave things as they are. Do you agree?"

"Yeh, I think that's the best thing."

"Good," Remi said. "So when you've secured things there come back to the station. I'll set up an incident room."

"Okay, sure."

Hentze rang off, then turned to Dánjal. "Technical are coming so we just need to preserve everything as it is. Will you go back to the car and get the tent and the large plastic sheets? If we do it between us I think we can rig something up to hold the rain off and keep the disturbance to a minimum."

"Okay," Dánjal nodded but then gestured to the graffiti. "It can't be a coincidence, can it? I mean, if she *is* one of the Alliance, and after the whale drive on Friday…"

Hentze cast a glance at the words, then shook his head. "It seems unlikely," he said.

As Dánjal turned to pick his way carefully out of the shelter and go back to the community hall, Hentze assessed the scene one last time. Very unlikely, he thought. Which was sure to make things even more complicated. But there was nothing to be done about that now.

He opened the forensic kit to look for a plastic bag large enough to accommodate the dead woman's head.

8

THE HOUSE ON MARKNAGILSVEGUR WAS LARGE AND DOUBLE-fronted, painted grey. Perhaps wisely the Alliance people had chosen to rent a property on the outskirts of Tórshavn rather than nearer its centre, and they had refrained from putting up any outward sign of who was living there. The only clue was the logo on the doors of the two cars parked outside.

Remi Syderbø stopped his car on the gravel drive in front of the house and got out. The head of CID was a man of medium build, lent a faintly steely air by his greying hair and rimless glasses.

"You'd better wait here for the moment," he said to the uniformed officer in the patrol car, which had followed him from the station. After Friday's *grind*, police uniforms might not be so popular in the Alliance headquarters.

The door of the house was opened by a young man, well dressed and Danish, who showed Remi in. Two rooms on the ground floor at the front had been turned into offices, but the place was quiet – just a couple of people typing on laptops – and if not for the campaign posters on the walls it might have belonged to an accountancy firm. This surprised Remi.

He had expected something more informal, if not bohemian.

He was led through to a smaller office where Petra Langley stood up and came round a desk as Remi introduced himself.

"*Politiinspektør* Remi Syderbø," he said, somewhat formally so she would be aware of his rank. "Thank you for seeing me."

For himself, Remi was well aware of Petra Langley's own details. As coordinator of the AWCA operation on the Faroes she'd naturally had her fair share of scrutiny and was the subject of an intelligence file: Canadian, forty-two years old, divorced, no children.

"So how can I help?" Petra Langley asked then. "On the phone you said it was important."

Remi cut to the chase. "Can you tell me if any of your group are unaccounted for?"

"You mean missing?" Petra frowned. "Not that I know of, but people come and go and today's Sunday. We don't keep track of them on their day off. Why?"

"I'm afraid that a woman's body has been found and we believe she may be one of your staff or volunteers," Remi said. "I have a picture here. It was taken of the body but it's not—" he sought the correct word "—not graphic. And of course, you don't have to look, but it would help to know if you recognise her."

Petra hesitated for a moment, then said stiffly, "Okay."

Remi took out his phone and summoned up the photograph Hentze had emailed to him, then held it so Petra Langley could see the screen. She looked for a second, then made a sound in the back of her throat before looking away.

"Do you know her?" Remi asked.

"Yes. That's— Her name is Erla, Erla Sivertsen. She's our photographer."

"Thank you." Remi put the phone away quickly. "I'm sorry to bring such bad news. How long have you known her?"

"About a year and a half."

"Was she a friend?"

"Yes. Not a close friend, but, yes, of course. Where is she? Do you know what happened?"

"Her body was found at Húsavík on Sandoy," Remi said. "We don't know what happened yet, but we are treating the death as suspicious."

"Suspicious?" The word appeared to surprise her. She looked away for a moment, to gather her thoughts. "I... I don't know what to say. You know she's – she was – Faroese. Her father lives here. On Suðuroy, I think."

"Thank you, that's useful to know," Remi said. "I'll find out so the family can be informed. Can you tell me, did she live here in the house?"

Petra shook her head. "No, she was sharing with some other people at the house on Fjalsgøta, number 82."

"Okay, in that case we'll need to have a look at her room. Do you know who has a key?"

"No, but I can find out. The landlord might."

"Thank you, if you would."

"Is there anything else I can do – any of us?"

"As a matter of fact, yes," Remi said. "We need to know what Ms Sivertsen was doing before she died, so we'll need to talk to all your people and find out when they last saw her.

How many are here at the moment, in the house?"

"I'm not sure. Only a few: most people go out."

"But you can contact them?"

"Yes, I'd think so, most of them, but—"

"Then please do that, and ask them to come back here as soon as they can."

For a moment it seemed that Petra Langley might raise an objection, but Remi Syderbø's tone had not left it as a request. Instead she nodded. "I'll see what I can do. Am I allowed to tell them what it's about?"

"It might be better if you don't – at least until they arrive. Some officers will come to take statements from them."

"Okay," Petra said, accepting the idea that some things were now inevitable.

"And if I can make one more request: I know that your organisation uses social media and the Internet to keep the public informed of your work, but for the time being – until we can notify Ms Sivertsen's family – I'd ask you not to make any public announcements. Can you agree to that?"

Petra Langley looked offended. "Sure, of course," she said. "We *are* decent people, too, you know."

Hentze caught the four o'clock ferry back to Streymoy and when he got to the station it was clear that Remi Syderbø hadn't been idle. He called Hentze straight into a side office, one along from the incident room, and made sure the door was closed firmly before starting to speak.

"The victim's name is Erla Sivertsen," he told Hentze.

"She was Faroese – from Suðuroy – but she'd been with the Alliance for about eighteen months: their official photographer, not a volunteer."

"Does she have any family?"

"Yeh, her parents. Jacob Poulsen is going to see them now to break the news." He paused, as if to indicate that it was not a job he had handed out lightly. "So, what can you tell me?"

"The scene is secured," Hentze said. "I've left six people to look after it. That's as much as we can do until Technical arrive."

"And you're still sure it was suspicious?" Remi asked as if he still had one last thread of hope that something might have changed.

"Definitely," Hentze said sombrely. "Apart from the stab wound – what *looks* like a stab wound – her jeans and underpants had been pulled down to her knees. I couldn't see any sexual injuries, but it also looked to me as if her body was moved to the place it was found – from how far, I don't know. It could have been just a few yards."

"And the graffiti?"

Hentze had a feeling this was the question Remi had wanted to ask all along. "There isn't much to add to what I said on the phone," he said with a shrug. "It looks as if it's written in marker pen and it seems fairly fresh – as if it was put there recently – but Technical might be able to tell us for sure."

"What's your feeling about it?"

"Given that she was working for the Alliance? It seems unlikely it's a coincidence."

"Yes." Remi adjusted his glasses. "Okay, well as it

stands now Ári is at the Alliance headquarters with a team to interview the AWCA staff and volunteers and two officers – Sonja Holm and Annika Mortensen – are conducting interviews at the house Erla Sivertsen shared with some other Alliance people."

"Has anyone examined her room there yet?"

"I've sent Oddur to do it, but until we know what her movements were before her death we haven't got much else to go on. Will you coordinate everything here and prepare a briefing on what you found at the scene? I'd like to get an overall picture as soon as possible."

"Sure. Are you taking charge?"

It was a loaded question, and although Hentze made it seem innocent enough he wanted to gauge Remi's response. The Tummas Gramm case was barely cold and its abrupt conclusion had effectively forestalled any judgement of the way Ári Niclasen had handled it. Even so, Hentze was sure that Remi Syderbø would not have forgotten his reasons for stepping in towards the end, so the question now was whether Remi was confident enough to put Ári in charge of what might be an even more high-profile investigation.

"For the moment I'll lead," Remi said, his tone neutral. "Until we know what we have. The involvement of the Alliance obviously makes this – complicated."

Hentze nodded. "Yeh, I can see that. Okay, I'll get on then."

9

VEERLE KONING WAS CRYING; A ROUND-CHEEKED YOUNG woman in her early twenties, with curly hair and slightly pouting lips. The tears didn't do much for her looks, which would not be outstanding at the best of times, Annika thought. Hard to tell how much of a meal she was making of all this, too. Although she knew it was an uncharitable thought, there was something about this young woman that made Annika suspect that her grief had an element of performance about it. Not that that necessarily made it less genuine; some people just didn't know how to react to moments like this and so relied on reactions learned from television dramas.

"It's okay, take your time," Annika told her. Veerle was Dutch and spoke no Faroese or Danish so Annika used English. "It's a shock, I know."

They were in the sitting room of the house on Fjalsgøta. The place had a distinctly student feel to it, with abandoned coffee mugs and discarded newspapers and magazines on various surfaces, and a tumbledown stack of DVDs in front of the TV.

Upstairs Oddur Arge was examining Erla Sivertsen's

bedroom, and in the adjacent room Sonja Holm was interviewing another AWCA woman who had arrived with Veerle about five minutes ago.

"How long have you known Erla?" Annika asked as Veerle blotted her eyes with a tissue.

"From May." Veerle sniffed, then made an attempt to focus. "We shared a room at the training camp before we came out here."

"Training camp?"

"Well, it wasn't really a camp – that's just what we called it. It was a conference centre outside Malmö. Those of us who were going to be here for the whole operation were there so we could get to know each other and learn what we were going to do."

"Oh, right, I see. And you've shared the house here since you arrived?"

Veerle nodded. "*Ja*. And when Lukas and I wanted to share a room here I exchanged with Erla. She said she didn't mind having somewhere smaller if we wanted the double. She was thoughtful like that. Always happy to help someone out, you know?" Veerle swallowed a lump in her throat, then ran a hand briefly over her cheek.

Annika said, "Is Lukas also a member of AWCA?"

"Yeh."

"Can you tell me his last name?"

Veerle sniffed. "Drescher. Why?"

"We need to know everyone who lives here so we can be sure to talk to them all," Annika said, noting the name down. Get as much information as possible, Remi Syderbø had told them, but find out especially who lived in the house and when they had last seen Erla Sivertsen. "So, can you tell me the last time you saw Erla?"

"Yesterday, after lunch."

"Do you remember what time?"

Veerle shook her head. "Not exactly. About two thirty or three o'clock I suppose. I'd been to the supermarket and when I got back Erla was working at the table in the kitchen. We had coffee and a sandwich together and a little later she said she was going out."

"Did she say where she was going?"

"I think she said she would go to some of the lookout positions. She took her camera bag. She never went anywhere without that."

"The lookout positions are where you're keeping watch for the whales?"

"Yeh."

"Okay. Can you tell me what Erla was wearing when she went out?"

Veerle thought back. "Jeans, an AWCA sweatshirt, and her red waterproof coat. She also had on a hat. It was grey, woollen."

"Okay." Annika wrote it down. "And she didn't come back after that? You didn't see her again?"

"No." Veerle shook her head.

"Were you here all the time? I mean, could Erla have come back while you were out somewhere?"

"I didn't go out," Veerle said. "Not till the evening. I cooked the meal for us – all of us in the house. We take it in turns. But Erla had said – she said she didn't know when she would be back, so not to worry about food."

As she said this Veerle looked as if she was deciding whether or not this memory was enough to warrant another overwelling of tears. In an effort to divert that, Annika shifted to more practical questions.

"So what time did you go out in the evening?"

Veerle swallowed, rubbed her eyes. "About half past seven or eight. I don't know exactly. We— We just went into the town."

"Who was 'we'?"

"Me, Lukas, Marie, Dieter: everyone from the house. We got back about midnight, maybe a little after that."

"That's early for a Saturday night in Tórshavn," Annika said. "You must have left just after things got going."

Veerle nodded. "When it gets busy there's sometimes trouble – because we're AWCA," she added in case Annika didn't understand.

"Yes, I see."

Annika scanned her notes. She was ready to wrap this up now. "The only other thing I need to ask is about Erla's private life," she said, looking up to Veerle again. "What can you tell me about that?"

"What do you mean?"

"Well, who was she most friendly with?"

"I— It's hard to say. She was friendly with everyone. Not just here in the house, but everyone in AWCA. She was that sort of person. She was easy to talk to, you know?"

"Did she have a boyfriend?"

"No, I don't think. She never said so."

"Okay." Annika made a note. "And was there anyone she *didn't* like – anyone she might have had an argument with?"

The question seemed to trouble Veerle for a moment, or at least to make her uncertain. "Do you mean in AWCA or…"

"Anyone."

"Not in AWCA, but…"

"Yes?"

Veerle hesitated, then said, "On Friday, after the *grind* on Sandoy, there was a Faroese man. I wasn't there but Erla said she'd had an argument with him. He wanted to erase pictures from her camera because they showed him cutting up a whale. But it wasn't… she said it wasn't a big deal. She made a joke about it. She said if the whale hunters' dicks were as long as their knives they wouldn't be a problem."

Veerle gave a half-hearted smile, which Annika returned sympathetically. "Maybe she's right. And this argument happened at Sandur?"

"Yeh, I think so. It must have been there."

"Okay," Annika said, writing it down. "Do you know what Erla did with the pictures she took?"

"I don't know. I suppose she would have put them on to her computer: maybe a hard drive. She always said she was paranoid about making copies in case she did something stupid like spilling coffee on the computer."

"Good, okay," Annika said. "*Stora takk fyri*. You've been very helpful – very brave."

"It's… I can't believe that… that she's really gone," Veerle said. She stood up and turned to look out of the window. "She was a really good person, you know?" She began to weep again.

Annika took a moment, then rose from her seat and more out of convention than empathy, she moved to put an arm round Veerle and give her a small, encouraging hug. But as soon as she did so Veerle made a small noise of pain.

Annika stepped back. "Oh. Sorry," she said.

Veerle shook her head. "It's just my bruises. A few days ago I fell – in the boat. I'm okay."

"Okay, come then," Annika said. "I think we could all use some tea."

When Veerle was settled in the kitchen with tissues and tea Annika went upstairs to find Oddur. Erla Sivertsen's room was at the top of the house, with sloping eaves and a single bed. The furniture, like that downstairs, was utilitarian and vaguely tired. The room was tidy and without clutter, though, and showed little sign of the person who'd inhabited it.

With surgical gloves on his hands, Oddur Arge was standing over an open drawer, searching under the bras and knickers. He was a rather lumpen man of deceptively plodding appearance and when Annika cleared her throat he looked up, vaguely embarrassed.

"Don't say anything," he said.

Annika shook her head. "I wasn't. Listen, have you found a computer or hard drives?"

"Yeh, a MacBook Pro." Oddur gestured to an evidence bag on the bed, which contained the computer. Beside it in another bag was a portable hard drive. "Looks like top of the range: 15 inches. Nice bit of kit."

Oddur was the technical guy when it came to electronics and he had an enthusiast's comprehensive knowledge of makes and models.

"Anything else?"

Oddur closed the drawer. "Photographic stuff: lenses, a flash gun. Nothing significant so far. Have you finished with the people downstairs?"

"Still waiting for a couple to come home. About the computer, though: one of the girls – Veerle – says Erla Sivertsen had a row with a man who was cutting up whales on Sandoy after Friday's drive. She took photos apparently, so it might be worth checking the laptop as soon as you can to see if we can identify him."

"Okay, I'll do it when I get back," Oddur said, then looked around the room. "Unless we start pulling up the carpet and taking the furniture to pieces I can't see that there's anything else here."

Annika waited while Oddur collected the evidence bags, then closed and locked the room. When they got downstairs they found Veerle Koning with a tall man whose dark hair and beard had the effect of making his complexion seem pale. He wore black combat trousers and boots below an AWCA fleece and he was damp from the rain.

"This is Lukas," Veerle told Annika. "I've told him what's happened." She put an arm through his and nestled up against him, as if he would be her support in this difficult time. He was a good five or six years older than his girlfriend, Annika decided.

"Hey, how are you?" Annika said.

Lukas Drescher gave her a stiff nod. "Do you have any more information about Erla?"

"Not yet. We're still trying to find out about her last movements. Would it be okay if I ask you some questions?"

"Sure, of course." Then he looked to the side as another man opened the front door and came in. "This is Peter Jessen," Drescher said.

Jessen was about Annika's age and wore nothing to show he was one of the Alliance. His hair was long and held back in a loose ponytail and his thin features reminded her of a hawk.

"Hey," Annika said. "Do you live here also?"

"*Nej*," Jessen said flatly in Danish.

Annika switched languages. "Are you with AWCA?"

"You want to question me too?" His tone made it sound as if he already knew it would be a waste of time.

"If you knew Erla Sivertsen, then yes, someone will need to speak to you," Annika said, keeping her tone coolly professional.

The man called Jessen chose to ignore that. Instead he eyed up the bags Oddur was holding. "Are you giving someone a receipt for those things you're taking?" he said.

"They've all been logged in my record," Oddur told him.

"Do we get a copy of that then? We don't know what you will do with them. It could be anything."

"A property list will be available to Ms Sivertsen's family if they request it," Oddur said flatly. Then he turned to Annika and said in Faroese, "You want me to stay and deal with this one?"

"No, it's okay." She turned to Jessen. "If you would go to the kitchen? I'll be with you in a minute... Thank you."

10

I'D AGREED TO MEET MAGNUS BEFORE GOING TO HIS MOTHER'S
house. It was to be an escorted visit, although he hadn't put
it like that. Instead he'd said it could be difficult to find the
house, so perhaps we should meet in the car park outside the
Eik bank on Heiðavegur.

After the cancelled sheep drive I'd driven back to Leynar
and changed, eaten a sandwich, then looked in on Fríða for
a few minutes before heading to Runavík. She was pleased I
was going to see Magnus and his mother, and although she
didn't say as much I guessed that she saw it as another step
forward on my reconnection programme. I didn't disabuse
her of that notion, although connecting in a brotherly way
with Magnus was not my motive for going.

What *was* in my head, and what I thought about on the
drive to Runavík, was my finished translation of the stiff,
cream-coloured cards that made up Lýdia's medical records;
the pre-printed boxes for dates, symptoms, comments,
diagnoses all filled in with blue or black fountain-pen ink.

Of course, the sensible thing would have been to ask
Fríða to translate it all for me, instead of spending hours with

an online dictionary and making semi-educated guesses. And maybe I would ask her later, just to check what I'd found, but I'd wanted to see it for myself first. For some reason that had seemed important.

So what did I have?

My mother: Lýdia Tove Reyná, born 21 June 1953 on the southernmost island, Suðuroy. On the medical cards I'd traced a sporadic list of childhood ailments and illnesses: mumps, measles, chickenpox; nothing remarkable. Aged eleven, a broken wrist; aged twelve, a chest infection. Then nothing for three years. A healthy girl, I assumed, until in July 1968 – aged fifteen – there were four appointments over three months.

In the doctor's notes for that period I found the word *sinnisrørdur*, which could mean rough, troubled, or unsettled. And there was – or seemed to be – anxiety, insomnia and restlessness. That was how I interpreted it, anyway. I couldn't make out what had been prescribed, but it seemed that something had; to be taken at night. Perhaps sleeping pills.

Then, a year later, the word *sinnisrørdur* again. And a different prescription in different handwriting. And perhaps this medication had worked, because there was nothing else for three years. Her next appointment was in August 1971 and I knew what it was for without translation. At eighteen, Lýdia was pregnant.

I suppose I'd always known she was young when I was conceived. She must have been, given our relative ages when she died: I was nearly five; she was twenty-three. Still, when I looked at the record of her pregnancy, so close to childhood ailments, it struck me how young she was to have fallen pregnant.

Fallen. An odd word for it. *Fallen from grace*; *fallen for an older man*. The latter was certainly true; the former, as well, I supposed, if you cared to look at it that way. I wondered how it had played out with family and neighbours in the conservative, godly Faroese community of the time. When Lýdia and Signar had finally married she'd been seven months pregnant: not something easily disguised.

The doctor's records made no note of the delivery – where it had happened or who had attended – perhaps because it had been uneventful, or because it had taken place at home. There was no way to tell. In fact the final record card had only one other entry, dated 5 September 1973. It said simply "Ørsted Sjúkrahús".

I knew *sjúkrahús* meant hospital, but there was nowhere called Ørsted in the Faroes. I could only assume, then, that it referred to the only place called Ørsted that Google had thrown up. It was in Denmark, which might fit with some of the other things I knew. Whatever the case it gave me a start on the questions I had for Sofia Ravnsfjall.

I was early by accident rather than design, and instead of just sitting in the car I got out and walked across the car park as far as a concrete wall. From there I had a view across the mist-obscured water of Skálafjørður: everything an almost uniform grey except for the four-square orange structure of the oil rig, planted like some industrial fairground attraction in the middle of the sound, yellow lights randomly dotted around the superstructure.

Then Magnus arrived, driving a dark blue Mercedes, which he turned and then waited for me to get in. I was expecting him to lay down the ground rules, like you might for a prison visit: no mobile phones, no prolonged physical contact, no unchecked gifts – and he did, after a fashion.

"Kristian has gone to Denmark," he told me. "My mother believes it is to look at a new business opportunity."

I nodded. "When did he go?"

"Two days ago. He may take a holiday also."

A long holiday, I guessed. I wasn't surprised. Even though there were no criminal charges against him, I couldn't see it being easy to carry on as if nothing had happened. Better to absent himself, lick his wounds. Not that he had any real injuries: others had suffered those.

Magnus drove back along Heiðavegur, and then turned up the hill, along a series of roads that took us up higher until we were on a road with no others above it and a commanding view over Skálafjørður.

It seemed appropriate to Signar's nature that he'd chosen to live up here, but the house wasn't as imposing as I'd thought it might be. It was a decent size, but with nothing to mark it out from the others nearby. White with a grey roof and a balcony across the front, it seemed pretty modern.

Magnus led the way to the side of the house where a disability ramp led up to a door. He'd told me before that his mother had arthritis and I guessed that the ramp was for her benefit. He knocked on the door and entered, calling out as he did so.

When I'd visited Signar in hospital – my only visit – I'd

been surprised by how much he'd changed in the twenty-five years since I'd seen him last. A man grown old. I had no younger image of Sofia Ravnsfjall to compare with the woman Magnus introduced to me now. Despite her being my stepmother – in a purely technical sense – we'd never met, so all I could see was a small woman in her late seventies. She had white hair, neatly permed, and a rather beady, bird-like manner; enhanced perhaps by the fact that she was dressed for Sunday, in a black skirt and a high-necked white blouse.

The introductions were stiff and awkwardly formal – half-Faroese, half-English – but Sofia shook my hand and directed us through to a sitting room with rugs on the wooden floor and heavy dark furniture. Then there was the formality of making tea, which Sofia insisted on doing herself despite the fact that she leaned heavily on a walking stick. When it was done she summoned Magnus to carry the tray to a coffee table in the centre of the room while she finally settled herself in a tall, high-backed chair; the sort for elderly people with mobility problems. I couldn't help thinking that with Sofia Ravnsfjall in it, it was somewhat throne-like.

"Magnus says you wish to talk about your mother," she said then, her English slightly stiff.

"If that's all right. Whatever you can tell me."

"Do you wish the good picture or the truth?"

"Mama…" Magnus said, but let it trail away when she gave him a look.

"The truth," I said.

Sofia nodded. "Lýdia was a difficult woman," she said. "For everyone who knows her. That is the truth."

I took that as it came. I hadn't expected her to sing Lýdia's praises. How many second wives would speak favourably of the first?

"How well did *you* know her?" I asked.

"Not very well," Sofia said with a shrug. "I have spoken to her perhaps two or three times. But that does not make it that I don't know how she was." She added the last part as if anticipating that I might dismiss her claims.

"So in what way was she difficult?"

Sofia Ravnsfjall considered that, then shifted a little. "She thinks of herself. In what she does. All the time it is what *she* wants to do. You understand?"

"You mean she was selfish?"

Sofia looked to Magnus. "*Sjálvsøkin*," he said.

"*Ja*," she said. Then to me, "With no thinking – no thoughts for others."

"You mean for Signar?" I asked.

"*Ja* – and also for you."

"Me?"

Magnus cut in. He spoke Faroese but I knew from the tone of it he was trying to divert her, or at least soften the tone of what she might say. But Sofia Ravnsfjall was no less assertive with her eldest son than she was with a stranger, and when she'd finished with him she looked back at me.

"I am the old woman," she said. "I do not spend time for sweetening *heilivágur* – the medicine. You understand?"

"Did you ever have time for that?" I asked her, guessing the answer.

She snorted. "*Nei*, not so much."

"Okay, so tell me."

She assessed me for a moment, then looked to Magnus and began to speak in Faroese.

It was clear that Magnus didn't relish being the interpreter for what his mother was saying, and I guessed that Sofia Ravnsfjall could probably have said what she wanted to say without a translator. So maybe it spoke something of her relationship with Magnus that she put him through it. Whatever the case, Sofia spoke with an assurance that trucked no demur.

Lýdia Reyná – as she was then – had been a good-looking young woman, Sofia wanted to emphasise. Everyone acknowledged that. But as a result she was allowed to get away with more than many others. She had a wild streak: rebellious or unruly – at least unconventional.

This didn't greatly disturb me. I suppose I thought it wasn't a bad impression to gain; of a girl and young woman who wasn't cowed by custom, who did her own thing. And maybe Sofia saw that in my reaction because her expression hardened a little. Through Magnus she said she was telling me this not so I would think it was good, but so that I'd understand when she said that Lýdia's death had not been the first time she'd tried to take her own life. She'd done it before.

I'd half expected it, I realised. Nearly a quarter of all people who kill themselves have already tried and failed at least once. I knew that, so I wasn't stunned by the revelation; just a little saddened to hear it.

"Only the family knew," Magnus went on, translating his mother's words. "Afterwards it was told – explained –

that Lýdia had to go to Denmark for an operation, but only Signar knew it was to a different sort of hospital."

"What sort of hospital?"

"A clinic for mental illness," he said, glancing at his mother for confirmation.

"Do you know where?"

"No, just in Denmark."

"She has to be made to go," Sofia said for herself now. "And even then she will not stay. She comes home again after a few weeks and so she makes a hard time for all: for a year maybe. She goes with the wrong people – never at home."

"What do you mean *the wrong people*?" I asked.

Sofia curled her lips. "They were at Múli," she said. "A place they call the Colony. Everyone knew what they did there."

"Which was what?"

But she shook her head, as if she wasn't interested in giving me details. Instead she dropped back into Faroese, speaking to Magnus as if she wanted to get back to the nub of the matter. And that was to tell me that Signar had been hard done by. She didn't say it directly, but that was what it amounted to. Here was a man whose wife had tried to kill herself, who then wouldn't accept treatment and instead sought out the wrong company. And if that wasn't enough, after a year she abandoned him altogether: took their young child and left the country; disappeared without trace for over a year.

It was only when Lýdia wrote to Signar from England, asking for money, that he was finally able to go and find her. He returned from this trip alone, though, and after that he neither saw nor heard from his wife again until he got the news that she'd killed herself in Copenhagen and I had been taken to England by Lýdia's sister, Ketty. By then, Sofia said, it was too late.

"Too late for what?" I asked, looking at her directly.

"For you to come home."

"Really?" I frowned. "Is that what Signar wanted?"

"Of course. You were still his son." She said it as if that made his desire to look after me an undeniable fact. But for the first time I knew that she wasn't telling the unvarnished truth she'd set so much store by. Sofia saw my recognition of that, too.

"He wanted to bring you here," she repeated resolutely. "I know this." Then she turned and said something to Magnus, before starting to push herself out of her chair. Magnus rose quickly to offer his arm and then her walking stick.

I stood up, too, out of politeness, and Sofia fixed me with a look for a moment. "Excuse me please," she said, then leaned on her stick and moved away.

Magnus escorted her out of the room and was gone for a few minutes. When he came back he was on his own.

"Perhaps we can call it a day," he said. "My mother is tired and her er – arthritis – isn't so good. It hurts her to sit here. She says she hopes you'll understand."

"Sure. Of course."

Outside we got into his car for the short journey back down the hillside. The misty rain was clearing and there were lengthening periods of sunshine.

"Thanks for arranging that," I said when he brought the Mercedes to a stop in the car park.

Magnus glanced at me. "You understand… my mother says things the way she saw them from the time after Lýdia left. She has told me before that things were not easy for Signar, to have lost a wife and his son."

There were a couple of things I could have said about that, but I thought Magnus had been given a rough enough ride already.

"Yeah, I understand that," I said.

"I am just sorry it had to be so…" He searched for a word.

"Blunt?"

"Yes."

I shook my head. "It was what I wanted," I told him.

"Yes. Even so…" He paused for a moment. "The things my mother told you – I haven't known them before. Maybe small pieces, but not as a story. Do you know what I mean? It can't be easy for you to hear things like that."

"Don't worry about it," I said. "Really. *Takk fyri* again."

I held out my hand and he shook it, then I got out of the car. I was a few paces away when the engine of the Mercedes stopped.

"Jan?" Magnus had opened his door and was getting out.

"I forgot there is something else I need to talk about," he said, coming across to me. "But if now isn't a good time…"

"No, go ahead," I said, wondering what was pressing enough after his recent discomfort.

"It concerns our father's will," Magnus told me. "There is a gift for you."

That wasn't what I'd expected. He'd referred to the will at the funeral, but I hadn't given it more than cursory speculation since then. I had no expectations, great or small; just vague curiosity.

"What sort of gift?"

"He has left you a house at Tjørnuvík," Magnus said then. "I don't know it or what it is like, but when all the details are finished I will let you know."

"A house?" I repeated. Stupid, but the only thing that came to mind.

"There is also some money," Magnus said. "I think it will be about five hundred thousand – krónur," he added quickly, in case I got the wrong idea.

I shook my head. "Listen, thanks, but no thanks. Signar can't play that sort of game just because he's dead."

Magnus frowned: a look of genuine confusion. "What sort of game? To leave something to a son is… It's a natural thing. What else would he do?"

"I don't know," I said, because I didn't. But for some reason I suddenly felt irritated by the whole thing. Because we were standing in a damp car park and he was telling me that the man who had barely acknowledged my existence in the last forty years had still deigned to remember me in his will.

What was that? Guilt? Remorse? Recompense? Or was it a way of trying to prove – as Sofia had put it – that I was still his son, no matter how far away he'd chosen to stay?

I realised that Magnus was watching me closely, still not understanding, it seemed from his look.

"Listen," I said. "Don't take this the wrong way, but I

don't want anything of Signar's. It's like I told you before: he was your father, not mine. So do what you want. Give it to the cats' home or something, okay? I'll see you later."

He stepped back when I started the car, but he stayed watching as I reversed, turned and pulled out on to the road. It was a grand gesture, I knew that, but at that moment I had nothing else.

11

REMI HAD CHOSEN ONE OF THE FRONT OFFICES OVERLOOKING the road to be the main incident room, but the office was too prone to comings and goings for Hentze's liking, so he'd taken over the adjacent room, just for some peace and quiet. One of the advantages of Sunday: there was no one around to lay prior claim.

Having a more private space also meant that the photographs of Erla Sivertsen's body were not on display for everyone to see; and to make sure of this, Hentze had lowered the blinds on the office windows. He had chosen to put up only six pictures from the scene: one showing the huts from a distance, three of Erla Sivertsen's body in situ, one close-up of the wound to her chest, and the last of the writing on the wooden beam.

He was just writing up the few facts they knew on a whiteboard next to the photos when there was a knock on the door.

"Yeh?" Hentze called.

Oddur put his head in at the door. "Hjalti? Have you got a minute?"

"Yeh, come in."

Oddur did so. He had a laptop – his own – under his arm.

"I've got some of Erla Sivertsen's photos I think you should look at," he said.

"You've accessed her computer already?"

"No, not yet. I need to clone the hard drive before I start digging around. These are from a hard drive I found in her room. Looks like she was religious about making backups," he added with a note of approval, as if that fact alone made Erla Sivertsen someone of sense.

"Okay. So what are these pictures of?" Hentze asked.

Putting his laptop on the desk, Oddur told Hentze what Annika had said about Erla Sivertsen arguing with a man after the whale drive at Sandur two days ago.

"It seemed like it might be a good lead so I looked at files dated for Friday and found the photos she took," Oddur said. He tapped the laptop's keyboard and half a dozen images filled the screen. "There are about three hundred from the day, but these are the only ones that specifically show someone cutting up a whale," he told Hentze, expanding the first photo so it filled the screen.

A man in waders was bending down to cut into the belly of a whale, his back to the camera. Oddur scrolled through the images one by one, until the final photo showed the man standing upright and facing the camera. His mouth was open in mid-speech, giving him a threatening look, and the knife in his hand pointed upwards.

"No, I don't know him," Hentze said. "Will you circulate it and see if anyone else does? Maybe without showing the knife or the background."

"Sure, no problem. I'll email it round," Oddur said.

"As a matter of interest, how many photographs did she have?"

"In total? I don't know. I've only looked at a couple of files, but altogether there must be several thousand."

"So many?" Hentze was surprised.

"It's not unusual for a professional," Oddur said with a shrug. "Actually, it's quite modest. She seems to have been selective about what she shot, rather than using a *spray and pray* approach."

"What about her emails and Facebook account and so on – can we check on those?"

"I'll get on to it as soon as I've cloned her laptop."

"Good, okay. Did you find a phone in her room by the way?"

"No – there wasn't one on the body?"

"No."

"She must have had one."

Hentze nodded. "You'd think."

When Oddur had departed Hentze picked up a marker and wrote the word *Argument* under a short list of other words on the left-hand side of the whiteboards. It was the only one not followed by a question mark: *rape?*; *whales?*; *location?*; *phone?*

He leaned on the table to survey the list. There was more space than information. Too much space to even start putting theories together. They needed a timeline, they needed a post-mortem, they needed some kind of framework – none of which would appear in the next few minutes. He went to make coffee, locking the office door behind him.

Outside the communal CID kitchen/canteen he met Annika Mortensen, heading the opposite way.

"Have you finished with statements at the house on Fjalsgøta?" he asked.

"Yeh," Annika said. "Five people live there, not including Erla. They're a pretty mixed bag: Dutch, German, English and French. And there was a Danish guy who was visiting."

"Do we know when they last saw Erla?"

"Yesterday afternoon, about three o'clock is the latest time. She was with a Dutch girl called Veerle, then she went out."

"Okay, good. That's useful to know."

"Listen, has Oddur talked to you about a man Erla argued with?" Annika asked then.

"Yeh, a few minutes ago. He's found some photos he thinks might be of the man. Was that your lead?"

"Sort of."

"Good. Thanks." And then, because there was no one else around, "So have you told Heri about your application to Vesterbro CID yet?"

Annika nodded. "A few days ago."

"And?"

"Yeh, he said it was a good thing to do."

"So it is," Hentze said. "You need a new challenge."

"As long as I get accepted."

"Nah, don't worry," Hentze said. "You will."

On his way back from the kitchen, coffee mug in hand, he met Remi Syderbø who had clearly been looking for him.

"So, how are we doing?" Remi asked.

"Come and see for yourself."

Hentze unlocked the office door and let Remi go in first. He sipped his coffee patiently as Remi surveyed the photos on the wall then moved in closer to look at the photograph of the wooden beam.

"This 'Fuck the Whales' bothers me," Remi said. "If you had just killed a person would *you* stay around to write something like that?"

"Perhaps, if I wanted to make a point about something," Hentze said neutrally.

"So we're to believe she was killed because she was opposed to the whaling?"

"Possibly. Or by someone who wanted to make it look that way – to distract us. There's no way to tell at the moment."

Remi let the issue lie for the moment. "Okay, well maybe we'll get a better idea when we collate the information from the interviews with her AWCA colleagues. The main thing we need to work out is what her movements were before her death, but even that's not going to be easy until we know *when* she died."

"I'd like to gather some more information about her background as well," Hentze said. "Do we have any intelligence on her?"

Remi cocked his head. "How do you mean?"

"I just wondered if there was a file somewhere. I assume our Danish friends didn't come empty-handed and it seems likely that they'd have information on all the AWCA staff, if not the volunteers as well."

"I don't know what information the Danes have," Remi said somewhat stiffly. "I can ask, of course. Have you checked for a criminal record?"

"Yes. She didn't have one."

"Well, as I say, I'll make enquiries about intelligence."

"Okay, thanks."

There was a knock on the door and at Hentze's call one of the younger uniform officers called Sólja looked in rather tentatively.

"Hjalti? Sorry to interrupt. I've just seen a photograph Oddur emailed round. He said you want an ID for the man in the picture?"

"Yes. Do you know him?"

"Yeh, his name's Arne Haraldsen: he's a friend of my father, from Sandur. I looked up the address for you, from the phonebook." She handed him a slip of paper.

"Thanks, that's great," Hentze said.

"Is he a suspect?" She sounded slightly concerned.

"No, just a potential witness."

"Oh. Right. Okay."

With a nod towards Remi Syderbø, Sólja departed. Hentze looked at the address, then at Remi.

"Who's this Haraldsen?" Remi asked.

"According to one of the Alliance people Erla Sivertsen had an argument with a local man on Friday after the whale drive. Looks like Haraldsen might be him."

"They argued about the *grind*?"

"I guess so. Of course, they must get into arguments all the time. It may be nothing."

"Yeh," Remi conceded."Still, you'd better check it out. And if you're going back to Sandoy you can meet the technical team when they arrive. It's probably best if you do that anyway, seeing as you've already looked at the scene."

There seemed to be a touch of expediency about the way Remi had grasped the opportunity to get him out of the office, Hentze thought, but he let it lie.

"Yes, that makes sense," he said instead. "Do you want me to wait and bring Ári up to speed when he gets here, or should I go now?"

"No, there's no need to wait," Remi said. "I'll fill Ári in."

Hentze ate an indifferent hotdog from the *Teistin*'s snack bar because there was nothing else to do on the ferry, and because he believed in the old policeman's maxim: never pass up the chance for the toilet, a coffee or something to eat. There was no telling how long any of them would be working tonight.

So far Remi Syderbø's leadership of the investigation had been positive and proactive, to say the least. That was no bad thing as far as Hentze was concerned, but by taking direct control, he wondered what sort of message Remi was putting out. He also wondered again whether Remi had had an ulterior motive for sending him out to Sandoy before Ári Niclasen got back.

Hentze and Ári had exchanged fewer than a dozen non-work-related sentences in the previous couple of weeks. Not that they'd exactly been bosom buddies before, but Hentze knew that Ári still felt burned over the Tummas Gramm murder, and that Ári saw him as the main cause of that.

The situation was unfortunate, but not really of Hentze's making. He had simply pursued the Gramm case as he would any other; but Ári had held back, which left him seemingly lacking when things had come to a head. Now, with another high-profile case so close to the last, Hentze knew that Ári would see any hint of reservation from Remi as salt in his wounds. Ári was senior to Hentze and known to aspire to Remi's position as head of CID one day. And because Ári held grudges the next few days might be tricky. So maybe it was better that he'd been sent off to do leg work, Hentze thought: out of the way. Let Ári stay close to Remi if that suited him. Hentze would just get on with the job, away from the politics. That suited him, too.

When the *Teistin* docked Hentze drove off the clanking ramp and then on up the hill, following the only road south. The light was already fading under a leaden overcast and it was a reminder that autumn was closing in, the days shortening ever more quickly.

Arne Haraldsen's house was on the west side of Sandur village, standing in the centre of a plot of flat grassland, a modern two-storey building with grey cladding and black eaves. It was far neater than the battered pickup truck parked on a patch of gravel outside.

Hentze checked the names on the mailbox – Arne Haraldsen, Marjun Haraldsen – then climbed the steps to the first-floor door and pressed the bell. There was a wait of a minute or so before a figure appeared behind the frosted glass panel and opened the door.

Hentze recognised the man immediately from the photos Oddur had shown him, but in person Arne Haraldsen was broader in the shoulders and a little taller than Hentze had assumed. He wore clean jeans and a sweater and stood in grey woollen socks.

"Arne Haraldsen?" Hentze asked. "I'm Hjalti Hentze from the police."

"Yeh, I know you," Haraldsen said with a nod. "What's up?"

"I'd like to ask you a couple of questions about the *grind* on Friday. Is that all right?"

"Friday?" A brief look of puzzlement crossed his face, but then he shrugged. "Sure, if you like. Come in."

Inside it was warm and Hentze took off his boots beside the door before following Haraldsen through to the kitchen. From the sitting room there was the sound of a TV showing some kind of sports event.

"You're Finn Sólsker's father-in-law, aren't you?" Haraldsen said, moving to fill the kettle. "Martha's father, right?"

"Yes, that's right," Hentze said. "How do you know Finn?"

"Oh, my boat's down there in the harbour with his," Haraldsen said. "The *North Light*. Take a seat. Would you like coffee?"

"No, thanks, not for me," Hentze said. Despite the old maxim he didn't think this was the time. Instead he pulled a chair out from under the pine dining table and sat down.

Arne Haraldsen left the kettle to boil and took a seat opposite Hentze. "So, what's this about?" he asked. "Someone complained about their share of the catch, is that it?"

"Not exactly. Did you have any trouble with the protesters during the *grind*?"

"Me? No. The police took care of them. They did a good job, I thought: got them out of the way pretty quick."

"What about afterwards – any problems then?"

"How could there be? They were all under arrest."

"Ah, okay," Hentze said with a nod. Then: "Do you know a woman called Erla Sivertsen?"

Haraldsen frowned. "No, I don't think so. I know Jógvan Sivertsen from Borðoy, but that's all."

Hentze took out his phone and swiped the screen a couple of times to bring up a photo.

"This is Ms Sivertsen," Hentze said, holding the phone so Haraldsen could see it.

The man squinted, and then – when he realised that this was not a photograph taken in life – he shook his head and looked away quickly.

"I don't understand. What's this about?" he said defensively.

"You haven't heard about the events in Húsavík today?"

"Húsavík? No, I've been here all day. Why, what's happened?"

"A woman's body was found there at around midday: this woman, Erla Sivertsen." He gestured to the phone. "We've also been told that you argued with Ms Sivertsen at the harbour on Friday afternoon. Is that true?"

"What? No." Haraldsen shook his head firmly. "Are you accusing me of something, is that it?"

"No," Hentze said, but left it a little less than definite. He put his phone on the table and set it to record. "However,

I do need to know what happened between you and Ms Sivertsen on Friday."

On the other side of the room the kettle came to the boil and clicked off. For a moment Haraldsen looked as if he might stand and go to it, but then changed his mind.

"Listen, there was nothing *between* us, as you call it. She was taking photos while I cut up a whale and I told her to stop it, that's all."

"And then what happened?"

"Nothing."

"Did she stop taking pictures?"

"Not straight away, no."

"So you threatened her?"

"No. Nothing like that – like you're suggesting."

"Is that true?" Hentze asked reasonably. "Only I've seen the photographs she took and you had a knife in your hand."

"Of course I had a knife in my hand," Haraldsen said curtly. "I was cutting up a whale, I told you. What else would I use?"

"But you're saying you didn't threaten Ms Sivertsen with it."

"No, of course not." Arne Haraldsen pushed back his chair with a jerk and stood up. "Listen, it was nothing like that – how you describe it."

"But you do look pretty angry in the photographs," Hentze said.

"Yeh? Well, I had a right to be," Haraldsen said. He paced the kitchen floor, then turned back. "Listen, I know what they're like, those Alliance people. They take your picture and next thing you know they've put it up on the internet or something, calling you a barbarian and a butcher. That's how they do things. Bloody foreigners. They should never have been allowed to come here in the first place."

Hentze cocked his head. "So you don't like the Alliance people?"

"Oh no," Haraldsen said with a wag of his finger. "No, no, you're not going to trick me like that. I'm just saying what most people think, that's all. I've got nothing against them personally: just against them coming here and telling us all what we should and shouldn't do."

Hentze knew that Haraldsen was correct in his assessment of the way most of the Faroe islanders felt, but he didn't want to start a debate. Instead he sat back in his chair.

"Have you ever used the phrase 'fuck the whales'?" he asked, giving it in English as it had been written, and watching for Haraldsen's reaction.

"What? No, I don't think so. Why?"

"I just wondered," Hentze said, passing it off. "So, as you're telling it, Ms Sivertsen took some photographs and you asked her to stop? Is that accurate?"

"Yes." Haraldsen gave an emphatic nod.

"And then what happened?"

"Nothing. She went away and I went back to the whales, like I'm entitled to do."

"Were there any witnesses to this? Anyone who can verify your version of events?"

"Sure, ask Høgni Joensen, he'll tell you," Haraldsen said. "And there was an English guy, too: some relative of

Finn's." Then a thought occurred to him. "Is it them who've put you up to this, is that it? Because if it is – if it's Finn who's accusing me of something, he wants to think again. 'Let him who's without sin…' – right?"

"Sorry, I don't follow," Hentze said.

Haraldsen came back to stand with his hands on the back of his vacated chair, as if he had a better grasp of the situation now. "This Sivertsen woman," he said. "I'd seen her a couple of times before Friday. Down there at the harbour, at the *Kári Edith*. More than once."

"You're saying she knew Finn?"

"Looked that way to me. Very friendly."

He gave Hentze a knowing, significant look, clearly pleased to have thrown new light on the inquiry.

"Well we'll be talking to everyone who knew her, of course," Hentze said, deliberately keeping it officially neutral. "But for the moment I'd like to concentrate on your movements yesterday and last night. Could you sit down again so we can go through them?"

Arne Haraldsen resisted for a moment and then gave an elaborate shrug. "All right, please yourself, but you're wasting your time. I didn't even know she was dead till you told me. Still, maybe it'll make the rest of them go away and leave us in peace now. That'd be something."

12

IT WAS ALMOST DARK BY THE TIME HENTZE LEFT ARNE Haraldsen's house and returned to his car.

Broadly speaking, Arne Haraldsen had had as much trouble recalling his recent movements as most people do. His memory had improved when his wife had returned home from visiting relatives in Skálavík, though, and after twenty minutes or so Hentze was prepared to believe that Haraldsen was a poor candidate for murder. Of course, without knowing exactly when Erla Sivertsen had been killed there was still room for doubt, but an argument over a few photographs seemed like a pretty thin motive, and any other – like rape – wouldn't be established until they had the post-mortem results. For the time being, then, Hentze was inclined to discount Arne Haraldsen as a possible suspect: not impossible, but unlikely.

He looked at his watch, tilting the dial to catch the last of the light. The flight from Copenhagen would be landing about now, but the technical team would still have to collect their baggage and make the fifty-kilometre journey from Vágar to Gamlarætt for the ferry. At least an hour and a half, he reckoned, before they reached Skopun.

So he had time. The question was, did he want to use it to follow up Arne Haraldsen's insinuation about Finn and Erla Sivertsen, or should he dismiss it as the muck-stirring it probably was?

Whatever the motive behind the innuendo, if Erla Sivertsen *had* known Finn Sólsker, Hentze knew he ought to follow it up. If it was anyone else that's what he'd do, and the fact that Finn was his son-in-law shouldn't get in the way. Besides, it had sparked a vague recollection in Hentze – so vague that he wasn't sure even it was reliable – and after a moment's more thought he reached for the ignition and started the car.

Just short of the ferry dock car park Hentze turned left, past the boats hauled on to land for repair, and drove on up the hill into Skopun. It wasn't much of a place: not pretty or quaint, and the fact that it was on a north-facing hill meant that even in daylight it always seemed to be gloomy. Now the streetlights lit the way and near the top of the hill he turned into a small estate of relatively new houses.

His daughter's house wasn't large – especially for a family with two kids under eight – but it was as much as the couple could afford, even with both of them working. Fishing was a fickle occupation, particularly for a man who ran his own boat, and Hentze knew there were many things that could unexpectedly push outgoings past income and leave a big hole in the accounts.

He left his car on the street and walked up the steps to the back door. The handrail needed a coat of paint, he noticed, and one of the external lights was still broken.

"Hey *babba*," Martha said, with a mixture of pleasure and surprise when she saw him on the porch. "What're you doing here? Come in. Quiet though, the kids are only just in bed."

The kids – Kári and Edith, aged seven and five – had school in the morning, and much as he loved his grandchildren, Hentze was glad not to have their distraction at the moment. Inside he let his daughter close the door quietly and took off his boots.

"Is it the body at Húsavík?" Martha asked then, meaning the reason he was on the island. "When I heard I couldn't believe it."

Hentze nodded. "The Technical team are on their way but I've got a little time yet, so I hoped you might make me some coffee."

"Sure, of course."

"You *do* know who it is?" Hentze asked, because so far he hadn't mentioned Erla Sivertsen's name.

"Yes." Martha's tight nod was enough of a signal that she not only knew but wouldn't choose to discuss it.

"Finn used to go out with a girl called Erla, didn't he?" Hentze said, because it was necessary. "Is it the same woman?"

"Yeh," Martha said. "It was years ago, though. She went away."

"So I understand."

Martha fiddled with the coffee pot, taking it apart and concentrating for a moment as she put in the grounds.

"So do you know anything yet – about how it happened?" she asked in the end.

Hentze shook his head. "We won't find out much till the technical people have had a chance to look at things. It will probably be a long night."

Martha digested that, then clearly decided not to go further. "Finn's in the sitting room with Høgni if you want to talk to him," she said. "I'll bring your coffee through when it's made."

"Are you feeding Høgni as well then these days?" Hentze asked with a nod at the dining table, which still showed signs of recent use.

"Only on Sundays. At least then he gets one proper meal in a week."

Hentze hung his coat on the back of a chair and went through to the sitting room, with its leather suite and sheepskin rug in front of the TV. Above that there was a large framed photograph of Finn, Martha and their two children. It was a good picture, Hentze thought: happy and relaxed, taken a couple of years ago.

"Hey, Hjalti," Finn said, raising a hand in greeting. "Martha didn't say you were coming. Have a seat. Have you—" He broke off when he put two and two together. "Are you working?"

"Yeh, I'm waiting to meet a technical team off the ferry."

"Right," Finn said with a sombre nod.

On the sofa Høgni Joensen was frowning. He looked to Finn for explanation. "What are you talking about?" he asked.

"About Erla," Finn said flatly.

"Oh. Oh. Yeh." Høgni looked away, as if he'd inadvertently said the wrong thing.

"When did you hear about it?" Hentze asked, sitting down in an armchair. He was speaking to Finn.

"This afternoon," Finn said. "One of Martha's friends from Húsavík called." He shook his head and scowled for a moment. "What do you say, eh?"

"You used to go out with Erla, didn't you?" Hentze asked, keeping it conversational.

Finn nodded, as if he'd anticipated the question. "A long time ago, while she was in college."

Hentze couldn't read the man's reaction to her death, but that wasn't so unusual. Everyone had had time to process the news and apply a filter to their feelings, whatever they were.

"Had you seen much of her recently?" he asked.

"No, not so much. She came to say hello not long after she got back."

"Here?"

Finn shook his head. "At the boat. And she was at the harbour on Friday for the *grind*."

"Yeh, I gather she had a set-to with Arne Haraldsen," Hentze said.

"He's an arsehole," Finn said flatly. He gestured with his beer bottle. "She took a few photos and he got shirty about it. Starts threatening her. You know Jan Reyná, right? He and Høgni had to break it up."

Hentze looked to Høgni Joensen. "What happened?"

Høgni shifted awkwardly. He was nervous around authority figures, and even if Hentze was part of Finn's family, the authority of the police was still there. It had a tendency to make him stammer. "A-Arne told her to stop taking his picture," Høgni said. "He told her to give him the camera."

"Did she?"

"N–no. And then he called her a whore." He uttered the last word without thinking and when he realised what he'd said he glanced quickly towards the kitchen door. Not a word to use in front of women.

"Then what happened?" Hentze asked.

"Nothing. I mean, I, I, I told him to leave her alone a–a-and he did. That was it."

Hentze nodded. Høgni wasn't nearly as tall as Arne Haraldsen, but he was built like a brick wall. There was also a direct simplicity about the man, which engendered the feeling that once he set his mind to something he'd push it through to the end.

Høgni shifted, uncomfortable at being the centre of attention. "Is it all right if I go for a smoke?" he asked Finn.

"Course it is, don't be daft."

Høgni looked grateful and headed for the kitchen like a condemned man who's just spotted an open door.

Finn watched him go. "He's only just stopped asking permission to take a leak when we're on the boat," he said with a hopeless shake of his head.

"How long's he been working for you now?" Hentze asked.

"Five years. You couldn't get a better baitman, though."

"That's what I hear – so when was the last time you saw Erla?"

The shift of topic stopped Finn for a second, then he said, "Friday, when she left the harbour. She gave Jan Reyná

122

a lift to Tórshavn so Fríða could stay and see the kids."

"Not since then?"

"No." Finn drained his beer bottle, assessed it for a second, then shifted in his seat, ready to stand. "Sorry, Hjalti, I should've asked before. Do you want a beer?"

"No, thanks. Martha's making coffee." And then, before Finn could move, he added, "Finn, listen. We're asking everyone who knew Erla, so I have to ask you too. Can you tell me where you were yesterday?"

"Are you serious?" Finn gave a disbelieving laugh.

"It's just routine, like I said."

Finn took a second, then sat back in his seat. "Yesterday? Okay, well, I was at the boat all day – except for a trip to Müller's in Tórshavn for a fuel pump."

"What time was that?"

"I got the two fifteen ferry there and the five fifteen back."

"What then?"

"Jesus, Hjalti, listen—"

"I told you, it's just routine."

Finn seemed ready to challenge that, but in the end he said, "I came back here, we had dinner, put the kids to bed and I went back to the boat for a couple of hours to put the fuel pump in."

"Was Høgni there – at the boat?"

"No, I was on my own."

"Okay, then what?"

"I packed it in about ten, came home, had a shower and after that we went to bed."

"Okay, thanks. That's all I needed to know."

Finn took a moment, then stood up. As he did so Martha came in with Hentze's coffee and then from upstairs there was a mournful child's call: Kári, the eldest.

"Oh, now what?" Martha said, looking weary. "They should be asleep."

"I'll go," Finn said. "You talk to your dad."

As Finn went upstairs Hentze gestured his daughter to the sofa. "Are you going to sit down?"

"No, I've still got the dishes to do."

"Okay, I'll come through then," Hentze said, standing up with his coffee. They went back to the kitchen.

"Is Høgni still outside?" he asked, glancing at the back door.

Martha shook her head. "No, he said he was going home. I think he's frightened of you."

"Me? Why?"

"I don't know. Maybe because of his father."

"Oh, yeh. Maybe then."

Høgni's father, Símun Joensen, had been a rare Faroese phenomenon; a man who stole and cheated so often that while Høgni was a boy he spent more time in prison than out of it. Finally realising he'd become the default suspect after any burglary on the islands, Símun had gone off to Denmark where the opportunities for a long-term career as a thief were better. He hadn't been seen since, which was no one's loss – apart from the Danes', Hentze supposed.

"So are you okay?" he asked, putting an arm on Martha's shoulder. She looked tired, he thought: stressed. Perhaps no more than usual with two small kids, though.

"Yeh, I'm fine. How's Mum?"

"Okay, doing well," Hentze said. "You could bring the kids over next weekend if you like."

"Okay, maybe I will." She leaned her head against him for a moment, then straightened and moved out of his embrace. "If you're going to be working late I'll make you a sandwich to take with you. Is lamb from the joint okay?"

"That'd be fine," he told her, pushing up his sleeves. "But only if you let me do the dishes."

13

"YOU PEOPLE HAVE TO STOP KILLING EACH OTHER," FORENSIC examiner Sophie Krogh told Hentze. "Having the highest birth rate in Europe is no excuse. Mind you, I don't know how *that's* possible either. You all go round looking like you only have sex once a year – if you're lucky."

"Maybe that's because we're too busy killing each other," Hentze replied flatly.

Sophie Krogh looked at him in the light of the car's dashboard and seemed to assess whether she might have misjudged her tone.

"Is it a bad one?" she asked.

Hentze shrugged. "No, not so much. Not in that way."

"So?"

Hentze sighed. "It's just been a long day, that's all," he said, realising it was true. Then he put it aside. "Did they send a pathologist with you?"

"No, not till tomorrow. Anders Toft is on a case in Odense. I don't know about the others. Maybe away for the weekend."

"We should have been doctors."

"Nah," Sophie shook her head. "Too many sick people. I

prefer corpses: they can't complain. So, tell me where you've got to with this one."

The drive across the island took as long as Hentze needed to give her the relevant details.

The number of uniform officers guarding the site had been reduced to three when it got dark. Now they helped unload equipment from the minivan while Hentze and Sophie Krogh suited up and went out to have a look at the scene. They each carried powerful flashlights to find their way along the common approach path.

At the stone huts the plastic sheeting Hentze and Dánjal Michelsen had hung over the alcove moved restlessly in the breeze, and Hentze stayed several metres away while Sophie went under it to take her first look at Erla Sivertsen's body. By Hentze's reckoning she might have lain there for more than twenty-four hours now, and he hoped Sophie wouldn't decide to leave things as they were until daylight. That seemed too long.

In an effort to distract himself he took out his phone and made a couple of calls until Sophie re-emerged.

"I think we'll leave the area search till the morning," she said. "But if we bring in some lights I think we can deal with the body and the area around it. It'd be too difficult to tent properly without disturbing things, so we'll get on with it now, before it starts to rain. We should be able to get her out of there in two or three hours unless we find anything unexpected."

"Okay, good," Hentze said. "The last scheduled ferry leaves

Skopun at ten thirty but I can arrange for the search and rescue boat to take her body to the mortuary when you're ready."

"Fine. Are you staying?"

"Do you need me?"

"Not particularly – unless you're looking for an excuse to pad out your overtime sheet."

"Not today, no." Hentze shook his head. They started back to the road. "In that case I'll leave you to it and see if there's any new information at the incident room."

Fríða's father, Jens Sólsker, had phoned with the news of Erla Sivertsen's death as we were finishing dinner. The rest of the meal was a fairly sombre affair; not just because Fríða and Erla had been friends but because the sudden death of anyone you know tends to shake up the jigsaw of things as they were and make you reassess the pieces.

When we'd finished eating Matteus cleared the table and started on the dishes without being prompted by Fríða. For a sixteen-year-old he was a lot less self-absorbed than most of his age, and because he was more used to reading his mother's mood than I was, I took my cue from him and joined him at the sink, leaving Fríða to make a couple of calls in private.

I did a little jigsaw reassessment of my own while we washed up, but not a great deal. I'd spent an hour or so in Erla Sivertsen's company and I'd liked her well enough. She'd seemed interesting and engaged, but beyond that it was unknowable now. Maybe I'd been dwelling on other deaths too much recently, or maybe the fact that my job deals with death all the time made it easier to draw down a detached distance. Whatever the case, that's what I did.

"Do you have any gin?" Fríða asked when she came back to the kitchen. Matteus had gone off upstairs.

"Does it rain here?" I stood up. "I'll fetch it. Tonic as well?"

She nodded, then changed her mind and said, "I'll come with you."

"Oh, okay."

She called up the stairs as we left, "Matts, I'm going next door for a drink with Jan, okay?"

"Yeh, okay."

In the guest house I found glasses, poured two drinks and brought them to the sitting room where Fríða had settled in the armchair, legs pulled up under her, staring thoughtfully at the unlit wood burner. I handed her a glass.

"*Ger so væl.*"

"*Takk. Skál.*"

"*Skál.*"

I went to sit on the couch, waiting to see what she'd choose to say.

"So how was your visit with Sofia?" she asked.

"She doesn't pull her punches, does she?"

"*Nei*, she's a tough one."

She sipped her drink.

"Do you know anything about her background?" I asked. "I mean how she and Signar got together?"

"Not so much. Her family had money – a shop in Runavík, selling supplies to ships – and I think she was in charge by the time she met Signar. And not so young, either.

I have heard some people say that she was looking out to find a husband before it was too late, but I don't know if it's true."

"Do you think… Do you know the phrase 'the power behind the throne'?"

"Yeh, I think so."

"Do you think that's what Sofia was? I mean, when Signar was alive."

She considered that, then nodded. "Yeh, I think it's possible, yeh. She has always been a strong woman: she knows what she wants."

I thought so, too. So I wondered if a recently widowed Signar might have seemed like a decent investment and opportunity to Sofia forty-odd years ago. I already knew that he'd bought his own boat at around the same time he'd married Sofia, and from then on his business interests had grown quickly, as well as gaining two sons – Magnus and Kristian – in quick succession. It wasn't such a leap to think Sofia might have been the moving power behind all that.

"Did you ask her about Lýdia?" Fríða said then. "That was why you went, wasn't it?"

"Pretty much, yeah."

So I told her what Sofia had said, boiling it down to the two most salient facts: that Lýdia had attempted suicide about a year after I was born and had been sent to hospital in Denmark as a result, although she'd refused to stay very long.

"I'm guessing," I said. "But it could fit with her medical record if Ørsted Sjúkrahús was some kind of psychiatric hospital."

"Yes, I suppose so," Fríða said, then looked at me over

the rim of her glass. "So how do you feel about that?"

It was said like a therapist, because that's what she was, and for a moment I debated whether I wanted to pursue it like that. Half and half. But before I could decide further my phone rang in the kitchen. I stood up. "Do you mind?"

"No, of course."

Hjalti Hentze's name was on the screen. "Hey," I said.

"I'm calling for work," Hentze said, as if to forestall any misunderstanding. "Have you heard about Erla Sivertsen?"

"Yeah."

"Okay." Said in a way that meant he could therefore dispense with the details, and he sounded grateful for that. "We think it's a suspicious death so you know how it goes now."

"Yeah, I know."

"You saw her on Friday, is that right?"

I knew why he was asking: he was building a timeline. "Yeah, at the *grind*," I said. "After that she gave me a lift back to Tórshavn. That was about half past six. I didn't see or talk to her again after that."

"Ah, okay, thank you, that was what I needed to know. And while she was with you did she say anything that might be useful to us?"

I ran back over the conversation, but only briefly. Hentze would only be interested in anything that might have given cause for concern and I already knew there was nothing like that. "No, not that I can think of. We just chatted."

"Okay, *takk*," he said, acknowledging that it had been a slim hope.

"Have you got a time of death yet?"

"No, only that she was last seen yesterday afternoon. Thanks for your help. I'll let you get back to your evening."

"Hjalti?"

"Yeh?"

"Statistically, the chances are that she knew the person who killed her – at least who they were. But more likely she knew them quite well."

"Yeh," he said flatly. He already knew that.

"Okay. If there's anything I can do, let me know."

"Yeh, I will, but this time it is our headache, I think. *Takk fyri, Jan.*"

He rang off and I put the phone back on the counter and plugged it into the charger, thinking about Hentze and his dislike of murders. Then I went back to the sitting room.

Fríða was still sitting as I'd left her but she'd finished her drink and when I offered another she said yes, then uncurled herself and followed me to the kitchen.

"It was Hjalti on the phone," I said, refilling glasses. "About Erla."

"Does he know any more?"

"Doesn't sound like it." And then, because I was curious, "How did you meet her? I mean, were you friends at school or neighbours or…?"

She took her glass and leaned against the counter top. "In the beginning, it was because of Finn. He was her boyfriend while they were at school, but it was always on again, off again: always a drama, you know? For a year, maybe."

"That's teenagers, though."

"Yeh, I guess. But they got together again when Erla went

to college in Tórshavn and then they became more serious. They were together for about three years. That was when I got to know her better."

"Like a big sister?"

"Yeh, maybe."

"So what happened between them?"

She shrugged, as if it was predictable. "It was what often happens here. The islands aren't so big, and if you want to..." she hunted for the word – "to *expand* yourself, you have to leave."

"Couldn't Finn have gone with her?"

"I guess, but he wanted to buy a boat and to fish. That's who he is. Erla's— She was more adventurous."

I nodded. "I got that impression."

"Did you—" She changed her mind halfway through the question. "Had you arranged to see her again?"

That came out of left field. I shook my head. "No. At least only if I wanted to go to a debate the Alliance are having at the Nordic House. Why?"

She shrugged. "I just wondered. I had the idea she might be your type."

"You think I've got a type?"

"Haven't you?"

"Yeah, maybe," I said. "Someone with a big stick."

She frowned. "A stick?"

"I'm not much good at reading the signals – the hints. I'm never sure I'm reading them right, so I usually need to be hit over the head to get the message."

"Is that how your ex-wife did it?"

I laughed. "Not exactly, but it *is* how she came to be an ex."

She smiled, but it was more polite than accepting; as if she thought I'd dodged the issue by making a joke. And I suppose I had, in a fashion. I wasn't sure why: maybe because I knew what Fríða did for a living; or maybe just because opening the door into one personal issue often leads on to others.

Whatever the case, Fríða seemed to see it as a marker of some kind. She took a last sip from her glass then put it aside. "I should get back."

I saw her to the door and when she'd gone I collected my drink from the kitchen and then sat for a while, thinking about Erla Sivertsen and a couple of *what-if* kind of thoughts. Too late, though. That sort of thinking always is.

"So what do we have?" Remi Syderbø asked. There were four of them in the room besides himself: Hentze, Ári Niclasen, Oddur Arge and Kim Stenburg, the uniform inspector for the night shift.

Ári Niclasen spoke up first, as if keen to show that despite his late entry into the investigation he was now up to speed. "We're still collating details from the interviews with the Alliance people, but basically the last time Erla Sivertsen was seen alive by any of them appears to be at about 15:00 hours yesterday."

He stood up and moved to the whiteboard. "At around that time her housemate – a Dutch girl called Veerle Koning – says Erla left the house at Fjalsgøta with her camera equipment but didn't say where she was going. However, she did say not to expect her for dinner. She was wearing jeans, a blue AWCA sweatshirt, red waterproof jacket and a grey hat. As you can see from the photographs of the scene, the jacket and hat are missing. The car she was using is a silver Volvo, registration DA 732. We're still trying to locate it."

"Was her camera equipment with the body?" Remi asked, looking to Hentze.

Hentze shook his head. "No, she had no possessions at all. I suspect that was deliberate on the part of her killer, either in the hope of making identification harder, or perhaps as a result of robbery."

"You think robbery was the motive?" Ári said, not trying very hard to keep scepticism out of his voice.

"No," Hentze said mildly. "I'm just saying that whoever killed her might also have taken the opportunity to rob her as well. She was a professional photographer, so I assume her equipment would be quite valuable."

"Or it may still be in her car," Remi said, acknowledging both points. "It would be good to find that as a priority."

"I've circulated the description to all the patrols," Kim Stenburg said. "We'll keep looking overnight and again tomorrow."

"Good, thanks." Remi looked back to Hentze. "Is there anything more from the scene?"

"Not so far. Sophie and her team will be there for several hours but I think most of the information will come from the post-mortem."

"You checked out the man she argued with at Sandur after the *grind* – Haraldsen?"

"Yeh. At least for the moment he seems to be in the clear. They did argue when she took his photograph, but it was nothing more serious than that."

"Despite the graffiti at the scene?" Ári asked. "That clearly points towards someone with a grudge against the Alliance."

"It might," Hentze allowed. "But after a public argument with Erla Sivertsen I don't think Haraldsen would have been stupid enough to draw attention to himself as a suspect like that."

As soon as he'd used the word "stupid" he knew it had been the wrong thing to do. Ári Niclasen was hyper sensitive at the moment, and now he appeared to take the word as an indictment of his theory.

"Well maybe he *is* stupid," Ári said. "Or perhaps he thought it would throw suspicion on other people who don't like the Alliance. Can we be so quick to dismiss this Haraldsen when we know there was bad feeling between him and the victim?"

"I want to come back to that in a minute," Remi said, cutting in before Hentze could reply. He turned to Oddur. "What about the IT side? We know she had a cellphone, yes? Even though we don't have it."

"Yeh," Oddur said. "I've talked to the service provider and asked for a list of all calls made and received. They weren't happy about it, being Sunday, but we should have something by the morning. They *were* able to tell me that the phone is switched off at the moment, though."

"Okay. What about emails, web posts, that sort of thing?"

"I've started going through her emails but there are a lot. So far there's nothing out of the ordinary."

"Right. Good. Okay, does anyone have anything else to add? Anything we've not covered?"

No one did.

"Then let's talk about the bigger picture for a moment," Remi said. "We all know the current situation with regard to the Alliance, and as Ári's pointed out, the graffiti above the body could – *could* – indicate that this crime is in some way related to their activities."

Ári Niclasen nodded when Remi said this, but Remi appeared not to see. "However," he went on, "I've spoken to the Commander and it's been agreed that we need to keep a tight control over things now. No doubt there are people who will assume that because Erla Sivertsen was a member of the Alliance, her death is somehow related to that. We can't prevent that idea, but we can avoid reinforcing it. So, outside this room I don't want any open discussion of the graffiti *or* any implication that we are linking Ms Sivertsen's death with her membership of the Alliance. We are not. We are keeping an open mind to all the possibilities. This is what I have told Petra Langley, the leader of the AWCA group here, and she has agreed that, except for a statement acknowledging the death, they will not publish any other comments on their website for at least twenty-four hours. They also realise that the situation won't be improved by allowing wild speculation, so discretion is in their interests, too. Okay?"

There were nods and Remi Syderbø looked satisfied. He checked his watch. "Right, then let's get as far as we reasonably can tonight and start again first thing in the morning. By then maybe we'll have something more from Technical to help us out."

As the meeting broke up Hentze didn't linger and instead went to his own office where he called Sóleyg to say he'd probably be home in an hour or so, but not to wait up, just in case. His wife, who had long since got used to a policeman's hours, told him not to worry about it.

"Who is it – the dead woman? Do you know yet?" she asked then.

"Her name's Erla," Hentze said, but no more than that. He protected Sóleyg as a matter of habit; it was as natural as taking off his shoes when he came into the house. As far as he knew Sóleyg had never met Erla Sivertsen, but he was still cautious in case there was some connection he wasn't aware of.

"Poor woman," Sóleyg said. "Just don't stay any later than you need to. Promise?"

"I promise," Hentze said. "I'll see you soon."

14

HENTZE WAS BACK IN THE OFFICE JUST BEFORE SEVEN AS THE SKY pinked up over Nólsoy and mixed with the orange of the streetlights. It was pretty enough, but he always found this pre-dawn time depressing, as if it spoke of lost hours and lost opportunities.

He went to make coffee in the CID canteen and found Sophie Krogh stirring from sleep on an uncomfortable two-seater couch. She accepted his offer of coffee with a grunt and put on her boots while he made it.

Erla Sivertsen's body had been removed shortly before midnight, Sophie told him; then driven to Skopun where the search and rescue boat had brought it to Tórshavn. Sophie had accompanied it, then overseen the removal of clothes and the taking of samples before the body was put into cold storage awaiting the arrival of the forensic pathologist. After that she'd grabbed a few hours' sleep.

Hentze stirred the requested two sugars into Sophie's coffee, then went with her out on to the grey steel fire escape so she could smoke.

"Anything you can tell me?" he asked. "Any indication of cause of death?"

Sophie thought, then said, "You didn't hear this from me because it's for the FP to say, but I noticed some blood and what I think is a fracture at the back of her skull. The thin part, here." She indicated the area she meant. "That's a very vulnerable area. A blow there can easily cause death."

"Right. I didn't see that," Hentze admitted.

Sophie waved it away. "No reason you would, unless you'd moved her."

"And did it happen there, do you think?"

"No, I don't think so. From most indications we found I'd say she was killed somewhere else and moved to the site after death."

"What about the stab wound?"

"I think it was made after she died," Sophie said. "If she'd been alive I'd have expected to see more blood on her clothing if not on the ground."

"Could there have been internal bleeding instead?"

Sophie made a so-so gesture. "It didn't look that way to me, but the FP will tell you for sure."

Hentze thought about that. "So if the stab wound was made *after* death, does that mean she was killed by the injury to the back of her head?"

"Well, there were no other obvious wounds..." She shrugged to let him draw his own conclusion.

"Okay," Hentze said. "And was there a sexual element, do you think? A rape?"

Sophie pulled on her cigarette and exhaled in a long

plume. "That's harder to say. I didn't see any of the usual signs – scratches or dirt and abrasions, either to the buttocks and thighs or to the palms and the knees, but of course, that doesn't rule it out until we get the PM."

"But the way she was found, with her jeans down..." Hentze said.

"Yeh, well, who knows what goes on in some people's minds," Sophie said with a throwaway gesture. "But if I were you, Hjalti, I wouldn't be in too much of a rush to take this thing at face value."

"Oh?" Hentze frowned. "Why not?"

She made a moue. "*Fuck the whales?* It's a bit obvious, isn't it? – I dunno, I need to look again, but the whole thing seemed just a little bit... *staged*. It could be a case of someone wanting you to believe one thing to cover up another. You know what I mean?"

"Yeh, I think so."

"Okay." Seeing he'd got the point, Sophie looked at her watch. "What time's the next ferry back to the island?"

"Seven thirty. It's the first."

"If I use the shower in your gym could I still make it?"

"If you're quick. I'll get someone to take you."

"*Takk.*" Sophie took a last, short drag on her cigarette, then stubbed it out and followed him back inside.

Still carrying his coffee Hentze went back along the corridor to Remi Syderbø's office. Remi was taking off his coat. He looked as if he might have had a slightly better night's sleep than Hentze, which wasn't saying a lot.

"*Morgun*," Remi said. "Anything overnight?"

Briefly Hentze told him that it looked as if Erla Sivertsen had been moved to the huts at Húsavík rather than killed there, but he said nothing of Sophie Krogh's unofficial assessment of the scene. This wasn't out of secrecy, but because he knew it would be jumping the gun to start tossing possibilities around without proper foundation. Besides, there was a protocol to be followed in terms of official reports and Remi was a big believer in protocol.

"Unless you need me immediately I thought I'd take Sophie back to Sandoy," Hentze said then. "I want to have a word with someone I couldn't speak to properly last night and it'll be easier to find him if I go now."

Remi frowned. "About the case? Who?"

"His name's Høgni Joensen. He was at the *grind* when Erla argued with Arne Haraldsen."

Remi adjusted his spectacles. "I thought you'd ruled Haraldsen out."

"Yeh, I think so, but Høgni also knew Erla so…"

A movement outside the office window took Remi's attention. Hentze looked and saw Ári Niclasen walking along the corridor. Ári didn't stop.

Remi had noted this, too. "Okay, if you think it's necessary to speak to this Joensen you'd better go," he said. "Just to be tidy."

"Sure, of course," Hentze acknowledged, wondering at the same time whether Remi had also just seen a way to avoid having him and Ári both working together in the incident room – for the moment, at least.

* * *

They made the ferry with a couple of minutes to spare and Sophie Krogh ate breakfast from the snack bar while Hentze stuck to coffee. At Skopun a car was waiting to pick Sophie up and Hentze said he'd look in at Húsavík later, then drove the short distance to Í Trøðum where Høgni Joensen lived in a small rented house.

There was no answer at the door when Hentze knocked, so he backtracked and went to Sandur instead. He left the car on the quayside near the access ramp and walked round to the wooden shed where Finn Sólsker kept his spare fishing gear and Høgni repaired the long lines.

One door of the shed was open and the strip light inside showed Høgni Joensen ambling around. There was no sign of Finn, which Hentze counted as good. He wanted to speak to Høgni without his son-in-law around as a prompt.

Perhaps hearing Hentze's approach, Høgni looked up. When he saw the policeman he started, then quickly came to the doorway. He was dressed as he usually was, in several layers of ill-kempt work clothes, topped off by a woollen hat.

"Hey, Høgni," Hentze said cheerily. "How are you?"

"Oh. Oh, okay, yeh," Høgni said.

Hentze had always suspected that Høgni was a little simple: not in any severe way, but just that he couldn't deal with complicated situations. Yes or no, in or out, suited Høgni far better, but now, caught on the hop, even that choice seemed beyond him. On the threshold of the shed he was apparently unable to decide whether to stay put or come out, but in the end he opted for stepping outside, then turned quickly to close the door behind him, as if something inside might escape.

"Finn isn't here," he said, turning back to Hentze.

"That's all right, it was you I wanted to see," Hentze said amiably. "You went off before I could talk to you last night."

"I, I thought you wanted to talk to Finn."

"And to you, too."

"What a–about?"

"About Erla Sivertsen."

Høgni shook his head. "I don't know anything," he said flatly.

"That's okay, it's just background questions," Hentze said. "It's all right, you're not in any trouble."

"Trouble?" The word seemed to make Høgni uneasy.

"How well did you know her?" Hentze asked. "Was it for long?"

Høgni frowned as if it was hard to weigh up. "Years. I don't know."

"So she was a friend?"

"Not— She knew Finn," Høgni said, as if that explained everything.

"Yeh." Hentze nodded, to indicate that Høgni had confirmed what he already knew. "He told me she'd been down to see him at the boat. Did she come down here often, do you know?"

"A bit. Sometimes." Høgni shifted uncomfortably. "I dunno."

"Weren't you here, too?"

"Yeh, sometimes."

"When was the last time?"

"The last time what?"

"That you saw Erla down here with Finn."

"I, I dunno. Friday I suppose. Yeh, Friday."

"At the *grind*?"

"Yeh." Høgni nodded vigorously. "Yeh, at the *grind*."

"You didn't see her after that – on Saturday, maybe?"

Høgni shook his head. "No."

"Are you sure? Were you busy on Saturday? Were you working?"

"No. No, the boat— The fuel pump was broken. Finn was fixing it. He had to get a new one. It took him all day." There was some relief in Høgni's voice now, as if they'd moved on to a safer topic.

"Did you help with that?"

"No, I went— I was in town."

"Tórshavn?"

"Yeh. I, I had some shopping to do."

"So Finn was here on his own? Only he told me that you came down to see him on Saturday night. Wasn't that correct?"

It was an easy trick to pull but Hentze didn't take any great satisfaction in seeing the way it threw Høgni Joensen into a foot-shifting shuffle of uncertainty.

"No, I— I mean, yeh. Yeh, I forgot. Saturday night? I did come down here for a bit, to see Finn."

"What time was that?"

"I, I dunno. I can't remember."

"Was it dark?"

"Yeh. Yeh, I think so."

"Okay," Hentze said, as if that verified what he'd thought. Then he cast a glance at the rain-leaden sky and shrugged up his collar. It was only spitting for now.

"Listen, is it all right if we go in out of the rain?" he said, gesturing at the shed. "No point standing in the wet, is there?"

"I-I, I'm going to the shop," Høgni said, shuffling awkwardly again. "I was just going."

"Can I have a look inside anyway?"

"W-what for?"

"No reason." Then, without giving Høgni time to work his way round that, Hentze moved to the shed and tugged the door open. He stepped over the rail on the threshold and went inside, waiting to see how long it would be before – or if – Høgni would follow.

Inside the shed two fluorescent strip lights illuminated the stainless steel filleting table and a collection of plastic-handled knives stuck to a magnetic strip on the wall behind it. Towards the back of the shed there was a collection of plastic bins, nylon lines, hooks and associated fishing tackle stacked up on the concrete floor or shelved on steel units along the walls. The place smelled dankly of fish, salt water and bleach but it was pretty clean and well kept.

"I, I need to go to the shop," Høgni said again. He was just inside the doorway now, looking uncomfortable.

Hentze said nothing but continued to look around the shed, finally casting a glance at several waterproof dungarees and yellow sou'westers hanging just inside the door.

"You'll have to go now," Høgni said, his voice more determined, as if he'd finally reached a decision.

Hentze took no notice, but stepped forward and moved the topmost waterproofs aside until he exposed the red

Gore-tex jacket whose collar had just been visible behind the bulk of the other coats. It wasn't a fisherman's jacket. For a start it was clean, but it was also designed for hill walking rather than boat work.

"Who does this red coat belong to?" Hentze asked.

"I, I dunno."

"It looks too small for you or for Finn," Hentze said, appraising it again.

"May-may-maybe it's Martha's," Høgni said.

Hentze shook his head. "I think you'd better start telling me the truth, Høgni," he said. "And properly now, okay? No more lies about where you were and who you were with."

The truth wasn't easy for Høgni Joensen – which, Hentze suspected, was because Høgni wasn't sure exactly what the truth was. In addition there was also the matter of Høgni's loyalty to Finn Sólsker, which made him reluctant to say anything that might be taken the wrong way. Finn was Høgni's best friend, not just his employer, and Finn was a good guy – something Høgni said several times, as if repetition would finally convince Hentze that it really was so.

So, the truth – at least as far as Høgni Joensen knew it – was that he had found the red waterproof coat this morning, when he'd come in to start sorting lines. He showed Hentze the place where it had been, lifting a crate of coiled hooks and line to reveal another beneath. It was in there, folded up, he told Hentze. He didn't know how it had got there, but he didn't want to leave it in with the hooks and the line, so he'd taken it out and hung it up with the other weather gear and when Finn arrived he was going to ask him about it.

For the most part Hentze believed this account, in as much as it described a sequence of events. What it didn't touch on, though, was what Høgni had thought about finding a strange coat amongst the fishing gear.

"Did you find anything else?" Hentze asked, stepping forward to look inside the box where the coat had been, then looking at Høgni.

"No. No, nothing."

Hentze believed that. He went back to the coats hanging by the door and removed the sou'westers, leaving the red waterproof where it was as he pulled on a pair of surgical gloves.

There was no name tag or identification mark on the coat's label; perhaps just a faint – very faint – suggestion of perfume from the fleece lining near the collar. Hard to tell for sure against the general odour of fish. Hentze checked the pockets and found them all empty, save for one on the inside from which he pulled out a grey knitted hat.

Høgni hadn't moved while Hentze carried out this examination, but when Hentze looked at him now he shifted his bulk in discomfort.

"This is Erla's coat, isn't it?" Hentze said.

Høgni gave a stage shrug. "I, I dunno. There are... there are lots like it."

"But Erla had one just the same as this, didn't she? And also this hat. We have a description of it and you'd seen her wearing it, hadn't you?"

A dumb nod.

"So, because you knew she was dead, you thought you'd better keep the coat hidden after you found it. Is that right? Høgni? Is that right?"

Finally pushed beyond yes or no, Høgni seized a breath, then spoke in a rush. "I was going to ask Finn what to do," he said. "I thought it was Erla's, but I didn't know. I didn't know why— what I should do with it, so I was going to ask Finn." He met Hentze's eye, more determined now. "She could've just forgotten it, couldn't she?" he said. "I mean, left it. That could be why it was here. She just forgot it."

"Forgot it when she came to see Finn?"

"Yeh. Yeh. Any time."

Hentze considered that for a moment, then moved to the doorway and took a look at the padlock and hasp on the door. "How many people have access to this shed?" he asked.

"Wh-what do you mean?"

"How many people have keys to the padlock?"

"Just me and Finn."

"And when was the last time you were in here before today?"

"On Friday, after the *grind*."

"Not over the weekend?"

Høgni shook his head. "I put the lines back on Friday. We hadn't used them because of the *grind* and we couldn't go out after that because of the fuel pump."

"Right," Hentze said. "And where were you really on Saturday night? I know you weren't at the boat with Finn because he told me he was there on his own."

Høgni shifted to avoid eye contact. "I was in Tórshavn," he said. "Till the last ferry."

"So, not with Finn."

Høgni Joensen looked at the floor and shook his head. "No," he said dully.

15

I WOKE LATE AND STIFF. MY SHOULDER HURT MORE THAN IT had for a while and I took a couple of ibuprofen with my coffee. A glance from the window on the upstairs landing had shown me that Fríða's car was gone.

I waited till nine thirty, which seemed like a decent time, then dialled the number for Rói Eysturberg listed on the Føroya Tele website. After our last, somewhat stiff conversation I wasn't sure that Eysturberg would be up for another. He was retired now, but still had an innate copper's caution about giving away more than you have to.

"*Ja?*" a voice said.

"*Er ta Rói?*"

"*Ja. Hvør er tann?*"

"*Tað er Jan Reyná,*" I said, and dropped back into English because I couldn't go further on my Faroese. "We spoke a couple of weeks ago, at your boat."

"*Ja,* I remember. What can I do for you, Inspector Reyná?"

Using my rank made a point, but I wasn't sure what it was. "I wondered if you had time to talk to me again. There are a couple of things I'd like to ask you about."

There was a short pause, then he said, "Sure, okay, go ahead."

"I'd rather meet up with you, if that's okay."

The pause was longer this time. "Okay," he said in the end. "You can come to my house. Do you want to know the address?"

"Is it the one in the phonebook?"

"*Ja*, it's the same."

"Okay. What time would be best?"

"Any time. I will be here."

From Sandur, Hentze drove to Húsavík and then – after speaking to Sophie Krogh and handing over the evidence bags containing the red waterproof jacket and woollen hat – he made his way back to Skopun. He arrived at the ferry with about two minutes to spare but it was enough time to see two uniformed officers standing beside a silver Volvo in one of the parking bays by the ferry dock. Even at a distance, he saw from the licence plate that it was Erla Sivertsen's missing car. Not missing any longer, then.

Hentze debated for a second whether or not to forsake the ferry and take a look at the car instead, but he knew it would be best left for a forensic team, so he followed the loading foreman's wave and drove across the ferry ramp and into the hold.

Forty-five minutes later he arrived at the main incident room and took Dánjal Michelsen aside.

"Is Remi around? He's not in his office."

"In a meeting." Dánjal raised his eyes skywards to indicate the fifth floor.

"Did he say for how long?"

"No, but he only went up about five minutes ago."

"Right. Thanks."

"Did you hear?" Dánjal asked. "They've found Erla Sivertsen's car in the ferry car park at Skopun."

"Yeh, I saw it. Has anyone told the technical team?"

Dánjal nodded. "They've said they'll look at it as soon as they can."

"Okay. Anything else new?"

"Well, there was one thing I wanted your opinion about. Have you time?"

Hentze debated briefly. "Give me five minutes, then I'll be back."

At his desk, Ári Niclasen was typing with alacrity, but he looked up when Hentze knocked and came in, closing the door behind him. "How are the technical team getting on?" Ári asked.

"Better now it's light," Hentze said. "They're searching the area inside the larger cordon. After that I think they'll be finished – at Húsavík anyway."

"Okay, good."

"There's something else," Hentze said after a beat. "I think I may have found Erla Sivertsen's coat and her hat. There's nothing to identify them, but they match the description we have."

"Where were they?"

"In a tackle shed at Sandur. Like I said, they're not definitely hers, but I've bagged them up and given them to Sophie Krogh for analysis."

"Who uses the shed, do you know?"

"Yeh, it's Finn Sólsker's. His baitman, Høgni Joensen, found the coat this morning. He wasn't sure who it belonged to so he put it aside."

"Wait." Ári held up a hand. "Finn Sólsker? Martha's Finn? Is that who we're talking about?"

"Yeh," Hentze said.

Ári paused. "Right," he said then. "I just wanted to be sure. Have you asked him about the coat and the hat?"

Hentze shook his head. "No, he wasn't there and I thought it was important to get them to Sophie so they could make the morning flight to Copenhagen with the rest of the samples."

He paused, momentarily debating whether to go on. But he'd started this now, so he said, "Also, I've already spoken to Finn about Erla. They'd been friends since school and went out together for a while, so I asked him when he last saw her, which he says was on Friday at the *grind* on Sandoy."

Ári took a moment to digest that. "So what are you saying?"

"I'm saying that if the coat and hat *do* belong to Erla Sivertsen, then clearly we need to find out how they came to be in Finn's shed. But I may not be the best person to do that."

"Because of your relationship with Finn?"

Hentze nodded. "I think it's possible that Finn may have seen Erla more than he wanted to admit – at least to me."

The trouble with vagueness, as Hentze well knew, was that while it avoided saying something specific, it did not rule out any other interpretation. And he could see that the interpretation Ári Niclasen had immediately made was the most obvious one. But at least he had the decency not to simply blurt it out, even if he did seem to savour the idea for slightly longer than was necessary.

"Okay, I see," Ari said eventually. "Well, in that case you could be right – I mean, that it might be better if someone else talks to Finn. Do you know where he is now?"

"Either at home or at his boat, I should think," Hentze said. "Høgni Joensen's probably told him what happened by now."

"Do you think Joensen could be implicated as well?"

"I'm not saying *anyone's* implicated," Hentze said, slightly more sharply than he intended. "Just that we don't know how the coat got there."

"Yes, of course," Ári said understandingly. Then he stood up. He seemed energised by the development. "Well, we'd better find Finn and ask him then. And don't worry, I'll deal with it, given that it's... sensitive."

"I'm not sensitive about it," Hentze said. "It just needs to be looked at."

"Yes, yeh, sure," Ári nodded, as if agreeing to a shared euphemism. "But, as there's a personal connection... you did the right thing."

"I'm glad you think so," Hentze said. He should have waited for Remi Syderbø after all, he realised, but it was too late now.

Back in the main incident room he got a coffee from one of the vacuum flasks by the window, then crossed to Dánjal's desk. He was working on the timeline of Erla Sivertsen's known movements: a tedious task of sifting and cross-matching information from statements.

"So what did you want my opinion about?" Hentze

asked when Dánjal stopped typing.

Dánjal reached for a sheet of paper on the desk. "I was going through some of the background info in the statements," he said. "Did you know Erla Sivertsen owned a flat in one of the blocks off Kirkjubøarvegur? In his statement her father says she let it out to a friend – a woman called Ruth Guttesen."

Hentze shook his head. "No, I didn't know. Do you think it's relevant?"

"Well, I just wondered if you thought it was worth talking to the tenant – I mean, if she was a friend of Erla's. Also, don't you think it's a bit odd that Erla stayed in a shared house if she had her own flat here?"

Hentze shrugged. "Like you said, if it's been let—"

Ári appeared in the doorway with Sonja Holm. "We'll be out for a while," he announced. "If there are any developments, call me. Or go to Remi, of course."

With that Ári moved on again briskly and Hentze knew that he thought he'd got a hot lead now – and that he wanted to follow up on it before Remi got out of his meeting. He really should have waited, Hentze reflected gloomily.

"Have you got the address of Erla's flat?" he asked, turning back to Dánjal.

"Yeh: Heimasta Horn 26, apartment 45."

Hentze put his coffee aside, hardly touched. "Okay, give this Ruth Guttesen a call and see if she's in. If she is I'll go and talk to her."

It would be better to go out and do something than sit around waiting for Ári to return.

16

THE FIVE-STOREY APARTMENT BLOCKS ON HEIMASTA HORN
had been built less than ten years ago, below the slope of
Lítlafjall and overlooking Argir and across the sound to
Nólsoy. They were of a modern, angular design but still had
something of the traditional about them, with the appearance
of wood cladding – although it was really dark metal – and
high pitched roofs. They were upmarket and – as Hentze
recalled – expensive.

He left the car in one of the parking slots beneath the
block at number 26 and went up in the lift to the fourth floor
– one down from the penthouse level. There were five flats
on the walkway corridor, all their doors painted yellow and
evenly spaced. At the door marked with the number 45 he
rang the bell.

Ruth Guttesen was in her mid-thirties, Hentze guessed; a
woman who presented confidently and with an open manner.
She was a geologist, she told Hentze after inviting him in and
asking if he would like coffee. She was currently working for
a Norwegian oil company, she said, which meant she often
spent up to a fortnight away in the North Sea, analysing data

from the rigs. In fact, she was in the middle of packing and due to catch a flight to Bergen that afternoon, to start another ten-day shift, but that troubled her because she was afraid she would miss Erla's funeral, although no one could tell her yet when it would be.

The woman appeared genuinely dismayed by Erla's death, but it was a quiet, reserved grief, for which Hentze was grateful. He didn't feel much like navigating emotional outpourings.

"Do you know how long Erla owned this apartment?" he asked when they were sitting at a glass-topped table. The view – even if this wasn't the penthouse – would certainly be a good portion of the apartment's value.

"Yes, she bought it off-plan before it was even finished," Ruth Guttesen said. "She used to say it was her pension. Then, when she started to work abroad more she decided to let it out. I was looking for somewhere to live at the time and so it worked out well all round."

"Can I ask how well you knew her?" Hentze said. "I mean, apart from being her tenant."

"Well, we used to be closer – I mean, before she left to do her photography. She was away most of the time for the last five years or so. But when she came back between jobs we'd usually get together if I wasn't working myself. She usually stayed over, unless she went to Suðuroy to see her parents."

"You mean she stayed here?"

"Yeh. There are two bedrooms, so it was no hassle – and she didn't ask as much in rent as she could have, so…"

Hentze considered that. "So had she stayed with you recently – I mean, while she'd been here working for AWCA?"

"Yeh, a few times."

For a moment she looked as if she was going to say something more, but instead she sipped her coffee.

"Would it be all right if I looked at the room she used?" Hentze asked.

"Of course. It's along there. The second door. I don't think she left anything, though. Maybe just a toothbrush. The clothes in the wardrobe are mine."

The bedroom was a decent size with the same view of the town and sea as the living room. The furniture was modern, uncluttered, and the only personal touch was an original oil painting of a gannet on a cliff top. More out of form than because he expected to find anything, Hentze checked the drawers but came up empty. The room told him nothing.

In the living room Ruth Guttesen had gone back to her laptop, but she closed it out of politeness when Hentze reappeared.

"Thank you," he said.

She nodded. "Do you have any idea about what happened?"

"It's still an early stage of the investigation. At the moment we're just trying to get a better picture of what Erla was like – what sort of person would you say she was? How would you sum her up in a sentence?"

Ruth frowned in thought. "I don't know if I could. She had guts, I would say. If she decided she was going to do something she didn't let anything put her off. She'd stick at it until she'd achieved it. So maybe it would be better to say she was determined. She wasn't afraid to set herself goals."

"Right," Hentze said. "And you say she'd stayed here a few times since she came back in July?"

"Yeh. I think when she wanted a bit of peace and quiet, you know? A bit of space away from the others."

"I understand. But in that case, couldn't she simply have come to live here – or wouldn't that have been convenient for you?"

"No, it would have been fine with me," Ruth said. "Half the time I'm not here anyway: there's work, and my boyfriend lives in Norway. I told Erla that, but she said she needed to stay with the AWCA people. I suppose because she wanted to be on hand to take pictures if anything happened."

To Hentze the idea of choosing to share a house with half a dozen people, all younger and idealistic, instead of using a flat like this seemed strange. And nor, from what he could tell, had Erla Sivertsen been one of those people who continue to live like a student well after they have passed the age to reasonably do so. She appeared to have been a woman who was far more grown up than that. Which might also account for the occasional need for some peace and quiet.

"Can you tell me if Erla was seeing anyone before she died?" he asked then. "Was she in a relationship of any kind, do you know?"

For the first time Ruth hesitated before she answered, as if framing an acceptable response. "I think there might have been someone," she said. "But I don't know who he was."

"She didn't talk to you about him?"

Ruth shook her head. "No, she— I only suspected it from a couple of things she said, and because once I came back and thought there might have been a man in the apartment while I was away."

"And while Erla was here?"

Ruth nodded.

"What made you think that?"

"Well, there was a smell of aftershave. I know that sounds silly, but I've always had a good nose for that sort of thing." She shrugged. "And also there was the toilet seat."

"Left up?"

"Yeh."

"But you didn't ask Erla about any of this?"

"No. I mean, it wasn't my business. And besides…" She trailed off, as if unwilling to voice the final assumption.

"Yes? Go on."

"Well, I thought, if she doesn't want to tell me, maybe there's a reason, you know? Like maybe she prefers to keep it quiet."

"Because he might be married?"

"I thought it was possible," Ruth acceded. "Something like that."

Hentze nodded. Asking leading questions wasn't good practice and he'd only done it because he was pursuing his own personal agenda. Which was also a poor approach. What was it Jan Reyná said: *If you don't know enough for a theory, don't make up a story instead*?

Hentze knew he was making up a story out of too few facts and too many suspicions, and he knew he should stop – at least, until he had more than just suspicion and worries.

"Would you like another coffee?" Ruth asked, breaking his train of thought.

Hentze shook his head. "No, thank you. There's just one

more thing I need to ask – was Erla anxious at all, the last time you saw her?"

"No, I don't think so. She was as normal."

"And you hadn't noticed anything odd or suspicious in the last week or so – maybe someone looking for Erla at the door or on the phone?"

"No, I don't think so. Except… there was a man I didn't know outside the flat about a week ago. A week last Saturday. I know it was then because I'd just come in on the last flight from Denmark. I'd sent a text to Erla to say I was coming – just so I wouldn't surprise her if I arrived and she was here. She hadn't replied, so I thought maybe she was busy." A shrug. "Anyway, when I came from the lift with my bags there was a man coming along the balcony from the flat."

"This flat?"

"Yeh. It couldn't have been any other because we're at the end. So I said, 'Can I help?' but he just shook his head and said, 'I'm on the wrong floor.' Then he got to the lift and went down."

"He was Faroese?"

"No, he spoke in Danish."

"Can you describe him?"

"Not really. Suit and tie. A raincoat. He was about forty-five, I'd say, but I didn't get a good look at him. I wasn't really paying attention, except that I remember thinking as I got to the door, 'Maybe that was Erla's guy and she'll be inside.' That was why I remember it now. And because I'd thought he wasn't her type."

"Oh?"

"I mean he was just a bit drab-looking: a bit urban, you know? Erla preferred the outdoors kind of guy."

"Right," Hentze said. "So would you recognise this urban man if you saw him again?"

Ruth shook her head. "I don't know. I don't think so, not for sure. Sorry."

"No, it's better to be honest about these things," Hentze said. "And just to be clear: was Erla here when you let yourself in?"

"No."

"Okay, well, thanks for your help, and for the coffee." Hentze pushed back his chair. "I'll let you get back to your packing. But just in case we do need to talk to you again, is there a number I can reach you on?"

"Yes, sure." She handed him a business card from a bag beside the table and Hentze took his leave.

Outside the flat he looked along the walkway as far as the lift and saw that Ruth Guttesen had been right: if someone had come this far along the walkway the only reason would have been to call at her flat. Of course, that didn't mean that the man she'd seen and who'd spoken Danish to her hadn't simply been on the wrong floor, as he'd said.

Something and nothing then? Maybe.

The one thing Hentze took some comfort from was the fact that Ruth Guttesen's description of the man appeared to rule out the possibility that he had been Finn Sólsker.

17

IN VESTMANNA I PARKED CLOSE TO THE EAST HARBOUR AND walked back along the road a short way. Rói Eysturberg's house wasn't hard to pick out: black and angular with a stand of spindly trees beside it. Their presence was unusual enough to draw your attention in the treeless Faroese landscape and beyond a small painted gate I made my way uphill along a path as far as a *hjallur* shed. The door was latched open and just inside Rói Eysturberg was standing at a wooden bench filleting a cod. He was in his mid-sixties, a peaked cap on his head, sleeves rolled back over bony brown forearms, and he sliced up the fish with the skill you only acquire from decades of practice.

"*Góðan morgun*," I said, watching his knife flick.

"*Hey*." Said flatly without looking up until he'd finished, then he tossed the filleted remains of the fish into a plastic tub.

"Good catch?" I asked.

"Some, *ja*. Not all." He turned a fillet round on the bench. "See there?"

I stepped closer and with the tip of the knife he pointed to small, brownish threads in the white flesh.

"Those are worms to spoil the meat," Eysturberg said. "They come from the *kópur*—" He shook his head in irritation as he tried to find the correct word in English. "Sea animals. Black."

For a moment I searched for something that might fit. "Seals?"

"*Ja*. Seals. The seals have the worms and they shit them out in the water. Then the cod eat the shit. It goes round, yeh?" He made a face. "People think the seals are *lovely*, but they don't know about the worms, eh?"

It sounded like a metaphor for something but I wasn't sure if that was his intention. It was hard to be sure of anything with Eysturberg, which may have been the way he liked it.

He cut round the infestation on the fillet, tossed the bad flesh aside and put the rest into a bucket. Then he took the last fish from a crate and started the process again.

"So, you have more questions about Signar Ravnsfjall, is that it?" He glanced at me for a second between cuts. "I heard that he had died. I'm sorry about that."

I knew he meant sorry for my loss, rather than sorry in his own right. As far as I'd been able to tell when we met before, he had no particular like or dislike of Signar.

"Actually I wanted to ask about something else," I said. "I remembered you mentioned that you knew my mother, Lýdia, when you lived on Suðuroy."

"*Ja?*" Half-statement, half-question.

"I wondered if you could tell me about her."

Another cut. "I don't know what there is to say. I didn't know her so well."

"She didn't stand out for any reason?"

He shrugged. "It's a long time ago." He started to clear the remains of the filleted cod. There were no worms in this one and once he had the parts sorted he began cleaning up.

I knew from our previous meeting that he liked to fence – to trade back and forth – so it was up to me to make a case for why he should tell me what he knew – *if* there was anything to tell.

I leaned on the doorjamb, then said, "I went to see Sofia Ravnsfjall yesterday. I asked her about Lýdia and, amongst other things, she said that when Lýdia was living on Suðuroy with Signar she tried to commit suicide."

Eysturberg was rinsing his hands and his knife in a bucket. "*Ja?*" The same half-statement, half-question; still flat.

"After that she was sent to Denmark for treatment at a place called Ørsted," I went on. "A mental hospital. That was in September 1973. She was there for about a month before coming home."

In poker they call it *going all in*. It was pretty much everything I knew, but I wanted to show him that I knew too much to be fobbed off with generalities. Either he could tell me something more or he couldn't, and either he was willing to or he wasn't.

He said nothing; not while he finished cleaning his hands, not while he dried them on a grubby blue towel and then took a fleece from a nail by the door. He stepped outside and took a pace, then turned back to me and gestured to the bench outside.

"You can sit," he said. "I will be back in a few minutes." Then he walked up the path towards the house.

He was gone for five minutes and I sat on the bench, forced not to slouch by the narrowness of the seat and the vertical side of the shed. Whether by accident or design there was a gap in the trees which let the sunlight through, unbroken, and it felt unusually warm there; sheltered from the breeze and against the black wood. It would have been a good place to close your eyes and doze, but oddly I had a feeling that if I did that I would lose something. Or that I'd wake up and find the world had turned to winter while I was gone. So instead I listened to the sporadic drip of the tap inside the shed and let my gaze wander over the garden until Eysturberg came back down the path.

He gave no clue as to what he'd been doing. Maybe explaining to his wife who I was, what I wanted to know. Maybe not, too. He was wearing his fleece rather than carrying it now, and when I stood up he gestured that I should go with him. He didn't break stride or speak until he'd opened the gate and gone through and I'd latched it behind us.

"Where is your car?" he asked, glancing along the road.

"At the tourist information centre."

"Okay, we'll go there."

Some people will talk more freely when sitting still, others need movement. With Eysturberg I suspected it was simply a way of controlling the situation. If I wanted what he might have I had to go at his pace, and where he led.

"Your mother's sister, she's still alive?" He asked it casually, but not quite casually enough to persuade me that it was just a passing enquiry.

"Ketty? Yeah, she's well."

"She's the one who looks after you in England, after Lýdia died?"

I nodded. "She adopted me – her and her husband."

"How old were you?"

"Nearly five."

He thought about that for a couple of steps, then said, "Before – when you asked about your father – it's because of the case with the men, Gramm and Mohr. Yes?"

"Yes."

"Okay. And that is all done now, as I hear. So now what is this?"

It was a good question: blunt, to the heart. What did I want?

I said, "I want to know what Lýdia was like; who she was. I'd like to know why she left here with me. I'd like to know what was going on in her head."

I looked to see whether he had understood this. It seemed that he had – at least the gist of it – because he gave me a nod.

"So who has said that I would know about your mother?"

"No one," I told him. "But if she'd tried to kill herself while she was living on Suðuroy I thought the police might have been involved and you're the only person I know who was there at the time. But if there's anyone else who could tell me…"

He considered, then shook his head, apparently satisfied. "The man – the police officer – who found her is dead. Maybe twenty years now. His name was Brimnes. We called him 'old uncle' because he had white hair and a big moustache. He had been a police officer on the island as long as we could remember, the young ones of us."

"But you know what happened as well?"

"Yeh. Yeh, I remember. I hadn't been to so many events – incidents – like that before, so…" He gave me an appraising look. "So you want to know?"

I nodded.

"Well, if I remember how it was, there was a telephone call to Brimnes at the police station. It is from a woman in Øravík. She has been looking after you for the afternoon because your mother has asked her, but now she has brought you back to the house and there is no reply at the door. Inside she can hear the radio and the lights are on, but the door is locked, which is not usual. So Brimnes calls me along and we go to see what is happening."

He glanced at me to make sure I was paying attention. "When we arrived at the house there are maybe six people there – the neighbours. You are a police officer so you know how it goes. They come to be looking, so Brimnes does not waste time. He tells everyone to stand away and kicks the door so it breaks. Then he goes inside and I'm to stay where I am to stop the others coming in. Two minutes later Brimnes is out again and tells us there has been an accident and to call for an ambulance.

"It takes maybe fifteen minutes, I don't remember, but when the ambulance people arrive your mother is taken to the hospital unconscious. Brimnes tells everyone to go home and for the woman you were with to take you to her home until your father arrives. Then he goes back inside."

He cast a look at me to see how I was following this; I sensed there was more so I kept quiet.

"I was still young in the job," Eysturberg said then. "So I liked to push my nose in – to see what is going on, you know? So after it is all quiet and I am still at the door I think I will be curious. I go inside to find Old Uncle in the bedroom and I see him with a paper sack where he's putting in bottles for pills and other things. I think it's for evidence, but when he sees me Brimnes says, 'You don't know about this, understand? You don't know it was here.' Then he takes the sack away and I don't see it again. We close up the house and that is that."

We crossed the road, cutting a corner and walking over a section of gravel for a while.

"So Brimnes wanted to cover it up?" I asked. "I mean the fact that it was a suicide attempt – is that what you're saying?"

"*Ja.*"

"Why?"

"Because it is nobody's business," Eysturberg said flatly, as if I should already know. "And because in those days…" He frowned as he tried to find the right phrase. "That sort of thing is to have a mark, do you know what I mean?"

"It was something to be ashamed of?"

"*Ja*, like that. Of course sometimes it cannot be helped that people know about it, but Brimnes would not encourage it. If someone has gone off a cliff it is an accident while they are trying to catch birds; or with a shotgun, it's an accident in cleaning. And if there is a goodbye letter maybe he shows it only to the husband or wife, or maybe it just disappears."

"Did Lýdia leave a letter – a note?"

Eysturberg shook his head. "I didn't see one, but it could

have been in the bag Brimnes took away."

"So if no one wanted to say it was a suicide attempt, how was it explained afterwards?" I asked. "What was the story?"

He shrugged. "Only that she had collapsed – *fainted*, yes? – and struck her head. She was required to stay in the hospital for a few days and then she was taken to Denmark. It was arranged between her doctor and your father, I think."

"Did Signar take her to Denmark?"

Eysturberg shook his head. "I don't know, but I would think so."

"And where was he when it happened?"

"I'm not sure. At sea, fishing, I think. Maybe somebody uses the radio to tell him, I don't know, but he isn't back at the house until evening."

Like all stories – all accounts trawled out of memory – I could see gaps and inconsistencies, but after forty years I hadn't expected anything different. If Eysturberg had told me he hardly remembered the incident, or not at all, I wouldn't have been surprised. Some things *do* stick, though. I could give chapter and verse on the first suicide I attended; the first dead kid I saw. Those things cling, and sometimes not for the reason you'd think.

We'd walked on a little way and Eysturberg had the look of someone who'd said as much as he cared to, but still hadn't quite left his own memory alone.

"Can I ask you something else?" I said.

"Can I stop you?" The forbearance seemed a little out of character for him but I didn't waste it.

"Did people think Lýdia was strange in any way?" I said.

"I mean the way she behaved in normal life."

He frowned, then shook his head. "Some people were jealous of her," he said. "The women because she was pretty, the men because she would…" He searched for a word, but seemed not to find it. "Because she was not interested in them. She would go for a walk or a dance maybe, but she didn't sit, stay still. You understand? Something would interest her, but then a different thing would be along and then that is what took her interest. But it was never with bad feeling," he added, as if he wanted to be sure I didn't get the wrong impression. "That was just how she was. People knew that." He drew a breath, then seemed to shift focus. "She was too young to be married to Signar Ravnsfjall," he said. "No one expects it. But I suppose because of the baby – you – she thought it was the best thing."

"Did that change the way she was? I mean, did she change after she was married?"

He shook his head. "*Nei*, I don't know. Everyone changes when they are married, don't they?"

"I suppose so," I acknowledged. "But I was told that she started going to something called the Colony, at Múli."

He shrugged. "Maybe. I don't know."

"But you know what it was?"

"Only from stories," he said, and I could sense him closing down again, like he realised he'd left the door open too long.

"What sort of stories? What kind of place was it?"

He made a dry grunt, dismissive. "It was for hippies: foreigners. I have never been."

Clearly it wasn't something he was interested in talking

about so I changed tack before the door finally closed. "What about Lýdia's friends, people she knew?" I asked. "Is there anyone else I could talk to? So far you're the only person who's given me an honest impression of what Lýdia was really like, but if there are others…"

I'd chosen the word "honest" on purpose, hoping it would flatter him. Whether it did or not, I couldn't tell, but he weighed up the request as we came round the corner of the harbour towards the information centre, then he seemed to decide.

"Eileen Skoradal is the only one I can think of," he said. "She has a shop for old things in Tórshavn: Magnus Heinasonar gøta."

"She was a friend of Lýdia's?"

"Yeh."

"Thanks. I'll try to find her."

He didn't react to that but instead gestured to the information centre. "I am going for coffee and to meet some friends now, so I will say goodbye."

"Okay. *Stora takk fyri*," I said.

I knew that was it, so I held out my hand. After a second he shook it, then walked away.

18

"WHY DIDN'T YOU WAIT TO TELL ME FIRST?" REMI SYDERBØ asked.

"Because you were in a meeting and I didn't think it should wait," Hentze said matter-of-factly. He took another forkful of pasta salad from his Tupperware lunchbox and chewed on it with deliberation. He'd come to his own office to eat to avoid being drawn into conversation in the canteen.

Remi sighed but had clearly decided there was nothing to be done about it now. "Do you know how it's going?" he asked.

"The interview?" Hentze shook his head.

Remi looked at his watch. Ári Niclasen had been interviewing Finn Sólsker in the second-floor office for nearly an hour. "Okay," he said. "I'll give it another ten minutes. If they haven't taken a break by then I'll interrupt it."

He looked round then moved a chair and sat down. There wasn't really enough space in Hentze's office for anyone else. The spare chair was mainly for show.

"So tell me what you think," Remi said. "Never mind about what's confirmed and what's not. Give me the picture."

Hentze considered as he finished a mouthful of salad.

Then he put down his fork and pushed the box away.

"I only know what I told Ári when I got back," he said.

"Which was?"

"That Erla Sivertsen's coat and hat – or two very much like hers – were in Finn's boat shed. In addition, there's a history between Erla and Finn; and on top of that the tenant at Erla's flat thought she might have been seeing a married man."

"Thought or knew?"

"Thought."

"So you've added that up and it makes Finn a suspect?" Remi's tone suggested that it was unlike Hentze to be quite so simplistic.

Hentze tipped his head, as if to acknowledge a fair point. "Yes, but also because Høgni Joensen gave me to understand that Erla had been to see Finn more often than he admitted to me last night."

"And you didn't consider putting these points to Finn yourself?" Remi asked.

"I considered it, yes, but I thought there was a conflict of interest," Hentze said. "Finn and I have never been particularly close – no reason we should be, I suppose – but even so, I hardly think he'd react well if I asked whether he was being unfaithful to my daughter."

As an answer it didn't seem to entirely satisfy Remi, but he accepted it. "So what are you doing now?" he asked, motioning to the file on Hentze's desk.

"Looking at those three burglaries in Klaksvík last week."

"Are you serious? We have a major crime and you're looking at a burglary?"

"Three."

"You know what I mean," Remi said, sounding slightly irritable now. "Leave the damn burglaries. I want you back on the murder. No one's going to question your impartiality, even if Finn does turn out to—"

He broke off when Ári Niclasen tapped on the door and came in. His presence made the office seem even more cramped.

"Has Hjalti told you?" he asked Remi.

Remi nodded. "You've suspended the interview?"

"Yes, just. Do you want me to fill you in?"

The question was clearly whether Remi wanted him to speak in front of Hentze.

"Of course, go ahead," Remi said.

Slightly uncomfortable, Ári Niclasen pushed the hank of hair back from his forehead. "Well, in short, he's saying he has no idea how the hat and coat came to be in his boat shed. He says he didn't put them there and that Erla Sivertsen hadn't ever been in the shed."

"Has he given an account of his movements on Saturday?"

Finn had, Ári confirmed, then recounted the same information Finn had given to Hentze the previous night: a day working on the boat, collecting a fuel pump and working again through the evening. And again there was no one who could vouch for this last part, and nor could Finn be specific about the times.

From his tone, Ári clearly saw the lack of any corroboration for Finn's account as a damning flaw in the story. Which it was, Hentze would have agreed, if not for the fact that most people would struggle to provide continuous alibis for themselves over the course of a day. Nevertheless, he didn't remark on that. Instead he said, "Did you ask him how many times he's seen Erla recently?"

"Well, he *says*" – Ári let the emphasis fall hard on the word – "only a couple of times in the last two or three weeks, including at the *grind* on Friday."

"So what's your opinion on what we should do now?" Remi asked, looking to Ári.

"I think we should hold him for now," Ári said. "At least until we get a time of death from the post-mortem. Then we can reassess his alibi, or lack of one."

"Hjalti?"

"I agree," Hentze said. "Without knowing when she died we're lacking a proper focus."

"Okay." Remi stood up. "See what you can get from Anders Toft at the mortuary. He probably hasn't finished yet but he might tell us something. Meanwhile, Ári and I will assess what we have from the collated statements of the AWCA people. I don't want us to jump the gun and focus on one potential suspect before we've considered other possibilities."

This last was aimed at Ári Niclasen, who nodded in response and said, "Sure, of course."

"Okay, then."

Ári opened the door and stepped out, with obvious relief to leave the small space.

"It might be a good idea to send someone to speak with Martha," Hentze said before Remi could leave as well. "She may be able to be more specific about Finn's movements on Saturday night. And I think she should be asked about his relationship with Erla as well."

"Wouldn't you prefer to do that yourself, rather than sending someone else?"

Hentze shook his head. "I'd very much prefer *not* to do it," he said. "I could ask Annika to go, though. She knows Martha a little, and woman to woman…"

Remi saw the logic of that. "Yeh, okay," he said. "If you're sure."

Annika Mortensen was just back from a patrol around Runavík when Hentze called her. They met up in the second-floor kitchen as Annika made one of her herbal teas.

"Does Martha know that Finn's been brought in for questioning?" she asked when Hentze explained what he needed.

"I don't think so. Martha would have been at work by the time Ári went to Sandoy and Finn hasn't asked to make any calls since he was brought in. Høgni Joensen could have called her, but I doubt it."

"So I'll have to break the news." A hint of uncertainty.

"Sorry."

Annika shifted, then shook her head. "It's okay. Is there anything specific you want me to ask her?"

"Times," Hentze said. "Most specifically what time Finn went back to the boat on Saturday evening, and what time he came home afterwards."

"Anything else?" She glanced round to make sure they weren't being overheard.

Hentze nodded. "Yes. Ask her whether she thinks Finn

was having an affair with Erla Sivertsen."

"Just like that?"

"Well I suppose you could dress it up a little," Hentze said, acknowledging her reservation. "But don't treat it any differently than you would if it was anyone else, okay? It's something we need to know, whether it's fact or suspicion."

"Okay," Annika said. "I'll do my best. I'll go now." She fished the scented teabag out of the mug and dropped it in the bin. "Would you like this?" she asked, offering Hentze the cup.

"I'd rather drink soap," he said. "But thanks."

19

HENTZE GENERALLY LIKED VISITS TO THE MORTUARY. HE LIKED Elisabet Hovgaard, the chief pathologist, and the fact that she always called a spade a spade with no concession to the police, or anyone else. Of course, she was as mad as a gannet, but Hentze liked mad people too. Perhaps because they fulfilled a role he himself couldn't play.

Unfortunately, because this was a murder, Elisabet Hovgaard could not conduct the post-mortem. Instead, a forensic pathologist from Denmark had been called in, and it was too much to hope that Anders Toft would have simply arrived at the mortuary, put on a gown and got on with the job.

Instead Hentze knew that Toft would have insisted on a little ceremony and show first, to mark his presence. Coffee and gossip, even some flirting if there was anyone pretty and female around. All this would have to be done before he finally got down to business, which meant that when Hentze arrived at the mortuary the autopsy was still going on.

The mortuary technician was a new guy and tried to insist that Hentze put on a mask and gown, which Hentze would have done if he'd had any intention of going close to the body. He did not, though, especially as Anders Toft was still working. Instead, after putting the technician in his place, Hentze pushed the door of the autopsy room open part way and remained on the threshold.

Anders Toft was dictating his observations as he worked, raising his voice for the benefit of the recorder placed on a stainless steel trolley. Elisabet Hovgaard was assisting where necessary, but seemed to be there mostly to field Toft's small talk. She had the look of someone who had been trapped in a corner.

"*Godmorgen*," Hentze said in Danish.

Anders Toft looked up and then gestured broadly in pleased surprise. "Officer Hentze. How are you?"

"Fine thanks, Anders. You?"

"Good, good, good. Put on a gown and come in. I'll give you the guided tour if you like. The more the merrier."

"Have you finished?"

"The first part, yes. In a moment we'll have a look at the brain."

"Well I don't want to interrupt you, and I'm on a tight schedule, but if I could borrow Elisabet for a few minutes…"

"Are you sure? Well all right, then." He glanced at Elisabet Hovgaard. "It must be time for a cigarette, anyway, eh? Okay, go ahead."

"*Oh, tak*," Elisabet said with a note of sarcasm that Toft appeared to miss but made Hentze smile.

It was raining so Elisabet pushed the fire door open to its widest extent and stood on the threshold to blow smoke outside. She was only partly successful.

"So, how's it going?" Hentze asked.

"Pah!" Elisabet said tersely. "I promise you, if he tells me about one more case and how it would all have fallen to pieces if he hadn't found this thing or that... And if it's not cases it's how pretty a nurse was, or a flight attendant, or even a victim's sister. A victim's *sister*, for God's sake. Jesus!" She shook her head, then took a hard pull on her cigarette.

"Yeh, well, the guest *is* the master," Hentze said drily, only half hiding his amusement.

"Yeh, yeh, at home, maybe," Elisabet said. "Not that I'd let him over *my* step."

She blew smoke again and appeared to have had enough of the subject. "You want to know when and how?" she asked.

"Of course. Unless it's too soon to say."

Elisabet shook her head. "He'll tell you it is, before he's made his report, but screw him." She flicked ash. "There was no record made of the body temperature by the doctor at the scene, but Sophie Krogh took a reading when she arrived. That puts the time of death in a three-hour window between eight and eleven on Saturday – give or take. Her stomach contents may also give us some idea, if you can find out the last time she ate."

"But we're definitely looking at Saturday night?" Hentze asked.

Elisabet nodded. "For sure."

"And cause of death?"

"A blow to the head."

"You're that certain?"

"If you mean because of the stab wound, then yes. It was

made by a fairly slim blade, maybe 12mm wide, but definitely post-mortem – and I'd say not less than an hour after she died." She shook her head. "No, the cause of death was blunt trauma to the back of her head from something roughly triangular and possibly associated with the earth. There are traces of grit and organic matter around the injury site."

"A rock then?"

"Could be, yes."

"So was it a fall or a blow? Can you tell?"

"No. The effect would be about the same. Although the skin was only abraded, the fracture was serious enough to cause immediate internal bleeding around her brain. We'll see better when Anders extracts it but I'd guess she died in less than five minutes."

"What about rape?" Hentze asked.

Elisabet looked a little more chary on this subject. "We've found what appears to be semen from unprotected sex," she said. "There's no evidence of injury or bruising that you might associate with rape, though, so I wouldn't say it was proven."

"That's what Sophie Krogh said, too."

Elisabet took a final drag on her cigarette and tossed the butt out into the rain. "You're concerned because of the way she was found?"

"I am if it seems that the killer was intending to mislead us."

"Yes, well, the knife wound and the way the body was presented could indicate that they were trying to make it look like a sexually motivated attack, I'd agree," Elisabet conceded. "But luckily that's something for you and not me."

* * *

They were sitting in leather chairs in the small, glass-panelled office of the Eik Bank, which was normally reserved for private meetings with customers about loan applications and rates of interest. Martha Sólsker was dressed in a neat grey business suit with a skirt, which made Annika Mortensen feel slightly less well presented than she'd hoped. Perhaps she should have stayed in uniform, but in the circumstances she still felt it was better not to look too official, especially as her arrival and request to speak privately with Martha had already caused a little disruption in the bank.

Annika was still hoping that Martha would feel able to speak freely in private, although the spartan office didn't lend itself to intimacy. And nor did Martha look as if she was going to loosen up when Annika told her why she had come. Not surprising, perhaps.

On the two or three occasions Annika had met Martha before she had formed the impression that Hjalti Hentze's daughter was a rather chilly person. Perhaps "chilly" was the wrong word. "Reserved" might be better. Undemonstrative, certainly. Annika didn't anticipate that Martha would collapse in floods of tears or panic when she heard about her husband, and nor did she. Instead Martha Sólsker stiffened and sat more upright in her seat.

"Why didn't my father call to tell me?" Martha asked. It was a question Annika had anticipated.

"He would have done, but he's been tied up with the investigation all day," she said. "It's been pretty full-on."

Whether or not the exaggeration – Annika didn't want to class it as a lie – was accepted by Martha was hard to tell. "I suppose so," she said. "Does Finn have a lawyer with him?"

"As far as I know he hasn't asked for one."

Martha considered that for a second. "So exactly what is it they want him to tell them?"

Annika was pretty sure Martha already knew – had guessed – what it was about, so she kept the account to a minimum: Finn had known Erla Sivertsen and all Erla's acquaintances were being interviewed, she said. However, the discovery in Finn's shed of a coat and hat that may have belonged to Erla obviously needed some explanation. It was purely routine.

Again, Annika found it impossible to tell whether this statement was accepted at face value because Martha said nothing and her expression remained fixed and distant.

"It would help if we knew exactly what Finn was doing on Saturday afternoon and evening," Annika said, trying to start a dialogue. "Can you remember what time he went back to work on the boat in the evening, for example?"

"Just before seven: about five to," Martha said flatly, still looking at the far wall. "He got back at just after ten." Then she brought her gaze back to Annika. "She couldn't just stay away, could she?" she said.

"How do you mean?" Annika asked.

"I mean *stay away*: go off and be glamorous and exciting somewhere else instead of here. Still, I suppose to *be* glamorous you have to be seen, and all the better if it's by everyone else who isn't as exciting as you are."

There was no doubt who Martha was referring to, but the obvious bitterness was not what Annika had expected and for a moment she had trouble shifting gears. "Had you seen Erla very much since she came back to the islands with the Alliance?" she asked.

"Me?" Martha said, as if the answer was obvious. "No. The first time was at the *grind* on Friday."

"But you did know she was here?"

"Yeh. Yes, of course. Finn had told me. And Høgni."

"Right, I see," Annika said. It seemed pointless trying to be subtle any more. "And had Finn seen her very often?"

Martha shook her head. "I don't know. More than he wanted to tell me, though; I'm sure about that."

"Oh? Why's that?"

Both women heard the faux-innocence of the question, but rather than react against it Martha seemed to take it as a signal that there was no need to avoid the truth.

"You know Finn used to go out with Erla, don't you?" she said. "Actually, they lived together for over two years before she broke it off and moved away. So…"

Annika nodded, although Martha wasn't looking at her. Her eyes were flitting round the room as she decided what to say next.

"If you want to know the truth of it, it's that Erla was one of those women who like to have men on a string," Martha said. "Especially men she can't – shouldn't – have. You might think I'm just saying that because Finn was one of them, but it's still true. That's what she was like. Maybe it made her feel good about herself – more attractive or glamorous – I don't know. I don't care. But she knew she could have Finn if she crooked her finger, so that's what she did and to hell with the consequences; to hell with his family, his kids or anyone else. So, if you want to know whether I think Erla Sivertsen was sleeping with Finn then the answer is yes. I can't prove it. I never caught them together, but I know how things have been since she came back here."

"Martha, listen—" Annika started, a conciliatory tone in her voice. But before she got any further Martha stood up and smoothed down her jacket.

"I have to get back to work," she said, a flat termination of any further discussion. "And then I have to be home for the kids. Not very glamorous, but there it is. So, can I show you the way out?"

20

IN THE OFFICE ADJACENT TO THE INCIDENT ROOM HENTZE DREW
a red zigzag on the timeline between the markers for Saturday
20:00 and 23:00. Alongside this he wrote, "Blunt trauma",
and then "No sign of rape. Recent sex."

He stood back to consider this, then let his gaze drift back
from the probable time of death to the blank space before it;
from 15:00 onwards when Erla had left the Fjalsgøta house.
That was the unknown: the five to ten hours, during which
Erla Sivertsen had done – what? Gone to a movie? Walked
on the cliffs? Sat in a bar and picked up a man? Anything was
possible and until they knew something – anything – about
where she had been in this time they would get nowhere.

He was still thinking about this when Oddur Arge
knocked on the door. Hentze had locked it, although he
wasn't sure why, but now he went across and flicked the latch.

"Am I interrupting?" Oddur asked. He had his laptop in
his hand.

"No, only thinking. What's up?" He looked at the laptop.
"Do you ever go anywhere without that?"

"Sure, of course," Oddur said, looking mildly hurt. "But

I thought you'd be interested in this. I've been going through Erla's photos from Friday and Saturday and comparing them with the statements from the Alliance people describing her movements over the same time. Because she was shooting digitally the date and time when each picture was taken is encoded in the metadata. But what's more interesting – more useful to us – is that she was also geotagging her pictures."

"No, you've lost me," Hentze said. "What does that mean?"

With a slight air of explaining to his grandmother – or *abbi*, Hentze thought – Oddur put the laptop on a table. "Her camera had what is essentially a GPS tracker attached to it," he said. "It means that whenever she took a photo the GPS – the geotagger – logged her location. For a professional the advantage is that you don't have to keep a manual record of where you take each shot. Even months or years later you can just look at the image's metadata and see exactly where it was taken and when."

"Okay, I get it," Hentze said. "So what did you find?"

"Well, overall the geotags confirm what we were told – except for Saturday afternoon. According to" – Oddur checked his notes – "a Veerle Koning, Erla said she was going to visit the Alliance lookout points when she left the house on Fjalsgøta. That's not what she did, though. No one from the Alliance saw her that afternoon."

"But she took photos?" Hentze said.

"Yeh, just one set: twenty-six in all, taken between 16:10 and 16:31 at Kaldbak."

"Can I see them?"

Oddur opened his laptop, brought up a Photoshop

window and started a slideshow of Erla Sivertsen's photos. Each picture was on screen for four or five seconds and at first Hentze didn't know what he was looking at. There were a dozen images of what appeared to be a concrete wall but surreally inlaid with plastic toys, kitsch sculptures and figurines. Then, abruptly, the location and subject changed to a minimalist view of a door in the side of a large building above a grass bank. And then to the harbour. Several shots of rusty chains and mooring rings. One of peeling paint on a wooden boat. And then a craggy, weatherbeaten face, looking up from a boat: a man in his seventies, Hentze knew.

The portrait was a good one, catching Jákup Homrum with an expression of openness but slight puzzlement, as if he couldn't quite understand why he would be the photograph's subject. There were three more of him, as if taken in rapid succession, but the first was definitely the best.

There was only one more picture, of an upturned palm against a background of what looked like the interior of a car. The red sleeve of a coat just edged into the frame.

"That's it," Oddur said. "Do you want to see them again?"

Hentze shook his head. "Was the last shot of the hand a mistake, do you think?"

Oddur shook his head. "Some photographers do that as a marker – a way of showing you've finished in one place. Like a full stop at the end of a sentence. It makes it easier when you're scanning quickly through pictures."

"Oh, right, I see." He moved to look at the timeline. "So what we're able to say now is that Erla was at Kaldbak between four and four thirty on Saturday. Well, that moves us forward a little, but still not close to her time of death. We're still missing four hours or more and—"

He broke off and fell silent for a moment. Oddur looked up. "What?"

"We've missed something," Hentze said. "The photos of Kaldbak were on Erla's laptop – correct?"

"Yeh, and copied to her backup drive."

"And the laptop was found in her room at the Fjalsgøta house," Hentze said. "So therefore Erla must have gone *back* to the house after Kaldbak in order to transfer the pictures from her camera to the laptop. Otherwise they'd still be on her camera, which we don't have."

"She *could* have had the laptop with her and transferred the photos while she was out," Oddur offered.

"Then how did the laptop get back to her room?" Hentze shook his head, convinced now. "No, she went back. So how come nobody saw her?"

He put the same question to Remi Syderbø five minutes later, who agreed it was worth talking to the other residents at the Fjalsgøta house again.

"Do you want to do it?" he asked.

Hentze shook his head. "It'll probably be quicker for someone who's already familiar with their statements. I'll go and talk to Jákup Homrum at Kaldbak, if it's all right with you."

"Because she took his picture?"

"No, because she made a point of telling her friend Veerle that she was going to visit the Alliance lookouts and then she didn't."

Remi considered, then nodded. "Okay, sure." He looked

at his watch. "But can you be back by five? I'd like a case conference then."

"Yeh, I'll be there. This shouldn't take very long."

So now he was driving the fifteen kilometres from Tórshavn to Kaldbak, following the same route Erla Sivertsen must have taken on Saturday afternoon, and at roughly the same time of day.

He thought he was gaining a picture of Erla – incomplete, for sure – but still, something. And what had begun to colour that picture was a growing feeling that Erla Sivertsen had not been a straightforward person. True, there appeared to have been nothing *overtly* odd or strange about her behaviour – or indeed about the descriptions of her from those she had known. No one had described her as, say, reckless or unreliable or short-tempered, or any of a dozen different adjectives that might be used to point to a significant character trait. Instead she was liked; viewed as professional, dedicated and accommodating.

And yet...

And yet Hentze felt this was not the entire case. This was also a woman who might have been conducting an affair; who felt the need to use the apartment at Heimasta Horn to get away from her colleagues from time to time; and who had specifically said she was going to do one thing on Saturday afternoon, and instead had done quite another. This was what bothered Hentze most.

Ten minutes out of Tórshavn, he turned off route 50 and on to the narrower road that doubled back on the north side of Kaldbaksfjørður, with near vertical mountainside rising up to his left above the shore-hugging road. Four kilometres on, the village of Kaldbak was the end of the road; a scattered collection of perhaps thirty houses, a grass-roofed church and a small harbour, beyond which were a couple of warehouse-like buildings set on the promontory.

Hentze parked near the church and walked a little way up the road to a modest, rectangular house where several racks of drying fish were hung neatly beside the door under the roof's overhang. The mailbox beside the door had two names: Jákup and Hansina Homrum, and it was Hansina who answered his knock. Early seventies, with round spectacles to match a round face.

"Hjalti, how are you?" she said, pleased to see him. "Come in, come in."

Hentze stayed put on the mat. "I'm looking for the old man, is he here?"

"Of course not. He's down at the harbour with his mistress. Where else? You can come in and talk to me, though."

"I'd love to, but I'm working," Hentze said.

Hansina chuckled. "Are you here to arrest Jákup?"

"I wasn't planning to, but I will if you like. What's the charge?"

"Neglect of his wife."

"Right, I'll run him in, then – or would you just like me to bring him home?"

"Oh, bring him home, I suppose. He has *some* uses – at least, when he's here."

The concrete harbour was small, with half a dozen boat sheds and perhaps twice that many boats in the sheltered, still water.

They were all of the traditional Faroese design, wooden hulled with upswept bows and sterns. Most had rowlocks and oars, but all had the internal well for an outboard motor. Why make life any harder for yourself?

There was no sign of Jákup Homrum in the boats, but when Hentze turned the corner of the quay he heard a movement from the darkened interior of one of the boat sheds and stopped to peer in.

"Jákup? Are you there?"

Out of the gloom Jákup Homrum appeared, dressed in a blue windcheater and a fur-lined hat with ear flaps, both of which appeared to have been bought for a man at least three sizes bigger than their current occupant.

"Hey hey," Jákup said jovially in greeting. "If Hansina's sent you to find me you could have saved yourself the walk. I was just coming."

"Not fast enough, according to her."

"If she expects fast on my knees she'll have to think again," Jákup said. He moved stiffly to kick away a brick that was holding the door of the boat shed in place, then closed it up.

"I need to ask you a couple of questions," Hentze said. "It's for work."

"Work, eh?" Jákup hung a padlock on the hasp of the door but didn't bother to lock it. "What have I done now?"

They started to walk up the slope, away from the harbour. Hentze slowed his steps to accommodate the older man. "Two days ago – Saturday just gone – you were here when a woman called Erla Sivertsen came to the harbour. She took your photograph, remember?"

"Sure," Jákup said. "There's nothing wrong with my memory. Why? Is she in trouble for something?"

"No, I'm afraid not," Hentze said. "She was found dead yesterday on Sandoy."

"That was her?" Jákup stopped walking for a moment. "I heard it on the radio but I didn't realise... Do you know what happened?"

"Yes, she was murdered," Hentze told him. "But that's not to go any further, okay?"

"Killed? Are you sure?"

"I'm afraid so."

"Poor soul. God rest her." Jákup shook his head.

"I'm trying to find out about her movements before she died," Hentze said. "Can you tell me anything about what she did while she was here?"

"Not much. She was taking photographs on the quay there," Jákup pointed. "Then she stopped to look at my boat. We chatted for a few minutes and then she left."

"What did you talk about?"

"I don't know. The boat, fishing... She asked if I lived here and she said she came from Suðuroy, I remember that."

"Anything else?"

"No, I don't think so. Have you talked to her friend?"

"Which friend?"

"Well I don't know who he was, but she was with him before she came down to the harbour. I saw them together. Tourists, I thought, because they were walking round the churchyard."

"Can you describe the man?"

Jákup shook his head. "Not really. They weren't close

enough for me to see him very well."

"Tall or short; young or old?"

Jákup considered for a moment, as if trying to focus on a blurred image. "I suppose medium height – about the same as her. I wouldn't say he was young. Middle-aged, maybe about fifty."

"What colour was his hair?"

"Brown, sort of."

"And what about his clothes – what was he wearing?"

"Some kind of raincoat," Jákup said then, without hesitation. "Yeh, I remember that. Because I thought they didn't look alike. She was dressed like a tourist but he looked more formal: city clothes, if you know what I mean."

"I think so," Hentze said. "And he didn't come down to the harbour with her?"

"No. I don't know where he went. I wasn't watching like that. I saw them together and then a little while later she was on her own. I didn't see him again."

At the top of the slope Hentze took his leave of Jákup Homrum, sending apologies to Hansina that he couldn't come back for coffee. He walked to his car and considered Jákup's description of the man Erla Sivertsen had met. Not Finn Sólsker, he was certain. Good. Hentze had been afraid that this meeting of Erla's might implicate Finn further. But it still left the question of who she had met and whether it was significant.

It needn't be, of course. The fact that Erla had talked to someone at the church could be entirely coincidental. She'd met someone, they'd exchanged pleasantries for a few minutes, then parted; there didn't have to be anything more to it than that. Until you remembered that Erla Sivertsen had come to Kaldbak despite saying she was going somewhere else. Then, you could say, the scales tipped a little away from coincidence and more towards something arranged.

Hentze opened his car and got in. Through the window he cast a look at the church and considered the churchyard for a moment, then started the car.

21

I'VE NEVER UNDERSTOOD ANTIQUES SHOPS. BRIC-A-BRAC, junk, second-hand goods, whatever you want to call it. It's someone else's cast-offs: stuff they didn't want, so why would I want it?

Apart from a few used books I have three things that are old: a set of poker dice I took from a boy called Sean when I was ten, and two Corgi toys – a blue tractor and a yellow truck – from about the same time. That's it. They're in a box somewhere, maybe at the back of a cupboard.

So the Reytt Bátur shop on the corner of Magnus Heinasonar gøta was an emporium of stuff I didn't want. I was in a minority of one, though. Tórshavn had been invaded by clusters of pastel-waterproofed tourists from a cruise ship in the harbour: Germans, by and large, with knots of Americans and French. It was the busiest I'd seen the streets, and despite the rain there was a slightly febrile urgency in the way they consulted maps and bustled from shop to shop, as if everything good might be gone before they got there or had to return to the ship.

I followed three of them to the Reytt Bátur shop but

didn't go much further than the threshold. It was poorly lit inside, although at the back of the room I could just make out a sales counter, topped by glass display units. Between it and me the aisles of dark wood furniture and worn leather chairs were narrow and already congested with tourists picking over everything from dusty wine glasses to old dolls and kitchen utensils. Their voices were raised and candid in the way people's are when they know they'll never be back and won't be understood by the locals anyway.

I guessed that feeling safe in their own language was the reason they weren't bothering to disguise their opinion of this plate or that trinket box, too. An American couple not far ahead of me were querying how much of this stuff was *really* "Faroe-ish". Hadn't they seen the same thing in a yard sale at home?

Behind the sales counter I caught a glimpse of a woman who might or might not be Eileen Skoradal. She seemed about the right age, but she was busy wrapping purchases and trying to explain money to a tourist.

Now wasn't the time, I decided, backing out of the shop as another knot of foragers arrived. Instead I went to find coffee and Wi-Fi, smug that I wasn't a tourist and wasn't on a deadline.

I gave it almost an hour and two cappuccinos, sucking the internet connection at the Dugni café. They didn't seem to mind. The tourists didn't have time to stop for coffee, so apart from a couple who came in to look at the knitted goods in the window I was pretty much the only customer.

Google gave me nothing on the Colony at Múli and including the word "Faroes" in the search often led me down links to semi-literate posts on social media sites, all decrying the "barbaric slaughter" of whales. Nothing about the death of Erla Sivertsen, though. Apparently humans didn't count for so much.

On a whim I checked the AWCA website and had some of my cynicism dispelled by an obituary on their home page. There was a decent photo of Erla in wet weather gear, looking happy against a grey ocean. Beneath that there were two paragraphs of text, which said simply that Erla Sivertsen had died on Saturday in her homeland of the Faroe Islands. After that there was a brief biography and mention of several photographic awards she'd won.

It was a tasteful and well-written piece by someone who had avoided over-sentimentalising. The fact that it said nothing about the circumstances of Erla's death was telling, too. It might have been as much as they knew, but I doubted it, partly because there was also no mention of the fact that Erla had been here as part of the anti-whaling protest. That, to me, suggested that AWCA had been requested not to go into details.

Not that it would be hard to figure out what Erla had been doing, given the content of the site's other pages. They'd opted for restraint in the obituary, but beyond that the story was different. The photos of the *grind* at Sandur were of the sort you'd expect and the editorial comments alongside them were filled with adjectival outrage that did little or nothing to inform. They were simply propaganda without subtlety or nuance. Killing whales was abhorrent; the Faroese killed whales, therefore the Faroese were abhorrent. I reckoned the average twelve-year-old would have got the idea in the first couple of sentences. After that it was simply patronising, repetitive and tiresome and I was sure that the person who wrote it hadn't written a word of Erla Sivertsen's obituary.

I read the obituary again, then I closed the browser. Whatever Hentze was doing on the enquiry, I knew better than to stick my nose in unless I had something to offer. Which I didn't. Not that it stopped me thinking about it for a while as I finished my coffee. Old habits.

By the time I left the café the rain had come on harder and the last of the tourists were heading towards the harbour with the spoils of their retail raids. I put up my collar and made my way back to the Reytt Bátur shop.

Reytt bátur means "red boat", but I was given a helping hand with the translation by the naïve-style painting on the signboard outside. Why it was the name of an antiques shop was still beyond me, though.

The building was an unattractive concrete structure, which had the look of something originally designed for utilitarian purposes. There were two floors of seemingly unoccupied offices above and the shop took up the ground floor, which might once have been some kind of showroom. Whatever the case, the place was empty of customers now; back to the way it normally was, I suspected: grey light from the plate glass and a few patches of brightness from lamps and wall lights.

I picked my way through the maze of precariously displayed bric-a-brac and when I got to the counter I spent a minute looking at various pieces of jewellery and metalwork while a figure clinked a spoon against china behind a curtained doorway.

When she emerged the woman had two mugs of coffee in hand and was slightly surprised to see me at the counter, making a quick, apologetic smile.

"*Hey, góðan dag,*" I said. "*Eg eiti Jan Reyná.* Are you Eileen Skoradal?"

She looked to be in her early sixties; a fairly small woman, with elfin features and an easy-going manner, but when I spoke she took on the slightly confused look I was getting used to when I mixed basic Faroese and English. I'd probably have done just as well to stick with English, but the Faroese was sometimes a useful flag that I wasn't just a tourist.

"*Ja.* Yes, I'm Eileen. Can I help you?"

"I hope so," I said. "My mother was Lýdia Reyná. I was told you might have known her."

She frowned for a second, putting it together, and then her face lightened. "Lýdia? *Ja* – yes, of course! *You're* Jan?" She seemed genuinely pleased to have made the connection. "I can't believe this."

"I was hoping I could ask you a few questions about her," I said. "If you have time."

"Yes, yes sure. Can you wait for a moment? I made coffee for my mother. Let me take it and I can come back. Is that okay?"

"Sure, of course. *Takk fyri.*"

Leaving one mug on the counter Eileen Skoradal moved away, weaving adeptly through the aisles, towards a far corner of the room I hadn't noticed before. Through the sea of furniture and objects I now made out an old woman – she had to be well over eighty – sitting under a standard lamp mostly covered in crocheted blankets. She was in an armchair and apart from her head the only part of her that moved were her hands, knitting with the regularity of a machine. Even when

Eileen brought her drink she didn't break off, but kept on clicking away as they spoke. It was almost hypnotic.

Rather than be caught watching them I turned and occupied the time by showing polite interest in the jewellery again: mostly silver rings and brooches with one or two gold and diamond rings in scuffed boxes. I was happy to look away when Eileen returned.

"Would you like coffee?" she asked. "Please, sit."

I took the chair she indicated at the end of the counter – well used and smelling vaguely of must – but declined the coffee, telling her where I'd been for the last hour while she'd been busy.

She laughed. "When the cruise ships come in the people are as if they were just set free from prison. They want to see and buy everything as soon as possible before they have to go back. It's like a race."

"Good for business, though," I said.

"*Ja*, as long as they pay. If you don't watch them they steal, too. They think it doesn't count if they don't live here. So, I have my mother to watch also."

The surreal image of the old lady rising from her blankets to tackle pilfering tourists made me wonder if she was joking, but she seemed quite serious as she pulled up a low, padded stool and sat down to face me. Coffee mug cupped in both hands, she leaned forward slightly, as if to be sure I was really there. She had rings on every finger, I noticed.

"So, you're Jan," she said again. "The last time I saw you... How old were you? Two years or three, maybe?" She shook her head a little.

"Probably," I said.

"Is this the first time you have come back?"

I nodded. I didn't think there was any need to go into the fact that I'd been back once before, when I was seventeen and intent only on confronting Signar.

"My father died so I came for the funeral," I said, again going for the easiest option.

"*Ja*, my mother tells me," Eileen said sombrely. "I am sorry to hear it."

"Thank you. Anyway while I was here I thought I'd try to find out something more about Lýdia – about what she was like when she was growing up, that sort of thing. I don't know very much about that and I've always wondered, you know?"

Maybe I was laying it on a bit thick, but on the other hand it was basically true. Rói Eysturberg had told me too much and too little not to take it further if I could.

Eileen Skoradal took the explanation at face value, though. "Of course," she said. "It would be a natural thing to do, I think."

"So what do you remember most about her?" I asked.

She sipped her coffee and composed herself in the way people do when they're delving into memory, seeming to wade through the undergrowth of recollection until she found something to latch on to.

We were going back more than fifty years, to her childhood, she told me. That was when she had first got to know Lýdia, when they were at school together on Suðuroy. They came from different ends of the same village: Vágur in the south of the island. The difference perhaps was more that her father was a manager in the Kommuna and Lýdia's father worked the fishing boats: white collar and blue. It made no difference to their friendship, though, and according to Eileen's account they were best friends from infant school right through to their teens.

"She always had a great – a fantastic – imagination, you know? For making up games and pretending to be princesses and rich ladies. And she would always be drawing in er... books with clean pages."

"Sketchbooks?"

"*Ja*, sketchbooks. She was very good. Pictures of people in dresses – the fashion – that we found in magazines. That sort of thing. She liked to look at photographs of film stars or pop singers and to draw them."

Not so hot on her schoolwork, though, apparently. Lýdia was usually in trouble for not working hard enough, although the teachers all knew she could if she wanted to. That was what annoyed them, Eileen said: the fact that Lýdia could have done well but chose not to. She wasn't interested in what she was *supposed* to learn, only in what interested *her*.

For ten minutes or so Eileen Skoradal strolled around in the past, describing what life was like for kids growing up in the Faroes back then. Very different to now; isn't it always? More basic, but somehow purer, she thought. They never felt the lack, she said as she told me about birthday parties and adventures or incidents and mishaps as children, and of teenage indecision about the future and what it might be like outside the Faroes in the barely-glimpsed wider world.

By and large Eileen's description of Lýdia fitted with

what Sofia Ravnsfjall had said yesterday, though this time it was told from the perspective of a friend rather than that of the woman who had succeeded Lýdia as Signar's wife. Boiled down, it seemed that Lýdia had been bright and lively but she'd had a rebellious streak: a nonconformist, but not one of whom the Nonconformist, church-going Faroese at the time would have approved much, I suspected.

"Did you stay friends after you left school and she married Signar?" I asked. "Did you still see her?"

Eileen nodded but she seemed more tentative than before. No one had expected Lýdia to marry Signar, she told me: much less to have a baby. As far as anyone was aware – even Eileen – Lýdia and Signar barely knew each other, so it was a surprise all round. But these things happen, she said with a shrug, and when they did Lýdia moved to Øravík to live, and after I was born, of course she was busy with looking after me and running the home.

I sensed something in that. "Didn't she like it?" I said. She had been only eighteen or nineteen, after all.

Eileen hesitated to pick her words. "I think it was harder than she expected," she said diplomatically. "It was a different life, you know? Sometimes she would say that she never saw anyone that she knew any more, or say that Signar was a long time away on the boat."

"Did she seem unhappy or depressed by it all?" I asked, thinking back to Rói Eysturberg's account of the suicide attempt.

"Yeh, yeh, a little sometimes," Eileen said. "But I didn't see her for some time because I was in Denmark to study jewellery-making for a year. She wrote to me a few times at the start and in the letters she seemed always happy. Sometimes I remember she would put a picture with the letter, but there weren't so many later." She shifted a little on the stool. "After she went away with you I hoped she would write to me to say where she was and what you were doing, but she never did."

I nodded to acknowledge her disappointment, then said: "Before she left I was told that she spent time at a place called the Colony, at Múli. Do you know anything about it?"

Eileen hesitated and straightened up slightly. "A little."

"It was some sort of commune, is that right?"

"*Ja*, something like that."

"Did you ever go there?"

"Maybe two times." Said in a way to deny any real knowledge.

"With Lýdia?"

She shrugged. "I don't remember. Perhaps."

I didn't press it. Instead I said, "So what did they do there?"

Eileen shifted again. She was clearly on the edge of her comfort zone and would have liked to shut this down, but didn't quite feel able to do it.

"It was… it was people who wanted to be er… self-sufficient," she said in the end. "To live differently, with the farming to grow what they need. In the summer people went to visit and help or just to have a holiday. Some lived in tents or little huts."

"People from the Faroes?"

She shook her head. "No, not so much from here. From Denmark and Europe, I think."

"Young people – hippies?"

"Yeh, some were hippies I guess you would say. All kinds."

"Was anyone in charge?"

"No, it was a commune," she said. "So everyone should be equal."

"It must have been someone's idea, though. Do you know who started it up?"

Again she shook her head. "Perhaps… I don't know. Maybe Rasmus Matzen. He was the oldest, I think. From Denmark." She stood up. "It was all years ago and they were not there long, so…"

As she let it trail off she moved to pick up a cloth from the counter and started to clean a brass box, as if it was something urgent she'd forgotten to do.

"So tell me what you do now," she said then; no way to disguise the shift in topic, except by not making eye contact, which she didn't.

"Oh, I'm on leave from my job at the moment," I said. "So it was a good excuse to finally come here." Perhaps better not to use the words *police* or *homicide*.

"And do you feel at home here?"

Now that she was sure we'd shifted away from the subject of the Colony, she appeared to feel secure enough to look up from the box she was polishing.

"No," I admitted. "Sometimes it feels very foreign, very strange: like nowhere else I could have gone."

Which was the truth. If I was truly, at heart, a Faroese then a large part of me was missing. That was how it felt. Or just possibly that I was missing something that anyone truly Faroese would have known.

I spent another five minutes with Eileen, for the sake of politeness and just to see if she would come back to anything I'd asked earlier of her own volition. She didn't, though. Instead she talked about Vágur again, saying that one day she and her mother would go back to live there.

"I was only supposed to have the shop for six months and I've been here for two years," she told me.

Had I been to Vágur? she asked. Did I know the house where Lýdia had grown up? When I said that I didn't she wrote down the address. Perhaps I should go. It was a nice house; not large, but always cosy. She said it with a kind of reminiscent look, as if she was remembering the place and time fondly, as well as Lýdia and their friendship.

I took the address and when I stood up ready to leave she suddenly seemed to be taken with an impulse and thrust the box she'd been polishing towards me. It was the size of a tobacco tin and looked old; the hinged lid embossed with a swirling design around a blank space clearly intended for an engraved name or initials.

"For memory of Lýdia," she said. "Please. I'd like you to have it."

"*Takk*," I said. "*Stora takk fyri*. It was good to meet you."

"Yes," she said. "I'm glad that you came."

I liked Eileen Skoradal despite the fact that she hadn't wanted to tell me everything she could have, and I was glad that I hadn't pushed her so far that she'd have shut down and not given me the box. I must have been feeling sentimental.

22

"HOW GOOD IS THE DESCRIPTION OF THIS MAN ERLA MET?" Remi Syderbø asked when Hentze had finished telling him about his conversation with Jákup Homrum.

"Not very," Hentze admitted. "Medium height, middle-aged, darkish hair, city clothes."

"Not Finn Sólsker then."

Hentze hadn't intended to point this out, knowing Remi was sharp enough to see it for himself.

"I wouldn't say so."

"But it's a description to fit a few hundred others," Remi said.

"Yeh," Hentze allowed. "Except that the tenant at Erla's apartment saw someone similar near the flat about a week ago."

Remi frowned. "Doing what?"

"Nothing. He said he was on the wrong floor."

"So maybe he was." Remi shook his head. "Without a better description I don't see how we could link those two things. It could be entirely coincidental."

"Yeh," Hentze agreed. "But I still have the impression that Erla's meeting with the man at Kaldbak wasn't an accident."

Remi thought it over for a moment, but in the end wasn't moved. "Well, mark it up on the timeline by all means," he said. "But I'd view it as a side issue. I don't think it should take up any of our time." His cellphone started to ring. "Okay?"

"Okay," Hentze said, though he allowed a degree of reluctance to colour it.

Remi nodded and answered his phone.

It was odd, Dánjal Michelsen thought. For people who obviously saw themselves as rebels against conformity, they all adopted a very uniform appearance: black jeans and heavy-metal tee shirts, piercings and tattoos, dreadlocks and/or ropey beards. And that was just the women, he added as a mental punch line, together with a rim shot.

But despite the easy caricature, Dánjal Michelsen's personal opinion of the Alliance protesters was not so black-and-white. He thought they might have a valid argument about there being no need to continue the *grind* in this day and age, what with the mercury and chemicals in the meat and blubber. So he might have been persuaded to at least declare himself ambivalent towards the *grind* if it wasn't for the way the Alliance presented it.

It was their attitude of moral superiority and their refusal to properly engage with the people they were bad-mouthing that got Dánjal's back up. It was just as one commentator had said recently: you can't have a meaningful debate with evangelists because at some point they always fall back on the unreasonable but unassailable point that they *know* they are right and you are wrong. They believe and you don't: they are the chosen and you are not. End of discussion.

So it was without any great relish that Dánjal followed Lukas Drescher – with tattoos, piercings *and* beard – through to the sitting room of Fjalsgøta 82 and was told that, yes, Veerle Koning was here; if Dánjal waited, the pallid German would go and find her.

Dánjal chose to remain standing, surveying the untidy room, until Drescher returned with Veerle Koning. They were followed by a man in his thirties who introduced himself in Danish as Peter Jessen.

Although Dánjal had anticipated speaking with Veerle alone, both Drescher and Jessen appeared determined to stay. And, since Drescher said that he lived there too, Dánjal decided not to make a point of asking them to leave. It didn't matter. In fact it was probably more useful to speak to as many residents as possible. All the same, he started by addressing Veerle when he finally sat down in the armchair across from her.

"When you talked to my colleague, Annika, yesterday you said that Erla left the house at about three o'clock on Saturday and that she didn't come back," Dánjal said. "Do you remember that?"

Veerle nodded. "Yes. It was after we'd eaten lunch."

"Well, the thing is, we now think Erla must have come back here at some point because she copied some photos she'd taken on Saturday afternoon on to her laptop."

Veerle frowned, as if this couldn't be right. "I don't know. I didn't see her."

"Were you here all the time?" Dánjal asked. "You didn't go out at all that afternoon, even just for a short time?"

"No," Veerle said, shaking her head. "Not until the evening." As if for confirmation she cast a quick glance at Lukas Drescher who was sitting on the arm of the sofa.

"You told Annika you went out at between half past seven and eight?"

"Yes."

From his position leaning on the arm of the sofa, the man called Peter Jessen shifted. "Are you accusing us of something, is that what this is about?" he said. "Because it sounds to me as if you're trying to make up even more bullshit against us, just because you don't like the fact that we're here."

"Listen—" Dánjal began, but Jessen was warming to his indignation.

"You know we have the *right* to be here and protest, don't you?" Jessen said, in Danish now. "Even your Prime Minister and Chief of Police have said that. Of course, that doesn't stop you arresting people for no reason as soon as we *do* protest. Your whole system is corrupt. You say one thing for the cameras and the press and then operate like a Nazi state as soon as you think no one's watching."

"Listen, Herre Jessen, is it?"

"Yeh. So?"

Dánjal held on to his temper. "So, this has nothing to do with protests or the whales. That is completely separate. What I'm investigating is the death of Erla Sivertsen."

"Yeh, I know that's what you *say*," Jessen told him drily. "But we all know it would be much better for the police to blame it on one of us and not on one of your own people. Forget that they are the ones who commit mass murder every time a pod of whales comes near. Because Erla was from AWCA, let's blame it on them."

Dánjal made an effort to keep any irritation out of his voice. These protesters had one-track minds, that was their problem. "As I said, no one is blaming or accusing anyone – yet," he said, flat and unimpressed. "So, if you'll let me ask my questions, I'll be gone. I'm sure that would suit us both."

Jessen gave him a pointedly unconvinced look but said no more and Dánjal turned back to Veerle Koning, speaking in English again. "Just so I'm sure; you're certain that you didn't see Erla again before you went out for the evening? It's okay if you forgot to tell us in your previous statement. Things were very upset, I understand that."

"No." Veerle shook her head, clearly pained by the apparent problem it caused. "I was here all the time."

"Listen," Lukas Drescher said, cutting in to take Dánjal's attention. "Veerle was here, I was here – some of the time anyway – and we were together. But even if Erla *had* come back we might not have heard. Some of the time we had music on in our room."

"You were in your room together – you and Veerle?" Dánjal asked.

"Yeh, that's what I said."

"And the music was loud?"

"Sure. Loud enough."

"Enough for what?"

"Shit." Lukas shook his head. "You want me to draw you

a picture? For sex, right? So the whole house doesn't listen, you know?"

Veerle shifted, a little embarrassed.

"But if there was no one else here…" Dánjal queried.

"Jesus!" Now Drescher was exasperated. "People come and go, yeh? Like, who knows when. In and out. So if you want a bit of privacy you play the music and they know you are there and what you are doing. Have you never shared a house with other people?"

Dánjal ignored the sarcasm. "So what you're saying is that while you were in your room with the music playing, it's possible that Erla came back to the house, then left again and you wouldn't know. Is that correct?"

"Yes, man. That's what I'm telling you."

"Do you remember what time this was?"

"I don't know." Drescher shrugged. "About five o'clock, maybe earlier."

He looked to Veerle, who agreed with a nod. "And I had a shower, also," she said to Dánjal. "So…"

"Right," Dánjal said.

"So have you finished now?" Jessen asked. "Are you satisfied? Or do you want to take our fingerprints and DNA?"

"No," Dánjal shook his head. "We'll only do that when you're arrested." He stood up. "Thanks for your help."

Neither of the two men moved as Dánjal made for the door, but as he got there Veerle rose and followed him into the hall, going ahead to open the front door for him. It was raining and Dánjal paused to fasten his coat.

"Do you know when the funeral will be?" Veerle asked,

still holding the door. "Annika, who was here before, said she would let me – us – know."

"I don't think it will be for some time yet," Dánjal said. "A week at least. Perhaps more."

"Oh. Okay. I see."

Her voice was flat, almost disappointed. She didn't move and Dánjal sensed that there was more she wanted to say.

"Listen," he said. "If you think of anything else that could help us – anything at all – you can call us any time."

"I… Yes, I will. I just wanted to say thank you to Annika, for when she was here before. She was really nice, you know? Kind. I thought—"

"Veerle?" Lukas Drescher called.

She turned her head quickly. "Coming." And then to Dánjal, "Will you tell Annika? If she ever wants to come here, for coffee or something…"

"Sure, of course," Dánjal said.

"*Takk.*"

Dánjal stayed on the step for a couple of seconds after the door had closed. Something not quite right there, but he couldn't put his finger on it.

23

THE CONFERENCE WAS HELD IN THE OFFICE ADJACENT TO THE main incident room. There were five of them there: Hentze, Remi Syderbø, Ári Niclasen, Oddur Arge and Sophie Krogh. They sat at two tables pushed together so they had a view of the whiteboards and when Remi called the meeting to order it was obvious he was going to keep this as formal as possible. Hentze had seen this before. Remi believed that formality brought order, as well as keeping things short.

"We are thirty hours into this investigation so we need to define what we do and don't know and decide on our next course of action," Remi said. "First of all I think we should look at the evidence from the body. Anders Toft had to take the afternoon plane back to Copenhagen, but Hjalti has a preliminary report on the post-mortem results from Dr Hovgaard and I think that's the place we should start. Hjalti?"

Hentze put on his glasses to read from the notes Elisabet Hovgaard had emailed across. "As Remi said, this is just a preliminary report," he told the group. "There are further tests to do and they'll be carried out when Anders gets to

Copenhagen, but in the meantime I think these bullet points will be enough."

The bullet points – time and cause of death, and the lack of indications of rape – were much as Elisabet Hovgaard had already outlined to Hentze at the mortuary, but there were a few more details about the stab wound.

"It was a narrow-bladed, sharp-edged weapon: something like a filleting knife," Hentze told the others. "The wound was 65 mm in depth, 10 to 15 mm wide and was directed upwards below the sternum but to the left of the heart."

"But definitely made after death?" Remi asked.

"Yeh, without doubt, according to Elisabet. Everything else – DNA sampling and so on – will be done as soon as possible, so we should have some results within the next twenty-four to thirty-six hours at the most."

"Okay, thanks. Any questions?" Remi asked, addressing the others. "No? Okay, let's move on."

Sophie Krogh was next, occasionally referring to an iPad on the table in front of her. "We've examined three sites," she said. "The huts at Húsavík where the body was found; the boat shed at Sandoy where the jacket and hat were recovered, and the car used by Erla Sivertsen. These have produced a lot of samples that need to be processed, along with clothing worn by the victim. So, I can't tell you anything from analysis yet. What I can say is that at the moment there's no evidence that the site at Húsavík was where she was killed. The boat-house is also clean."

"So what's your best estimation of events?" Remi asked.

"Without a full analysis it would only be an informed guess."

"That's okay, I understand."

"Well, in that case what I'd say is based more on what we haven't found than what we have. I'd say she died at an unknown location, and I suspect that the body was put in the boot of her car, possibly so it could be moved to Húsavík. There are certain things that indicate this might be the case, but we need fibre and soil analysis to be sure. After that I think her body was placed where it was found and the clothes arranged to suggest a sexual attack. That may also have been when she was stabbed, but it's not possible to say for sure."

"What about the graffiti?" Remi asked.

"We've managed to remove the section of wood it was on for analysis. I didn't think you would want it left there anyway. I don't think it will show very much, though. Certainly nothing specific in terms of when the words were written."

"So it may or may not be related to the body."

"There's nothing to say that it is," Sophie said.

"It must be," Ári put in. "It's too much of a coincidence for that not to be the case."

Sophie Krogh clearly didn't think it was worth reiterating her previous statement so she just shrugged.

"How soon do you think we might have some results?" Remi asked. "On anything."

"Perhaps twenty-four hours. I've asked for the samples which might provide the most information to be fast-tracked."

"Good. Thank you. Is there anything else we should note?"

"Not directly relating to forensics, except for the cellphone SIM card in her car. It was found under the driver's seat in a fold of the carpet after the car was brought back to be properly examined."

"When you say it was under the seat, do you mean it was hidden?"

"Possibly, yes; or just lost. Of course, we don't know how long it was there or who it belonged to yet, but Oddur has it for analysis."

"Okay, thank you," Remi said. "Would you mind staying in case there's anything we need to clarify?"

Sophie shook her head. "No, I'm happy to."

"Okay." Remi looked at the others. "So, now we come to our own investigation. Ári?"

Ári Niclasen rose to his feet, moving round the tables to the whiteboard from where he could address the others. This was what he'd been waiting for, Hentze thought: his moment in the spotlight. Then he chided himself for being uncharitable. Still, it was hard to be generous in the face of Ári's rather superior, lecturing tone, which suggested that he – alone amongst the others – had already seen the light.

"We've collated more than forty statements from members of the Alliance, as well as Ms Sivertsen's family and friends," Ári said. "These have enabled us to compile a timeline for her last known movements, which is shown here." He tapped a section of whiteboard with the end of a marker pen. "I can assume we're all familiar with it?"

He glanced round the room to confirm.

"I think so," Remi said.

"Very well, then." Ári nodded. "So, we've established that Erla must have returned to her room at the Fjalsgøta house some time after 16:30 hours. She didn't speak to any other residents, but at some point she must have left again. There are no sightings or reports of where she may have gone, but as the post-mortem shows, between 20:00 and 23:00 she was dead. So, that leaves us with four to seven hours unaccounted for, during which time she either went to or was taken to Sandoy."

He moved to indicate a block of times written at the end of the whiteboards. "If we look at Saturday's ferry timetable from Streymoy to Sandoy there are only four sailings she could have been on – either alive or dead. If she was on either the 17:15 or 19:15 sailings she was clearly alive; 21:00 or 23:45 she may have been dead, in which case – if Ms Krogh is right and her body was moved in her car – it would be the driver of the car we need to find. However, we've canvassed the *Teistin*'s crew and passengers as far as we're able and no one remembers seeing either Ms Sivertsen or her car."

Again Ári Niclasen paused to let his audience assimilate this information, then he moved to another section of the board.

"I think there are several other things worth noting. First, her car was found at Skopun, which could suggest that after dumping her body, the killer used it to return to the ferry and then travelled back to Streymoy as a foot passenger, leaving the car at the ferry terminal to distract us.

"Second, we haven't recovered her phone or her camera equipment, or any personal possessions that she may have had with her at the time of her death. Her pockets had been emptied.

"Third, we're now able to access her phone record and email account. Oddur?"

Oddur Arge half made to stand, then decided against

it and cleared his throat instead.

"Her emails are what you'd expect: a mixture of personal messages to family and friends and those related to her work with AWCA. There's nothing that jumps out as suspicious or odd. Her phone calls are more or less the same."

"But her cellphone service provider *has* identified the numbers she called," Ári said, like a lawyer prompting a reluctant witness. Ári was making his case, Hentze realised; he had this planned out.

"Yes, all but a few," Oddur said.

"So in the last week, who had she called besides AWCA colleagues?"

Oddur cleared his throat again. "Her parents' home and Finn Sólsker's cellphone."

Hentze raised his mug and realised it was empty. He leaned forward to pump fresh coffee into it from the Thermos jug.

"How many times?" Ári asked.

"Her parents twice, Finn Sólsker eight."

"When was the last time she called him?"

"On Saturday at 19:03."

24

THE SEA WAS GETTING ROUGHER AS THE WIND BACKED TO THE west, but the beat and vibration of the *Teistin*'s engines didn't vary. Outside the sky was heavy and leaden, almost all the light gone.

The case, as Ári Niclasen had made it, was not without merit. Hentze acknowledged that. On top of the known history between Erla and Finn Sólsker, Annika's report of her meeting with Martha was clear: Martha believed that her husband was having an affair with Erla Sivertsen.

Obviously, this wasn't known for a fact, as Ári had been at pains to point out. It was a wife's suspicion. But when you also remembered that Finn had no alibi for Saturday evening, that he could offer no explanation of how Erla's coat and hat had come to be in his boat shed, and that he refused to admit to having seen or spoken to Erla Sivertsen more than twice in the last two months… Well, something was clearly not right.

Of course, Ári had said, if Finn *was* viewed as a viable suspect, then they could only speculate on what might have happened. The apparent staging of a rape, stabbing the body and leaving graffiti about the whales could all have been designed to obscure the truth. But whatever the case, if and when the technical lab matched samples to Finn, he would have no choice but to explain properly. In the meantime, Ári advised, it would be in everyone's best interests to continue to hold Finn until the test results were known.

"You want a coffee, Hjalti?" Sophie Krogh asked, bracing her knees against the roll of the ferry, a hand on the back of the vacant seat beside him.

The rest of the police contingent had gone to sit in the forward lounge near the snack bar, but Hentze had gone to a table in one of the side galleries. It maintained the distance he had insisted on to Remi. He wasn't part of the team and was only there because he wanted to speak to Martha.

"No, thanks." Hentze shook his head.

"Company?"

"No. Thanks."

"Okay. I'm going for a smoke then."

"Watch your footing on the deck," Hentze told her.

"Don't worry, I'm told I've got the reflexes of a cat. At least, I think 'reflexes' was the word they used."

She gave him a grin, then moved on towards the aft deck.

Hentze turned his head to look out of the window. In Remi Syderbø's place, he would have made the same decision. With no other suspect and the weight of circumstantial evidence, it made sense to hold Finn in custody overnight pending DNA analysis and other forensic tests, and when this was decided the meeting had broken up. Remi had held Hentze back, though.

"You agree?" he asked.

Hentze nodded. "It's the best way."

"You know we'll have to search the house."

"Yeh. I'll call Martha and get her to take the kids away if that's all right with you."

"Of course."

"I also think I should leave the investigation. More now than before."

"I've told you, no one will question your impartiality."

"Not here, maybe, but if or when it goes to court a smart lawyer could use it to muddy the waters. That doesn't mean I think Finn did it; just that if we can't rule him out I think we should play safe."

Remi could see Hentze had a point. He didn't seem to like it, but in the end he said, "Let's talk about it in the morning when we see how things are going, okay?"

"Okay," Hentze agreed, although in his head he was already stepping aside.

So now Finn was being driven to the holding cells in Klaksvík and Hentze was on his way to Skopun and a meeting with his daughter to which he was not looking forward. She had said barely half a dozen words when he called her to say that she should probably arrange for the kids to stay the night with friends. It could be disturbing for them to have several uniformed officers searching the house.

On the table in front of him Hentze's phone rang. It was Jan Reyná.

"Hey, Jan," Hentze said.

"Hi. Can you talk?"

For a second Hentze debated. "Not so much now."

"Okay. I just wondered if Finn Sólsker was going to be held overnight."

"Yeh, to the morning."

"Okay, thanks. Can I call you later or tomorrow?"

"Tomorrow, yeh."

"When would be best?"

Hentze decided. "Would you like to have breakfast?"

"Sure. Where? Hotel Tórshavn again?"

"No, there's a café on Niels Finsens gøta: Smyrjibreyðsbúðin."

"You're spreading your favours around?"

"*Ja*, something like that. Is seven too early for you?"

"No, I'll be there."

"Okay, I will see you then."

Hentze rang off, then sat back in the seat and closed his eyes.

In the forward lounge of the ferry Dánjal Michelsen was sitting with Annika Mortensen, a table away from the three uniform officers who'd also been assigned to the search. Most of the other passengers – fewer than half a dozen of them – looked as if they were on the way home from work. The *Teistin* in choppy weather was no pleasure cruise.

Dánjal tidied used sugar packets into his empty cardboard cup.

"I forgot to tell you, I talked to Veerle Koning at the Alliance house earlier," he told Annika. "She said you should call in any time if you felt like a coffee."

"The Dutch girl?" Annika asked. "Curly hair, looks like a milkmaid?"

"Yeah, I suppose so."

Annika shook her head. "Don't think I will. She's a weeper, that one. Turns it on too easily."

"You mean fake? She didn't strike me like that."

"No, not fake: just too emotional. Anything will set her off."

"She was okay today," Dánjal said, then shrugged. "Anyway, I said I'd tell you. And at least she was more cooperative than those arseholes she lives with: Jessen and Drescher. I don't like being told I'm no better than a Nazi."

Annika nodded, but didn't follow it up. Instead she cast a glance at the opposite table, then lowered her voice. "What do you think about Hjalti?"

"What about him?"

Annika gave him a look as if to question whether he was being purposely dense. "You think he's okay?"

"Sure," Dánjal said, but then decided it needed qualification. "It's not like Finn Sólsker's a proper relative, is it? I mean, only an in-law. And anyway, if he did it I'll swim home."

"You don't think so?"

Dánjal shook his head. "If he'd killed her he could've put the body on his boat, gone twenty kilometres out to sea and that would've been that." He looked up as Sophie Krogh came to the table and sat down next to Annika.

"Ask Sophie," Dánjal said, swapping to Danish.

"Ask me what?"

"How would you dispose of a body if you lived here?"

"Put it on a boat and take it a long way out to sea," Sophie said, as if she'd worked this out a long time ago. "Strip it naked, weigh it down – chains round the torso is best – then over the side. I'd send the clothes after it with more chain, then sail away. Any help?"

Dánjal smiled. "I must remember never to seriously piss you off."

"No," Sophie said. "It wouldn't be a good thing to do."

25

"THEY'RE HOLDING HIM TILL TOMORROW," I TOLD FRÍÐA.

She hadn't wanted to call Hentze herself, despite the fact that she probably had more of a legitimate connection to him than I did. She might have thought I'd get more information, copper to copper.

"Is there... Did he say anything else?"

"No, he sounded as if he was up to his eyes – busy," I told her. "But I said I'd meet him tomorrow for breakfast. I'll see if I can get more details then."

She nodded, even though it clearly wasn't as much as she'd hoped. "Have you eaten?" she asked.

"Yeah, in Tórshavn."

"Would you like a drink?"

"That would be good. *Takk*."

"Beer?" She moved towards the fridge.

After talking to Eileen Skoradal in her shop I'd walked through the town centre for a while and then been seized by an idea and found my way to the library – *býarbókasavnið* – in another ugly building: flat-fronted, office-block design. Inside it was more welcoming: lots of Scandinavian open

229

space and primary colours, bright and warm and with helpful staff. Yes, they had copies of newspapers from the 1970s on microfiche and if I wanted to browse through them I was welcome; the assistant could show me where.

I knew my Faroese wasn't up to it – nowhere close – so I declined the offer and said I'd just wanted to check if the resource was available. I might come back later with someone to help me. Sure, that was fine.

After that I walked down to HN Jacobsens bookshop by Vaglið square and bought a large-scale map and a few items of stationery. I was precise and picky about this or that notebook, this or that pen. I recognised the preoccupied behaviour but I didn't try to suppress it. I was on an upswing and to a certain extent I welcomed it because it brought focus and gave me a purpose after days of just walking the hillsides.

It was just getting dark when I got back to Leynar and started down the steps to Fríða's guest house. The lights were on in her place and she must have been watching for my car because she opened the door in case I didn't intend to call in.

"Jan, do you have a few minutes to come in?" Fríða said. She was wearing one of her long knitted cardigans, wrapped round her as if she was feeling the cold, and her voice was oddly formal.

"Sure, of course," I said. "What's up?"

"The police have arrested Finn," she said. "It's about Erla."

So now we were in the kitchen, each with a beer, and Fríða was clearly mulling over the fact that we'd found out no more from Hentze, other than the fact that Finn Sólsker wouldn't be released tonight.

"Do you think they believe he did it?" Fríða asked in the end. "Would they hold him like this if they didn't?"

"Professional opinion?"

She nodded.

I said, "I don't know about here, but in England it's not unusual for people to be arrested or held for questioning even if they're not a firm suspect. The police want to make sure they've got all the facts before deciding to charge or release. And if someone's refused to answer questions, being arrested can make them think twice. It tells them you're serious, and that it's in their interest to tell the truth."

Fríða looked thoughtful, then shook her head. "With Finn it might not be so easy. He doesn't like to be accused. It makes him stubborn."

"He'll probably do better if he's not."

That didn't make her feel any better. "How long can they hold him?"

"Twenty-four hours from the point when he was arrested, or they can ask for an extension."

I'd picked up that much from spending time with Hentze. No different to the UK, though some other things were. By British police standards their arrests and interviews were less codified and rigorously recorded; not necessarily a bad thing, depending on which side you were on, of course.

"So he might not be free in the morning."

"Maybe not. I'll ask Hjalti tomorrow, though."

I wondered how much Hentze would be involved with the case now, given his relationship to Finn. I could well imagine Ári Niclasen being keen to lead and perhaps being glad of an excuse to sideline Hentze. True, my opinion of Niclasen had never been very high, but I knew the type. I also knew that Hentze was the better copper.

"Finn wouldn't do something like that," Fríða said then, decided. "The police must have something wrong."

"Could be. It happens a lot. More than you'd think."

A platitude. Without more information it was all I could offer. There could have been a hundred reasons why Finn had stood out to the police as a potential suspect and there was no point in trying to guess what they might be.

"Why *would* he kill her?" she said. "There could be no reason. It doesn't make sense."

I remembered the tension I'd noticed in Martha Sólsker when Erla and I had come to Finn's boat after the *grind*. There were a couple of conclusions you could draw from that. "You think he was still fond of her?" I asked.

"Sure, of course. Why not?"

"*How* fond?"

She knew what I was asking, but rather than answer it directly her voice took on a slightly reminiscent note. "My father used to say that Erla was Finn's dark princess. You know the idea? That everyone has someone who may not be good for them, but they find it hard to resist going back. But that was a long time ago. Now…" She shook her head.

Whether she didn't want to think about the obvious possibility or didn't believe it, I couldn't tell. Whichever it was, it was enough to make her move to the sink and rinse out her empty beer bottle.

Then I heard the front door open and close and Matteus

called, "*Hey!*" from the lobby followed by the thud of a bag being dumped. He came into the kitchen.

"*Hey*," he said again, slightly breathless as if he'd been walking quickly, "*Hevur tú hoyrt?*" then switched to English for my benefit. "Have you heard? About Uncle Finn?"

"*Ja*," Fríða said.

"It's been on the news."

"*Ja*," Fríða said again.

"Do you know why they're saying it? It must be bullshit, right?" His conviction had a sixteen-year-old's certainty.

"Don't say 'bullshit'," Fríða chided him, but without any real force.

"Yeh, but it is, right?"

He looked towards me, as if he thought I'd give a professional opinion.

"Chances are it's only a routine arrest so they can ask questions," I told him. "There's a big difference between that and being charged. I wouldn't worry too much about it."

I caught Fríða's glance and a small, grateful nod. "*Takk, Jan.*"

It was my get-out, to leave them in private, so I took it and made for the door. "Just shout if you need me, okay?"

Hentze and Martha stayed in the kitchen while the others searched the house and garage. He'd made a couple of attempts to be close to his daughter, but when Martha had side-stepped and moved away he'd given up and sat down at the table.

Martha continued to keep herself busy in a determined manner, sorting laundry and cleaning the sink. She was angry in a way Hentze recognised from her childhood: closed down tight, containing the pressure inside her like a moka pot on a low light. All the while they could hear muted noises from the activity in the other rooms.

"So, have you talked to him?" Martha finally asked after a silence of several minutes.

"Not today, no. Ári Niclasen took the interviews."

"And he doesn't believe what Finn said because he was sleeping with her." She wouldn't use Erla Sivertsen's name, as if it was a point of principle not to let her into the house.

Hentze shifted. "You said that to Annika, but do you know it for certain?"

"I'm not stupid."

"Of course not."

She cast him a black look. "Don't patronise me, Dad."

"I wasn't. I didn't mean to."

Martha's expression made it clear that she didn't believe this, but she said nothing more.

It had been a mistake to come with the others, Hentze realised now. It would have been better later. He'd only wanted to reassure her, but she was a grown woman and well capable of dealing with this. Instead, he'd probably made things worse. Bad enough to have your privacy invaded by strangers, but more humiliating when witnessed by people you know, trying to do good.

Not for the first time he wondered whether he was overprotective by nature, or – where Martha was concerned –

whether it was his way of showing that she was just as valued as her brother had been, despite Sóleyg's apparent evidence to the contrary.

Of course, Sóleyg had never meant her grief over Jógvan to be taken that way. It was an illness she couldn't control, and over time – with Hentze's protection – Sóleyg had improved. Working part time in the pre-school, as she did now, had acted like an inoculation, strengthening her resistance. But still Hentze couldn't help keeping up his constant vigilance for things that might trigger a re-infection of grief. So perhaps it really was his nature, to watch, to guard, and to worry when he could not.

And he couldn't now. That much was clear. Martha had retreated and didn't want protection.

Hentze pushed his chair away from the table. "I'll see how much longer they're likely to be," he said, standing up. "Then I'd better get back."

26

Tuesday/týsdagur

THERE WAS A GROWING, PINKISH LIGHT IN THE SKY AS I LEFT Leynar the next morning. The particular stillness amd clarity of the air was something I'd come to associate with Faroese dawns. They were like nothing I'd seen anywhere else; the rising light caught the underside of the clouds, while the sea and vast mountainsides remained dark. It was like that for ten minutes or so and then it was gone and the world shifted into a different phase.

By the time I was through the two tunnels and driving alongside Kaldbaksfjørður the car was warm and the voice on the radio was still incomprehensible. It didn't much matter. I was only listening to see if I heard any names I recognised – Erla Sivertsen, Finn Sólsker – but I didn't.

I parked on a side road off Niels Winthers gøta and walked up the hill past a construction site where a concrete-framed building was already well advanced and men in hard hats were starting things up for the day. At the top of the pedestrianised part of Niels Finsens gøta I found the Smyrjibreyðsbúðin café, newly fitted out and smartly finished in black wooden cladding.

Inside it was subdued, just open, with only two other customers, but there was already a smell of pastries and bread. There was no sign of Hentze so I took a table by one of the side windows and ordered coffee and two croissants, then ate, drank and waited. It was unlike Hentze to be late, but he was.

He arrived just after seven twenty. Not a man to appear flustered, he looked as if he had more things on his mind than he could easily deal with, and that prioritising them was a job in itself. He had lost the relaxed groundedness he'd had the last time I'd seen him by the sheep sheds.

"I'm sorry to be late," he said. "I had something to do."

He didn't volunteer more, so I didn't ask. I let him order coffee and decline anything to eat. I got the impression that he didn't expect to be here for long.

"You wanted to ask about Finn?" he said, cutting to the chase.

"For Fríða. Only what you can tell me."

He took a few seconds to put his thoughts into order – editing them, maybe – then he said, "A coat and hat we think were Erla Sivertsen's were found in Finn's boat shed at Sandur. He was brought to the station to explain how they were there, which he says he doesn't know. He also says he hasn't seen Erla since the *grind* on Friday, but we know that she spoke to him on the phone on Saturday night when he says he was working on his boat – alone," he added, because he knew I'd ask.

"Any forensics?"

"Yeh, but we don't know the results yet. Today, we hope."

"So it's circumstantial."

He nodded, then sipped his coffee. I knew there had to be more because a coat and a phone call on their own proved little. Anyone with a half-decent imagination could explain them away – at least until forensics showed something damning.

"We also believe he was having an affair with Erla," Hentze said then. "Martha thinks so and there are other reasons to believe it."

His dark princess, I remembered.

"Has he confirmed that?" I asked.

"*Nei*. At first he answered questions, but after that he has been difficult."

From the way he said it I could tell that he thought Finn had taken the wrong path. It didn't necessarily mean that Hentze thought he was guilty; more that Finn wasn't helping himself. You get people like that: suspects who stand on principle or are just bloody-minded in refusing to talk, even when simply giving an honest account would be in their best interests.

"How long have you got left on the custody clock?"

"Until midday, unless we ask to increase... for an extension."

"Depending on the forensics."

"Yeh."

I was going to ask him about the post-mortem, but it wasn't anything more than professional curiosity, and because he hadn't volunteered any details I decided to leave it. He looked as if he could do without anyone else picking at him for information.

"I'll tell Fríða, if that's okay," I said. "She wanted to know how long he might be held."

"Sure, that's okay."

"*Takk*," I said. Then: "So who's in charge?"

"Ári, but Remi Syderbø is watching over it."

"Right."

I got that. If I'd been Syderbø I'd have been watching over Niclasen, too.

Hentze glanced at his watch. There was something else I wanted to ask before he had to go, so I shifted.

"Listen, changing the subject," I said. "Have you heard of a commune that was set up at Múli on Borðoy in the mid-seventies? They called it the Colony."

He was silent for a moment. "*Ja*, yeh, I knew of it, from when I was a teenager."

"Anything specific?"

He shrugged. "There were always rumours – gossip – about what went on there," he said. "A few boys would go out to see if they were true but I wasn't one of them."

"Rumours about what?"

He made a "huh" and shook his head. "That they all went around naked and the women would have sex with anyone; that you would be given marijuana cigarettes and get drunk on homemade beer. If you could imagine something, that was what happened. So of course, it was very attractive if you were thirteen or fourteen. We would dare each other to go there, or make plans for how to go for a weekend when our parents didn't know."

"And *did* any of that happen?"

"Not as far as I know. That didn't stop the ministers making sermons in church, though; and the older people saying how could such a thing be allowed. I think there was a – what do you call it: petition? A petition to the government, but in the end it didn't matter because they left."

"Any idea why?"

He made a dismissive gesture. "It's not a good place – an easy place – to live. In the winter there are storms and gales and not so much shelter. I think it was just too hard for them."

"Does anyone live there now?"

"No. The houses have been empty – abandoned – for years."

"But you can still get out there?"

"Yeh, for sure. In good weather there is a beautiful view from the headland. The road isn't good, though – are you thinking to go?"

"I thought I might have a look," I said. "Apparently my mother spent some time there, so…"

"You're on your own investigation still?"

"Like you said, if I don't do it now…"

"Yeh, of course." He made an apologetic expression. "I'm sorry I haven't had chance to look for your mother's doctor yet."

I waved it away. "Doesn't matter. You've got enough on your plate."

"I won't forget, though," he said, then checked his watch again. "I'm sorry, I have to go for a meeting."

Outside we parted with a handshake and went in different directions. As I walked back to the car I called Fríða and told her what Hentze had told me. Most of it, anyway. It was hard to assess what she thought.

"So we won't know until midday what's going to happen," she said.

"No. They'll either charge or release him or ask for an extension of custody. They won't decide until they get forensic results."

"Okay, I see. Thanks for finding out." A moment of silence. "What are you doing today?"

"I thought I'd go north to Borðoy and have a look around."

There was a brief pause, then, "Okay. I'll see you later when you get back."

The meeting was delayed by almost an hour. There was no explanation, but neither Ári nor Remi were anywhere around.

To occupy the time Hentze dealt with some of the housekeeping tasks for the investigation, but without knowing the forensic results or having the strategy meeting there wasn't much the team could usefully do. Tidy up loose ends and catch up on reports, that was about all.

Then Sophie Krogh arrived and parked herself on the edge of the desk Hentze was using.

"I was summoned," she told him. "A royal command from Ári."

There were others around so Hentze let the slightly derisive tone pass rather than draw attention to it. He knew it as an indication of solidarity, though; Sophie wasn't known for her love of Ári.

"So, are you all finished?" he asked.

"Yeh, unless you've dug up anything more I'm back to civilisation on the afternoon plane."

In the background a phone rang. Dánjal answered, then called across the office. "Hjalti? Ári says can you go to his office. Sophie, too."

"What shall we give him," Sophie said, shifting off the desk. "A Broadway duet or a comedy routine?"

Ári wasn't alone in his office. For whatever reason, Remi Syderbø had come here rather than use his own. He was standing while Ári sat behind his desk and Hentze tried to read what this arrangement might signify, but as Sophie closed the door Remi put an end to any speculation.

"We have a problem," he said. "The forensic samples that went off to Copenhagen yesterday didn't arrive."

"You mean they were delayed?" Hentze asked.

"No, they've been lost – for the moment, at least."

"Shit!" Sophie said with some feeling.

"Are we sure they didn't just miss the flight at this end?" Hentze said. "Could they still be at Vágar?"

"No." Remi was definite. "The case went through baggage handling here. It was tagged and scanned but it didn't come through at the other end. I've asked for a thorough check in Kastrup but if it was wrongly diverted, to another plane for instance, it could be anywhere now."

"So what do we do?" Hentze asked.

"For the moment? Just wait, but we have to assume the worst, I suppose," Remi said. He looked to Sophie Krogh. "Can you stay in case we need to gather new samples?"

"I can, but you know some can't be reproduced, right? The clothing and other items can't be replaced and there are some samples we can't take again: those prior to the post-mortem, for example. They have to be taken at the time and in situ or they're no use as evidence."

"Well, can you go through the list of samples you took and identify the ones you *could* take again and which would still be valid as evidence?"

Sophie shook her head in disgust. "Yeh, yeh, okay. I'll see what I can do."

"Thank you," Remi said, somewhat drily. He turned to the others. "So then, that leaves us with the problem of what we do about Finn Sólsker. I've talked to Rógvi Dam in the Prosecutor's office and he doesn't believe that we can justify a charge based on what we have at the moment. Nor does he think a judge will grant an extension to custody, unless perhaps we could give a definite time by which we'd have forensic results. Clearly we can't do that. So we'll have to release him."

"We still have a few more hours," Ári said. "And now that he's had all night to think about things I'd like to try another interview."

"Hjalti?"

Hentze shook his head. "I think you should leave me out of this."

"Yeh, yeh, but if it was anyone else – any other case – what would you think?"

"With nothing new to put to him? I don't see why he would say any more now than yesterday, but by all means try."

243

"All right, then, but will you also sit in on the interview with Ári? Be a friendly face."

"I don't think Finn will see me that way," Hentze said. "But if that's what you want."

"Thank you," Remi said, as if Hentze had selected the most tactful option. "And after that – assuming that he *doesn't* admit anything more – what then? Have we other lines of enquiry to follow without forensic results to guide us?"

"If we have to release Finn I think we should look at Høgni Joensen again," Ári said immediately. "As soon as possible, before he and Finn have a chance to talk."

"Høgni?" Hentze said, unable to keep his surprise out of his voice. "Based on what?"

"Based on the fact that he had the same access to the boat shed as Finn. And didn't you say he tried to give Finn a false alibi?"

"Only because I put the idea in his head, to see what he'd say."

"So he's proved he'd try to cover for Finn," Ári said, as if Hentze had made his point for him. "So who knows, maybe they were acting together, or Høgni helped Finn after it happened. Or maybe Høgni was secretly attracted to Erla and tried to make something happen between them. Then, if she rejected him... A man built like him could easily kill someone – accidentally or on purpose."

"Høgni hasn't the mental capacity to move or leave the body like that," Hentze said. "He's also as good at lying as Sophie is at hiding her opinion."

"So maybe Finn helped *him*," Ári said, unwilling to be

swayed. "Whatever the case, I think Høgni Joensen should be interviewed."

It was a peculiar sort of madness, Hentze decided: to jump from one scenario to another, with nothing to say that any one of them had *actually* happened, but to still give each one credence. He looked to Remi Syderbø for some show of rationality.

"Let's cover all possibilities," Remi said. "It can't hurt to talk to Joensen again."

"Well, if we're covering *all* possibilities maybe we should also be trying to find out more about the man Erla met at Kaldbak on Saturday," Hentze said.

Given that Remi had already set Kaldbak aside, Hentze intended it only as an indication that he thought it was as futile as interviewing Høgni, so it struck him as odd when Remi agreed.

"Okay, that too, then," Remi said. "And in the meantime let's hope that the airline can locate the forensic samples in lost luggage."

Outside Sophie Krogh followed Hentze down the corridor to the CID canteen. It was empty. "And you say *I'm* the one who doesn't hide my opinion," she said as Hentze switched on the kettle.

"I'm just tired and cranky today."

"Which makes it harder to pretend Ári Niclasen's not an arsehole."

"Something like that." Hentze spooned Nescafé into two mugs. The coffee in the jug on the hotplate already smelled stewed.

"I still can't believe those fucking samples have gone missing," Sophie said, aggrieved. "Everyone tells me how safe and reliable it is to send them on their own. 'Bags never get lost between here and Copenhagen,' they said. Well apparently they *do*."

"Don't feel too bad about it," Hentze said. "It wasn't your fault. If it got lost anywhere it was probably at the other end."

"So it could have been diverted to Abu Dhabi or some other godforsaken hole."

"Will it ruin the case?"

"I dunno, I'm no legal expert. I don't think it would help if a lawyer could challenge the validity of replacement samples, though. And like I said, some *can't* be replaced. Luckily, though, I don't have so much faith in airline efficiency."

Hentze looked at her. "You've got duplicate samples?"

"Of the most important ones, of course. What am I, an amateur?"

He handed her a coffee. "No, 'amateur' is not the word I would use. What's the word the Americans have: 'ballbreaker'?"

"Tcha!" Sophie said. "They deserve to suffer a bit, just for the fact that I'll have to spend the morning cataloguing what I *do* need to take again. *And* I won't get the afternoon flight. Katrina's going to be very pissed off."

"Katrina? Is she new?"

"A month or so. I only managed to get her into the sack last week but now she's a *very* enthusiastic convert. She especially likes—"

"Stop." Hentze held up a hand. "Too much information." Sophie grinned broadly, which made him laugh. "Just don't leave Remi in purgatory for too long before you tell him all isn't lost," Hentze told her. "Okay?"

"Okay. But I think he can live with it for an hour or so."

"Yeh, all right, fair enough."

He laughed again. Sometimes Sophie Krogh was just what you needed.

27

FINN SÓLSKER DIDN'T LOOK AS IF HE HAD SLEPT WELL, HENTZE thought. Hardly surprising. The cells in Klaksvík were as comfortable – or not – as those anywhere. But he was also glad that Finn didn't look too well rested. In his experience those who slept well in a cell were, more often than not, guilty. The guilty could sleep because now they'd been caught they could finally relax. The innocent had too many things on their mind.

"I thought you might want some coffee," Hentze said, putting the mug down in front of Finn. "Have you had breakfast?" Finn nodded. "Okay. Good."

Ári Niclasen and Finn's lawyer settled themselves. The recorder went on. The time was logged.

Hentze sat back in his chair almost leisurely. "Feel like talking?" he asked.

"I've already told him everything I know." Finn gestured at Ári without looking at the man.

"But not me."

Finn took a moment, then sipped his coffee experimentally. "Are you going to ask anything different?"

"Probably not. But there might be details you'd forgotten last time."

"I didn't kill her," Finn said, putting the coffee mug down. "That's the only thing that matters, right? Did I or didn't I? And I didn't. I keep on saying it and now I'm sick of saying it. I did not kill Erla. Okay? End of story."

Hentze didn't say anything. Give it time; let the first hard resolve dissipate…

"Okay, so let's start again at the beginning, shall we?" Ári said flatly. "Saturday afternoon."

The moment crashed to the floor and shattered.

For the next half an hour Hentze barely spoke. There was no need and no point. Ári was going to push this as hard as he could, as if badgering and cynicism would wear Finn Sólsker down rather than simply strengthen his obstinacy. It took two minutes for Finn to start saying, "On the advice of my lawyer I have no comment to make," but still Ári pressed on, until he had been through his list of questions, each one pushing Finn Sólsker further away.

"Do you have *anything* to say before I conclude this interview?" Ári asked finally.

Finn didn't bother to reply.

"Finn, now *would* be a good time," Hentze said mildly. It was a final appeal but he knew it wouldn't work. Finn shook his head.

"Very well. This interview is concluded," Ári said.

Ári didn't hang around. He was off to Sandoy to find Høgni Joensen, Hentze knew. Clutching at straws.

Because it was the easiest way, Hentze dealt with the

CHRIS OULD

release; the return of possessions, the signing of forms. Throughout it all Finn said no more than he had to, then followed Hentze to the back door of the station.

"Call Martha," Hentze told him, unlocking the door. "Then go home. Get some sleep if you need it. When the test results come from the lab there could still be more questions."

Finn shifted. "These tests, will they—" He changed his mind. "They'll show you I didn't do it. I'm telling the truth."

"Yeh? Just not all of it, though – right?" Hentze opened the door.

For a moment Finn Sólsker looked as if he might say something to that, but then he set his shoulders and walked out.

"Call Martha," Hentze repeated, then went back inside.

He took the open tread stairs to the third floor but as he pressed his key fob to the sensor the door opened anyway and Jósef Dimon came out.

"Hey, Jósef." Hentze nodded.

"Hey," Dimon said. "How's it going with your murder case?"

Dimon was lead officer on the islands' four-strong drugs squad; a compact, athletic man in his mid-thirties with brush-cut hair and a short-cropped beard. He was generally close-mouthed and slightly remote from the others, but a decent guy just the same.

"It might be a lot better if the airline hadn't just lost the forensic samples," Hentze said.

"*Lost* them? Shit. Maybe we should both just go home for the day."

"Your day's not so good either?"

"You could say." For a moment Dimon seemed to debate how much he wanted to say, but then he gestured Hentze to move along the short corridor to the glass wall of the stairwell.

"I've just had an operation cancelled," Dimon said, keeping his voice low. The stairs carried sound well. "We've been setting it up for a fortnight, all set for today, and then it's called off. Not from our side: the Danes. No explanation, it's just off. Complete waste of time. Maybe anything to do with the airline is jinxed."

"Your stuff was flying in?"

"Yeh, the lazy way. You'd think they'd know better, but they don't." There was the sound of footsteps and voices below and Dimon took it as a cue to become more circumspect. "So now I have to find something else to do for the day. Or maybe I'll just go fishing. Sometimes it's all you can do, right?"

"Yeh, sometimes," Hentze said.

On a map the *norðoyar* – the northern islands – look like long thin ripples of rock spreading away from the ragged coastline of Eysturoy. In reality, or if you look more closely at the map, they aren't ripples but ridges, some over two and a half thousand feet high. You get the sense that they're the crenellations of a drowned world.

It took me an hour to reach Klaksvík, the second largest town on the islands, and once through its strangely disorientating road system I followed route 70 north until it made an abrupt turn into a mountain.

So far all the tunnels I'd been through had had two traffic lanes, and they were all lit. The Árnafjarðartunnilin took me by surprise because it had no lights and the road narrowed to a single lane. It was like driving into a mine, with no indication of how far and how deep you would have to go. It was unnerving and the roughly cut passing places carved out of the rock didn't make it any less so.

I was lucky, though. I made it through without meeting anything coming the opposite way and was finally ejected into the light on a long stretch of downhill road with a view of the narrow strait separating Borðoy from Viðoy. A bridge spanned the gap to the scattered buildings of Hvannasund on the far side, but before I got to it I slowed and took a turn to the left.

There was no sign to point the way down this side road, but if Múli was deserted I guessed there was no need. Who'd go there? Still, for the first half-mile or so the single-lane road was metalled and relatively smooth, until I crossed a cattle grid and started hitting potholes and patches of eroded tarmac. I slowed down a lot and from then on the road was a track, in places hardly more than a ledge perched on the hillside, with a two hundred foot slope to the sound on my right.

It seemed to go on for ages like this, but finally I rounded a curve in the hillside and saw a small cluster of buildings that could only be Múli, sitting in the scoop of a valley near the toe of the headland. Around the buildings there was a patchwork of fields, a few divided by dry stone walls, but most only delineated by streams and ditches, the usual Faroese way. The green-yellow shades of the grass were the colours I'd come to recognise when hay had been cut. Even if no one lived here the land couldn't be wasted.

By the time I got to the outskirts of the place the track was just two ruts with grass in between. I let the car idle along at little better than walking pace, as far as a stone shed where there was room to pull in without blocking the way. Force of habit. Nothing moved, there was no sign of life and when I switched off the engine the only sound was the breeze through the half-open window and the *tick-tick*ing of hot metal from the car.

When I got out the same absence of sound told me the place was deserted. It felt that way, too. It's odd to be sure there isn't another soul within miles, but I was. You could feel it. It was the sort of sensation that makes you want to walk quietly and make a noise, both at the same time.

I left the car and followed the track between several stone outbuildings, varying in size and proximity, with greying wooden doors and rusted tin roofs. Past them there were two houses, one higher than the other on the slope, separated by a track and a patch of overgrown grass. The larger one was also the highest so I went to look at it first: double-fronted with gabled dormers in the red tin roof and an undercroft of white-painted stone.

From a distance it had looked fairly well maintained, but that was an illusion. Closer to it I saw the window frames were rotting and the paint on the stones was flaking away. The door to the undercroft was secured by a small rusting padlock on a hasp; the same at the door round the back.

The windows were greyed with dirt and I cupped my hand

against one to see through it. Inside, back-lit by an open door to a front room, there was a kitchen: cabinet doors ajar, two chairs and a small table, all looking as if they dated from the fifties. In the centre of the table there was an arrangement of dusty artificial flowers and a half-burned candle in a gilt candlestick.

I went back to the door. It wouldn't have taken much to prise the hasp from the wood, and for a moment I was tempted. Wasn't that why I'd come: to walk in places Lýdia had known; to pass through the doors and go up the stairs to see what sort of view she might have looked out at?

I tugged at the padlock; rattled it hard and then harder. And then I stopped and let it drop because I recognised this for what it was. I stepped back. Drew a breath. Forty years on, it was too late to hope to walk in anyone's footsteps.

Back at the main track I took a look at the second house, but only in passing. I felt the need to strike out and I followed the path towards the headland beyond the houses and sheds, past an overgrown potato patch and several small stone-built enclosures. On the hillside down to the sea most of the fields had been cut and the grass was baled up in green plastic bags, scattered or stacked in threes and fours, awaiting collection.

The ruts of the track finally gave out at a stone wall, but I hadn't gone far enough so I climbed over at a low place, then followed the faint outline of a path through the wet sod. After a while, even that path faded, but it didn't matter. I stuck to the contour of the land and followed the curve of the hill around to the west until Múli disappeared behind me and all there was was the hillside and the exposed ribs of rock strata beneath the conical summit of the mountain.

Eventually I slowed as I came to a sheepfold. Far enough. I sat down on the stones to look at the view and simply to stop. The breeze was stronger out here and across the strait the sun shone on Viðareiði's tiny white buildings. I wished I had a cigarette to smoke, just to mark the moment, but I hadn't.

So, had I got what I wanted?

I'd come here because it was a place she had been. But the question wasn't really about the place; it was *why* had she come? It was too far from Suðuroy to make the journey without reason; too far to simply drop in for a visit. Two hours by ferry, just to reach Tórshavn, and I guessed that forty years ago – before tunnels and good linking roads – it would have taken all day to get here. So she must have stayed, at least for a few days, when she came here.

Had she brought me with her, then – had I been here, too? I guessed so. If not, I was sure Sofia Ravnsfjall would have cited it as another damning indictment of Lýdia's behaviour: young mother abandoning her baby as well as her husband to go to the ends of the islands.

And still: *why?* What was the attraction – compulsion – to come to a hippy commune almost as far north as you could go?

They wanted to live differently, that was what Eileen Skoradal had told me. Was that what had drawn Lýdia here then? A girl who looked at pictures of the outside world with her best friend: was this as close as she could get to that outside, to living differently?

I came back to the word *compulsion*. Wasn't that really what I was trying to understand? Even though I knew it couldn't be done – not if what I believed about Lýdia now was correct.

And believed about myself?

The light was shifting, less brilliant now: grey cloud from the west. Shadows on the land. I was starting to feel the chill. I stood up to head back.

I heard the sound of an engine as I got closer to Múli: something rougher than a car and too constant for that. When I climbed the wall at the end of the track I saw a man dressed in overalls and a peaked denim cap guiding a self-propelled mower towards a patch of uncut grass. At the front the machine had a three-foot blade of triangular cutting teeth.

When he saw me approaching the man throttled back the engine until it was just ticking over.

"*Morgun*," I said, coming to a halt.

"*Morgun*." He looked me over. "Alliance?"

It seemed like an odd question out here but I shook my head. "*Nei. Eg eiti Jan Reyná. Duga tygum enskt?*"

"*Nei*. Small." Then he pointed to himself. "Eyðun Thomsen."

We exchanged nods and greetings all over again, then I turned to point at the houses and took in the fields with a gesture, then pointed at him. "Is this yours? Your land. *Hús*. You?"

"*Nei, nei. Hoyggja.*" He gestured at the mower and hay so I'd understand, which I more or less did.

"Who owns it? Er… *Hvat navn?*" I made another gesture at the houses and fields.

"*Oh, ja. Múli*," he said.

The name of the place, not the owner. Then I had a bright idea. "*Duga tygum dansk?*"

"*Dansk? Ja.*"

"Okay. Hang on."

I fished out my phone, swiped the screen and searched for the translation app. It didn't have Faroese, but it did have Danish. Thomsen cocked his head and peered at the screen as I pecked out the question, "Who owns this land?" then tapped the translate button which turned it into *Hvem ejer denne jord.* I held the screen so he could read it.

"Oh, okay." He nodded. "Justesen – Boas Justesen."

He looked to see if I got it. I showed that I did, then typed out "Do you know where he lives? I would like to talk to him."

He read the translation then looked at me again with just a hint of suspicion. "You... er – buy? This?"

"*Nei, nei.*" I shook my head and tried to show that it was the last thing on my mind. "I just want to talk to him. *Tale.*"

Whether he fully understood that I couldn't tell. I started for the translator again, but he stopped me. "*Fuglafjørður,*" he said. "*Ennivegur fimm.*"

"Ennivegur?"

"*Ja, nummar fimm.*" He held up a spread hand to show the number five.

"Okay, *takk,*" I said. "*Stora takk fyri. Hav ein góðan dag, ja?*"

"*Ja. Sjálv takk.*"

I started away. After a couple of steps he called after me, "Hey. No problem!"

I waved back. "No problem."

28

"THIS TIME I'M TAKING THEM MYSELF," SOPHIE KROGH SAID, holding up the aluminium flight case in her hand. She had her coat on and a rucksack over her shoulder, ready to go.

"Will there be enough to give us answers if the other evidence can't be found?" Hentze asked.

"*Some* answers, yeh, but without her clothes for analysis..."

Hentze got the point. "You'll tell them it's urgent?"

"Yeh, of course."

"Okay. Thanks. Safe home, then."

"*Takk*." She made to move on, then turned back. "Listen, Hjalti, take it easy, okay?"

"Sure. Of course."

"Okay then."

When Sophie had gone Hentze leaned back in his chair and wondered if it was so obvious that he had *not* been taking it easy over all this.

Little surprise, perhaps. He should have insisted that Remi remove him from the investigation altogether and it bothered him that Remi had not, even when he'd suggested it yesterday. In fact, when it came down to it, Remi's recent behaviour bothered Hentze in more ways than one – not least because he was letting Ári Niclasen run around like a headless chicken.

Perhaps, as he'd considered before, Remi felt that a show of faith was in order, to bolster Ári's position after the Tummas Gramm case. If so, then giving Ári a degree of latitude in how he led the investigation might be expected – at least in public. But in private it would certainly be possible for Remi to direct or divert Ári away from pursuing contradictory lines of enquiry, or those based only on wild speculation.

But Remi had not, and that bothered Hentze. It was almost as if Remi was deliberately letting Ári set himself up for a fall. Was that it then? Was Remi giving Ári enough rope to hang himself?

No, Hentze doubted that. Remi was more direct. If he wanted Ári gone he would just do it, or simply step in.

What then? On such a serious case – not to say sensitive, given the involvement of AWCA – how did it make sense to let Ári run wild?

Hentze sat up. Damn it all. He'd been dragged into thinking exactly the way he despised most: letting office politics become the subject of his attention. What he did was police work. He wasn't interested in vying for position or pushing for credit. Leave that to others; he just got on with the job, which was exactly what he should do now.

"So where are we up to?" Hentze asked when he found Oddur, not in the incident room, but alone in a room two doors along. "Have we anything new to be looked at? Anything at all."

Oddur Arge seemed a little thrown by Hentze's rather resolute tone. "Anything?" he asked.

"Yes, whatever you have."

"Well, we've found nothing more on her email or social media accounts: nothing that's interesting to us, anyway. Same for her photos and video."

"But?"

Oddur still seemed uncertain, but then took the plunge. "You remember the SIM card Technical found in her car? Well, it got me thinking. Like, why did she have it, why was it hidden? So I went through the data and—"

"Hold on," Hentze cut in. "Wasn't the SIM card with the samples that went – *should* have gone – to Copenhagen?"

Oddur shook his head. "No, it came up negative for prints so there was no point sending it."

"Okay, go on then." Hentze pulled a chair round and sat down.

"Well, it turned out to be a pay-as-you-go card with two hundred krónur credit," Oddur said. "But when I looked at the call history the curious thing was that it had only been used to send text messages. There are no voice calls at all and no messages received. And then it gets stranger. Look." He turned and opened a document on the laptop and a list appeared: three columns of text. "On the left is the date," Oddur said, pointing. "In the centre is the phone number the text was sent to, and on the right is the message. As you can see, the recipient number is always the same. I checked: it's another pay-as-you-go cellphone."

Hentze squinted at the screen, then got out his reading

glasses. The right-hand column was a series of letters and numbers: P 1500; S 1130; Q 1845; S 2100; Q 2200.

"*Are* those messages?" he asked.

"Yeh, that's what was sent," Oddur said.

"What do they mean, do you know?"

Again Oddur seemed slightly hesitant. "I think they could be rendezvous codes." He glanced at Hentze. "The letter stands for a location, the numbers are the time. For example, if P was the football ground in Klaksvík, then sending 'P 1500' would mean 'Meet me at 3 p.m. at the football ground.'"

"That's all a bit James Bond isn't it?" Hentze said.

Oddur looked slightly defensive. "Well, yeh, maybe, I suppose," he said. "Listen, I'm a nerd, right? I know what everyone thinks, but the SIM card *was* hidden in the car and I don't see what else the text messages can be if they're not rendezvous codes."

One thing about Oddur was that he stuck to his guns, even when doing so only confirmed most people's scepticism. It was something Hentze respected, even if most of the time he had no interest in whichever conspiracy theory Oddur was embracing.

Hentze looked at the screen again. "Is there a pattern to the dates when the messages were sent?"

"No, but that *could* be because they were only used to rearrange missed meetings," Oddur said, then leaned in, warming to his subject. "What you'd normally do is arrange your next meeting while you're together. So you agree the time and the place in advance. *But* if you can't make that meeting for some reason, then you send a coded message to rearrange a new one. Or, if you've got something you need to pass on right away, you could also send a message to call a crash meeting."

"A *crash* meeting?"

Oddur shrugged. "I read a lot of espionage novels."

"Okay, so you know what you're talking about," Hentze said, with no trace of irony. "But say that you're right, why would Erla Sivertsen need to arrange secret meetings?"

"She wouldn't, not unless she was doing some sort of undercover work."

"Against who? The Alliance?"

"Why not?" Oddur said, as if he'd already got this far in his thinking. "We all know there are contingency plans for Alliance protests, so wouldn't it also be useful if we had someone on the inside who could give advance warning of what they were planning to do?"

Hentze thought about that. "She couldn't, though, could she?" he said in the end. "The Alliance can't know in advance when a *grind* will take place any more than anyone else, and last Friday at Sandur everyone was caught on the hop."

"Yeh, I hadn't thought about that," Oddur admitted. He looked at the messages on the screen. "But even so, what else could this be?"

"I don't know," Hentze said. "I tell you what, though: why don't you compare the dates and times in the text messages with that geotagging thing on her photos. Would that be possible? It might tell us more – perhaps where she went."

Oddur brightened. "Yeh, sure, of course, it wouldn't be hard."

"Okay then," Hentze said. "See what you find." He stood up. "Have you told Ári or Remi about this?"

"Hardly."

"No. Right. Okay."

29

BY THE TIME I GOT TO FUGLAFJØRÐUR I BADLY NEEDED COFFEE
and food. Beyond Tórshavn cafés are a rare thing in the
Faroes, but I found one with a view of the harbour and ate and
drank and listened to the chat going on around me. It didn't
matter that I didn't understand more than the odd word. It
felt companionable, and when I left I felt better. Sometimes
you just get moments like that, in passing.

Afterwards I walked back to the car and drove on around
the bay, past the long dockside where large pressed-steel
buildings edged close to the quay and three decent-sized
ships were tied up.

The harbour industry buildings went as far as the end
of the road and on my left the houses became more thinly
spread out. There was no other traffic, so it was easy to
track the house numbers and finally spot number five, with
a couple of cars parked outside on some gravel, neither of
them anywhere near new.

I drove past and made a U-turn, then parked and walked.
The house wasn't large: two bedrooms, maybe; a stone
undercroft and white boarded walls above it, most showing

their age. There were steps up to a side door and that looked like the best bet, so I climbed them and knocked on a uPVC door that seemed slightly out of keeping with the rest of the place.

A minute or so later a young woman – maybe twenty – opened the door. She was heavily pregnant, wearing a floral print smock.

"*Hey*," I said. "*Duga tygum enskt?* Do you speak English?"

"Yeh, of course. How can I help you?"

"I'm looking for Boas Justesen. I was told he lives here."

"Yeh, he does. But downstairs – in the cellar."

For a second that caught me off guard, until I worked out that she must mean the undercroft.

Behind her a guy about the same age came to see what was happening. They both had that bright-eyed, clean-cut Scandinavian aura, as if anything was possible. Or maybe it was just youth.

"You want Boas?" he asked. "He's there. I saw him come in half an hour ago. Just knock on the door. But knock hard, yeh? Sometimes he doesn't hear it so well." He performed a drinking mime. "But now he should be okay. He was walking straight when I saw him."

"Okay, thanks, I'll do that."

"You're English, right?" he asked. "I lived there for six months. I love England. It's a great place."

"It can be," I said. "Sorry to disturb you."

Back down the steps I went round to the door of the undercroft and knocked on the frosted glass panel. This door was wooden and the broken paint showed it had been at least four different colours in its lifetime.

Nothing.

I tried again: a copper's knock. "Harra Justesen?"

This time there was an annoyed call – a couple of words – from inside. I knew it wasn't an invitation – more like the reverse – but you can always trade on ignorance. I tried the door and it opened so I took a step into the gloom inside.

"Harra Justesen?"

Off to my right there was what sounded like a repeat of the words I'd heard from outside, just as truculent. The only light was from a couple of net-covered windows but it was enough to get an impression of the place: cramped and cluttered, seemingly a self-contained, one-room bedsit. The plasterboard on the walls was only partly skimmed and in various places electrical wiring protruded from holes. It had the look and feel of something intended to be temporary but which had become permanent.

I located the man through a grey haze of cigarette smoke, half reclined in an armchair. He was in his mid-sixties, perhaps older: sallow-faced, with white stubble and deep crevasses. He was dressed for the outside, in a woollen coat that looked two sizes too big for him; as if he'd come in and sat down without bothering to do anything else. By his feet there was a carrier bag. I couldn't tell how drunk he was, but enough.

"*Hey*," I said, deliberately making it sound upbeat, as if I'd failed to register his tone. "*Eg eiti Jan Reyná.* Do you speak English?"

"*Nei. Fara burtur! Eg eri sjúkur.*" A rejection in any language, leaving no room for doubt.

"I'm a policeman, from England," I told him. "*Ein politistur, ja?*"

I hoped it might get through and add a touch of authority, even if it was spurious. What it got me was a sulky, bad-tempered repeat as he waved at the door. "*Eg skilji ikki. Eg eri sjúkur.*" Then a definite gesture. "*Fara burtur!*"

"I'll come back in a minute," I said and went to the door.

I could have left it at that, but I didn't want to; not because of the language barrier. I doubted that Boas Justesen would cooperate if I tried Danish as I'd done out at Múli, though, so I went back to the steps at the side of the house and up to the door where I knocked again. The young man answered it this time.

"Hey. Everything okay?" he asked.

I shook my head. "Language problems," I said. "Could you do me a favour and translate for me? I could pay you for your time."

"Shit, you don't need to do that. Sure, I'll come. Hold on."

He went back inside to put on a pair of trainers, then came out on to the steps, closing the door behind him.

"I'm Aron," he said. "My wife is Kirstin."

"Jan," I said. "Thanks for doing this."

"It's no problem. We're just waiting – for the baby to come. Any time now."

"Boy or a girl, do you know?" I asked for politeness.

"A boy," he said with some pride.

"Any names yet?"

"*Ja.* He'll be Jógvan Hallur, after my father."

This took us as far as the undercroft. I opened the door

and went in with just a cursory tap. It made Boas Justesen jerk round from his kitchen counter where he was now trying to find a relatively clean glass amongst half a dozen that weren't. Aron followed me in and when Justesen saw him there was some back and forth between them, in the middle of which I heard the word *politistur*.

In the end Aron turned to me and said, "He says you're a cop. He doesn't talk to the cops."

"It's not official," I said, not sure whether Aron might have the same reservations as Justesen. "It's a personal matter. I was told he owns the houses and land at a place called Múli. Can you ask him if that's true and how long he's had it?"

The explanation took a while, but in the end Justesen gave a grudging answer before going to the sink to rinse a glass. He leaned on the counter.

"He says it's his family's place," Aron told me. "They've always had it."

I nodded. "There was a commune there in the 1970s. They called it the Colony and I'd like to talk to anyone who was there. Can you ask him if he remembers any names?"

"A commune – like with hippies?"

"Yeah."

"Okay."

He got Justesen's attention again and explained. The answer was a lot shorter than the question: an irritable shake of the head and a "*Nei.*"

"What about someone called Matzen – Rasmus Matzen? I think he was Danish."

While Aron translated I watched Justesen again. I'd already seen a brief reaction when he heard me say the name. Now he wasn't quite as quick to say no. Instead it was something like a "maybe".

"He says he doesn't remember. Maybe there was someone called Matzen but it's too long ago."

"Is there anyone else I could ask?"

But even as I was saying it Justesen cut in. "He says he's ill – sick," Aron said. "He doesn't know anything. He wants to be left alone."

I knew there was no point and no way to pursue it, especially not when hampered by the language. "Okay, will you say thanks and if he remembers anything I'd appreciate it if he called me?"

While Aron translated that I dug out a card with my mobile number on it and held it up for Boas Justesen to see, then placed it on the counter in a relatively clean spot. He didn't bother to acknowledge it.

Outside in the fresh air I thanked Aron for his time and apologised again for interrupting his day.

"It was no problem," he said. "It's good to practise my English again. I hope you get the information you need. Boas isn't very – er – *fond* of the cops at this time. They put him under arrest a few days ago."

"Oh? For what, do you know?"

"For drunk driving. I know because he asks me to bring his car back afterwards."

"That might explain it, then," I said. "But thanks again for your help."

"Any time."
"And good luck with the baby."
"*Takk*. It'll be fantastic, I know."

30

HØGNI JOENSEN WASN'T UNDER ARREST, ALTHOUGH DÁNJAL Michelsen doubted that he had recognised the distinction. When Dánjal and Ári had found him on Sandoy and "requested" that he go with them it probably hadn't even occurred to Høgni that he had the right to say no.

Dánjal knew that Ári had chosen him as second officer because he'd wanted to take someone who looked like he meant business. Ári's tall, gangly frame wasn't the sort to cut an imposing figure in the macho world of fishing and boats, whereas Dánjal looked as if he'd square off for a fight at the drop of a hat. It was a misconception, but useful if – like Ári – you wanted to bring in a man who was built like a bulldozer.

That bulldozer of a man was crying now. That's what Ári had brought him to in the last hour. Ári might not be imposing on a quayside, but in an interview room he could be brutal and Dánjal felt genuinely sorry for Høgni Joensen. The man just wasn't bright or fast enough to match or counter the scenarios Ári was putting to him, one after the other: drumming away and inserting a knife blade in any small crack he found.

Hadn't Høgni lied in an attempt to give Finn Sólsker an alibi?

Well, yes – no – not really, he just thought—

So *why* had he lied? Was he trying to help Finn to cover up the murder, or had Høgni participated in that as well?

No! N-n-no of course not. He liked Erla.

Really? Liked her how – in what way? Was he attracted to her? She was a good-looking woman. How could he not have been attracted to that?

B-b-*because*!

Because what? Because she rejected him – was that it? She rejected him and he killed her, wasn't that more like the truth?

The more Ári pressed, the more Høgni stammered and now he could hardly even get a single word out, even to deny what Ári was saying. He just shook his head and tried to sniff back the tears.

Then Ári gave it a moment, as if reassessing or reaching the end of his tether.

"All right then," he said. "I tell you what: if you *were* in Tórshavn on Saturday night as you say, just give us the name of someone you saw. Anyone. Then we can check. Who were you with? You *must* remember that."

"I-I…" Høgni began, then shook his head.

"Anyone," Ári repeated. "Or are you making it up?"

"No!" Then Høgni let out one sobbing breath. "I-I was with Sal."

"Sal? Who's that then?"

"S-Sal M-Moretti. He, he's a friend."

"Okay, at last we're getting somewhere," Ári said. "Where can we find him?"

"A-at, at the pizza takeaway; on, on N-Niels Finsens gøta."

Høgni hung his head, as if he'd just condemned himself out of his own mouth. It was enough, Dánjal decided. Too much.

"Maybe we should take a break," Dánjal said without looking at Ári. "Would you like a drink, Høgni? Coffee or tea, or something cold?"

Høgni sniffed, nodded, but didn't look up. "C-cold, please," he said.

"Okay, just wait there for us, eh? I'll sort something out."

They left Høgni wiping his face and went out into the corridor. As he closed the door behind them Dánjal knew Ári was pissed off. Ári didn't say so, but his manner was peremptory, as if he suspected there was some implicit criticism behind Dánjal's unilateral move.

"You'd better check out this Sal Moretti then," Ári told him. "It shouldn't take long if he's at work. If he can't or won't verify Joensen's alibi I want to get back to interviewing as soon as possible, okay?"

"I'll go now," Dánjal said, although in his head he reckoned he could make sure it took the best part of an hour. Enough time to let Høgni Joensen recover.

The pizza and sandwich shop on Niels Finsens gøta was at the bottom of three concrete steps, hidden away from the other shop fronts, as if it didn't fit in with the image the street wished to give of itself. This was the slow period of the day –

after the lunch trade – and there were no customers waiting when Dánjal went in and asked if Salvatore Moretti was there.

A minute or so later Sal Moretti came out of the kitchen. He looked to be in his late twenties, with a thick quiff of black hair and a high-cheekboned face. He was slightly built, snake-hipped, and wore a chef's smock over a pair of baggy jeans.

Yes, sure, he knew Høgni, he told Dánjal as he came around the counter and into the shop. "Why, what's the matter?" His Faroese was rough and he dropped into Danish when necessary, though it was scarcely any better. Even so, his concern about Høgni came through.

"Can you tell me if you saw Høgni over the weekend?" Dánjal asked.

"Sure. Yes, I did," Salvatore said without hesitation.

"From when until when?"

Salvatore frowned as he deciphered the question. "The last time I see him is Sunday – the morning. About ten o'clock."

"Okay. What time did he arrive?"

Salvatore frowned. "No, he didn't. Not Sunday. He came Saturday evening."

"You mean he was with you from Saturday night until Sunday morning?"

"Yeh, yeh, that's right."

"Okay. What time did you meet him on Saturday?"

"I don't know," Salvatore shrugged. "Maybe seven o'clock. He comes here, we go for… to eat, yeh? A few drinks. Later to my place."

"So you were with him all the time?"

"Sure. Of course. I'm saying that. Listen, what's

happened? Is Høgni okay? Please. Is there trouble?"

"No, no, he's fine," Dánjal told him. "We just had to ask him some questions."

"What about?" And then he realised. "About the woman who was dead?"

"It's related to that," Dánjal allowed. "Do you know any reason why Høgni wouldn't want to tell us what he was doing on Saturday night?"

Salvatore frowned for a moment and glanced at the back of the shop, then he turned a little so that the conversation was more private.

"He was with me," he said. "*Together*, yeh? You know what I mean? Høgni and me."

"You're gay?" Dánjal asked, hearing the surprise in his own voice.

"Sure, of course," Salvatore said, as if it should be as obvious as a tattoo on his forehead. "But Høgni doesn't feel good to tell anyone. I say, 'For Christ sake, Høgni. It's the twenty-first century.' But it doesn't matter. He is afraid of what people say, you know? Other men to work with. He thinks they give a hard time."

Dánjal nodded. It was easy enough to imagine the attitude amongst the fishermen. Gay pride in the islands had been around and accepted by most for several years, but the old conservative values still held sway behind some closed doors.

"So Høgni was with you all the time?" Dánjal asked, to be clear. "From Saturday evening until Sunday morning."

"Yeh. All the time."

"Is there anyone else who could back that up?"

"Sure. Plenty when we were out."

"Okay," Dánjal said. "That's all I needed to know. Thank you."

"So he's okay now?" Sal asked, still concerned. "No trouble?"

"Not now, no," Dánjal said.

"I can call him?"

"I'd leave it for half an hour, but yeh, after that. Thanks for your help."

Dánjal left the shop and climbed the steps back to street level as he took out his phone and called Ári Niclasen. "It's Dánjal," he said when Ári answered. "Høgni's alibi stands up. He was out on the town from seven on Saturday night. Sounds like he had quite a bit to drink and slept on Sal Moretti's couch. Anyway, he can't have been on Sandoy."

"Are there other witnesses to that?"

"Quite a few, yeh. I can try and track them down if you like, but I think it'll be a waste of time. His mate's solid."

"So why was he so reluctant to tell us if he was simply out on the town?"

"Well, you know what the Plymouth Brethren are like about drinking," Dánjal said. "He probably didn't want word getting back."

He had no idea whether Høgni *was* Plymouth Brethren, but it seemed to satisfy Ári.

"All right then, you'd better come back," Ári said. "There's a *grind* out at Norðragøta and things are getting hectic, but I'll tell Joensen he's free to go."

And an apology would be nice too, Dánjal thought, but he didn't say it.

31

THE ALLIANCE HOUSE ON MARKNAGILSVEGUR WAS ALIVE WITH activity. As Hentze arrived three people hurried out through the front door and jumped into a pickup truck, which then sped away.

"I'm sorry, we're a little busy right now," Petra Langley said as she led Hentze inside. "Some whales have been seen, but you probably know about that, right?"

As a matter of fact Hentze didn't know. The news must have come in while he was on his way there. If he *had* known he might not have come, although he knew that if he didn't follow up on Oddur's theory now he would probably have talked himself out of it by the time things calmed down. After all, it *was* Oddur.

"If it's a bad time to talk now I can come back later," Hentze offered. In the AWCA office people were on phones or speaking into radios, and at the back of the room a group of four men and women were gathered at a map of the islands, tracing routes, pointing out features, as if preparing for battle. Which was, Hentze supposed, exactly how they saw it.

"No, it's fine," Petra said. She gestured to a man in a

sweater holding two phones, one lowered, the other to his ear. "Charlie's our action coordinator. At times like this I take a back seat. Shall we go somewhere quieter?"

She led Hentze to a room at the back of the house: a sort of communal area with two large sofas and a view of the sea through its large window. There was no one else there and once they were inside Petra closed the door and invited Hentze to a seat.

"So, how can I help?" she asked, sitting opposite him. "On the phone you said it was about Erla? Have you found out any more yet?"

"We're making some progress," Hentze said. "But you'll understand it takes time."

"Of course. I don't suppose it's ever as easy as you see on the TV."

"Not so much, no."

He assessed her for a moment. She seemed like a level-headed person; or at least, not one to be thrown into a fluster by the activity of the moment. And she was clearly waiting for him to get to the point.

"I'd like to find out some more information about Erla's background," Hentze told her. "For example, I wondered why you – the AWCA organisation – chose her for the job."

Petra Langley considered the question. "We hired her because she was a good photographer and because she fit in well with everyone else."

"Had she been involved with other campaigns like yours before she joined AWCA?"

"No, not as a campaigner, but she had done a lot of

wildlife and documentary work."

"Oh? I thought you would look for someone with experience of protests."

"We're not short of activists," Petra said. "What we needed was someone who could take great pictures. That was the brief. Of course, she had to support the issues we campaign on, but that wasn't the reason she got the job."

"Okay, I see," Hentze said. "And when you hired her did you already have plans to come here?"

"To protest the *grind*? No. That only came later."

"And how did she feel about that?"

"You mean because she was Faroese?"

"Yes. Did she think it might be difficult for her?"

"No." Petra was definite. "Just the opposite. I remember we talked about it – while the campaign was still under discussion – and she said it could be an advantage because she knew the language."

"So she was enthusiastic to come?"

"Sure. Like the rest of us, she thought the *grind* was unnecessary in this day and age. I don't see what this has to do with her being killed, though. How is it relevant?"

Before Hentze could answer, the door behind them opened and someone looked in, then withdrew again quickly. The interruption reminded Hentze that he still hadn't got to the point – if he had one.

"It's just for background information," he said. "I'm sorry to take up your time, but there is just one thing more I would ask."

"Sure, go ahead."

"In your time here, or maybe before, do you ever find surveillance of what you are doing? Does anyone think that they are being watched, for example?"

Petra gave a dry laugh. "Surveillance? I'd have thought you'd know about that better than us. Don't the police have a stake in all that?"

"Perhaps in other countries," Hentze allowed, already regretting going this far. "But if it happens here I don't know. That's why I ask."

"Well, no one's told me that they think they're under surveillance," Petra said. "Besides, we've got nothing to hide. The whole point of our being here is to raise awareness. That's why we have a website and why Erla's pictures were important: we *want* people to know what we're doing and why."

"Yes, I suppose so," Hentze said. He stood up. "Well, thank you for your time. It's been very helpful."

He walked back to his car, chiding himself. It had been an unprofessional interview; badly thought out. Of *course* there was no reason why the AWCA people would be under surveillance. What would it achieve?

He cast a look back at the house and wished Oddur hadn't started him thinking about codes and secret agendas. Not because he thought Oddur was wrong – quite the opposite. But if coded messages and rendezvous times really had nothing to do with AWCA's activities, then they could only indicate that something else must have been going on in Erla Sivertsen's life.

And in her death?

Yes, well, that too, Hentze concluded as he turned the key in the ignition. What else was there to think?

* * *

The road out of Fuglafjørður passed through a valley between two mountain ridges before turning south at Gøtuvík bay. By the time I got to Norðragøta there was a light rain and I'd noticed an increase in the number of vehicles ahead of me, slowing down to form a tailback. Any kind of traffic hold-up was unusual in the Faroes, but here it was compounded by the fact that many of the cars ahead of me were pulling in by the side of the road and parking.

I stayed in the line of traffic, moving at little more than walking pace until I reached a spot where I caught a glimpse of the bay and then saw what all the activity was about. A mile or so from the shore a flotilla of fishing boats was progressing into the bay and ahead of it a pod of pilot whales was breaking the surface.

Before I could see much more than that my attention was called back to the road. Ahead of me a people carrier pulled in on a margin of flat ground beside the tarmac and, on the spur of the moment, I did the same.

Outside the car the wind was cold and blustery off the sea. People from other vehicles were pulling on coats and fleeces as they headed briskly back down the road towards Norðragøta. I didn't follow them. By this bend in the road there was a good enough view and below in the bay the drama had already started.

The line of fishing boats was still moving shoreward, but now I could see two rigid-hulled inflatables buzzing across the water, kicking up spray. Both flew the blue AWCA flag;

one boat chasing back and forth in front of the whales in an obvious attempt to frighten them off; the other being pursued by a patrol craft: larger, grey and flying a Danish Navy flag.

Then, overhead, there was the sound of a helicopter engine and as I glanced up a naval Lynx swooped in, nose down until it came over the water, then swung round and hovered above half a dozen kayaks, which were being paddled frantically out towards the approaching whales. I saw several of the kayakers look upwards, but they kept going, strung out in a line of Alliance blue, which made them easily visible against the dark water.

All this played out in an almost stage-managed way; as if it was part of a choreographed spectacle laid on for the entertainment of tourists, perhaps. But when a second naval pursuit craft appeared around the headland things seemed to take a more serious turn. The first naval craft broke off its chase of the outermost AWCA boat and instead sped around the fishing boats to go after the Alliance boat closest to shore.

Then the helicopter turned on its axis and I thought I heard some kind of loudspeaker warning or command to the kayakers below. It was too broken up by the wind and the sound of engines to be sure, but whatever the case, the kayaks kept on going and for a few seconds there was no change, until the Lynx suddenly tilted and dropped half its altitude so that it was only about fifty feet above the sea. Then it moved, in that oddly articulated manner of helicopters, to position itself a little to one side of the lead kayak so the downdraught of the rotor blades buffeted the occupant, before tipping him sideways into the water.

I wasn't the only one watching from the crash barrier, and about twenty yards away a knot of people let out a cheer when they saw the kayak capsize. It wasn't over yet, though, because the Lynx moved down the line of kayaks, tipping them each in turn until all but one of their occupants was out of their boat and clinging to it.

Job done, the helicopter gained height again and swung round, as if to reassess the situation below. And by now the naval pursuit boats were also winning. One Alliance boat had been pinned against a rocky shore and the other was being chased out into open water as a grey frigate appeared from the north.

And even after all this the whales and the fishing boats behind them were still heading for shore, not much more than three hundred yards distant by now. Because of the slope of the land I couldn't see who or what was waiting for them on the beach, but after Sandoy I had a pretty good idea and I didn't feel compelled to see it again. Instead I put up my collar and walked back to the car.

32

AS HENTZE PULLED INTO THE YARD AT THE BACK OF THE station two of the blue vans sent over from Denmark were heading out in a hurry. There were three of these vans altogether, provided for the transport of prisoners if – as had been predicted – the Alliance protests resulted in mass arrests. So far the vans hadn't been needed, but with this second *grindadráp* less than a week after the first, someone had obviously decided to make a show of strength.

A second whale drive was bad luck, to Hentze's way of thinking. If nothing else it served as a distraction from other police work, and it was hardly going to make Alliance witnesses feel more willing to come forward to talk about Erla Sivertsen's death.

Inside the station there was more activity than normal and Hentze climbed the stairs with Hans Lassen, who was hurrying between the ground floor and fourth.

"We've got five or six Alliance people under arrest at the moment," Lassen told him, taking the steps two at a time. "There'll be more, though. The navy are still fishing them out of the sea."

"The navy?"

"Yeh. The Alliance used boats this time: a couple of inflatables and others in kayaks. Those are the ones who ended up tipped in the water."

"Was anyone hurt?"

"None of ours," Lassen said, as if that was all that mattered. "And we're seizing the kayaks and boats as evidence. At least that'll stop them being used again for a bit."

Lassen went on up the stairs as Hentze headed into CID and the incident room. Only Dánjal Michelsen was there: as a SWAT-trained officer, Sonja had been called out as soon as the *grind* was announced, and there was no sign of Ári either. He was definitely not SWAT-trained.

"How did it go with Høgni Joensen?" Hentze asked when Dánjal looked up from his computer. "Did you bring him in?"

"Yeh," Dánjal said. "He had an alibi for Saturday night, though, so we let him go."

"Right." Hentze wasn't particularly surprised. "So where's Ári now?"

"Gone to a Response Team meeting for the *grind*. Listen, have you got a minute?"

"Sure. What's up?"

Dánjal glanced round, then stood up and gestured towards the corridor. "Okay if we go to your office?"

"All right, if you like."

Once inside Hentze's office Dánjal closed the door as Hentze sat down at the desk.

"So what's up?" Hentze said again. It wasn't like Dánjal to be so covert.

"I think you should know, I pulled a fast one on Ári," Dánjal said.

"What sort of fast one?"

Dánjal gave Hentze a brief *précis* of Høgni Joensen's alibi for Saturday night and the reason why he hadn't wanted to admit where he was.

"I wouldn't have guessed," Hentze said with a thoughtful nod. "Still, at least the alibi takes him out of the equation."

Dánjal nodded. "I just thought you should know – I mean, that I didn't tell Ári the full story. I didn't think he needed to know that Høgni's gay, but just in case it comes back later for some reason I thought you should be in the picture."

"I can't see why it would come back," Hentze said. "But okay – is that it?"

Dánjal shook his head. "Actually, no." He paused, then straightened up. "I think Ári went too far when he was questioning Høgni. I mean, he had him *crying*, for God's sake. And I think he enjoyed it. It was like a power trip, to see how brutal he could be. Christ knows what he'd have said if he'd known about Høgni's sexual orientation. The guy would probably have ended up weeping under the table."

He broke off for a moment, as if he realised he might have gone too far, and then his tone became slightly more conciliatory. "Listen, I know Ári wants— I know we need to move the case forward, and okay, Høgni didn't help himself by lying. But there are ways and there are ways of doing these things, right? You can't just tear someone apart simply because you think they *might* have done something – at least, not unless you've got more than your own half-baked suspicion to go on."

Hentze considered that thoughtfully for a moment, then said, "No, of course not. But I'm sure Ári handled it the way he thought was right."

"Hjalti, come *on*," Dánjal said, reanimated by the political answer. "You know what I'm talking about. You out of everyone. Ári was trying to *bully* Høgni into confessing. That's the long and short of it and I don't think it's right. In fact I think someone needs to speak up about it – to Remi, at least."

This was more than Hentze had expected and now he leaned forward, shaking his head. "Listen," he said evenly. "I understand what you're saying, okay? And yes, if Ári acted the way you say, he went too far. But if you go to Remi about it – if you make it official – you're going to set a boulder rolling down the hill and there'll be no stopping it."

"Yeh, well, maybe that's what's needed."

"You think Ári would be squashed?" Hentze shook his head. "He's too quick on his feet. Was there a recording of the interview?"

"Yeh, on Ári's phone."

"Were there any other people present – a lawyer?"

"No."

"Has Høgni made a complaint?"

"No, but—"

"So, where does that leave you? What do you think Ári will say when – *if* – Remi calls him to explain? He'll say he conducted the interview with vigour, but nothing more. And because it went nowhere he deleted the recording. He will also say that you were being oversensitive, that you misinterpreted his line of questioning, *and* – when he finds out – that you deliberately failed to report the full facts of Høgni's alibi."

Dánjal shook his head, but Hentze could see that he knew all these things to be true. You only had to know Ári to know that. "It's bullshit," Dánjal said, deflated.

"Yeh, I agree," Hentze said. "But that's how it is." Then, relenting a little, he said, "Listen, leave it to older heads, okay? You're still too far away from your pension. Let's just get through this case and after that, when we see how it's gone... Well, like I said, there are older heads who can consider everything as a whole. You understand?"

Dánjal was still clearly reluctant, but in the end he nodded. "Okay, if you say so," he said.

"I do."

When Dánjal had gone Hentze turned his chair to the small window. Nothing but sky to be seen, which was fine.

Damn it.

He'd been able to keep his own reservations about Ári in check – more or less – but if the others like Dánjal were starting to see cracks, too... It didn't bode well. Ári Niclasen wasn't stupid and he could be subtly vindictive if he got a sniff of dissent or personal criticism from those on his team. Fortunately things rarely got that far, but in the past it hadn't been unknown for certain CID officers to gradually lose their positive assessments and find themselves taking uniform shirts out of the wardrobe again.

And still... And still... There was something else. Not just Ári's desperation to find a viable suspect – that could be taken as normal – but the fact that Remi had not reined him in, not even a little. It was almost as if Ári's activities were being allowed to serve as a distraction, a smoke screen, hiding... What?

There was a knock on the door. Oddur Arge was looking pleased with himself and Hentze's heart sank. Now what?

"I think I've identified one of the meeting places," Oddur said before he was fully inside. "It's 'Q' in the codes. Both times it was used Erla took photographs at Hoyvík near the time of the rendezvous."

"Do the pictures show anyone we could identify or talk to?"

"No, just the museum buildings in the first group and some of the cove in the second. But it does prove we were right."

Hentze noted the "we" with some reluctance. "What about the other locations – the other code letters, if that's what they are."

Oddur shook his head. "No, there was nothing. If she took pictures at those meetings she didn't keep them."

"So we're not much better off," Hentze said.

"No, only a little," Oddur acknowledged. "But while I was thinking about all this I wondered if we'd overlooked something obvious, so I called a friend of mine in Copenhagen – Ulrik. He works in the intelligence branch so I asked if they – the Danes – had a file on Erla – you know, because she worked for the Alliance."

"And?" Hentze asked.

"No, nothing." Oddur shook his head, but didn't seem downhearted.

"Nothing at all?"

"Well, not that Ulrik could find. There *are* files on some

of the other AWCA staff members – above Ulrik's clearance, unfortunately – but that's the point, isn't it? You'd expect there to be *something* on Erla, too. So, the fact that there's nothing could very well mean that her file's been removed or restricted to protect a covert operation."

It was more than apparent that Oddur had completely bought into the idea that they'd uncovered some kind of conspiracy, but on top of everything else it was a step further than Hentze was willing to take. Yes, he still felt there was something amiss, but he also believed in grounded police work: building a case from the facts, not the other way round.

"So, what do you think we should do next?" Oddur asked, his expression expectant. "Should we take it to Ári or Remi?"

Hentze appeared to give that some serious consideration. "It's good work so far, and that could be the next step, but without anything more specific maybe we should give it more thought. Overnight. If we shout out too soon, well, it might be too easy to dismiss. You know what the others can be like, eh?"

Oddur did know. "Yeh, yeh, you're right," he told Hentze. "We need something else to make up the rule of three."

"Rule of three?"

"Yeh. You know: once is accident; twice is coincidence, but three times is enemy action. It's James Bond. *Goldfinger*."

"Oh, right, of course," Hentze said without any irony. "Well, let's see if we can find a third then, okay?"

"Okay, sure," Oddur said, showing no sign of dampened enthusiasm. "I'll get on it."

James Bond. God help him. Hentze shook his head as Oddur went out.

33

HENTZE DECLINED WHEN I OFFERED HIM A BEER. IT WAS GONE six o'clock – my own, fairly flexible sun-and-the-yardarm point in the day – but I wasn't surprised when he said no. Still, I thought I sensed a bit of regret when he accepted coffee instead, standing in the kitchen as I made it. He had something on his mind, but wasn't ready to share it just yet. In its place he said, "So, how has your day been? Did you go to see Múli?"

"Yeah, it was interesting," I said, spooning Nescafé. "Not as rundown as I'd thought. I also found the guy who owns the houses there: a man called Boas Justesen. He wasn't much help, though."

"So a dead end?"

"More or less. What about you? I saw the *grindadráp* at Norðragøta on my way back. It looked like the Alliance pulled out all the stops."

Hentze nodded. "They were able to get their boats there this time. It's unfortunate."

"Why?"

"Because when we have the navy and helicopters chasing

around it makes us look bad: like we use a big hammer on a small nut."

Which wasn't Hentze's style, I knew that.

"Were there many arrests?"

"Yeh, quite a few and some whales escaped, so now there are some people saying the Alliance should pay compensation."

"Do you think they will?"

"I don't think so, but their boats have been taken as evidence, so maybe it goes to the courts to decide. I don't know. *Takk*." He accepted his coffee, like punctuation putting an end to the subject.

"I want to ask your opinion about the Erla Sivertsen case," he said then. "Your thoughts. Do you mind?"

"Not if it's useful," I said. "Come through and sit down."

He followed me to the sitting room and we sat in the chairs by the French windows. Too grey and cold to go outside, but an interesting sky thick with cloud, which I watched while he told me the bones of the case.

It took him about ten minutes – sometimes going back over a detail when I queried it – but by and large he left out any chunks of extraneous detail, giving me the impression that he'd already been paring away at the whole thing for some time. What he wanted – as much as to tell me – was to clear his own line of sight, so he could see the wood for the trees.

By the end of it I knew there was only one real question to ask. "Do you think Finn killed her?" I said.

"No." He was definite on that. "An affair with her, yes, that's possible. I don't like to think so, but…" He shrugged helplessly. "But I don't think he killed her."

"Why not?"

"Because if he had I don't believe he would have left her body like that. That's what I don't think is right with all this."

"Because it was staged – the body was arranged to make it look as if something else had happened?"

"Yes." Then he shook his head in frustration. "But I don't see what it achieves, to do that. Anyone who is intelligent enough to think about what they are doing, they must also know that there will be tests made. We will find out how she died, we will know if there was a rape, *and* that the knife stabbing is done after she's dead. So what was the point of trying to deceive us?"

"Maybe you've got a psychopath on the loose," I said, deadpan.

"Are you serious?" A deepening frown crossed his forehead.

I'd been trying to lighten the mood, but it was misjudged. "No, I'm not serious," I said. "I don't think a psychopath's very likely. Statistically you'd be very unlucky if it was."

"Good then," he said with a touch of relief. "So, why would someone want to confuse us? No, that's a stupid question. Why *not* make things harder for us? He doesn't want to be discovered."

"So why leave her body there, then?" I said, batting it back. "That's the most obvious question. If he doesn't want to be discovered, why take all that time and trouble when he could have put her in the sea? If he'd done that there was a chance that she wouldn't be found, but not by leaving her the way he did."

"So it's done on purpose."

"Or in blind panic. But then…"

"The killer would not have arranged her body."

"No, I wouldn't think so."

I stood up, just for want of something to do, and also to think. "What about the people at the house where she was living?" I asked. "And other members of AWCA? You didn't get anything from them?"

"No. They all have alibis for Saturday night."

"That's convenient."

"Yeh." He nodded, but I could tell his thoughts had moved on. He shifted and took a piece of paper from his pocket, unfolded it and held it out.

"What do you think this means?" he asked.

It was a tabulated list: five letters each followed by four numbers. I shook my head. "Are they flight numbers? Times?"

"Times, yes. Each one is a text message sent by Erla Sivertsen to the same phone number. We think – Oddur thinks – they are times for meetings at arranged places."

I looked at the list again. "Any idea where the places are?"

"Only one. Oddur thinks 'Q' is Hoyvík."

"And the messages were on Erla's phone?"

"No, on a SIM card. It was hidden in her car, so I think it must have been hers." He seemed to debate for a second, not sure if he liked what he was thinking of saying. "Oddur has a theory that Erla was an undercover person to watch the Alliance."

"Working for who?"

"If you believe it, then not for us, I'm sure about that. Maybe the Danes. There are some Danish officers here and there is a saying – a what do you call it – a proverb? 'If one Dane comes into a room more Danes will probably follow.'"

"If I was playing devil's advocate I'd ask why anyone would *want* to put an informant in with the Alliance," I said. "I mean, they're not exactly secretive about what they're doing, are they?"

"No, that's true. I'm not saying I believe Oddur's theory."

"But you've tried to check it out?"

"Yeh. As far as I can tell there's no sign that Erla Sivertsen has ever worked with the police and she has no criminal record. Of course, Oddur says that if she was undercover, the people she worked for would make sure there was no way to find out, but anyway I don't see how it is possible. She joined AWCA more than a year ago, before they had any plans to come here to protest."

I could see why he didn't think it was a likely theory but I stayed with the devil's advocate role. "Even so, if she *was* undercover or some kind of informant it could give you a motive for her murder – if someone in the Alliance found out what she was doing."

"Someone kills her because of that?" He shook his head. "These people are vegetarians."

I shouldn't have laughed, but I did.

"Yeh, well, you know what I mean," he said, slightly embarrassed. "But okay, for the moment, let's say Oddur is correct and Erla Sivertsen is an informant for the Danes. Someone in the Alliance finds this out and she is killed. Okay. But if that is true it would mean that the person who knows most would be the person she works for – her controller. So why has he not made himself known to us? Even in private, why not say *this is what I know*?"

I shrugged. "I've only known a couple of people who worked undercover. They were pretty close-mouthed about it, even afterwards. Have you asked anyone higher up about it?"

"Yeh, I asked Remi Syderbø. He says he doesn't know of anything like that."

"So you're stuck between a conspiracy theory you can't prove and a suspect you don't think is guilty."

"Yeh, it looks like it." He sounded unhappy.

I sat down again. "What's your main worry?" I asked. "That Finn will be charged with something he didn't do, or that the real culprit gets away?"

"Both, of course," he said without hesitation. "But also that we won't find the truth because we are not looking in the right places. I don't say that Oddur is correct with his conspiracy theories, but I know – it's my feeling – that something *is* hidden, and if that is true we cannot wait a long time to find out. In a month, maybe, when the Alliance have left and the Danes also go, then how are we left?"

He was right, I knew that. If Erla's death *was* tied to some kind of undercover work then the chances of resolving it would disappear as soon as the Danes pulled out, maybe even before. If an undercover operation goes wrong you don't want to shout about it; instead you clean house, remove the evidence and depart as quietly as you can. It wouldn't be their problem if they left the Faroese police with an unsolved or unsolvable case. That's what Hentze was worried about; that and the possibility that, without any other suspect, Finn

Sólsker might be left to carry the can.

We sat there in silence for a minute or so. My beer bottle was empty and so was his coffee mug. I stood up.

"Another?"

"*Nei, takk.*"

I headed for the kitchen. "You know, there is one way to set the cat amongst the pigeons – to stir things up," I called into the other room as I flipped the cap off another beer.

"Yeh? What's that?"

"Send another text message – another meeting code – as if it's from Erla."

There was no reply so I wasn't sure he'd heard me, but when I went back to the sitting room he was frowning. "What would that do?" he asked. "They know she's dead, so it can't be from her."

"No, of course not. That's not the point. You'd be sending a signal. You'd be saying, 'I know what you're up to.' And if you send it from a number they can't trace or they don't know, then they're going to worry about who's sniffing around and why. That might flush somebody out."

"To come to a meeting?"

"Why not? You said you knew one of the locations she used, right?"

"Yeh, Hoyvík, we think."

"Okay, so you send a text, then set up an obbo – surveillance – and keep watch. If no one turns up you're no worse off, but if they do come maybe you'll find out what you're dealing with." I gestured with my bottle, then took a pull. "In fact, if you want, I'll send the text and go to Hoyvík to see who shows up. All you have to do is watch."

He gave a dry laugh. "You want to be there for bait?"

"Nah, I'd just be an innocent tourist doing a bit of sightseeing. Nothing wrong with that, is there?"

He gave me the vaguely troubled look he reserved for moments when he realised we weren't so much alike. Even so, he didn't dismiss the suggestion out of hand, and now I realised I was hoping he wouldn't. In my head I'd latched on to the idea with the same infatuation you get for some notions after five or six drinks. The fact I was only on my second beer didn't seem relevant.

"Let me think about it," Hentze said, then scrubbed at the side of his head in vexation. "This secret stuff – all whispers and closed doors – I don't like it. I wish for straightforward crime, so you know where you are."

"So *make* it straightforward."

He looked thoughtful for a moment, then nodded. "Yeh, maybe you're right to say it," he said. "Maybe that's what we need."

He considered that conclusion for a moment longer then slapped his hands on his knees in a decisive manner. "I should be going," he said, as if he'd reached the end of the road. "Thank you for your ideas."

He pushed himself out of the chair and I walked him to the door. I wasn't sure anything I'd said had been much use. Sometimes it doesn't matter, though; all you need is a sounding board and Hentze did seem a little less burdened as he went up the steps. If he was I'd at least done one useful thing that day.

* * *

I'd lost the impetus to cook, so I made a sandwich to go with the second beer. I ate in front of the TV and an impenetrable Danish current affairs programme about wind farms, and let my thoughts wander until it was either have another drink or do something else. I chose something else: the grown-up alternative.

It was pretty dark and the chilly wind hadn't eased off as I crossed the paved yard to Fríða's door. I was in the habit of knocking and walking in, so that's what I did. I called out, though, and I heard Fríða's voice from beyond the kitchen.

She was working in the small room that served as her study, off the sitting room with a window that – in daylight – had a view over the beach. The room was barely eight feet by eight: one wall of books, a desk and a laptop illuminated by an expensive-looking Anglepoise. The only thing not scrupulously tidied away was the pad of paper she was referring to as she typed. Upstairs I could hear the faint sound of bass from Matteus's room.

I stood in the open doorway because there wasn't space for two in the room.

"Hey," she said with a slightly distracted smile. Her head wasn't fully out of what she'd been doing. "Was that Hjalti Hentze's car I saw by the road?"

"Yeah, he came for coffee."

"Just coffee?"

"He likes someone to tell him he's wrong, just so he knows he isn't," I said. Then, "You know they released Finn?"

"Yeh, Hjalti called me. I think he was afraid Finn wouldn't let me know."

"Why wouldn't he?"

"Because he's proud." She shrugged, still upbeat. "Anyway, I called him and he sounded okay. He was going home. He said all he wanted was a shower and some sleep now it was over."

I couldn't tell whether she knew that Finn had only been released because the forensic samples had gone missing and not because he'd been ruled out as a suspect, but I didn't think so. Telling her would have been the honest thing to do, but I didn't particularly want to be the one to put a dampener on her mood at this point. If Finn hadn't told her I didn't see that it was my place to speak up.

"What?" she asked then, because I'd gone quiet.

"No, nothing," I said and shifted in the doorway. "If you're working I'll leave you alone. I just thought I'd say *hey*."

"No, that's okay. I would have called to see you anyway. Do you feel like going out?"

"Now?"

She shook her head. "Tomorrow evening. I have an invitation for a charity event." She searched for a word. "An *auction* of art. It's at the Nordic House, with drinks and canapés. I thought you might like to go with me."

"Sounds a bit upmarket," I said. "I'm not sure I've got the wardrobe for it – not here, anyway. I had to borrow a jacket from Hjalti for the funeral, remember?"

"Yeh, but this will be casual – perhaps not *so* casual," she amended with a glance at my sweater. "Jeans and a jacket would be fine, though."

"Sure?"

"Yes."

"Okay then. I'd like that. What time?"

"We can leave here at seven."

"Okay, I'll be ready."

It seemed a good point to leave her in peace, but I remembered the thing I'd come over to ask.

I said, "Before I forget, do you know anyone I could pay to do some research and translation for me?"

"I can translate something if you have it."

"I don't know if there is anything yet. I wanted someone to trawl through the newspaper archives to see if there are any articles about a commune at Múli. Someone who can think for themselves would be good: follow up a lead if they find one."

She didn't ask why, but maybe she'd guessed. "This is the Faroese newspapers you mean?"

"Yeah, although I suppose there might be some Danish, too."

Fríða thought for a moment, then said, "Yeh, I might know someone who could do that. Her name is Tove Hald, but I'm not sure if she's still on the Faroes or has gone back to Denmark. She's a student in Copenhagen: very bright. I know her parents from when I was there: Ralf is Danish, Maibritt is Faroese."

"Sounds as if she'd be ideal," I said. "Could you find out if she'd be interested? I don't think it would take her too long – a few hours. Would a hundred and twenty krónur an hour be fair?"

"Yeh, I think so. Let me find out if she's here."

"Okay, *takk*."

I said goodnight then and left her to work, but about twenty minutes later she sent me an email to say Tove Hald was in the Faroes for a few more days and would be happy to do the research I wanted. She'd given her my number and she would call me tomorrow.

I sent back a *takk fyri* and went to weigh up my wardrobe, such as it was. I already suspected it would come up wanting on the smart-casual front, and so it proved. I ought to do better, if only for Fríða's sake, I decided. Why not?

34

Wednesday/mikudagur

MAKE IT STRAIGHTFORWARD, AS REYNÁ HAD SAID; THAT'S
what he'd decided to do. Cut away all the entanglements and
unnecessary complications and go back to the beginning with
a cold eye.

Alone in the office next to the incident room, Hentze
had his head propped on his hand as he read through the
transcribed interviews with the AWCA personnel. These
were the actual statements as noted down by the interviewing
officers, rather than the bare, collated details. If there was
something they'd missed, it would be here: something that
had not been abstracted because it had seemed unnecessary
or spurious; something overlooked in the pressure of the
moment, but which would stand out when he saw it: a
coincidence of names, times, locations or activity; perhaps
just an off-kilter remark.

That was what he hoped, but it was still a tedious task
after three cups of coffee and most of the statements were
repetitious in their vagueness. "I was with X, Y or Z... I

think we left about six thirty... I don't think I'd seen her since Thursday..."

It was to be expected because people have less than perfect recall, but still, Hentze read with attention. So far there was nothing. He occasionally made a note of a name or a place, but mostly he just read.

Not long after nine he reached the end of the statements, just as Remi Syderbø came looking for him.

"There's good news," Remi said. "The original forensic samples have been tracked down at Kastrup. Apparently they'd been wrongly directed to a cargo handling area – something like that. Anyway, the important thing is that they're now on their way to the technical lab and I've requested that they be dealt with as a matter of urgency, so perhaps later today we'll at least have something to move things forward."

"That would be nice."

Perhaps because his response didn't seem sufficiently enthused, Remi cocked an eyebrow and gestured at the desk. "What are you working on?"

"The statements from the Alliance people."

That got a deeper frown. "I thought we'd been through them."

"I didn't think it would hurt to look again. They were the people Erla had most contact with. In fact, she doesn't seem to have spent much time away from them, which I think is a bit strange given that she had friends and family here. She hadn't been to see her parents for three weeks, for example."

"Well, if she was working... And they do live on Suðuroy."

"Yes, that's true, but I also keep wondering why she chose

to live at the Alliance house when she could have used her own flat. The tenant, Ruth Guttesen, works away half the time and she told me she'd suggested that they share the place, but Erla wanted to stay at the house on Fjalsgøta. I just think that's strange, unless she had some particular reason to do so."

"Like what?"

Hentze hesitated, but only briefly before deciding to take the bull by the horns. "Oddur has a theory that Erla may have had some role with the intelligence service."

"Really?" Remi did a good job of looking surprised and dubious at the same time. "Why?"

"Because there are some strange text messages on the phone card we found in her car. He thinks they're a code of some sort."

"Didn't Oddur also have a theory about CIA involvement in 9/11?"

"Yeh, he probably spends too much time on the internet," Hentze acknowledged. "But even so, this does look odd. And there's still the matter of the unknown man Erla met with at Kaldbak the day she died. When you consider that, together with the attempt to make her death seem sexually motivated or even related to the anti-whaling protest…"

"It still seems a little fanciful to me," Remi said. "Although maybe not for Oddur." He clearly meant this to be enough to write off the idea, but Hentze didn't choose to take it that way.

"Do you know if there *is* a security service presence with the Danish contingent?" he asked. "It might only be one man."

Remi made a moue. "To do what? I can't imagine that an

organisation like the Alliance is seen as much of a threat to national security, especially when they're all the way out here. They're a pain in *our* arse, but why would the Danes care about that? If it was a G20 summit meeting in Copenhagen they were disrupting, then the security services would take an interest, but over a few whales? I doubt it very much."

"Even though we originally thought there could be mass protests – hundreds of people on the beaches?"

"Which clearly hasn't happened." Remi shook his head. "Listen, I'm not saying some people weren't jumpy when we first heard about all this, but it's been pretty clear for some time that the Alliance talk big but deliver very little. How many volunteers and members have they got here – about forty? Hardly an army. So if there *had* been any covert interest in them I think it would have evaporated by now."

He shifted and looked at the whiteboards, as if he'd tired of the subject and was ready to get things back on track.

"Listen, Oddur can amuse himself with his theories, but in his free time. It's okay to be thorough, but I think he's chasing a barren cow, especially as it's agreed that – pending the Technical reports – Finn Sólsker is still the prime suspect."

"Agreed?" Hentze asked. "By who? When?"

"Hjalti…" Remi said with a mildly reproachful air.

"You know what I mean," Hentze said, discovering that he was suddenly unwilling to give ground. "If Finn *is* the prime suspect – and I'm not saying he shouldn't be – but if he is, then why is Ári giving people like Høgni Joensen a grilling? Was it just to fill the time? It can't be both ways. If we're convinced Finn is guilty, why pursue anyone else?

And if we're not, then surely we should be looking at *all* possibilities, even Oddur's."

As much as this was an indictment of Ári Niclasen, Hentze knew it could also be taken as one of Remi Syderbø for failing to keep Ári in check. He waited to see how Remi would take it, not caring much either way. He was spoiling for a fight, he realised.

For a moment Syderbø seemed troubled by Hentze's uncharacteristic intransigence. Not that Hentze couldn't be stubborn, but usually he was far more subtle about it.

"Listen," Remi said in a conciliatory tone. "We both know that we need the Technical reports, either to confirm that we're going in the right direction, or to show us that we're not. Until we get them I don't think there's much to be gained by anyone chasing shadows." He made a gesture to show he was including the absent Ári in this. "We should have something from the lab soon, but until then I'm scaling back on the incident room staff. Ári, Dánjal and Sonja can handle it for the moment. Meanwhile we have the Alliance arrests from yesterday to finish processing and I'd like you to make sure we haven't been overlooking the more normal cases in the midst of all this. Those burglaries in Klaksvík you were talking about, for example."

The same burglaries Remi had been quick to dismiss the other day, Hentze remembered, but he nodded as if Remi had made a valid point and he'd accepted it. "Okay, if that's what you think best. I'll go through the log and make sure we're not falling behind."

"Thanks. It would help."

* * *

"Want to hear something strange?" Jósef Dimon asked, coming in from the fire escape after a smoke and finding Hentze in the kitchen stirring his fourth coffee.

"Strange how?"

"Peculiar," Dimon said. "You know that operation I was talking about yesterday – the one that got cancelled? Well, I got annoyed about it, so I called a guy from the Copenhagen drugs squad. His lead set the whole thing up, so I thought he might know what had happened. Anyway, long story short, they were *told* to lay off."

"By who?"

"Yeh, well that's it. Officially, the drugs squad commander decided that they didn't have enough information to justify the operation. This is after at least two weeks' preparation, remember. *Un*officially, the word is that the security services told them to close it down because it crossed with something they already had in place. And security always takes precedence, of course." He pulled a face. "Anyway, this is bullshit because Eric knows the guys we were targeting went right ahead and did what we expected them to do. They sent a shipment through, but because we'd been stood down, there was no one to drop the net when they did."

Hentze sipped his coffee. "Any idea who was collecting the shipment at this end?"

"Not for certain, no. We think it was two Icelandic boys we've had our eye on, which would make sense if they were using us as a waystation before moving it on to Iceland. We needed to have eyes on the consignment to really be sure who collected it, though. But what really pisses me off is that the security services can swan in and cancel a perfectly good operation without having to account to anyone. Just two magic words – *national security* – and everyone does as they're told."

"That's true," Hentze agreed. "So, when you were told that the operation had been scrubbed, who did that come from?"

"Here? From Remi, but I'd already been told by the squad leader in Copenhagen."

"So why was Remi telling you again?"

Dimon shrugged. "Just confirmation, I suppose: to make sure I didn't spend hours sitting at the airport for nothing. I should be grateful for that at least, I guess."

35

"JAN? IT'S RICHARD KIRKLAND." WHICH I KNEW. I TOOK THE fact that he hadn't said "Superintendent" to be an indicator that now he'd finally got hold of me, he was going to take an I'm-not-just-your-boss-I'm-your-friend approach. Which wouldn't work.

"Yes, sir," I said, because he was never my friend.

"Where are you?"

"Still in the Faroes."

I was leaning on my car, keys in hand, on the point of driving to Tórshavn.

"Right. Has— Have you had the funeral yet?"

I enjoyed the fact that he found it awkward to ask. "Yeah, a few days ago."

"Ah. Okay. And how are you feeling – medically, I mean? Are you able to travel now?"

"I think I probably could if necessary," I said.

"Okay, good. Well, the reason I'm ringing is because the DPS has rescheduled your interview for next Tuesday, the first. So if there's no reason you can't attend this time – no medical reason – I thought you'd want as much notice as possible to make any arrangements: travel and so on."

"I appreciate that, sir."

"I imagine flights might be limited from there."

I imagined that he probably knew exactly how many flights there were and at what times. He would have looked it up.

"There are usually two a day to Copenhagen," I said.

"Right, good then." He sounded satisfied to have disposed of the final reason I might find not to show up. "So we can confirm the first?"

"I don't see why not," I said and waited to see if he'd say "good" one more time. Some people called him Goody Kirkland, but I wasn't one of them.

"Okay, then."

I waited again, just because I could.

"Jan?"

"Sir?"

"You might do well to leave yourself some time to prepare."

"I'm already prepared," I told him. "But I'll bear it in mind."

I thought – hoped – there was a trace of uncertainty in the slight pause he left before saying, "Good, well, okay then. The first: nine o'clock. There'll be an email to confirm. I'll see you then."

"Yes, sir," I said. "Bye for now."

I rang off.

Goody Kirkland. I was glad I'd taken the call. It had made me realise that I'd already made a decision; I just hadn't let myself acknowledge it till then.

* * *

Tove Hald was about average height, but that was about it as far as average went. When I'd asked her on the phone how I'd recognise her she'd said, "Oh, I'm blonde." It didn't strike me as a particularly outstanding feature in a country where every other person was fair-haired, but when I saw her I knew who she was. Her white-blonde hair stood out even here: short-cropped and slightly tousled. She had clear, ice-pale skin, light-blue eyes and her features were as Nordic as it seemed possible to be, even amidst the Scandinavian looks of the other customers in the SMS mall.

"Tove? I'm Jan."

"*Hey*, nice to meet you," she said with an easy smile and a good, businesslike handshake.

I bought us coffees at the Baresso counter and as I followed her to the seating area I saw she had a row of tattooed flowers – daisies, maybe – down her spine: three of them between the base of her skull and the collar of the quilted plaid jacket she was wearing.

We perched on a pair of high stools at a narrow counter running the length of the back window. "Did Fríða tell you what I needed?" I asked.

Tove shook her head. "Only that it was family research and translation from the newspapers."

"Yeah, sort of," I said. "I'm trying to find out about a commune at Múli between about 1973 and '74. All I know is that it was called the Colony and it might have been run by a Danish man called Rasmus Matzen."

"Okay, just a second."

She dug in a pocket and came up with a pen and a small hardback notebook. I saw it was already half full when she flipped through to a blank page, then started to jot down the key names I'd used in quick, fluid handwriting.

"Do you know any more?" she asked.

"Only that the houses and land at Múli are owned by a man called Boas Justesen who lives at Fuglafjørður. He told me yesterday that they'd been in his family for some time, but I don't know how long. He wasn't very helpful."

The name Boas Justesen went down in the notebook.

"Okay. Anything else?"

I thought, then shook my head. "No, that's about it."

"Okay. So why do you think that there would be something in the newspapers about the commune?"

I couldn't quite shake the feeling that I was being interviewed, but there didn't seem to be anything behind it except efficiency.

"Well, I was told that people at the time didn't approve of the commune, so I thought there might be some coverage. Letters to the editor, that sort of thing."

"Okay, I'll check that. And what's your objective to the search? It would be helpful to know."

I said, "My mother spent some time at the commune, so if possible I'd like to trace anyone who might have been there with her."

"And her name?" Pen poised.

"Lýdia Tove Ravnsfjall. That was her married name. Before that she was Reyná."

313

She wrote it down and when she'd done that it was like a switch had been flicked. "She was Tove, like me," she said, as if she thought that was a plus to the job. She closed her notebook. "Okay, I'll see what I can find out for you. The day after tomorrow I'm going back to Denmark, but that should be okay if I start work this afternoon. I don't think it will take too long. Fríða said you could pay one hundred and twenty krónur an hour."

"If that suits you."

"Yeah, that's good, *takk*." She knocked back her coffee like a shot of vodka and got off the stool. "Okay, then, I'll call you as soon as I'm done. Good to meet you, Jan."

"You, too," I said, shaking her hand again. "And thanks."

It was only as I watched her walk away, into the central hall of the mall, and then turn towards the exit that I realised she hadn't asked me a single personal question.

Then my phone rang. It was Hentze.

"You remember you volunteered to do something last night?" he asked.

"Yeah."

"Are you still ready?"

"If that's what you want. When and where?" I didn't bother to ask if he was sure. He wouldn't have rung if he wasn't.

"Hoyvík at two thirty. Can you be there?"

"Yeah, that's fine."

"Okay, *takk*. I think by the harbour would be best, past the museum. You can drive most of the way and then walk."

"What about the message?"

"Do you have a pen?"

I found one and wrote down the phone number and meeting code he gave me on the back of the receipt for the coffees. "I'll send it now," I told him. "See you later."

"*Nei*, I hope not."

I knew what he meant: if I saw him, so could anyone else.

I rang off and sent the text he'd dictated. I didn't expect a reply and I didn't get one. Still, I gave it five minutes, finishing my coffee, and then I went to look for a jacket in the smart-casual range.

Hentze had offered no explanation when he left the station on Yviri við Strond, but there was no reason he would. Coming and going was part of the job.

There was a veil of sea mist cutting the visibility on the road to a hundred metres or so and it showed no signs of dispersing as he drove out to Hoyvík, then took the side road to the Hoyvíksgarður museum. It was a winding, single-track road, descending into the small valley beside a mown field where geese foraged in the grass.

When he got to the collection of buildings that comprised the outdoor museum Hentze parked in a bay by the administrative building. Two lights in a first-floor office and a single car outside were the only indication that anyone was inside. Except for a few hours each Sunday and Thursday the museum was closed for the winter season and the preserved buildings of the old farm were locked up. Unless you worked here there was no reason to come.

He checked his watch then got out of the car and crossed

the tarmac towards the old, stone buildings. There'd be a wait, but that was okay. He'd be in place when Reyná arrived and then things would develop or not.

Initially he'd had some reservations about involving Reyná in this, despite the fact that it had been his idea. He liked the man in the way of complementary opposites, but he also knew that Reyná was a complex individual: a good copper, yes, but still, complicated and hard to predict, especially his disregard for authority.

The alternative, though, had been to ask Dánjal or Oddur, which Hentze was unwilling to do. It was one thing to expose himself to possible repercussions, another to entangle them. And if – as he half expected – this vaguely ridiculous subterfuge turned out to be for nothing, then at least it would be a relatively private embarrassment and afterwards he could put it to rest.

The tarmacked track hairpinned back on itself, going downhill. After a minute or so I passed the museum buildings I'd read about while I killed time over lunch – stone walls and grass roofs: a preserved traditional farm. Not that I could see a great deal of it in the mist.

Past the buildings the track became gravel and there was more winding for a short distance until I saw the roofs of boathouses and pulled in at a wide spot on the corner of the track. I stopped the engine and checked the time. Two twenty-five was about right, so I got out and pulled on my coat, then followed the slope to the quay.

Heljareyga was a small, natural cove no more than a hundred yards wide at its midpoint. Beyond that I couldn't see much. The mist hung like a damp dust-sheet over the headlands and above the almost mirror-smooth water it appeared to ebb and flow slightly, gossamer fine. The stillness made you want to hold your breath. Nothing and nobody moved.

The quay was quite short with half a dozen wooden boathouses in varying states of repair. In a couple of places nets and ropes had been dumped in disorganised piles, as if waiting for collection or disposal. An upturned oil drum rusted gently under the rainwater collected by its rim.

There was no natural landing place – no beach, just a litter of boulders and rocks – but a concrete slipway ran down to the water. Beside that a narrow jetty stuck out about twenty yards from the shore so I picked my way down to it and then went out along its length, as far as a ladder going down into the clear water. I was as visible as it was possible to be, so now I just had to wait. I leaned on a short rail and looked back at the land.

I hadn't seen any sign of Hentze but that didn't matter. He'd be there somewhere – perhaps near the museum buildings for easy cover. There was only one way in or out of the place, which has advantages and disadvantages depending on whether you're the watcher or the watched. I was neither. I was just the bait. The only question was whether I was alluring enough.

Ten minutes. Fifteen.

I waited, hands in my pockets. The only movement was from a pair of lost gulls, which came in to alight on the sea;

the only sounds were vaguely watery and damp. I waited. You get used to just waiting when you're a copper, sometimes for hours. And then my phone rang, as alien in the stillness as it was possible to be.

Hentze heard the sound of an engine ten minutes after Jan Reyná's car had gone past. In the stone doorway he was concealed well enough, with a view of the track to the cove and any person or vehicle that went down it.

He straightened slightly, straining to follow the sound of this second car and judge its approach, which seemed leisurely or cautious, perhaps because of the mist.

It didn't come past the corner of the building, and from the sound of gravel under tyres and a few seconds of reversing Hentze concluded that it had turned and backed up in the spot where he'd left his own car. The occupant or occupants might leave their vehicle and walk, so he stayed still, waiting to hear the engine stop.

But it didn't. The engine – a diesel – continued to tick over; the sound muted but carried well enough by the damp in the air. There was no sound of doors being opened or closed, either. Just the engine.

Hentze checked his watch. It was nearly five minutes after the rendezvous time. He wondered how much leeway would have been agreed between Erla Sivertsen and her handler. How long would either of them wait beyond the agreed time before calling it off? Ten minutes? Fifteen? Half an hour?

But of course, Erla Sivertsen could not make this

rendezvous, and if anyone was coming they knew that. So they would come on time or not at all.

The engine ticked over and Hentze made his decision. He moved out of the doorway and along the side of the building as far as the corner, then stepped out around it. In the parking lot across the way the idling car was an anonymous silver Nissan, medium-sized, with one occupant – a male. It had turned, as Hentze had imagined, and was facing the road from a spot directly in front of Hentze's own car, blocking it in.

Hentze crossed the short distance at a businesslike pace, waiting to see if there would be a reaction. He half expected the car to move off, but it didn't. Instead he heard the whine of the driver's window being lowered.

The man in the car's driving seat was in his mid-thirties, Hentze estimated as he approached. Hard to tell from this angle but he looked fit and well built. Certainly not the man Jákup Homrum had described as meeting Erla Sivertsen at Kaldbak.

"I'm a police officer," Hentze said in Danish. "Will you tell me your name and your business here?"

"You're requested to return to your office," the man replied flatly, also in Danish. "Vicekriminalkommissær Syderbø would like to speak to you."

"And you are?" Hentze asked, taking his phone from his pocket.

"I don't think that's relevant, do you?" the man said mildly. "And you can tell Mr Reyná to go home also." He shifted and put the car into gear. "Please, return to your office."

Hentze had activated the camera on his phone by now, but even as he brought it up to the level of the car window the driver let out the clutch and started away. There was no squealing of tyres, no apparent hurry, but even so, all Hentze got was a slightly blurred shot of the top of the man's head, then a second of the car's rear number plate. It was Faroese and he could remember it anyway.

He watched the car make the winding ascent up the valley road until it was lost in the mist. Then he called Reyná.

"You can come in now," he said.

36

REMI SYDERBØ LED THE WAY UP TO THE FIFTH FLOOR, conspicuously keeping a couple of steps ahead of Hentze as they ascended the stairs. They had exchanged fewer than a dozen words since Hentze had returned to the station to be met by Remi at the door to the CID department. Hentze took both the reception and the silence as an indication that Remi was annoyed, but whether that stemmed from what Hentze had just done was harder to tell.

There were fewer offices on the top floor of the building and they were all large. It was also quite quiet, with none of the coming and going of the lower floors, but more of a studious – perhaps even a library-ish – air.

Remi knocked on the door of the Commander's office and went in as if he knew they were expected. Hentze followed.

The office had a fine view of Nólsoy when the weather was clear, but now the large, sloping windows looked out on the obscuring mist. The Commander, Andrias Berg, had his desk facing the view, but he was sitting with his back to it, swivelled round in his leather chair. He was a stocky man with prematurely white hair and he wore his uniform with evident pride. No matter what the time of day his shirt always looked freshly ironed. By and large, Hentze had no particular opinion of the man. He seemed personable enough, but kept his distance from the lower ranks, which was about as much as you could ask.

Berg didn't get up from his chair when Remi and Hentze entered. Neither did the man who sat in an armchair with his back to the wall. He was middle-aged, unremarkable in a slightly bank-clerkish way, tending towards the jowly. A man who looked as if he would wear a raincoat over his suit, Hentze judged. A man not unlike the one Jákup Homrum had seen.

"Thank you, Remi," Berg said. A dismissal, but perhaps also an indication that he might be required again.

Remi left the room, closing the door. Hentze remained standing.

"Thank you for coming," Berg said, but only out of convention.

"It was no problem," Hentze said.

"This is Herre Munk," Berg said, switching to Danish. "He's with the national security services."

"*Goddag*," Hentze said in acknowledgement.

Munk's only reaction was a slow blink.

"Could you explain to us what you were doing at Hoyvík just now?" Berg asked then.

"Yes. I was testing a theory," Hentze said.

"Which was?"

"That Erla Sivertsen was working for or had some connection with the security services."

He waited to see if Berg would ask why he would think

that, but the Commander either knew already or didn't care.

"Did you discuss this theory with anyone besides the British inspector, Jan Reyná?"

Hentze shook his head. "No. At least, I didn't tell anyone else what I was doing, but the idea that Erla Sivertsen might have been involved in something clandestine wasn't mine originally."

Again, Berg gave the impression that he knew this already. "And why did you involve this Reyná? Why not one of your colleagues?"

"He volunteered," Hentze said simply.

"For what reason?"

"I suppose because he's a police officer and also a friend."

"You didn't think that was inappropriate if you suspected there might be security service involvement?"

"To be honest, I didn't give it much thought. But if I can say—?" He paused and Berg nodded. "If Herre Munk hadn't sent someone to Hoyvík I'd have been none the wiser about their involvement. All he had to do was do nothing."

There was a faint twitch at the corner of Berg's eye, but it was impossible to tell what it signified. He looked towards Munk.

"I think we can stop the silly games," Munk said then, shifting his weight in the chair as if finally provoked into life. He had an unexpectedly light voice. "In the interests of national security you're to make no further enquiries about Erla Sivertsen's death with any members of the Atlantic Wildlife Conservation Alliance. Nor are you to direct, suggest or imply that others should do so, either police officers or civilians. In other words: leave them alone."

Hentze absorbed that for a couple of seconds. He said, "So Erla Sivertsen *was* working for you."

Munk shook his head. "I'm not able to say."

Which meant that she was.

"And if evidence comes to light that shows someone from AWCA may have been involved in her murder?" Hentze asked.

This time Berg fielded the question. "If at any stage it becomes necessary to make more enquiries with the Alliance, Remi will oversee it," he said. "But at the moment it *isn't* necessary."

Hentze looked back at Munk. "Do you know who killed Erla Sivertsen?"

Munk was unfazed. "If I knew I'd pass that information to the senior investigating officer. However, I can say that no members of AWCA were involved."

"If you don't know who killed her how can you be sure of that?"

"Because I know more than you do."

"I don't doubt it," Hentze said flatly.

"All right," Andrias Berg said with just a hint of a warning now. "We don't need to prolong this. You understand you've been given a direct order not to have further contact with members of the Alliance?"

"Yes."

"Okay, then you can go back to work. Thank you."

Hentze turned for the door.

Outside Remi Syderbø was loitering a few yards along the corridor, flicking through a magazine, which he immediately put aside when Hentze emerged. He fell in beside him but didn't speak until they were in the stairwell.

"You've only yourself to blame," he said to Hentze then, without any sympathy. "I told you to leave it alone."

"When you said that, did it come from the Commander or Munk?"

Remi just shook his head, whether in hopelessness or denial wasn't clear. "You're to have no further part in the Sivertsen investigation," he said. "And this time, for God's sake, do as you're told."

37

I DIDN'T KNOW HOW LONG IT WOULD BE BEFORE HENTZE showed up; or *if*. He'd said he would, though, so I settled in to wait. I didn't lack for company, however. Outside the Smyrjibreyðsbúðin café, about ten yards away through the window, I was under surveillance.

He'd followed me from the car park, his own car turning in at the entrance about fifteen seconds behind me. Any other day I probably wouldn't have registered it, but Hentze's little adventure had made me more aware. So when the man with angular Nordic features, leather jacket and jeans matched my pace and direction as I walked through the town, it was easy to recognise what he was doing.

Just for the sake of bloody-mindedness I went into Maria Poulsen – a department store for upmarket lighting, cookery equipment and gifts – and wandered around for ten minutes. He didn't follow me in, but when I emerged he was waiting, and when I continued up the incline of the street he fell in a regulation twenty yards behind. There was no attempt at subtlety.

Now, while I stirred sugar into a cappuccino, he simply stood as impassive and lifeless as a lamppost across the road.

He might have been waiting for a bus, except this part of the street was pedestrianised. He might have been waiting for a date, but he didn't look at his watch or for anyone coming along the street. All he looked at was the window where I was sitting: a steadfast gaze, almost resigned.

It was a crude attempt at intimidation, if that was the intention. I doubted it was, though. More of a demonstration; just so I'd be in no doubt that they knew who I was, and that they didn't mind wasting this time to let me know.

For about forty minutes I leafed through an out-of-date edition of the *Times Herald* from the magazine rack by the door, bought a second coffee and a pastry, used the facilities, thought about Kirkland's phone call that morning. I wondered if Tove Hald was in the library down the road. I flicked through my notebook. I speculated about how close to my credit card limit I was getting after buying a Jack Jones jacket at the SMS mall. I debated when I should ring the airline and change my ticket. There are worse ways to spend your time on a Wednesday afternoon – like standing outside watching a man drink coffee, eat a pastry and think his thoughts.

I saw Hentze arrive when he opened the door. As he approached my table I glanced out of the window. The man across the street had gone.

"Sorry to keep you waiting," Hentze said.

I shook my head. "Coffee?" He hadn't sat down yet.

"*Nei*." He cast a glance at the three other customers nearby. "Shall we walk?"

We left the café and turned right, then across Bøkjarabrekka at the constantly bleeping pedestrian crossing. There was still a light mist in the air, like a high ceiling, but not as dense as it had been by the sea. I glanced back a couple of times, but if we were being followed it was being done properly now. I didn't think we were, though.

"So, I'm taken off the Erla Sivertsen investigation," Hentze said in the end, as if it had taken him this long to frame the sentence.

"Because of this afternoon?"

"I would say so."

We walked up Niels Finsens gøta at a stroll while he told me about his summons to the fifth floor. He related it matter-of-factly, so it was hard to tell how he felt about it. When he'd finished I described the man who'd followed me and Hentze looked thoughtful.

"He doesn't sound like the same man I spoke to at Hoyvík," he said. "And if he isn't we can say there are at least three of them here, if we include Munk."

"You're sure they *are* spooks – security services – rather than from a branch of the Danish police?"

"That's what Andrias Berg said: the national security service. And I'm to do as I'm told as a matter of national security."

"National security trumps everything."

"Even a murder, it seems," he said flatly.

We walked on a couple of paces, then Hentze seemed to make up his mind.

"I'm going to say that Munk was Erla's boss: her contact," he said. "That's the only thing that makes sense.

He was the one who went to meet her when she sent a message. Maybe others did too, but Munk is the one we've heard described. And when they meet she tells him things about what the Alliance is doing: what their plans are, how many people they have…"

Most of which you could find out just by watching them from a distance, I thought: no need for any kind of undercover operation. Still, I didn't say so. I could tell Hentze needed to get this out of his system, so I just let him talk.

"Then someone in the Alliance finds out that Erla is an informant," he went on. "And on Saturday night she is killed and the murderer leaves her body in a way that will make it look as if she was killed by a Faroese person. Maybe he knows we won't believe this, maybe he doesn't, but when we arrest Finn Sólsker he must be happy because he knows we are on the wrong path." He looked at me. "Yes?"

"Okay."

"Good."

"Why good?"

"Because it shows Finn didn't do it, or at least, that Munk doesn't think so. It must be the case, otherwise Munk wouldn't care if I go to the Alliance asking more questions. No. Munk knows it is someone in the Alliance who killed Erla, but, whatever his reasons, he doesn't want this person found: no interference."

"He'd have a reason if his operation is still ongoing," I said. "In fact, it must be. Otherwise, like you said, why would he care?"

"So, if Erla's death hasn't stopped Munk's operation, he

has a reason to keep us from looking at AWCA until he can do whatever it is he plans."

"That makes sense," I agreed. "And if Munk wanted to delay the murder investigation it might explain why your forensic samples went missing as well. Without test results Finn is still the prime suspect, which means that no one looks for alternatives. It's all part of the smoke and mirrors routine."

"*Smoke and mirrors?*" He frowned.

"Illusion, misdirection. What stage magicians use so you don't see what they're really up to."

"Ah. Okay." He seemed to chew the phrase over for a moment and I had the sense that he was storing it away.

"Okay," he repeated. "But in that case, why did they not just destroy the samples? Why let them be found again?"

"Didn't you say Sophie Krogh had duplicates? Maybe the delay was all they needed."

"So their operation could be nearly over."

"Maybe," I said.

We came to a side street and Hentze turned down it. I noticed his pace had increased slightly, as if it was linked to his thought processes.

"So, we know that Munk's operation is based on the Alliance, yes?" he said, as if he wanted to confirm where we stood. "And because Munk wants to keep us from investigating them he must think that someone from the group was Erla Sivertsen's killer. He either thinks it or knows it. Yes?"

"Probably," I allowed. "But it doesn't mean Munk's target and the killer have to be the same person. Munk could just be afraid that a police investigation of the Alliance will frighten his target, even if he's not the killer."

Hentze considered that, then shook his head. "Why would it do that? Unless Munk's target, as you call him, is guilty of the murder then he has nothing to fear: he can carry on as normal. No, I think it must be the case that Munk's target is also the one who killed Erla. He realises she is spying on him, so he kills her. Maybe not on purpose, we know that, but still…" He looked at me. "What? You don't agree?"

"No, yeah, you could be right," I said. "Trouble is, I can't see what you can do about it. It's not a case you can work from the outside. The Alliance are the obvious people to look at, but if you're off the investigation you can't go in and question them; not without ending up like me, anyway."

"Yeh, well, I wouldn't want that," he said drily.

"So you're dead-ended," I said. "At least, until the forensic tests come back. But if you're right about Finn, the forensics will put him in the clear and then Remi Syderbø won't have any choice. He'll have to look for alternative suspects and he won't be able to ignore the Alliance then."

I'd meant it as a degree of consolation, but Hentze didn't seem encouraged. "You think?" he said. "What if Munk and his colleagues have a reason to want a – what did you call it the other day? A *scapegoat*? What if they can use 'national security' as a reason to interfere with the tests and make sure Finn remains as a suspect?"

"Now you're being paranoid."

He didn't accept that. "Smoke and mirrors, you said. Why not?"

The best I could manage was a shrug. I couldn't see

the point in trading conspiracy theories. What he had was a situation he couldn't get around, and knowing Hentze, that was what really bothered him. He smelled something rotten in the fridge, but he couldn't find it to throw it out. Hentze was a man who liked his fridge clean and smelling good, and the fact that it didn't was going to piss him off in that quiet, clamped-down way the Faroese have.

We came to Bøkjarabrekka again, still walking downhill, and he didn't say any more until we'd crossed between the traffic, which was starting to get heavier in the build-up to what passes for Tórshavn's rush hour.

"Finn is being stupid," he said when we were on a quieter street and able to walk two abreast. "He won't tell the truth because he thinks being innocent is enough. But for something like this it's not enough to *be* innocent: you have to *show* it, even if that means being uncomfortable with the result."

"You mean admitting he was having an affair with Erla?"

"If it's the truth, *ja*."

"Have you told him that?"

"Of course. No difference."

I gave him a rueful look. "Well, if I was Finn I'm not sure it's something I'd want to admit to you."

"To me? Am I so frightening?" He shook his head. "No, it's not that. Finn has always the idea that to do something because someone tells him to do it is to lessen himself. Even if it is to his advantage. Do you know what I mean?"

For a second I wondered if he was implying the description would fit me as well, but then I saw that he was simply venting his frustration. "Yeah, but sometimes there's nothing you can do about it," I said. "He's made his bed, so now he's got to lie in it."

I looked to see if he knew the phrase. He nodded. "*Sum tú reiðir, skalt tú liggja*," he said.

"How long till you get forensic results?"

"Now? By the morning – that's what they promised."

But I could tell that he had little faith in what they would show.

We walked back as far as the car park together. Hentze didn't say much else because he was thinking, but as we came to my car he seemed to put his thoughts aside.

"Thank you for coming to Hoyvík," he said. "I appreciate it."

"Go and do something else," I told him. "Forget this for a bit."

"Yeh, maybe I will."

I doubted he would. Then, for no reason I could think of, I said, "By the way, I spoke to Kirkland this morning – my superintendent. I have to be back in the UK next week."

He frowned, as if I'd added something more to trouble him, which hadn't been my intention. "Are you— Will you go this time?" he asked.

"I don't think I've got a choice – not if I still want my job."

"Do you?"

"I'm still thinking about it."

Which was more or less true, if slightly glib. The longer I was away the more distant – irrelevant – it seemed. I opened the car door. "You know where I am if you want to annoy anyone else," I said. "And let me know what the forensics say – if they'll tell you."

"If they don't I can find out," he said.

"Okay. See you later."

"Yeh, I'll see you."

He started away towards the mist-laid stillness of the west harbour. I glanced around but there was no sign anyone was watching. Which didn't mean they weren't, but I wasn't going to go there.

38

IT WAS HARD TO HAVE ANY PROLONGED PRIVACY IN THE staff kitchen. That was why Annika was making the most of the fact she was cooking. As long as she was there Heri couldn't get into a long conversation about her going to Denmark without the chance that someone would wander in and overhear.

Cooking for the shift wasn't something done every day – perhaps once a week – and when Jón Danielsen had suggested it yesterday Annika had volunteered because she was on the control desk tonight. The others brought in the ingredients and she started the stew soon after going on shift, so it would be ready to eat around nine.

For the moment, Annika and Heri Kalsø had the kitchen to themselves because Jóhanna Dam had gone off to look at a reported child endangerment. Heri had a copy of the *Copenhagen Post* spread out on the table in front of him.

"It says here that the rent for some flats in Frederiksberg is over thirty thousand krónur a month – a *month*. Can you imagine?"

"Yeh?" Annika said. "That's not the sort of place you'd

live unless you were really successful, though, is it?"

"No, maybe not," Heri allowed. "Still, it's city prices wherever you are."

"I suppose. Some things are probably cheaper, though, without transportation costs."

"Yeh, Lego, maybe."

Over the past couple of days Heri had started to take an interest in all things Danish – particularly those relating to Copenhagen living. It wasn't very subtle, although on the surface it was done in a supportive manner. But somehow the drawbacks always came to the fore. It was hard to miss, but Annika refused to be drawn. If they were going to talk about it – *when* they talked about it – she was going to do it properly.

She adjusted the heat under the large pan as Hentze entered the room, sniffing appreciatively.

"I think I might work late tonight after all," he said. "Hey, Heri."

"Hey." Heri nodded.

"If you're here at nine you're welcome," Annika told Hentze as he dropped down on to the worn leather sofa beside the table.

Seeing that Hentze didn't seem to have anywhere else to be, Heri put the *Post* aside and stood up. "I suppose I'd better do some work," he said with no real enthusiasm. "See you later."

"Okay, see you," Annika said.

"Did I interrupt something?" Hentze enquired mildly once Heri was out of earshot.

Annika shook her head and rinsed her hands under the tap. "No, not really. He was just pointing out how expensive it is to live in Copenhagen."

"Oh. Right," Hentze said, understanding.

Annika reached for a towel. "There's no need for him to take it that way. He's known for ages that that's what I wanted to do – CID, I mean."

"But he thought you'd do it here?"

Annika nodded. "And I might. Probably. Afterwards. But first I want to see what else is out there, you know? I want to be in plain clothes with some good experience on my record before I get married and need time off for kids."

"Married and kids? With Heri?"

"I mean in general. I haven't discussed it with Heri. I'm not even sure that's what he'd want. And if he doesn't…" She shook her head. "It's all right for you men, but it's not like I've got so long to do it all, so I need to get on with things. Here, taste this."

She brought a spoon across from the pan and he duly tasted the stew.

"More salt?"

"A little," Hentze said. "It's good, though. You'll make someone a great wife."

"Yeh, I will," she said, ignoring the wisecrack. "But not till I'm ready. Do you want a coffee before I go back to the desk?"

"No, thanks. Will you do something else for me when you're there, though? I need a check on this car: owner, address…" He held up a slip of paper with a registration number on it.

"Sure, of course."

"Wait, don't be so quick. If anyone asks about why you're interested in it tell them straight away that you're doing it for me. I'm hoping no one *will* ask, but if they do, that's what you say. Don't make something up."

"Why would I?" Then she got it. "Oh. Because you don't want to look it up yourself."

Hentze nodded. "I'm trying to stay off the radar. But I don't want you to get into trouble if anyone takes an interest."

"Why? What's it about?"

He debated for a second, but he knew Annika was reliable. He said, "There are some national security service people here, on the islands. This is one of their cars."

She frowned. "If it's national security is it wise to be… I don't know – poking into their business?"

"If they poke into ours, yeh, I think so."

"What are they doing?"

"Interfering in the Erla Sivertsen case."

Her frown deepened. "How?"

He shook his head. "It's too complicated. You don't know anything about that, okay? I'm serious: don't put your head above the wall. If anyone asks, all you know is that I asked you to check the car and there was no reason you wouldn't."

She gave him a vaguely dubious look but then nodded. "Okay, if you say so. But if they're security services won't the car details be false?"

"I'd expect so, but even that might say something." He wasn't sure what, but it was the only thing he'd been able to come up with that didn't involve doing nothing.

"Okay," Annika said. "Let me just finish this and I'll

check it out. No email, right?"

"Right."

"Where will you be – incident room?"

"No, I'm not on the case any more."

"What? Hjalti…"

He shook his head to fend it off. "I told you, it's too complicated. I'll be in my office. Probably not long enough for stew, though."

39

FRÍÐA AND I MADE THE ROUND OF THE PAINTINGS AND sculptures displayed on temporary panels and plinths around the lobby area and café of the Nordic House: a very Scandinavian place, naturally. Lots of stone, pine and glass.

There was a jazz quartet playing off to one side, not making much of an impression on the noise of the two hundred or more people milling around. The charity art auction may have been the stated reason for coming, but clearly it was as much an excuse for the professional classes to mix and mingle. I didn't get the impression that there were many fishermen or shepherds amongst us, but if there were they'd scrubbed up well, just like me.

It was the sort of gathering where I might have expected to see Magnus, but he wasn't there. Instead, Fríða introduced me to several knots of people she knew; some professionally, others through various and convoluted paths of association that I didn't try to untangle. The Faroes are a small place and even three degrees of separation is a lot.

I hadn't watched the news that day but I quickly gathered that yesterday's *grindadráp*, on top of Erla Sivertsen's death, had made the subject of the Alliance the default conversation starter for a lot of people. For the rest – often older – the subject was like religion, politics and sex: not one to be raised in polite company. For those who did bring it up, though, the fact that I was a foreigner made me a general barometer of the outside world. They wanted my opinion, and even when it was equivocal they still seemed gratified when I said that, as far as I was aware, no one outside the islands really knew about the *grind* or the protest. It seemed to satisfy them just to know that their reputation wasn't being tarnished. I didn't like to say that for the islands to be tarnished, the outside world would first have to know that the Faroes existed.

About an hour after we'd arrived I lost Fríða in the way that you can do accidentally in a large gathering. Freed up from more introductions I wandered a little, exchanged an empty beer bottle for a full one and wandered some more. I ended up a little way out of the main hub, just watching until I spotted Fríða about halfway across the space. I was about to head in her direction when a guy in a blue jacket and crisp shirt approached me. His tie was loosened and he had a couple of days' worth of blond stubble.

"*Hey*," he said when he saw he'd caught my attention. "You're English, yes?"

"Yeah."

"I thought so. I saw you with Fríða a little while ago. I'm Jens Kjeld, by the way."

"Jan Reyna." It had become habit these days to pronounce it with the Y and not the hard J; I was getting used to it as much as saying *takk* and *ja* or *nei* in conversation.

"So, what do you think of all this – this *art*?" He made rabbit ears to show that he used the word loosely. "Will you buy any?"

I couldn't decide if it was just clumsiness to ask if I'd buy something he'd just derided, or whether it was arrogance in assuming I'd naturally share his assessment. I said, "There are a couple of pictures I like, but I'm not sure I'd like the price."

"So you're not here with a cheque already signed?"

"No, just to look."

"You might be wise. Most of this is just average – not bad, not outstanding."

Again, the slightly superior tone, but then he shifted to cast a look in Fríða's direction. "So, have you known Fríða long?" he asked.

I wasn't sure whether I disliked him for the directness or found it refreshing for the same reason, but I had a feeling it was going to be one or the other quite soon.

"Sort of," I said, just to show I wasn't a pushover.

"Ah. Are you being cagey?"

"No, not really. It's just a long story."

"That makes it sound interesting."

He was fixed on me now, with that focus that tells you you're not going to get away unless you make a point of being brusque. It might also be a pretty good indicator of how much he'd drunk, I decided.

"We're cousins," I said. "I knew her when we were kids but I hadn't seen her again until recently."

"Oh. Okay, now I'm confused. Your name is Jan – are you Faroese?"

"By birth, yes. Are you?"

He laughed. "Okay, tit for tat, yeh? Fair enough. Yes, I'm Faroese. I work for Faroil, I lived for ten years in the UK and I'm here because the company is a sponsor of the event, and because there is free food and drink. Cheers."

"*Skál.*"

He clinked his glass with the neck of my beer bottle, but I wasn't entirely misdirected.

"You missed out how you know Fríða," I said.

"Oh, yeh," he couldn't help another swift glance in her direction. "It's a small place, so… one tends to meet the same people. Especially at events like this."

Which wasn't an answer, but I'd decided I liked him well enough now, so I let it go for the moment.

"Listen," he said then. "You want a tip? Come over here." He gestured and moved, so I followed a few paces and he pointed out a landscape painting. "Buy that. It doesn't matter if you don't like it. I know for a fact that the artist – his name's Djurhuus – will be selling for five times today's price by the end of the year, maybe more."

I must have looked dubious because he shook his head. "I'm serious," he said. "There's a collector in New York who is just getting into Djurhuus in a big way. She may not buy up the smaller stuff like that one, but where she leads…"

"You mean Djurhuus will become fashionable."

"Sure. And he paints *very* slowly, so there is a limited stock, which means that when it starts to be sought after by others the price will go up more sharply. Supply and demand."

"So why don't you buy it?"

He shrugged. "I have four already – slightly bigger. It doesn't do to be greedy, does it?" He flagged down a waitress who was passing with a tray of drinks, knocked back the one he already had and took a fresh one. "Do you smoke?" he asked, patting himself down to locate a pack of Prince. "I need to breathe some pollutants."

"You go ahead," I told him. "I'll have a look at the Djurhuus."

"Good." He nodded. "Up to ten thousand krónur would be a bargain; up to fifteen would be a decent price. I wouldn't go more, though – unless you like it, of course."

With that he gave me a friendly smile and a wave of his cigarette pack and headed away towards the open fire doors. Nice enough guy, pissed as a newt.

I was still looking at the Djurhuus when Fríða found me again a few minutes later. By then I'd decided that, good investment or not, I didn't care for it much.

"Hey," she said, drifting in beside me. She had apple juice in her glass and she looped her free arm through mine, which was nice.

"Do you like this one?"

"It's okay," I said, aware that that was probably as damning as a no. "Do you?"

She considered it, then shook her head, unmoved. "Not so much."

"Your friend Jens Kjeld says it would be a good investment. Apparently he has insider knowledge."

"If he says so it's probably true."

"Even though he works for an oil company?"

344

"He looks after investments," she said. "He's very smart. Did he say anything else?"

I shook my head. "No, but the silence was deafening. And he knew where you were in the room most of the time."

"So you were being detective?" I couldn't sense how she felt about that.

"It was fairly obvious. Ex-boyfriend?"

"Why do you think ex?"

"I'm a detective."

She gave a dry laugh then. "Yeh. We dated about three years ago."

"And he's still carrying a torch?"

She took a second to work that one out, then shook her head. "I hope not, but it was a good thing for a while and he's a nice guy. So…"

She gave a matter-of-fact shrug, as if that laid it to rest. Sometimes she seemed very grown-up and comfortable with her choices. It was more than I felt most of the time, and I envied her.

The Djurhuus was late in the auction and went for 21,000 kr, maybe because someone knew what Jens Kjeld knew, or maybe just because by then there were only a few lots remaining for people to demonstrate the depths of their pockets.

I did bid, but not in person and not on the Djurhuus. I didn't trust my Faroese anywhere near enough to follow an auction, or to keep track of the price in krónur against that in sterling. Instead I registered a commission bid on a paired lot of two canvases about eight inches square, one showing a boathouse and the other the rocky harbour beside it.

The bidding in the room ran out 200 kr short of my limit, so I got them but didn't tell Fríða until I'd paid and collected them, now bubble-wrapped, and got them as far as the car. They were under my coat because it was raining and because I hadn't wanted to give them to her publicly. Now I handed them over in the glow of the courtesy light.

"I bought you something."

"Really?" she asked, as if she was genuinely puzzled either by the objects or the fact I was giving them to her; I couldn't tell which. She unwrapped one then the other before she spoke again. "Are you sure?" she asked, still seeming perplexed.

"You won't take any rent, so I'm hoping you weren't just being polite when you said you liked them."

"Well, they're not the Djurhuus…" she said somewhat hesitantly, then laughed when she saw she'd nearly caught me. "I'm never polite about art," she said then. "They're great. *Takk fyri*."

She leaned across and kissed my cheek warmly, then straightened up, handing the pictures to me so she could put the keys in the ignition.

"Of course, if they're rent you know what this means?" she said then.

"You'll have to declare them for tax?"

She chuckled and started the car. "No, but to be fair I'll have to let you stay for at least another week."

She cast me a sideways look, part grin, and pulled out of the parking space.

"Yeah, well about that…" I said. "I talked to my boss today."

"And he wants you to go back?"

"'Wants' is the wrong word," I said. "But I'll have to go anyway. I've used up my excuses, so I can't put it off any more. I have to be there next Tuesday."

She knew I'd been suspended and had asked me a little about it while I was laid up on her sofa with concussion ten days ago. She'd left it alone when she realised that I didn't want to go into details, though, and hadn't raised it since, which I appreciated.

Now she pulled out of the car park on to the ring road and let the subject hang for a few seconds.

"You've never told me how serious it is," she said.

I shrugged non-committally, but in the darkness I wasn't sure whether she saw it. "Serious enough, I suppose."

"But you don't want to tell me."

I almost did, but then I said, "No. It would only sound like I was justifying myself – or an apology. Which it wouldn't be. I didn't tell Hjalti Hentze for the same reason. Whatever I say, that's just my version and it's more complicated than that."

"Is it a criminal offence?" she asked. "Could you go to prison?"

"No. They call it *a breach of the standards of professional behaviour*, but that's just a catch-all. What it really means is that they think I did something I shouldn't have, but because they don't know for sure they have to do a dance to prove they're taking it seriously."

"So you *didn't* do it – whatever it was?" she asked.

347

"No, I did it," I said. "It just wasn't wrong, that's all."

She cast me a look. "In *your* opinion."

"Yeah, in my opinion," I said. "But it's the only one I care about – as far as that's concerned, anyway."

"Isn't that a bit arrogant? To think you know better than anyone else?"

"Maybe, but it's not meant to be," I said. "I just don't care what anyone else thinks – anyone else in the job – because I know the full circumstances and they don't."

I could tell she didn't like my answer – or maybe it was just the fact that I was refusing to admit that there could be a doubt.

"So will you tell them these circumstances when you go back?" she asked.

I shook my head. "I don't know yet. I'm still thinking about it because I'm not the only one involved – listen, let's change the subject, okay?"

"Okay," she said. Her tone was accepting, but it didn't fully convince me that I hadn't just put a damper on what should have been a better end to the evening.

40

Thursday/hósdagur

HENTZE WAS DEEPLY ASLEEP AND THE NOISE OF THE PHONE TOOK more than a minute to penetrate his consciousness. By then Sóleyg was also stirring. He felt her turn under the duvet and he muttered something soothing as he finally silenced the phone.

"Hold on," he said into the illuminated screen, as softly as he could.

The bedroom had grown chill. He scooped up his sweater from the chair as he padded to the door, cursed silently at its squeak, then went down the hall to the bathroom.

"Yeh, okay, who's this?" he said into the phone.

"Hjalti, it's Karl Atli Árting. Sorry to wake you. Do you need a minute?"

"No, go on, what's happened? What time is it?" His eyes were still blurred from sleep and without his reading glasses his watch hands were indecipherable.

"Ten after three. I'm out at Múli. There's been a fire – well, actually, there still is a bit – but there's also a body. It's in the house."

349

"Bloody hell." Said with more irritation than he meant. Hentze rubbed one eye with the back of his hand.

"I wasn't sure if I should call Ári Niclasen, but Hans said it'd be you."

"Yeh, no, it is," Hentze said. "Okay, listen, have the firefighters said anything – I mean they're sure it *is* a body, not someone hurt?"

Even as he said it he knew his brain was still lagging a step behind his mouth.

"Oh yeh, no doubt about that."

"Okay, I'll come out. Just leave everything as it is and try to keep the damn firemen from doing anything they don't need to. I'll be with you— I don't know, as soon as I can. Okay?"

"Okay, thanks, Hjalti."

Hentze rang off and stood for a moment to gather himself. He needed to wake up and he contemplated taking a shower, but he knew the noise of the pump would disturb Sóleyg. He settled instead for scrubbing tepid water on his face in the basin and brushing his teeth. Afterwards he crept back to the bedroom. It was harder to see in the dark now that he'd been in the light, but he managed to locate his clothes on the chair. He didn't dress but made for the door again.

"Are you going out?" Sóleyg asked, voice blurred from sleep.

"Yeh, to a fire. Go back to sleep. I'll call you at breakfast time if I'm not back."

"Is anyone hurt?"

"No, I don't think so." He leaned down and kissed her on the soft warmness of her upturned cheek. "Go back to sleep."

* * *

The only other vehicles on the road were a few Samskip and Blue Water trucks moving containers between Tórshavn and Klaksvík. The previous day's mist had been cleared by the rain and a westerly breeze in the evening, but now it was still and clear again and occasionally Hentze got a view of the moon between the dark peaks of the mountain valleys. Not a bad time of the day to be out and about, although it was a long time since he'd worked shifts. Except for Fridays and Saturdays this time of the night was generally peaceful.

He had the radio on but turned low. He sipped from a Thermos mug of coffee and thought back over yesterday and whether he'd lost more than he'd gained by getting himself thrown off the Sivertsen case.

He'd known it was a provocative strategy to try and show that Erla had been involved with the security services, but in some ways he supposed he could count the move as a success. There was no longer any doubt that Erla Sivertsen *had* been involved in some sort of clandestine activity, but whether that proved it was related to her murder was another matter.

At least Remi Syderbø now knew that there should be a new light on the case, but if the man Munk was able to call the shots and effectively ban any further investigation of the Alliance, what then? If Remi's hands were tied, what good did it do?

It stank. National security or not, in Hentze's view the interference of people with the apparent authority to suppress the truth – or at least, the seeking of truth – couldn't be right.

Without transparency how was anyone to know that the interference was justified? And besides, who were the Danes to say that their concerns trumped those of the Faroes? Such attitudes put wind in the sails of the independence movement, of which Hentze didn't count himself a member, but still…

All of which was why he'd asked Annika to check on the car used by the man at Hoyvík. Not so much in the expectation of learning anything of merit, but in order to show – if only to himself – that he hadn't been entirely cowed by the order to leave things alone.

Of course, Annika being Annika, she had gone further than he'd wanted; not only finding out that the car was a rental, but also getting details of the hirer. Hentze hoped there'd be no comeback from that, especially as the information took him no further. The car had been rented to a Dane called Lund with a Copenhagen address but there was no way to check beyond that without alerting Munk to the fact that he *was* checking. And in any event, he knew Lund's details were probably false.

So there it was. He had been stopped and he could see no way, short of direct and certainly futile disobedience, to go forward. Leave it to others, he told himself; leave it to Remi and Berg to fight it out – or not. It had been taken out of his hands, but it still stank.

It took him just over an hour to reach the turn-off from route 70 for Múli and then he drove more cautiously because the track was uneven and full of potholes, and because the road edges were unmarked. It wasn't until he had passed the halfway point and rounded an outcrop of land that he finally saw the lights from the fire trucks in the distance: points of brilliance, but still small and some way below.

When the rough gravel track finally gave out and became nothing but a pair of ruts Hentze drove until he found a flat patch of ground, then pulled the car on to it, out of the way. From the passenger seat he picked up a long Maglite torch, then took a pair of surgical gloves from the box in the glove compartment. He didn't bother with anything else. There'd be time enough for evidence-gathering later, once he'd assessed the scene.

Using the Maglite he followed the track until the torch became unnecessary in the lights of the emergency vehicles. He passed a police patrol car, pulled on to the verge, and then the line of fire trucks – three of them, nose to tail – brought up short of the buildings by the narrowness of the path.

The burned house was on the higher side of the track. There were no living flames in what remained of the building by now. The semi-acrid smell of damp smoke mixed with burned plastic infused the air, and grey wisps of smoke caught the spotlights as they rose from charred wood, waiting to be doused by the last two firefighters still damping the structure down.

Hentze navigated carefully over the red hoses that snaked underfoot until he had passed all the vehicles and found Officer Karl Atli Árting with the chief fire officer – a large man called Jónas Simonsen, the only professional amongst the volunteer firefighters. They exchanged greetings, then turned to look at the house.

"Is there any indication of how it started?" Hentze asked.

"No, there's no way to tell at the moment," Simonsen said. "It'll have to wait for daylight. The victim's on the first floor, the room to the left."

"Can I have a look?"

"From a ladder, yeh, I think so. I'll get someone to fix one up for you."

"Thanks."

Simonsen trudged off and Hentze looked to Karl Atli, a wiry little man, despite the bulk of his police uniform. "Who called it in, do you know?"

"Someone from Viðareiði, I think," Karl Atli said. "They saw the flames across the sound." He gestured along the track. "There's a car parked back there, beyond the last shed. I've checked on the owner. It's a Boas Eli Justesen from Fuglafjørður."

The name surprised Hentze. "Justesen? Are you sure?"

"Yes. Why?"

Hentze shook his head. "No, nothing. Someone mentioned his name the other day regarding something else, that's all. I think he owns this property."

"Yeh? Well the body could be him then: his car, his house. That'd make sense."

Hentze nodded. "Could you do me a favour and ask a patrol car to check on Justesen's home and see if he's there?"

While Karl Atli went off to do that Simonsen came back to say that a ladder was in place, and he and Hentze made their way towards the house. Against the darkness and with the stark shadows cast by the floodlights there was an illusion that the upper storeys might still be there, just not illuminated. It wasn't until Hentze looked more carefully that he realised that between the stone gable ends where the upper floors would have been there was, in fact, a void. On the right-hand side a blackened chimneystack and a few vertical timbers remained; to the left a single sheet of roofing tin clung to a gable end. The rest of the roof had collapsed and now its sheets lay scattered and overleafed with each other, sometimes caught on beams or masonry.

The ladder was propped against the stone wall of the undercroft with a firefighter to steady it. Hentze unfastened his coat, gripped the Maglite and climbed the rungs carefully until his head was about a metre above the lower wall. He paused for a moment to change his grip, then shone the torch in, illuminating the charred remains of the floorboards.

"It's over to the right," Simonsen called up. "About halfway back."

Hentze shifted the torch and then saw the shape of a head and shoulders, an arched back and the rigid angle of an arm. For the moment he was glad the body was facing away from him, though the cindered remains of hair adhering to the browned skin over the skull were enough to forewarn him of what the body would look like.

He adjusted his stance on the ladder, prompting an immediate call from Simonsen below. "Don't go any further."

"Don't worry, I don't intend to."

Hentze swept the torch beam across the space for a last look, then started down the ladder. "What can we do about examination and recovery of the body?" he asked Simonsen when he was on the ground again.

"Nothing until we've done a proper assessment of the structure and decided what we need to make safe. The floor's not so good and the gable walls could collapse."

"So, the morning at the earliest?"

"At the earliest."

Which meant that there was nothing Hentze or anyone else could usefully do now, so after instructing Karl Atli to stay at the scene until someone from the day shift took over, Hentze turned his car round on the narrow track and set off for home.

Halfway there he got a call from Rúni Jensen to say that Boas Justesen wasn't at home, but had been seen by his tenants leaving the house in his car at about nine o'clock the previous evening. Hentze thanked Rúni and decided that on the balance of probabilities, it was likely to be Boas Justesen's body in the ruins of the house. Which meant that tomorrow – today – things might be simpler when it came to identification. Simpler was good.

41

HENTZE AWOKE TO SÓLEYG'S HAND ON HIS SHOULDER. IT WAS just after seven – already late by his standards – so he didn't bother to rush. Instead he showered, dressed in a better selection of clothes than he'd grabbed in the dark, then ate breakfast with Sóleyg. It wasn't something they usually did during the week, which made it a pleasant change.

He'd arrived back in Hvítanes just as the faintest light was starting to show in the sky: too early to start the day, too late to get a good night's sleep. He let himself into the house quietly, found a blanket in the linen cupboard and wrapped himself in it, still clothed, to try and catch at least a little more sleep on the sofa. But his brain had refused to shut down and he was plagued by images and disconnected thoughts to the point where he was ready to admit defeat and get up again. The next thing he knew, Sóleyg was gently shaking him.

After breakfast he drove to the station. It was eight thirty by then and he was aware that there was still a certain wilfulness in refusing to hurry. In fact, he wondered if his deliberate break from routine was really a way of thumbing his nose at Andrias Berg. Not that Berg would even notice.

Still, to Hentze it seemed as if he'd crossed some kind of Rubicon in the last twenty-four hours. The only question now was where did he go from here?

On Thursdays it was usual for CID to have a morning meeting, but when Hentze strolled down the third-floor corridor the conference room was empty. He doubted that he'd missed the whole thing, so he guessed that it had been cancelled or postponed, which probably meant that Remi Syderbø and Ári Niclasen were otherwise engaged. This turned out to be the case when he got to his office – after a diversion to make coffee – and checked his email inbox. There was a round-robin email from Ári saying the usual meeting had been postponed until tomorrow. No explanation.

For ten minutes or so, Hentze occupied himself with the routine housekeeping tasks presented by the overnight and early morning emails and then he called Jónas Simonsen to ask about the state of the building at Múli.

"I know you need to get in there to remove the body," Simonsen said. "So I've got the boys to support the floor as best we can. To be honest, though, the whole structure's pretty unstable. I wouldn't want to vouch for the walls in a strong wind."

"Is it windy there at the moment?"

"No, it's quite calm."

"Okay, in that case I'll come out as soon as I've got the equipment I'll need. I'll see you in about an hour."

During the call Remi Syderbø had opened the door. He had a manila folder tucked under one arm and Hentze could guess what it might contain.

"You're going out?" Remi asked as Hentze hung up the phone.

"There was a fire at Múli last night. One dead. The building was too unsafe to recover the body but it should be okay now."

"Yeh, I saw the log," Remi said. Clearly this wasn't the reason for his visit. He took a step further in and half closed the door.

"We have the first set of results from the technical lab," he said, touching the folder under his arm.

"Good, it's about time." Hentze drank the last of his coffee: just the dregs, more or less cold.

"Would you like to know what they said?"

Hentze shook his head. "It's not my concern."

"Oh for God's sake, Hjalti, don't sulk," Remi said irritably. "I'm not— Don't tell me you aren't interested."

"Of course I'm interested," Hentze acknowledged. He put his mug down. "Can I speak freely?"

"I thought you already were."

Hentze ignored the tone. "Yesterday Andrias Berg made it very clear that I'm not to be involved with the Erla Sivertsen investigation, which is fine. But in that case you shouldn't come in here like a quay hen, flashing your legs and asking if I'm interested. The security services man, Munk, said there had been enough silly games. I agree. So, if you don't mind I'll stick to investigating the fire and the body at Múli. Unless you'd like me to leave that alone, too; which would also be fine, and in that case I'll go back to the burglaries in Klaksvík because God knows I've seen enough bodies recently."

For a second or two Remi Syderbø's eyes hardened behind the lenses of his glasses and it seemed as if he might finally react to this uncharacteristic diatribe. In the end, though, he opted for a stiff nod.

"All right, then," he said. "You'd better carry on with the fire investigation and let me know what you've got at the end of the day. In the meantime it will be common knowledge soon anyway, so you might as well know now that Ári's on his way to Sandoy to re-arrest Finn Sólsker. When he gets back Finn will be charged with Erla Sivertsen's murder, based on the forensic results."

Hentze considered that for a moment, then said, "I see. Thank you for telling me."

"Believe me, it was no pleasure," Remi Syderbø said, then he turned and left Hentze's office. The manila file stayed under his arm.

Had he gone too far, Hentze wondered. Probably. Still, it was another mark of the line he had crossed that he felt no regret. Some things should be said. Some things should not be left to pass. Maybe he had caught Jan Reyná's disease.

On the ferry from Gamlarætt, Dánjal Michelsen watched the most southerly point of the island of Hestur go past the window. Wisps of grey cloud licked down the slope towards Skútin, and Dánjal ran through a mental list of the birdlife it was possible to see there. Bird watching was something he greatly enjoyed. He was not enjoying anything else about this trip: not the reason for it, and certainly not Ári Niclasen's company. The only thing to be grateful for was the fact that Ári seemed to have more than enough tasks to occupy himself on his iPhone.

Dánjal knew that ever since they'd brought Høgni Joensen in for questioning, Ári had come to view him with some mistrust. Rightly so. Dánjal had had no great faith in Ári's judgement since the Tummas Gramm case, but after seeing him bully Høgni as he had, Dánjal had lost what little respect he'd had left for his boss. If Hjalti hadn't warned him against it he would have taken it further – to Remi – and now that Hjalti had been dumped off the case Dánjal was left feeling isolated and uncertain.

Because of this he'd said little during the case conference in the incident room when Remi and Ári discussed the forensic reports. DNA sequencing had matched the semen found during Erla Sivertsen's post-mortem to Finn Sólsker, so there was no doubt that Finn had had sexual relations with Erla shortly before her death. In light of his constant denials of this, Finn must now be viewed as an even more likely suspect in her death. That was Ári's strongly made contention – why else would Finn lie so persistently? And in the absence of any contradictory evidence, Remi Syderbø had concurred, so now Dánjal and Ári were on their way to re-arrest Finn.

But Dánjal wasn't happy. It wasn't that he disagreed with the evidence, but he had doubts about Ári's conclusion. Sure, Finn must have been having an affair with Erla, but did that mean he'd killed her? Dánjal didn't think so and he wondered if either Remi or Ári had ever cheated on their wives. He thought not. Ári wasn't imaginative enough and Remi was too cold a fish. But Dánjal had, and it was something that still filled him with shame.

It had happened three years ago, on two consecutive nights while he'd been in Denmark for training. Thank God the woman he'd shared those nights with had not turned out to be a home wrecker. He hadn't heard from her since, but when he thought of what *might* have happened, Dánjal still got cold sweats. He could have lost his wife, kids and home for the sake of a couple of fucks.

So his unfaithfulness was a secret he'd take to his grave. Even if he was accused of murder he wasn't sure he would admit to an alibi of adulterous sex. All of which meant that Dánjal understood why Finn Sólsker might deny an affair with Erla Sivertsen, even when told he was suspected of killing her. And in Dánjal's estimation what that denial didn't do was place Finn's guilt beyond doubt as Ári Niclasen seemed to think that it did.

Once the ferry docked at Skopun it took less than ten minutes to drive to Sandur, slowing down on the narrow streets through the village, avoiding a couple of wandering dogs as they descended the concrete ramp to the harbourside.

Finn Sólsker's boat, the *Kári Edith*, was moored beyond the fish-processing building at the far end of the quay, between a larger steel vessel and the ferry *Sildberin*, which made the infrequent journey to Skúgvoy. Dánjal brought the car to a halt a few metres from the edge of the quay and almost before he'd switched off the ignition Ári Niclasen was opening his door.

There was no sign of life on the other two vessels, but the *Kári Edith*'s engine was ticking over and Høgni Joensen had stopped to look up from unhitching a stern line from a mooring ring.

When he saw who it was, Høgni clearly felt several conflicting urges to move in different directions, all of which resulted in no movement at all. As if to confirm that that was the right thing to do, Dánjal made a gesture that Høgni should stay put while Ári Niclasen approached the edge of the quay.

The relative heights of the boat and the quay meant there was a good half-metre drop to the *Kári Edith*'s deck, over side rails and between the line haulers. For a second Ári Niclasen hesitated, then turned and clambered down awkwardly, due in part to his attempts to keep his suit from touching the rails.

His feet had barely hit the deck when the door of the wheelhouse banged open and Finn Sólsker came out. He was dressed in waders and an oil-stained sweater.

"Get off my boat," Finn demanded before Niclasen could speak. "Unless you want a job on the lines."

Ári straightened up. "You need to come with us," he said. "Switch off the engine and come to the car."

"Fuck you," Finn said, his stance becoming more resolute. "I'm going fishing. You've already cost me two days when I could've been working. If you want to talk to me you can wait till we get back." He turned to look for Høgni who was still at the stern line. "Cast off, for Christ's sake. Don't just stand there!"

"Listen—" Ári started, but Finn cut him short.

"You've got ten seconds to get off or you'll be with us all day. Please yourself."

He started towards the bow and the rope there but Niclasen went after him and grabbed his arm. In an instant Finn Sólsker spun on his heel and swung a solid right hook, which sent Niclasen sprawling on the slippery deck.

For a moment everything was frozen, as if no one had expected what had just happened, but then Dánjal was first out of the traps.

"Shit! Finn, are you mad? Stand still!" With an agile jump Dánjal was down on the deck, putting himself between Finn and Ári, still supine on the deck. "Okay, that's enough," Dánjal said, even though Finn had made no further movement. "You're under arrest for assault. Turn around, hands behind your back."

Finn only reacted when he saw Dánjal pull the handcuffs from his belt. "All right, you don't need those," he said.

"Yeh, yeh, I do," Dánjal said. "Turn around now." He glanced at Høgni who was now standing over them, still on the quay. "Stay out of this, Høgni, it doesn't concern you, all right?"

The last thing Dánjal wanted was Høgni Joensen weighing in. Luckily, however, Høgni seemed even more thrown by the situation than Ári and he just stood looking down as Dánjal fastened the cuffs round Finn's wrists.

42

ÁRI NICLASEN HAD BEEN DESPATCHED TO THE HOSPITAL TO have his elbow examined. He'd hit it on the deck of the boat when he fell and was complaining of pain and pins and needles when he moved it. He was also developing an amazing black eye, so Remi Syderbø had instructed him to attend the emergency department. It was not a request.

In some ways it helped matters that Ári was unavailable to interview Finn Sólsker. But even before that, Remi had decided that a different approach might be in everyone's best interests. Perhaps contrary to appearances, Remi Syderbø was more in touch than people imagined and he had picked up on the growing groundswell of concern about Ári's handling of the Sivertsen case. He also knew of Dánjal Michelsen's disquiet, and Hjalti Hentze's misgivings were more than evident if you knew how to read the signs.

All of this gave Remi Syderbø cause for concern, but not half as much as the involvement of the man, Munk, from the security services. Remi didn't like the feeling that his instructions from the Commander – about what direction to push the case in and who to take off it – were being driven by motives unconnected with the best interests of the investigation. He also knew that information was being withheld from him and that, by implication, he wasn't deemed trustworthy.

In that respect, Remi thought, he and Hjalti Hentze were probably on the same track, which had made it all the more irritating that Hentze had refused his olive branch that morning. But then – phlegmatic as he was – even Hentze wasn't immune to bruised pride.

Thinking this through as he watched a boat heading for Nólsoy, Remi Syderbø made a decision. He turned in his chair when Dánjal Michelsen knocked on his office door and came in.

"How well do you know Finn Sólsker?" he asked as he waved Dánjal to a chair.

"Not very well," Dánjal said, with just a touch of caution. "Just in passing."

"Because of Hjalti?"

"Yeh, I suppose so."

"And at the boat, when you arrested him, he didn't try to take a swing at you, too?"

"No." Dánjal shook his head, hesitated for a second, then said, "For what it's worth, I think the only reason Finn hit Ári was because he'd reached the end of his rope and he snapped. He must have been under a lot of strain for the past few days and when Ári said he had to come back with us…"

"Maybe," Remi said, not convinced either way. "But if he's got a temper that's something we should bear in mind. Anyway, I want you to take the interview."

"Er, okay. Just me?"

Remi nodded. "I think it needs a change of tack. The Prosecutor's already agreed that we should charge him with Erla's murder, and that's what we'll do after this interview – unless he can come up with a better explanation of events than he's given until now. And 'no comment' won't cut it any more. He needs to realise that and to tell us – you – the truth."

"Okay," Dánjal said, still slightly surprised that Remi Syderbø wasn't going to take part. "I'll see what I can do."

"Take your time," Remi said as Dánjal stood up. "You don't have to go straight for the jugular." He didn't add "this time" but he knew Dánjal heard it.

"Okay," Dánjal said.

"Have you spoken to Hjalti today?"

"No, not today."

"Right." Remi left it at that.

At Múli the fire tenders had gone, but in their place were several cars and a flatbed truck from a scaffolding company. Four men in fire officer uniforms were stacking corrugated roof sheets on a patch of grass, but the activity gave the impression that it was merely to pass the time rather than being essential.

Hentze and Mikkjal Godtfred left the car and walked down the track that led to the burned house. Mikkjal was in his forties, slightly scruffy in a recently-divorced-man sort of way, but like a third of the Faroes CID personnel he'd had extra training in a specialist field, and in his case it was fire: its causes and effects, accidental and deliberate. That was one reason Hentze had brought him along; the other was that this was Mikkjal's first day back from holiday and he'd had no involvement in the Erla Sivertsen case.

Squeezing past the scaffolding truck they found Jónas Simonsen drinking tea from a Thermos as he gazed dubiously at the remains of the house. If anything, the building looked even more gutted than it had in the dark and from the front it reminded Hentze of a child's doll's house, opened up to reveal the inner structure. Modern timber-framed houses would have had fire retardant boarding, but this one looked over a hundred years old and the timbers were probably resinous pine. It had been a blaze waiting to happen, Jónas Simonsen told them, and Mikkjal Godtfred concurred as they stood together assessing the wreckage.

"So is it safe now?" Hentze asked.

"Well, I wouldn't call it *safe*," Simonsen said. "But it's *safer* than it was. We've supported the main joists of the first floor so you can walk on it without it collapsing, but everything above that…"

"You mean it could still come down?"

"Put it this way: if you didn't have to go in to recover the body I wouldn't let anyone near it. I think it should be demolished – especially the gable ends – so it doesn't come down unexpectedly. You'll be probably be safe enough, but I wouldn't spend any unnecessary time on it, or do any tap-dance routines."

A faint gust of damp wind blew in along the track. Hentze cast a distrustful look at the stone end walls of the house. "We'd better get on with it, then," he said.

* * *

Mikkjal and Hentze put on forensic suits – as much to protect their clothes as to avoid contamination – then climbed up the ladder. Hentze went first, stepping gingerly off the ladder and on to the charred wooden floor above the undercroft. Despite Simonsen's assurances that it wouldn't collapse he had no desire to tempt fate.

Mikkjal followed him up and after he'd taken video and photographs of the scene they moved to the body, which lay on its side. The clothes on the top half of the body were scorched and badly burned, but oddly the jeans and shoes seemed relatively unscathed. They were male clothes, however, and despite the fact that the facial features had been distorted by the flames and the heat it was still possible to make out where sideburns and whiskers would have been.

While Mikkjal took more photos Hentze considered the dead man's frame against the information from Boas Justesen's arrest record. Both the height and weight – 175 cm, 60 kilos – seemed about right. Added to the fact that the house was Justesen's property, that his car was parked by the outbuildings, and that he hadn't been home since last night, Hentze was left with little significant doubt that he was looking at all that was left of Boas Justesen. It wasn't conclusive – there would have to be dental identification for that – but for the time being he was content to accept the obvious conclusion.

After a couple of minutes Mikkjal announced himself satisfied that he had everything he needed, so they spread a sheet of plastic on the floor beside the body. Mikkjal went to the feet and Hentze moved around to the torso, preparing to lift the body by the shoulders.

"Up, across and down," Hentze said. "Ready?"

The action was made easier by the fact that the body was in rigor and didn't sag, but during the process Hentze spotted something and now kneeled closer to look, carefully folding back a piece of brittle fabric to expose the man's neck. There – although charred and blackened – was a piece of blue nylon rope about a centimetre thick. It appeared to encircle the neck and a loose end about fifteen centimetres long was part-welded to the lower shoulder.

"What do you make of this?" Hentze asked, beckoning Mikkjal closer.

"Looks like some kind of noose," Mikkjal said, squinting. "Like you'd hang yourself with."

Hentze looked for a knot and found it – so he thought – under Justesen's collar at the back of his neck. It was hard to be sure what sort of knot it was because the nylon was partly melted, but in Hentze's limited experience of hangings – three in twenty-odd years – all had had the knot in roughly the same place.

"What do you think?" Mikkjal asked when Hentze straightened. From his tone he seemed to expect Hentze to pronounce a verdict.

"It could be a suicide," Hentze said. "I've seen others like it. Let's wait till we hear what the pathologist says. Shall we get him bagged up and moved? Less weight on this floor would make me feel better."

* * *

"We know you had sex with her, Finn. The DNA proves it. That's all they need."

It was just the two of them in the room, with the digital audio recorder sitting on the edge of the table where Dánjal Michelsen hoped it wouldn't be a distraction.

Finn Sólsker sat with his arms folded. He said nothing. There was a small chip in the varnish of the table and his gaze was fixed on it. Finn had not raised his eyes since Dánjal had sat down.

Dánjal let the silence continue for a few seconds, then he opened a manila folder and took out two photographs. He placed them side by side over the chip in the varnish.

"If you did this, just say so. If not..."

There was a slight movement of Finn Sólsker's head – perhaps a shake, but perhaps just the movement as he looked at the photographs. Nothing more.

"Okay then," Dánjal said. He retrieved the photographs, then placed them back in the folder. He stood up.

"I didn't kill her."

Dánjal paused. "Do you want to say what did happen?" He barely placed any stress on the word *did*, not wanting to make it sound like a demand.

Nothing.

"It was an affair?"

A moment, then Finn nodded – once.

"Okay," Dánjal said. And then because he couldn't think of anything better, "I understand."

He put the folder back on the desk and sat down again.

43

ONCE JUSTESEN'S RIGID BODY HAD BEEN REMOVED, MIKKJAL
Godtfred started a step-by-step examination of the
woodwork and burned contents of the room. With nothing
much to contribute to that Hentze made his own appraisal
of the wrecked house. He considered the mechanism of
hanging and assessed the original height of the room. It was
hard to do given that most of the ceiling above had collapsed
or burned away, but he estimated it had not been an especially
high room and that a man of average height would have had
about thirty centimetres of head clearance. Not exactly a
great amount of space to hang yourself in. Still, people could
hang themselves from doorknobs and shower rails if they
were determined enough.

He moved carefully towards the back of the building,
trying to assess which part of the floor above – if it had
remained in place – would have been over the spot where
Justesen's body had lain. He moved delicately around canted
beams, peering around and underneath them until finally,
after about five minutes' searching, he spotted something
protruding from a charred joist.

It was a blackened metal hook and had the look of something that might have been handmade by a blacksmith: sturdy and, by Hentze's estimation, capable of supporting a decent weight. When he looked more closely it seemed that he could make out the residue of melted plastic.

"Mikkjal, I think you should have a look at this," he called.

Mikkjal wanted to remove the hook intact by cutting it out of the beam, but Jónas Simonsen declared it too dangerous to go sawing through timbers. There was no way to know how precariously balanced other things were above it. Instead, Mikkjal had to satisfy himself with close-up photographs and scrapings of the residue on the hook. He declared himself happy enough, though.

"If this residue turns out to be the same nylon as the rope round his neck it'll make some sense of things," he told Hentze, once they were well away from the beam.

"In what way?"

"Well, did you notice how the upper part of the body was more burned and smoke-blackened than the lower part? His legs especially."

"I just thought it meant part of him was closer to the blaze than the rest."

"Yeh, it does," Mikkjal confirmed. "But heat travels upwards and away from the source unless it's confined or has no other fuel to go to. So, if Justesen hanged himself from that hook before the fire started, the heat would have risen and spread out across the ceiling. Imagine an upside-down waterfall. That would account for the fact that there's more burning to the upper part of the body, which takes place until the rope melts and the body falls to the floor. By then the fire's got hold of the ceiling beams and the wooden floor above and keeps moving upwards. That's also why there's not much damage to the undercroft."

"So you think the fire started here, on this level, not below?" Hentze asked.

"I think so. On a sofa of some sort. Perhaps over here."

Mikkjal moved to a spot where a pile of ash lay in a roughly rectangular outline. The remains of the sofa were so badly burned it was almost impossible to tell what it had been, but a few metal springs gave them a clue.

"I still need to take samples," Mikkjal said. "But if you look at it in the context of everything else it seems to me that's the seat of the fire. Was Justesen a smoker, do you know?"

"No, I don't know. Why?"

Mikkjal squatted and used his pen to point out a soot-blackened glass dish in the ash of the sofa. "That's an ashtray," he said. "And here…" He stepped back a short distance and pointed to a couple of smoke-browned spirit bottles. "Smoking, drinking, old sofa… At least a third of all household fires are started by fallen cigarettes."

Hentze weighed it up. "So what do you think – that he comes out here to commit suicide and hangs himself after a last cigarette? And then, by chance, the cigarette falls on to the sofa and starts a blaze."

"It doesn't have to be by chance," Mikkjal said. "He might have kicked the ashtray over when he was hanging: perhaps if he panicked. He might even have set the fire on purpose just before he hanged himself. I saw a report on a similar case about a year ago in Sweden or Finland – I forget which. Apparently the guy didn't want his wife or kids to come home and find his body hanging, so he started a fire in one room, then went next door and strung himself up."

"Fantastic," Hentze said drily. "So not only is he dead but the family's left homeless as well." He shook his head, then his phone rang. It was Annika.

"I thought you'd want to know that Finn's been arrested," she said. It sounded as if she was moderating her voice so she wasn't overheard.

"Thanks. Remi said he would be."

"Yeh, well it wasn't so straightforward," Annika said. "He hit Ári."

"Are you serious?"

"Yeh. Ári's gone to hospital with an injured elbow."

"So Finn's being held for assault as well now?"

"Yeh."

Hentze could hear the discomfort in Annika's voice, perhaps at the conflict of loyalties between duty and friendship. "Okay, thanks for letting me know. I'll see you later."

He rang off, then looked towards Mikkjal. "Listen, unless you need me I'm going to go and check out Justesen's car."

"No, go ahead," Mikkjal told him. "I'll be a while yet."

Dánjal Michelsen knew very well that sometimes, once they've passed the point of acknowledging a truth, people will talk as if a tap has been turned on. Finn Sólsker wasn't like that, however. What he said came as slow droplets, one at a time, forced through tightly sealed valves. Whether it was shame or the scrutiny that bothered him, Dánjal couldn't tell. At a guess it was somewhere in between: perhaps the embarrassment of a strong man having to confess to a weakness, to the fact that he had no control over certain things, and that one of them was his feelings for Erla Sivertsen. Dánjal had had no such feelings for the woman he'd been unfaithful with, but he understood just the same.

After more than an hour and a half Dánjal called a halt. Until then he'd been reluctant to pause in case the slow trickle of information dried up altogether and couldn't be restarted, but by the end of that time he knew as much as he needed. He had taken each drop of Finn's explanation, examined it, questioned it and finally he had enough. If Finn Sólsker had killed Erla Sivertsen then Dánjal was going to quit CID and go back to traffic.

Once Finn had been taken to the holding cell with a coffee and a sandwich, Dánjal quickly collated what had been said and went to find Remi Syderbø. He didn't look to see if Ári Niclasen was back yet, nor did he care. He hoped Ári had been given sick leave for a week – or better, two.

In the office next to the incident room Remi took a seat as Dánjal stood by the whiteboards.

"Finn admits the affair," he told Syderbø. "It had been going on for the last four or five weeks."

"No surprise there," Remi said. "So what about Saturday night?"

"He says Erla called him at just after seven on Saturday night to say she'd be on the next ferry: that's the 19:15 from

Gamlarætt. She had her car and they arranged to meet at a layby beside route 30 next to Norðara Hálsavatn lake. Finn says he was there first and when Erla arrived she left her car and he drove them up the track towards the sheds at Hamarspjalli. He parked in a sort of old quarry pit."

"So they couldn't be seen from the road?" Remi asked.

"I guess so. I don't know the place, but on the map it looks secluded and it would have been dark by then."

Remi squinted at the timeline on the board. "So that would be what – about eight o'clock? Maybe a bit before. How long does he say they were together?"

"About an hour. They had sex – outside, he says – and afterwards they talked in the car. He says Erla wanted to get the nine thirty ferry back from Skopun because she had some photographs she needed to edit and put up on the AWCA website. He also says they had a bit of a row about that. Maybe 'row' is too strong a word for it: 'disagreement' was the word he used. He said that she was helping the Alliance tell lies about the *grind* on the website rather than showing the truth. She disagreed."

Remi considered that for a moment. "It's not the strongest of motives to kill someone."

"No, well, he says that when he took her back to her car in the lay-by and she went off for the ferry he thought they'd parted on bad terms. He sat around thinking about it, then after a few minutes he went after her. He caught up with her in the car park before the ferry arrived and they walked to the harbour and made up. Then the ferry arrived and Erla got in her car and drove on board. He says that was the last time he saw her. After that he drove out to Sandur and spent a few minutes on his boat before going home just before ten."

"Hold on." Remi shifted. "Why did he go to the boat? If he was at the ferry quay his house was just up the road."

"I asked him the same thing," Dánjal said. "Eventually he admitted it was so that when he got home he'd have engine oil on his hands as if he'd been working on the boat."

"Right. The alibi for the wife." Remi frowned and looked at the timeline again.

"What does he say about her coat being in his shed? How does he account for that?"

Dánjal shook his head. "He can't. Like before, he says he has no idea how it got there. He claims Erla didn't go near Sandur that night and he's positive she had the coat with her when she left him because it was raining and she'd put it on to walk round the harbour."

Remi rubbed the side of his chin. "You know what Ári would say if he was here, don't you? The Prosecutor will say the same thing."

"Yeh," Dánjal said flatly. "That he could still have killed her between eight o'clock and ten and taken her body to Húsavík."

Remi nodded. "We've got nothing to prove that she *was* on the nine thirty ferry back to Gamlaraett, and the fact that her car was found in the car park at Skopun suggests she never left the island. And Sólsker's also admitting they had an argument."

"Yeh, I know," Dánjal said. He could sense the balance of Remi's opinion shifting. His decision now was whether to go with the flow or to say what he thought. He said, "The thing is, though, why would Finn mention an argument if it wasn't true? He must know it wouldn't help his case, so why raise it? He'd say everything between them was fine, wouldn't he?" He shook his head. "No, to me it rings true. And there *is* an alternative."

"Oh? What's that?"

Dánjal rifled through a folder and came up with a sheet of paper: a print-out of the Strandsfaraskip ferry timetable. Four sailings were highlighted in orange. "If Erla *did* get the nine thirty ferry as Finn says, then she'd have been back in Tórshavn about ten fifteen. So, if she was killed at some point in the next hour – between, say, ten and eleven thirty – it's possible that someone could have taken her body back to Sandoy on the last boat at eleven forty-five."

Remi assessed the times for a moment. "Okay, just say you're right. That would mean the killer would have been stranded on Sandoy until the first ferry on Sunday morning. And on top of that, *who* would he be? We either have Finn Sólsker, who was having an affair with Erla and could have had any number of motives for killing her, *or* we have nothing: no other viable suspect; no one who even *looks* suspicious."

"Maybe not yet. But how far have we looked? Since Ári—" Dánjal broke off, corrected himself. "I mean, once Finn looked like a suspect we didn't really consider anyone else, did we?"

He fell silent. For several seconds Remi didn't meet his eye, but instead seemed to run over the points on the whiteboards again, as if matching something to them in his head. Finally, though, he drew a dissatisfied breath and looked at Dánjal.

"So you don't think Finn did it." A statement, not a question.

Dánjal shook his head. "No."

Remi's lips tightened. Then he stood up. "All right. I need to talk to the Commander. In the meantime we can hold Finn on the assault charge: that's good till tomorrow." He turned towards the door. "Don't wander off, I might want you. And don't discuss this with anyone else, okay? And I *mean* no one, understood?"

44

BY THE TIME MIKKJAL GODTFRED HAD FINISHED COLLECTING samples and examining the undercroft it was well past midday. And because he wanted to get back to Tórshavn to start on his report as soon as possible, Mikkjal said he'd go with the private ambulance that had arrived to transport Justesen's body to the mortuary. It left Hentze free to do as he pleased, and given his need for coffee and something to eat he drove straight to Fuglafjørður and Muntra, the restaurant overlooking the harbour.

As he'd hoped, there were several occupied tables – mostly men from the boats or the harbourside businesses. One or two were familiar to him and he exchanged a few nods and greetings as he passed, but didn't engage in conversation.

With a plate of beef stew and a stick of bread, he settled himself at a table by a window and ate hungrily for several minutes, interspersing that with sips of coffee. Then, with his immediate requirements satisfied, he finally allowed his gaze to wander around the restaurant. As he'd hoped, this didn't go unnoticed and one of the men he'd acknowledged earlier took the opportunity of passing his table to stop and make conversation. Shortly afterwards a second man joined them and before long there were three, with others listening in from nearby.

News of the fire at Múli was already common knowledge, as – inexplicably, but unsurprisingly, too – was the fact that the body found there was believed to be that of Boas Justesen. So it didn't need more than an indication of interest from Hentze for his fellow diners to offer their thoughts on the matter, and on Boas Justesen's life. This wasn't speaking ill of the dead, as all the contributors to the conversation were keen to point out, but in view of such an unusual circumstance, there was clearly a justification for candour, especially to an officer of the law.

Hentze sipped coffee and listened. Not much else was required. The consensus was that Boas Justesen had been an unfriendly and disagreeable man who, over the last forty years, had somehow managed to fund both his drinking and smoking without any regular or serious appetite for work.

Of course, at nearly sixty-five he'd been too old for work now, but even so there was some speculation about how he'd managed to go for so long without any visible means of support. Perhaps his money came from renting out the land around Múli to Eyðun Thomsen; but maybe that hadn't been enough, given that Boas had recently moved into the undercroft of his house so he could let out the upstairs to a young couple who couldn't afford better. And over the summer there had also been a rumour that he was planning to sell the land out at Múli, which had made Eyðun Thomsen worry about his hay crop.

When all the gossip and stories were taken together, the general opinion was that if a fire hadn't killed Boas then a drunken fall into the harbour or a crash in his car would have been just as likely to do it. And furthermore it wasn't expected that his only known relative – a niece from Eiði – would be too upset by his passing. Why would she be? As far as anyone knew she'd had no contact with the old man for twenty-odd years, and wouldn't she inherit? Even at Múli, land was land, and no one could turn up their nose at that, especially if it came to them free.

There was nothing like a touch of envy to keep gossip alive, Hentze decided as he finally left the restaurant and walked back to his car. Though by the sound of it, there had been little to envy about Boas Justesen.

He found Justesen's house easily enough, identifying it as much from its rundown appearance as from the number. It was raining quite heavily now and Hentze pulled up the hood of his jacket as he walked up the path to the door of the undercroft, then knocked. He waited for a moment, hoping no one would answer, because if Boas Justesen himself opened the door it would present him with a new set of problems. But no one answered, and when he tried the door handle it opened. Does a man who is thinking of suicide bother to lock his door when he leaves? Perhaps not.

Inside there was gloom and the stale smell of cigarettes and beer. Out of habit Hentze pulled on a pair of surgical gloves and searched for a light switch. When he found it he looked round at the untidy and uncared for apartment and then started to search.

The best he could hope for was a suicide note. That would simplify things greatly, but amidst the discarded newspapers, utility bills and other detritus there was nothing that was a final *farvæl*. Too much to expect, perhaps, from a man who lived amongst chaos and had no one to whom he'd address such a note.

In the back corner of the room an unmade single bed was piled with unwashed laundry and next to it the door to a small bathroom stood half open. The smell was enough to indicate the state of the facilities, but Hentze had seen worse and he wanted to be thorough so he went in and looked round to find it much as he'd imagined. The only difference was an unusually large number of pill bottles and blister packs – some empty, some not – arrayed on a sheet of chipboard over the stained bath.

For the most part the names of the drugs were unfamiliar to Hentze. A few, like codeine and diclofenac, were obviously for pain relief, but the rest could have been anything. He debated for a moment, then took out an evidence bag and collected half a dozen. He would ask Elisabet Hovgaard what they were.

Back in the main living room he took one last look around. It was a depressing sight; a dismal legacy to leave the world. When he went he wanted to leave things clean and tidy at least. But perhaps that wasn't something you were ever given a choice about. No doubt Boas Justesen would have preferred to leave the world with people thinking well of him, rather than simply envying the person who might inherit his land. But there again, maybe Boas Justesen hadn't cared. The evidence of his house would seem to suggest not.

There were no keys to the door that Hentze could find, so he simply closed it behind him as he left.

"I'd like your opinion on whether we should still go ahead with the murder charge against Finn Sólsker," Remi Syderbø said. He'd had to wait for over two hours to get this meeting with Andrias Berg and so he'd had time enough to decide to get straight to the point.

Berg was chewing an antacid tablet. "Of course," he said with a nod. "I thought that was already decided."

"It was," Remi acknowledged. "But I'm having second thoughts. Sólsker's finally given an account of his movements and confirmed he was having an affair with Erla Sivertsen, but despite that he still maintains that he didn't kill her."

Berg made to speak but Remi pretended not to notice. "It's also been pointed out that if we take Sólsker's account at face value – i.e. that he saw Erla leave Sandoy on the nine thirty ferry – then it's clear that she must have been killed on Streymoy."

"Possibly," Berg said, "but why *should* we take what he's said at face value? Is there anything to corroborate his account? More to the point, why's he gone until now without telling this story when – if it's true – he could easily have told us two or three days ago? Is it just because he knew we'd finally got DNA evidence to prove he had a relationship with the victim?"

"I'm sure he wanted to keep the affair quiet," Remi said. "But that alone doesn't give us a motive for murder. In fact, as far as I can see, the main reason he was so conflicted about the whole situation was because he was in love with her instead of his wife."

Berg's expression was one of distaste. "Yes, well, we've all heard of cases where someone is supposedly in love with their victim but has still killed them. A row, a moment of anger… And by the sound of what happened to Ári Niclasen, Sólsker *does* have a temper."

Remi Syderbø wasn't sure whether Berg's pursuit of this tangent was deliberate or not, but he knew the Commander well enough to recognise the signs of impatience.

"Well that may be true," Remi acknowledged. "But all the same I think we should allow him at least the benefit of the doubt. After all, the case against him is still circumstantial. I'd feel more comfortable about charging him if we were sure there weren't any other viable scenarios – especially as we may not have been given all the facts by some people."

Berg shifted. "If this has come from Hjalti Hentze…"

"It hasn't," Remi said. "He's out on a fire investigation at Múli at the moment. He hasn't even seen the forensics report. He refused to look at it, in fact. Whatever you said to him yesterday obviously had an effect."

Berg wasn't convinced. "So you've taken up his cause instead?" Again the look of distaste as he reached for another indigestion tablet.

"*Is* there a cause?" Remi Syderbø asked, although he knew it sounded disingenuous. "Isn't it just a matter of making sure that we know all there is to know, rather than just pursuing the easiest course?"

"So what are you asking for?"

"I'd like to talk to whoever Erla Sivertsen was working with or for in the national security service and to find out if they know anything about her movements on Saturday night. Do they know if she went back to Streymoy as Finn says? Did she meet with them? When was the last time they saw her? At the moment it feels as if we've simply ignored someone who may have important information."

Berg shook his head and leaned forward. "They haven't been ignored. *I've* spoken to the people concerned and I've been assured that they can't give us any relevant information."

"Can't because there isn't any, or because they have their own reasons for saying nothing?" Remi Syderbø made an open gesture. "You can see my problem here, in terms of a full and proper investigation. I understand the need for discretion – well, actually, I'm not sure I do – but it seems to me that we can't tell whether we've been told all the facts, or whether information is being withheld because it suits some other purpose."

"What other purpose?" Berg fixed him with a suspicious look.

"I don't know," Remi shrugged. "I don't know why there are security service people here at all, but they must have *some* reason. They must be doing *something*."

But Andrias Berg had clearly had enough. "That's not your concern," he said bluntly. "And regarding Finn Sólsker, if the Prosecutor's office hasn't raised any new concerns then I'm happy to go along with their original recommendation to charge him. Unless there's direct evidence to say we shouldn't. Is there?"

"No," Remi admitted. "Only what I've said."

"All right then. So let's stop chasing phantoms. It's as if the whole of CID has started seeing trolls in broad daylight. Let's just get on with the job, all right?"

"Of course," Remi said with a nod.

But as he headed back to the stairs he wondered just how he could get on with the job when – even in broad daylight – it was hard to believe, let alone trust, the assurances of people who might not even officially exist.

45

THE TRIP HENTZE MADE TO EIÐI IN SEARCH OF BOAS JUSTESEN'S
niece was fruitless. It turned out that the niece was in
Copenhagen with her husband. Her neighbour provided this
information, along with the niece's cellphone number, and
Hentze managed to speak to her while she was walking along
a street in Strøget.

Giving the news of Boas Justesen's death over the phone
wasn't ideal, but as it turned out there was no great emotion
from the woman. She was Justesen's *great*-niece, it transpired,
and she'd had no contact with him since she was a little girl.
Her greatest concern was whether she would be required to
pay for the funeral, on which matter Hentze couldn't help.
When he rang off it felt to him that Boas Justesen had been
even more alone in the world than he'd imagined before.

He drove back to Tórshavn under a prematurely dark
sky and by the time he pulled in to the hospital car park it
reflected his mood.

"I haven't got anything for you," Elisabet Hovgaard said
when she saw him coming along the corridor. She meant
regarding Justesen, Hentze guessed. "I'll X-ray his teeth for an

ID and circulate the pictures, but at this time of day I wouldn't expect any of the dental community to respond till tomorrow."

"Is someone coming out to do the forensic PM?"

"Yeh, it'll be Eric this time. Anders has gone off us, I think."

"Oh? Why?"

"He seems to think he's being blamed for misplacing the samples from the Sivertsen autopsy."

"Not by me."

"No, well, you know what he's like."

By now they were at Elisabet's office and Hentze followed her inside. It was as any normal hospital office, save for a rocking chair in the corner containing more than a dozen stuffed toys.

"Are you in a hurry? For the PM, I mean," Elisabet asked.

"Have I any need to be?"

Elisabet shrugged. "I haven't given him more than a cursory look. I can tell you he's dead and there's a rope around his neck. That's about it. Are you treating it as suspicious?"

"Not at the moment."

"Good."

"Why good?"

"Haven't you got enough on your plate already?"

Hentze chose to leave it as a rhetorical question. Instead of replying he fished out the bag of drugs he'd taken from Boas Justesen's house. "Can you tell me what these are for?" he asked. "They were in Justesen's bathroom, plus a lot more." He handed her the bag and she examined the labels through the plastic.

"Well, oxocodone is a very strong pain killer and

heparin is to prevent DVT... With the rest I'd say he may have had cancer."

"Can you check his records?"

Elisabet Hovgaard hesitated for a second, but seemed to intuit that Hentze was not having the best of days. "Hold on," she said.

After a little faffing around to enter the hospital database and then find the appropriate records she examined the results, chewing on the cap of a pen.

"Well, assuming that your body *is* Boas Justesen then yes, he was being treated for inoperable cancer of the liver. Terminal."

"Any idea how long he had?"

"You can never be sure. At a guess, six months."

"That might explain why he strung himself up then," Hentze reflected. "Better that than six months just getting worse on your own."

Hovgaard gave him a look under the angle of her fringe. "Are you feeling sorry for him or yourself?"

"For myself? I haven't got cancer, unless there's something you're not telling me."

"So why the face like a cod on the line?"

"Leave me alone."

"Well, there's one thing that might cheer you up. Your body in there *is* Boas Eli Justesen." She tapped the screen. "It says in his record that he's missing the lower joint of two fingers on his left hand and all his little finger. So is your corpse. Accident at sea twenty-two years ago."

"Really? I never noticed."

"That's not like you. Anyway, it means we can dispense

with the dental X-rays for identification. Doesn't that make you feel better?"

"Not much, but thanks."

As Hentze was on his way back to the station – having run out of reasons to stay away, he realised – Sóleyg called him to say that she was going to see Martha and the kids. She was on her way to catch the five fifteen ferry.

"Oh, okay," Hentze said, trying to sound casual. "Any reason?"

"Of course there's a reason," Sóleyg said. "Haven't you heard about Finn? Why didn't you tell me?"

"I didn't want to worry you. I don't think—" What didn't he think? That it was serious? That Finn was guilty? Neither of these would stand up to scrutiny. "I don't think you should stay too long," he said, knowing it was feeble.

"I'll see when I get there," Sóleyg replied. In her voice there was something of the determined streak she'd once been known for – something Hentze hadn't heard for a long time. "Mar will need help with the kids anyway. I'll stay as long as she wants me to."

"Sure, okay," Hentze said. "Will you let me know when you're coming back, though?"

"Of course."

"Give Martha my love, then."

"I will."

He rang off and wondered for a moment if he shouldn't divert to the ferry. But maybe that wasn't such a good idea after last time. Maybe Sóleyg's presence would moderate things in a way in which his could not.

No, he decided, he wouldn't go to the ferry. He wouldn't follow his instinct to jump in and protect. You can't guard against everything, even if you'd like to. He thought of Boas Justesen. You can't guard against cancer or dying alone.

On his desk he found a sealed envelope, propped against the computer. There was no writing on it, so Hentze slit it open and pulled out the contents. The first page was a print-out of an email from Sophie Krogh at the technical lab in Copenhagen, addressed to Remi Syderbø. Hentze scanned it for a moment before going back to look at the time the email had been sent. Two hours ago.

The rest of the pages were a forensic examination report on fibres, fluids and other trace evidence from a number of locations, including Erla Sivertsen's car. Hentze patted himself down to locate his reading glasses, then he read on.

Maybe it says something about your connection to a place when it's familiar enough that you know where you can park and where to suggest meeting someone for coffee without thinking too hard. Learning your way around places is easier than navigating people, though. You think they're becoming familiar and then you find out that the landmarks and road junctions aren't where you thought they were after all.

I hadn't seen Frída that morning, but I'd have liked to

have done. Something about the way things had been left last night still bothered me. I wasn't sure exactly what it was: just a generalised feeling that I'd said either too much or too little and it had changed something between us. But her car was gone by the time I got up.

Telling Fríða about Kirkland's phone call had brought the whole thing into sharper focus for me, though. I'd put off doing anything about it until now, but I knew I couldn't let it go any longer. If nothing else I needed flights – from Vágar to Copenhagen, and then on to the UK – and having left it this late I knew I'd have to take whatever was available.

As it turned out a helpful man at Atlantic Airways gave me a choice: leave tomorrow on the afternoon flight, or on Monday morning at eight. I opted for Monday, as reluctant to make hurried farewells as I was to get home any earlier. There would be little joy in sitting around over the weekend just waiting to see Kirkland on Tuesday. Better to cut it fine.

Online there was a greater number of flights between Kastrup and Heathrow and while I was still being decisive I did the necessary entering of credit card details and then it was done: I *was* going back.

There'd never really been an alternative, of course. Occasionally it might have felt like there was, but in reality I'd never been under any illusion that I belonged here. True, I knew places to park and where to get coffee, and over the last three weeks I'd entangled myself in the place and with some of its people. I didn't know if any of that had given me a greater insight, but I was sure of one thing: whatever my roots, I didn't belong here.

I thought about that while I was walking to Válur, skirting the mountains and pushing myself hard. It was a five-hour walk but I did it in four; not exactly punishing myself, but conscious that I might have been trying to sweat the Faroes out of my system, ready to go home.

When I got back to Leynar I had a call from Tove Hald as I took off my boots. Brisk and straight to the point, she told me she'd finished the translated research I wanted and if I was free to meet her in two hours' time I could have it. I said that I was and that would be fine, and when she rang off I called Fríða. On Thursdays she often had late afternoon consultations and I thought she might like to meet up when she'd finished. Her phone went to voicemail, though, so I left a brief message and then went to shower and change.

Because I had time in hand I took the slightly longer, alternative road to Tórshavn; route 10, undulating and winding round the mountains down the spine of the island. There were massing grey clouds to the south-west and the light had a strangely luminous quality as I left the car in the quayside car park at Tinganes.

I'd arranged to meet Tove Hald at Kaffihúsið, a café beside the west harbour, and despite the threatening clouds and chill breeze she was sitting at a table outside. She was talking to a young man of about her own age across the barrier which separated the café's seats from the quay, but when she saw me approaching she said something briefly and he moved on with a wave.

"*Hey*," I said, navigating to her table as she stood up.

"*Hey hey*, are you okay?"

"Good, yeh. Coffee?"

"Sure, *takk*. Shall we go inside? It's going to rain."

Inside we got drinks and went to sit at a table by the window. Tove took a stiff manila envelope and a USB stick from her bag.

"Okay, the good news is that I have found several things about the Colony," she said, dropping into her abrupt business manner. "I didn't make any discretions about what you would want to see, so it is all here: photocopies of the originals and my translations."

I slid out the contents of the envelope – at least two dozen pages.

"You translated all this?" I asked.

"Sure. I'm a fast typist. It wasn't so hard. In 1973 and 1974 there are seventeen letters to the editors of the three newspapers, *Dimmalætting*, *Norðlýsið* and *Sosialurin*, plus eight news reports. I also did a little research about the man Rasmus Matzen, who ran the group. I discovered an article about him in a Danish magazine, *Provokation*, from 1976. I thought you might want to read it, so it is also translated."

"*Takk fyri*," I said, still slightly surprised by the amount she'd managed to do. "How long did it take you?"

"I will say twelve hours," she said without needing to work it out. "That includes time at the library, travel to and from there, online research and then the translation. It may have been longer but I was interested in something I found while I was looking at the old papers, so I think that's fair. Do you agree?"

I laughed. "Sure. I think I got a good deal."

"Good. So it is one thousand four hundred and forty krónur," she said, still in business mode.

I got out my wallet. "Did you find any references to Lýdia anywhere?"

"No, I didn't see her name, but I was only scanning for articles about the commune, so if she was mentioned in another context I might not have seen."

"No, I'd have been surprised if she was," I said. "I just wondered."

I handed her the hundred-krónur notes, which she looked at briefly, then said, "Okay, you will need sixty krónur change."

She started to look in her bag but I waved it away. "Don't worry about it."

That seemed to surprise her, but then she nodded. "Okay. *Takk fyri*." She folded the notes and pushed them into her jacket pocket, smiling again now that business was all over. "It was a fun project. I enjoyed it."

"I'm glad it wasn't a chore," I said. "When do you go back to Denmark?"

"Tomorrow morning, the first flight." Then she pushed back her chair and stood up. "So, good luck with your research, Jan. It was good to see you again."

"You, too. And thanks," I said, just about getting it in before she strode away. She was a strange creature, that was for sure.

"You read it?" Remi asked. They were in his office and the door was closed.

"Yeh." Hentze had the envelope in his hand. "Do you want it back?"

Remi shook his head, then leaned back a little in his chair.

"We didn't— I wasn't given any choice about charging Finn," he said, then raised his eyes towards the ceiling, indicating upstairs. "And maybe that's the right decision. But from what Finn has told us – finally told us – Dánjal and I both think there's at least a possibility that Erla wasn't killed on Sandoy. And if Sophie Krogh's report is correct in saying that Erla's body was in the boot of her car for some time after death, that could support the possibility. It certainly doesn't tally with the theory that Finn killed her and then dumped her body as quickly as possible. So, as of tomorrow, we're going to start re-interviewing all the AWCA people Erla was closest to, concentrating on where they were and what they were doing between nine thirty and midnight on Saturday. I'm also going to put out an appeal for anyone who was on the *Teistin* from Skopun to Gamlarætt between the same times." He paused and gestured upwards again. "For obvious reasons I can't involve you in any of that. It would be going too far and draw too much attention, but I'll keep you up to date on the side, okay?"

Hentze considered that for a moment. Then he said, "Unless I miss my guess, I'm pretty sure you'll get attention as soon as you start talking to the Alliance again. I was told to leave them alone."

"No one's said that to me."

"Even so, wouldn't it be better if I were to do it? I'm already in the doghouse and that way it'll be me Andrias Berg comes after rather than you."

Remi thought about it, but only briefly, then shook his head. "No, I think this needs to come from someone they can't just reassign – at least, not without creating a stink. They'll realise how it will look if they try, so maybe they'll decide it's less damaging to let things run their course."

"You can hope."

"Well the worst-case scenario is that they *do* take me off the investigation, in which case they'd have to pass it to you in terms of seniority."

"What about Ári?"

"He's been signed off sick for a week. Hairline fracture of his elbow and a severe dent in his pride. I imagine his suit will need cleaning as well." Remi leaned forward again, shifting the subject. "What about the fire death?"

Acknowledging that Remi had made his decision, Hentze said, "Boas Justesen. At the moment it looks as if he committed suicide by hanging himself and the fire was started accidentally. That's Mikkjal's opinion, and according to his medical records Justesen was terminally ill. Anyway, there's nothing suspicious so far."

"Thank God for that."

"Yeh," Hentze agreed. "So I'll make a start on the preliminary report, then wait for the PM to firm it up."

"Okay. And regarding Erla Sivertsen, just keep your head down," Remi said.

"Thanks. But I don't think it's me they'll be shooting at once you start talking to the Alliance."

46

I HEADED BACK TOWARDS THE TOWN CENTRE AFTER AN unproductive hour in the SMS mall, waiting to see if Fríða would call and vaguely hoping to find something I could take back to England for Ketty. But neither one had happened, and I'd given it up as the stores started to pull down the shutters. I was getting hungry and I decided that if Fríða hadn't rung by the time I reached Vaglið square I'd better eat alone.

I'd walked to the mall after leaving Kaffihúsið, which might have been a mistake because now, as I crossed Bøkjarabrekka, it started to rain. There were just a few seconds of forewarning drops, and then a cold, heavy downpour: the sort that bounces off tarmac. I sheltered in a shop doorway, but the street was already perceptibly darker and I knew this wasn't just a shower you could wait out. Instead I dashed a hundred yards or so to the Marco Polo restaurant on Sverrisgøta.

It was the first time I'd been back there since the day I arrived and now, as before, I was the only customer in the place. The waiter didn't seem to mind me dripping on the carpet, though, or the fact that he had to put his book down.

"Any place you like," he said with a gesture.

I ordered, then ate undisturbed, straining to read some of Tove's translations in the weak light of the wall lamps. I was just finishing my pasta when Hentze called.

"The other day you told me you'd been to see a man called Boas Justesen," he said. "About the commune at Múli, do you remember?"

"Sure," I said. "Why?"

"Well, one of the houses there – at Múli – burned down last night. Boas Justesen was inside."

"You're serious?" I asked, although I knew he was. "Is he dead?"

"Yeh, I'm sorry to say it. So if you have time I need to ask you a few questions – just about how he appeared to you, his mood. Is that okay?"

"Yeah, no problem," I said. "Now?"

A pause. "Would you like to go for a drink? Are you at Leynar?"

"No, I'm in Tórshavn: at the Marco Polo. But a drink would be good."

I guessed he wanted a chance to talk face to face, and perhaps not just about Boas Justesen.

"Okay, *takk*," he said. "If you stay there I can pick you up. Is twenty minutes too long to wait?"

"No, that's fine. I'll see you then."

Beyond the forecourt lights it was dark now, and the rain hammered on the steel awning over the pumps of the Magn petrol station. Annika Mortensen had to put a finger in her free ear to hear the voice on the phone above the din.

"I didn't... I didn't tell you the truth. The other day. About Erla."

Annika frowned. "How do you mean?"

"I saw her," Veerle Koning said. "She... she came back to the house. Please, can you come here? I don't know when the others will be back. I need to talk to you."

There was a catch in her voice, as if she was short of air.

"Okay, of course," Annika said, turning to spot Officer Rosa Olsen beyond the plate glass of the shop window. "You're at the house now – Fjalsgøta 82?"

"Yeh. Yes."

"Okay, don't worry, I'm on my way. I'll be there in five minutes."

"This is my colleague Rosa," Annika said as Veerle held the door open and let them in to the hall. As before she used English with the young Dutch woman. She glanced towards the back of the house. "Are you on your own?"

Veerle nodded. "Yes, all the others are... they went out." She looked as if she'd been crying and there were dark circles under her eyes.

"Okay," Annika said, taking off her dripping coat. "Let's go and sit down, eh? Then we can talk."

Veerle led them through to the sitting room. The two officers sat on the sofa and after a moment's hesitation Veerle perched on the edge of an armchair. "On the phone you said

402

you didn't tell us everything before – about Erla," Annika said, trying to keep her tone engaging. "What did you mean by that?"

For a second Veerle seemed uncertain. She cast a quick glance at Rosa Olsen, as if debating whether to speak in her presence, but then she looked back to Annika and said, "Lukas didn't want me to tell you. He said it would just make trouble, but I *did* see Erla again. She came back to the house in the late afternoon."

"Why would it have made trouble to tell us that?" Annika asked, keeping her tone neutral so Veerle wouldn't feel she was being reproached.

"Because—" Veerle broke off and swallowed, then tried again. "Because Erla had found out something, and Lukas knew from what she said."

"Found out what?"

Veerle hung her head, as if coming this far had exhausted her. She said nothing.

"I'm sorry, I don't understand," Annika said. "What had Erla found out?"

"About Lukas."

For a moment longer Veerle remained still, then – without making eye contact – she stood up and turned away from the two officers. She reached round to grip the bottom edge of her sweater and shirt, and in an effort that obviously caused her discomfort, she pulled up the clothing so that Annika and Rosa could see her back.

Veerle's pale skin was almost invisible under the mottled yellow, green and purple of bruises, some clearly older than others. Just below her ribs on her left-hand side the skin was still red from recent blows.

"Did Lukas do that?" Annika asked.

"Yes," Veerle said, barely more than a whisper. Then she lowered her clothes and when she turned to face Annika and Rosa again her cheeks were wet with tears.

"I didn't know what to do," Veerle said. "Erla knew, but I couldn't— I'm afraid now."

Annika stood up and took the three steps to Veerle before she had even thought about it. She took her in her arms and felt Veerle sag.

"It's okay, you don't have to be afraid of him any more," Annika said. "We'll sort him out, don't worry."

Veerle shook her head against Annika's fleece. "No, no, it's not that," she said, her voice slightly muffled. "*Ja* – yes it is that. But I'm also afraid of what they will— what they're going to do now."

"Now? What do you mean?"

Veerle pulled back from Annika, enough to wipe a sleeve across her face. She made an effort to compose herself. "It's all of them from here," she said. "And others. They are going to do something big tonight. Something—" She struggled to find the right words. "Something that everyone will look at, you know? That's where they have gone."

"You mean the Alliance are going to do something?" Rosa asked.

"*Neen*, it's not AWCA. It's just Lukas, Peter, Marie… Some others, too. I don't know. Lukas said— He said they will open people's eyes – to make them look."

The phrase sounded ominous in its simplicity. Perhaps just a product of being translated from Dutch to English, but even so Annika could see the worry on Veerle's face.

"Do you know where Lukas and the others are now?" she asked after a moment.

"No, I don't know," Veerle said. "They didn't tell me."

"Have you heard them mentioning names or places maybe," Annika asked. "Have they talked about anyone you didn't know, or perhaps an unusual place?"

"No, I don't think so. They never talked about anything like that – except the garage, maybe."

"The garage? You mean a petrol station?"

Veerle shook her head. "No. It's a— I don't know what else to call it. It's an old building. We stopped there one time maybe a week ago – when I was with Lukas. I thought it was closed – I mean, not in business – but he told me to wait in the car while he went inside. There was a door at the back and he went there like he knew where to go. Like he'd been there before."

"Did he say *why* he was there?"

"No, he just said it was to see someone." She hesitated. "I didn't ask more."

Annika nodded. She knew why Veerle hadn't asked. Questions brought beatings.

"Was there a name or a sign outside this place?" Annika said. She tried to sound conversational, to keep things unpressured.

"A sign, yeh. I don't know what it said. It was in Faroese, but there was a picture of a big *autoband*—" She searched for the word in English. "For the wheel on a car: a tyre? Yeh, tyre."

"It sounds like Gregersen's old place on Falkavegur," Rosa said. "It's been empty for a couple of years."

"Yeh," Annika said, then looked back to Veerle. "Do you think they could have gone there now?"

"Maybe. I don't know."

"Okay," Annika said. "Why don't you sit down for a minute? I just need to talk with Rosa."

In the hall Annika and Rosa spoke Faroese again.

"What do you think?" Annika asked.

"About her story? Sure, I believe it. From those bruises... Yeh."

"What about the rest of it – this thing the others are up to?"

Rosa shrugged. "There's no way to tell, is there? It sounded a bit far-fetched. What sort of thing could they be planning anyway?"

"Not a demonstration, not at this time of night and in this weather." She shifted. "Listen, can you stay here with Veerle? I'm going to go and have a look at the garage."

"Wouldn't it be better to take her back to the station first? Then we can tell Hans and see what he thinks." Hans Lassen was duty inspector.

Annika checked her watch, then shook her head. "It'll be faster just to go and look. If nobody's there then Hans can decide what to do – who to tell..."

"And if there *is* someone there?"

"I'll call it in." Annika took her coat from the hook and put it on. "I'll probably be back in fifteen minutes. Okay?"

47

I WAS PRETTY SURE HENTZE WOULD BE PROMPT AND HE WAS, pulling up on the narrow street outside the restaurant almost exactly on time. The rain hadn't stopped so I made a dash down the steps and across to his car, but even that short distance was enough to get me soaked all over again. "You picked a good night for it," I said, dropping into the passenger seat.

"Yeh, I think so," he said without any irony. "I thought we would go to Hotel Føroyar. Have you been there before?"

"No. Isn't it a bit classy?"

"For you, maybe. Perhaps we'll stay in the bar." He gave me a look to say he was joking, then put the car into gear and pulled away.

I let him negotiate the side streets as I adjusted the seat belt, but once we were on the ring road I said, "So do you want to ask me about Boas Justesen now, or wait till we've got a drink?"

"No, I can ask now and get it out of the way," he said. "It's only one question: how did he seem to be when you saw him?"

"Annoyed," I said with a shrug. "He didn't want to talk

to me. That was about it. He'd been drinking."

"He wasn't depressed?"

"Not that I could tell. Why?"

"I think he may have committed suicide at the Múli house. It isn't sure yet but that's how it seems."

He might have been about to say more but then his phone rang. It was clipped to a holder on the dashboard and when it chimed he looked at the screen, then back at the road before swiping it to answer.

"*Hey, Annika.*"

From the background noise behind Annika's voice I guessed she was also on speakerphone, perhaps driving. More than that I didn't get because she was speaking Faroese. I did pick up Erla Sivertsen's name, though, and a few seconds after that Hentze flicked the indicator and turned off the ring road, pulling in to a side street.

For a minute or so he continued to listen as Annika spoke. I caught a couple of other names, then Hentze cut in with a question and whatever Annika Mortensen's reply was, it made Hentze pause. He glanced at me, then gave Annika what seemed to be instructions. The last thing he said was "*Fimm minuttur. Bei.*"

He tapped the phone screen to ring off, then put the car back in gear.

"Did you understand that?" he said as he hauled the steering wheel round to make a U-turn.

I shook my head. "Too fast. Only something about Erla."

"Yeh." He checked traffic at the junction, then accelerated quickly, back the way we'd just come, towards town. "One of the people Erla lived with, a girl called Veerle Koning, has called Annika to give her new information."

"About the killing?"

"Maybe, yeh – but also about the other Alliance people in the house. Veerle says there is something being planned – some kind of protest action, maybe."

"And it's happening now?"

"Yeh, she thinks so. The people from the house have all left together, to meet others, she thinks."

"So where are we going?"

"Annika is on her way to look at a place Veerle has told her about: an old garage on Falkavegur. She will be there in a couple of minutes; we will be there in five – unless I let you out here."

Despite the lashing rain he was doing about 90 kph so it wasn't much of a question and I didn't bother to answer. Instead I said, "Any idea what *sort* of thing they're planning to do?"

"*Nei*." He shook his head. "All the Veerle girl knows is that it is 'something that will make people look'."

Out of context it was a statement you could take any way you wanted – from an explicit threat to an empty piece of rhetoric.

I said, "If it's serious – I mean, if the Alliance really *do* have some kind of plan for direct action – it would explain why your spooks have been taking an interest."

"Yeh, I think so," Hentze said flatly. He flicked the wipers on to double time. "That's why we are going."

As we came off the ring road and took the first exit off the roundabout Hentze called Annika again. He was driving at less than forty now and scanning the buildings we passed. It wasn't an area of the town I'd seen before: a mixture of light industrial and commercial buildings, some looking rundown, others newer and smarter. In the rain and the darkness it was hard to tell how far it extended but there was an air of unusual neglect in some of the cracked concrete frontages and worn brickwork we passed.

Annika's voice on the phone was low and slightly guarded, as if she was talking us in. We rounded a corner and Hentze let the car bump on to a concrete apron beside a brick wall. He turned off the ignition and the headlights.

"Which building is it?" I asked.

"There," he pointed across the road at an angle. "The one with the tyre sign."

It was about a hundred yards away, hard to define through the rain on the windscreen, but cast partly in light by the lamps on a neighbouring building.

Then there was a movement beside the car and the rear door opened in a gust of wind and rain. Annika Mortensen got in quickly and closed the door after her. She was soaking wet, without a coat or hat. I guessed she'd gone without to make herself less visible.

"Hey," she said. And then to me, "We do this again, eh?" She had to raise her voice over the sound of the rain on the roof.

I gestured at Hentze. "He won't leave me alone."

Hentze wasn't in the mood for banter, though. He watched the garage for a moment longer, then twisted in his seat to look at Annika. "Have you seen anyone?" he asked.

"*Nei*, no one. But there is a light on inside the building.

From the back you can see it, not here. And there are also two cars there, both Skodas."

"Where's your car?"

"Back there, round the corner," Annika said with a gesture. "I didn't think it was a good idea to be seen."

"No, not so good." Hentze considered for a second. "So all we know is that some Alliance people from Erla's house have gone out together – maybe on a secret operation, maybe not; maybe here, maybe not."

Annika pushed her wet hair back and nodded. "Veerle says her boyfriend, Lukas Drescher, and others have been coming here. She doesn't know why but she knows it's not usual."

"So why is she telling you this now? Why not before?"

"She's scared," Annika said. "Drescher beats her; I've seen the bruises. And he beat her tonight – maybe because she asks too many questions – so then, because she was afraid of what they will do next, she called me."

"Okay," Hentze said. He looked back at the garage, assessing, and I knew what he was trying to work out: whether to go in to look and then deal with whatever he found, or to call out the cavalry and make a big deal out of something that might prove to be nothing.

"Have you seen anyone – anyone else watching?" he asked.

"*Nei*." Annika frowned. "Who do you think would be watching?"

"Security services."

He glanced out of the window, as if saying the words might summon them, then looked at me. "What do you think?"

411

I shrugged. "If the spooks *are* here they'll have seen us," I said. "But if they didn't do anything when Annika went to look at the place…"

"Yeh – maybe they do nothing at all," he said flatly. "Maybe that is their plan." He turned to Annika. "How many entrances are there?"

"To the garage? Only two. An ordinary door at the back and the big doors in front."

Hentze took a couple of seconds and then he shifted. "Okay, we'll go and look. I've had enough of this nonsense."

We got out of the car into rain that was as heavy as any I'd known on the Faroes: hard, cold drops the size of coins. Hentze strode ahead and, as we passed the corner of the last building before moving into streetlight, I felt an instinctive prickling in the centre of my back. I wondered how far we'd be allowed to get if we *were* being observed by a security services team.

Then I saw headlights, illuminating a wall down the side street we were all heading for. The lights shifted as the car they belonged to swung around and I felt Annika tug my arm. We stepped quickly back into the cover of the corner we'd just passed as the car swung into the side street, then came towards us before turning left on the road in front of the garage. There was no way to tell if we'd been seen, and if we had whether it meant anything to the car's occupants. Two silhouettes were all I made out.

Hentze already had his car keys in his hand and he passed them quickly to Annika. "Follow them," he said. "Find out where they go."

Annika was good enough that she didn't question or debate it. Instead she started back to Hentze's car at a run. "Can you go with her?" Hentze said to me. "I prefer it."

I hesitated for only a second, then took a leaf out of Annika's book. "Okay," I said. "Call for backup, all right?"

"Yeh. Go."

I ran. By the time I got to the car Annika was already starting the engine. I pulled the passenger door open and got in beside her. She looked at me briefly, then banged the car into gear as the engine caught.

"You get bored with your holiday?" she said. By then we were moving, thudding over potholes until we hit the tarmac.

"Yeh, something like that."

She grinned. "This time maybe you stay conscious."

48

WE HADN'T AROUSED ANY ALARM, THAT MUCH SEEMED CLEAR by the way the car ahead was being driven: cautiously, as if the driver was wary of the rain-wet roads. Annika had caught up with the car easily enough because it had stuck to the speed limit and even indicated its turns in good time.

Within a couple of minutes we'd turned out of the industrial area and on to a better road, heading south towards the centre of Tórshavn. There was very little traffic and what there was the rain made anonymous. From a hundred yards back it was an easy tail and now that the initial urgency had subsided a little I glanced at Annika.

"So, what's the plan?" I asked.

She pushed her sodden hair back from her face. "Just what Hjalti said: follow and see where they go – what they do. If it's nothing…" She shrugged. "But if we find Lukas Drescher I will arrest him."

"For beating his girlfriend?"

"Yeh."

"Okay, fair enough."

We were on a street I recognised now: Tórsgøta, downhill

towards the Hotel Tórshavn on the corner and the harbour beyond that. Annika held our car back as the Skoda reached the junction and slowed. Its brakelights flashed for a moment, then it turned right and as soon as it did so Annika sped up again, as far as the junction, then braked and edged out enough to see the Skoda moving along the street parallel to the waterfront. By holding back I knew she was trying to make our continued presence less obvious, but when the Skoda passed a curve in the road and disappeared Annika pulled out quickly, spinning the steering wheel one-handed.

"Unless they are blind they will see us soon," she said. "And I don't understand where they are going, unless to the harbour. There's nowhere else."

We passed the curve and for a moment there was no sign of the Skoda. We both craned forward.

"Can you see them?" I asked.

"*Nei*." And then, "Yes. There," Annika said, immediately slowing the car and suddenly taking a right into a side road. I saw the Skoda sideways on for a second as it entered the car park across from the harbour, then my view was obscured by other vehicles.

Annika bumped the car half up on a kerb and stopped the engine quickly to kill the lights.

"I'll take a look," I said opening my door. "Hang on."

The rain was as hard as before – just as cold – but at least here there wasn't much wind. I crossed the road quickly, as far as the closest cars in the car park, then used them for cover.

In the day time the Skálatrøð car park was usually pretty full, but now there were fewer than a dozen cars. Even so it took me a few seconds to locate the Skoda, because it had pulled in at the rear of the car park, close to a rock outcrop and as far back from the streetlights as possible. I saw its headlights dim as its engine was switched off, and then they went out altogether. Then nothing.

I gave it a couple of seconds, then jogged back to Annika. She was out of the car, standing by the open driver's door. "They've parked," I told her over the dinning rain on the roof. "Lights out. A hundred yards away at the back."

"Okay. Let's see, yeh?"

We crossed the road briskly together until we were back in the lee of the parked cars.

"Over there, by the wall." I indicated, but it became redundant when the courtesy light inside the Skoda went on and the doors opened.

There were two figures, both dressed in dark clothes. It was impossible to see more than that because of the rain and the darkness, and when the interior light went out again there was even less detail. The figures appeared to go round to the boot of the car, though, disappearing when the lid went up. I thought I saw the faint glow of another interior light but couldn't be sure.

"What now?" Annika said. "You think we have the right people?"

"They're up to something," I said. "Otherwise they wouldn't have parked way over there."

As I said it the boot of the Skoda was closed and the two figures started away from the car. No one walks slowly in the rain and neither did they. But this was more than just briskness:

there was an urgency to it, and as they moved across the centre of the car park I could see that each of them was carrying a bag – a large holdall of some sort – obviously heavy. And they weren't heading towards us or the town centre; instead they were taking a direct line towards the waterfront.

Annika and I both backed up a little way to stay behind cover. I could tell she was trying to decide on the best next move.

"I think we should stop them now," she said. "Let's see how they account for themselves. Yes?"

"Okay."

We ran the short distance back to the car and before I had my door fully closed Annika had started the engine, banging the gears into reverse and backing up just far enough to turn on to the harbour-front road again. She didn't floor it, but instead gauged the speed so that we approached the car park as the two bag-carrying figures were crossing the road.

The streetlamps gave enough light to see them better now: a man and a woman, both in their twenties, I thought. The only part of them visible was their faces, below knitted hats and above zipped-up fleeces. The holdalls they were carrying were heavy enough to make their movements awkward and lopsided.

The man glanced in our direction as they reached the top of the short flight of steps down to the waterfront path, then he moved a little faster, hurrying the young woman who was slightly ahead.

Annika didn't do anything until the last moment, then pulled sharply across the road and braked hard enough for a short skid at the kerb. We were both moving as soon as the car stopped but Annika was closest and I heard her call out in Danish, voice raised over the rain; an instruction to halt in any language.

The couple from the car were now on a walkway next to the water, four or five feet below street level. They'd both stopped moving at Annika's command, and as we went down the steps to their level she continued to give instructions in Danish.

The man and woman exchanged glances, but they both put their holdalls down on the ground. Then the man turned to Annika and from his tone I could tell he was asking what the problem was.

Annika wasn't taken in by the forced innocence any more than I was, even in Danish. In response she gestured to the bag at his feet. The man shrugged and made to bend down and open the holdall, only to be brought up by Annika's sharp instruction to stop and step back. She repeated it to the young woman, who seemed less willing to comply but said nothing as she moved back half a pace.

"He says his name is Lange and they are just taking supplies to their boat," Annika told me. "Can you look?"

Her hand was resting on the grip of the pistol and I knew why she'd asked. If this was innocent enough she didn't want to wave a gun in their faces, but if it wasn't she wanted to keep them in sight.

"Okay. Hold on."

I sidestepped around her and went the half dozen paces along the walkway to where the woman's bag sat. I kept to the outer edge by the water so I didn't block Annika's view, then squatted and looked at the holdall. It was bulky and nylon, larger than carry-on size and beaded with rain. There was a zip down the centre which I tugged open along its full length, then I folded the sides back so I could see better in the light from the nearest streetlamp.

Inside the bag there were three plastic fuel cans in a row: gallon-sized. They were the sort you carry in the boot of your car for emergencies, except these all had black tape wrapped around them, securing some kind of plastic box at one end. I saw wires, too, and that's when I left them alone.

As I started to straighten up I was looking towards Annika and she knew it wasn't good. She might have seen what was inside the holdall, but whether she had or not she was already drawing her pistol and barking at the woman and the man called Lange to stay still.

I took a couple of steps back towards Annika as she reached for her radio with her free hand. But before she could use it I heard the sound of over-revved engines approaching at speed and then two sets of headlights swung in: a car and a van.

I think we all looked in their direction for a moment, except the young woman. As the two vehicles skidded to a halt on the road above us there was a quick movement off to my left and I saw her breaking away at a run. She'd snatched up one of the fuel cans from the holdall, and now it swung out like a pendulum weight as she rounded a post and sprinted on to a jetty five yards away.

With a shout Annika went after her before I could move, and out of instinct I looked back to check on the man who'd called himself Lange. He hadn't been as quick off the mark as the woman, but now that Annika was off in pursuit he was tugging at the zip on the other holdall, clearly intent on making his own play.

Without thinking about it I ran towards him, making a lunge at the same time that I glimpsed half a dozen men in black combat gear and ski masks piling over the top of the embankment. They were yelling in Danish, but it was too late to stop and I struck Lange hard enough to knock him to the ground.

What followed had little finesse. Beneath me Lange was writhing and kicking, but my grip on his arm was suddenly pulled away by one on my own. There were at least two of them hauling me off, and seconds later I was flung down again and pinned to the tarmac by a knee in my back. There were orders being barked from all sides so I stayed very still. In any language it's the best thing to do when automatic weapons are being pointed at you.

"Okay! It's okay," I said, loudly and clearly.

I spread my hands slowly to show they were empty but even as I was doing that there was a small, sharp *crack* in the background, followed by an immediate exhaled *whumph* in the air. Even face down I saw an orange ball of flame rise over the harbour. I saw its reflection in the dark waters as it rose and balled upwards, and then there was running and shouting and I couldn't see Annika Mortensen anywhere on the jetty.

49

IT WAS ONE THING TO CALL FOR BACKUP BUT ANOTHER THING to wait and do nothing. The nearest patrol car was five minutes away at Kerjabrekka, the second closest— Well, what did it matter? Even five minutes was long enough for things to change or go wrong.

From the shelter of the industrial unit Hentze looked again at Gregersen's garage across the road. There was no sign of life, or alarm. Impossible to know, then, whether anyone remained inside. There had been two cars parked at the back, Annika had said. Now one. And if that one set off, too, then what would he be left with? Nothing. Again.

Hentze made up his mind and moved out of shelter, crossing the road briskly. Where were the spooks when you needed them? Nowhere, of course; or else off chasing their own hares.

He took the shortest route to the unpaved track that gave access to the back of the garage, ignoring the large roller door at the front. Even from here he could see that the Judas gate was fastened with a padlock.

Down the side of the dirty redbrick building he passed

out of the reach of the streetlights and into shadow. He half stumbled when he trod in a hidden pothole of water, soaking his foot, but he didn't stop until he reached the rear corner of the building, then took a moment before risking a look round the corner.

It was as Annika had described it: a rear door and, a little further along, a frosted window of what might have been an office. There was a light on behind the glass, casting a faint patch of yellow on a Skoda Octavia, which was parked on the rough gravel, rain bouncing on its roof.

Hentze withdrew again and for a few seconds he allowed himself to reconsider. He wasn't carrying his pistol and without knowing who and how many might still be inside the building it would be a rash move to go in alone. But, if anything, coming this far had increased his resolve, so he moved round the corner and kept close to the wall as he made for the door.

He took the two concrete steps outside it, then paused to listen for any sounds from within. If there were any they were lost in the sound of the rain on the roof and in the drainpipes, so he put his hand to the doorknob and turned it gently, waiting to see if it stopped. It didn't. He felt the catch give and the door jerked inwards a little, as if badly hung.

Now he was committed. He opened the door wider and stepped forward, into a short corridor lit by a striplight; a pair of swing doors at the far end and one just to his left. The nearest one stood halfway open with a light on inside, so Hentze pushed it the rest of the way and stepped in quickly, ready to speak if there was anyone there.

The room was unoccupied; a stripped-out office lit by a single bare bulb. On the floor were two mattresses with sleeping bags on them and various personal possessions scattered around, but Hentze didn't pause to inspect anything. Instead he backed out into the corridor again and moved quietly to the doors at its end.

The swing doors would open into the old garage space itself, he knew, and although he'd never been in there he had an idea of the size it must be. How many people were inside? Doing what? He paused for a moment, then pushed the doors inwards and stepped boldly through.

Under twin rows of fluorescent lights the workshop echoed with the sound of the rain. Some of the equipment from its former use still remained: the posts of a car lift; an empty tyre rack along one wall; an oil-stained bench and a metalwork lathe. But what stood out most because of its incongruity was a white bedsheet fastened to the far wall in front of a tripod, a video camera and two mounted lights.

Not far from this a woman in her late twenties was sitting in a camping chair, engrossed in a laptop, which was balanced on her knees. She was dressed for the cold in a large parka coat and Hentze had taken two steps into the workshop before she sensed his presence. When she did she glanced up and then did a double take when she realised that he was a stranger. Quickly she snapped the laptop shut and started to rise.

"I'm a police officer," Hentze called, raising his voice over the din of the rain. "Stay there please. Are you alone?"

He was already crossing the space towards the woman, who continued to rise, but was hampered by the computer.

He reached her before she could fully stand up and because she was still off balance he was able to push her back into the seat. Ignoring his instinct for courtesy, he kept a hand on her shoulder, firm and controlling. In response the woman spoke quickly and belligerently in German, aggrieved and protesting. Hentze took no notice.

"*Polizei*," he said, cutting her off. "*Polizei, okay?*"

He glanced quickly round again but there was no sign of anyone else in the workshop. Satisfied, he let his attention focus on a pair of flimsy wooden tables a couple of metres away. One of them was cluttered with used coffee mugs, some papers and general detritus, but the other was bare except for four mobile phones. Each one was laid out on a separate piece of paper, on which was a written a different six-figure phone number.

There was a significance to this, that was easy to see, but when the woman shifted and tried to free herself from his grip Hentze looked away.

"*Sprechen sie Englisch?*" he said. He took his hand from her shoulder and stood back a little.

"*Nein. Deutsch.*"

"*Was ist das?*" he asked, gesturing to the phones. It was about as much German as he knew.

In reply the woman launched into a diatribe of protest, gesturing angrily to go with the words. It was cut short, however, when the swing doors and the Judas gate in the building's main entrance simultaneously crashed open, followed a split second later by a sudden influx of men in black tactical gear, submachine guns unslung.

"Armed officers! Armed officers! Stay where you are! Do *not* fucking move!"

In the time it had taken to manhandle Hentze to the back wall of the garage and check the ID from his pocket, the German woman had been spread-eagled face down on the floor and searched. Then her hands had been bound and she'd been hauled to a sitting position and told not to move. The instructions were all given in German, Hentze noted.

Beyond this activity two men in civilian clothes who had entered the building after the others were now at the wooden table. They carefully placed the mobile phones into a container much like a cooler box, with thick sides and a locking lid. When that was done one of the men took the container away while the other came over to Hentze.

The man spoke in Danish – was Danish; a rotund face, heavily freckled. "Kriminalassistent Hentze?"

"Yes," Hentze confirmed. "Who are you?"

The man ignored the question. "You're free to go. Please report directly to your superior officer at the police station."

Hentze shook his head and indicated the woman. "I need to know by what authority that woman has been detained, where you intend to take her and what crime she's accused of."

"You'll have to take it up with your superiors," the freckled man said. "Leave now please. That is not a request."

Outside Hentze had anticipated more of a circus. Instead when he stepped out of the garage there were only two cars – dark-coloured Volvo estates – and a windowless van. They blocked access to the garage building and two black-clad men with submachine guns stood by as sentries. They didn't look round as Hentze emerged and went past them to where Karl Atli Árting was standing beside his patrol car on the approach road.

"Hjalti, are you okay?" Karl Atli asked, glancing uncertainly at the building. "What's going on?"

"Security services," Hentze told him. "Listen, has there been anything on the radio – any other incidents?"

"Yeh, five minutes ago," Karl Atli nodded. "There was a report of an explosion at the west harbour just as I got here. I wasn't sure where you were but when this lot arrived…"

"Okay. Try and get Annika on the radio, will you?" Then his phone rang. It was Remi Syderbø.

"You need to come back to the station," Remi said as soon as Hentze answered.

"Listen, there's been some sort of incident at the west harbour," Hentze said. "And if—"

"I know," Remi cut in. "This is serious, Hjalti. That's why you need to come back here. Right now."

Despite his personal inclination to do otherwise, Hentze recognised the grim tone in Remi's voice. "Okay, I'll come now," he said.

He rang off and turned back to Karl Atli who was still listening for a response on his radio. "Annika's not replying."

"Okay, come on," Hentze told him. "I need a lift to the station."

Karl Atli drove quickly while Hentze tried Jan Reyná's mobile number. It went straight to voicemail.

He thought for a moment, then turned to Karl Atli. "Listen," he said. "I need you to do something for me. As soon as you've dropped me off go to the AWCA house at Fjalsgøta 82. Rosa's there with a Dutch girl called Veerle. Take both of them to the Runavík station and wait there until you hear from me."

"Runavík?" Karl Atli looked at him questioningly.

"Because there'll be no one else there," Hentze told him. "Veerle is a key witness in the Erla Sivertsen case and there's a chance that someone will want to stop her telling us what she knows. We need to prevent that – to protect her – so when you get to Runavík, stay there until I tell you different, okay? Stay off the radio and don't let anyone talk to Veerle or take her away, not even if the Chief Prosecutor turns up."

"But if—"

"It's my responsibility," Hentze told him. "A direct order, okay?"

"Okay," Karl Atli said, although he still didn't seem overly happy.

"Okay, good. You can drop me off here."

Karl Atli stopped the car on the corner of Djóna í Geil gøta opposite the grey police building and Hentze got out quickly. "Fjalsgøta 82," he said again before closing the door. "As fast as you can."

50

INSIDE THE STATION THE STAIRWELL ECHOED WITH CLATTERING feet, going up and coming down, but on the the third floor Hentze found the CID corridor as quiet as normal for that time of night. It surprised him, given what seemed to have occurred, and he walked briskly to Remi Syderbø's office.

The door was open and Remi was on the phone, saying little but listening carefully with a serious frown on his face. As Hentze entered, Remi said, "Okay, I understand. Yes." He rang off and gestured Hentze further in. "Tell me what you know," he said without any preamble.

Hentze took a second to regroup his thoughts, then told Remi as briefly as possible what had occurred. He went as far as the security forces breaking into the garage but didn't mention his instructions to Karl Atli regarding Veerle Koning.

"Right," Remi said when Hentze came to a stop. "And you've heard there was an explosion at the harbour about ten minutes ago?"

"Yeh, just," Hentze nodded. "Do you know any details?"

"No, but we have to assume it's connected to what you found – especially as the national security service has closed off the area." He gestured at the phone. "That was the Commander. We're instructed to comply with all security service instructions for the duration of this emergency."

"Which emergency?" Hentze asked. "The explosion or something else?"

Remi shook his head as if the distinction didn't matter. "Apparently counter-terrorism have several operations in progress across the islands. That's all I know, except that Hans Lassen is going spare in the operations room. He's got patrols being held back at the harbour and reports coming in of men with guns at Runavík and on the approach to the Northern Isles Tunnel. I hope, though I'm guessing, that they're security forces and not something else."

"Have you called anyone in – from our department, I mean?"

"Only Oddur so far. Dánjal was on duty anyway and—"

His phone rang again and he picked it up straight away. "Yes?"

Remi listened for several seconds, face cast in a deepening frown. "They're taking them to hospital?" he asked in the end. "Okay, I'll get someone from uniform to be there – no, there's no point. Yeh, bring him here."

He hung up.

"That was Dánjal. He's at the west harbour. Annika Mortensen was hurt in the explosion. It sounds as if she was trying to catch one of the Alliance protesters with a petrol bomb and it went off."

"Shit – how badly hurt?"

"Burns; that's all the Danes will say. Also, Jan Reyná was

detained with another man, but he's being released."

Hentze nodded, already taking out his phone. "I'll call some people I know in the hospital ED. They'll tell me how Annika is whether the Danes like it or not."

When your hands have been zip-tied by a professional it hurts for the first two or three minutes, then you start to lose sensation below your wrists. After fifteen minutes I couldn't feel my hands at all – not even if they were still there. I couldn't check because the guy who'd fastened the zip tie round my wrists was a pro and they always make sure your hands are behind you.

There was no point in complaining, though, even if there'd been someone to complain to. The guys in black tactical uniforms and masks were – at the least – anti-terrorist squad, perhaps special forces, and neither would give a damn about my discomfort. All they're ever interested in is making sure you're incapable of pressing, pushing or releasing anything that might make something go bang.

To that end I'd also been thoroughly and roughly frisked and my mobile, wallet and keys had been taken away. My only small consolation was that I hadn't been hauled off and thrown in the back of a van with a hood over my head like Lange, the man I'd been holding when the tactical squad had arrived.

So I sat awkwardly in the back of an unmarked car and tried not to rest my weight on my tied hands. From this sideways position I watched with a limited view as black-clad figures came and went with brisk efficiency, and then as two ambulances arrived and were allowed through the blockade on the road. Their crews carried rucksacks and bags quickly towards the harbour jetties, but then I couldn't see any more. I still didn't know how badly Annika Mortensen had been hurt, but I guessed that she must have been injured from the fact that there were two ambulances. The woman she'd been chasing when the petrol bomb exploded was probably the worse off. I hoped it was that way round, anyway.

Finally, about five minutes after the ambulances had arrived, a woman wearing what looked like a police jacket but bare of insignia approached the car with a tall man whose face was still masked. The rear door of the car was opened and the woman looked in. She was about forty and very brisk. "Mr Reyná, you can get out now."

That was easier said than done without working hands, but once I'd shuffled along the seat and got my feet in the doorway the tall guy reached in without ceremony and hauled me to my feet. As soon as I was upright he turned me around, then I heard a *snip* and felt the release of my wrists.

"*Takk*," I said with relief. He said nothing, just stood there. The rain hadn't stopped, but it was slackening off, and now that I was out in it again I felt cold.

The woman seemed to wait for a prescribed time while I refamiliarised myself with my hands, then she shifted. She had the dry, pragmatic air of someone who had a long list of tasks to carry out. "For the moment this area is restricted," she said. "So you will be escorted to the barrier and passed into the authority of the local police force. They will wish to ask you some questions. You will not speak to or try to communicate with anyone else until you have been released by the local police. Do you understand this?"

It was a *pro forma* speech so I nodded. "Do you know what happened to Annika Mortensen, the police officer I was with?"

The woman considered that briefly. "She has some injuries, but they are not a danger to life."

"And the girl she was chasing?"

She wasn't going to go that far. "You may be told more information by the local police. They will also return your personal possessions. Now…"

She gestured across the car park towards the road where Annika and I had left Hentze's car and the guy beside me shifted as an additional hint. I started moving and he followed, to my left and slightly behind, as I took the shortest course towards the blue lights from two patrol cars. All the while my hands were throbbing back to painful life; pins and needles pulsing through them, intense and burning.

My escort didn't say anything but a couple of yards from the railing at the edge of the car park he stopped and watched me walk on until I was met by Dánjal Michelsen, one of maybe half a dozen people – both uniformed and plain-clothed – standing guard.

"Jan, are you okay?" Dánjal asked.

"I'll live." I ducked under the railing.

"You have to come with me to the station," Dánjal said flatly. I knew he'd been given an order.

"Yeah, okay," I said, looking round. "Is Hjalti here?"

"*Nei*. I'm just told to take you to the station." He glanced back in the direction I'd just come. "No one knows anything," he said bleakly. "Only that something is really fucked up."

The atmosphere in the station on Yviri við Strond was one I recognised: tense and pressured. I'd been confined to an office on the third floor and when people passed the window they were all moving briskly and their expressions were set. In situations like that there's always the thought at the back of your mind that if things are like this now, how much further might they go?

Dánjal Michelsen had left me saying he'd try to find out what was happening and come back when he knew. I didn't see him again that night. Instead a young uniformed officer came in a few minutes later, asked if I'd like coffee and went off to make it when I said that I would. He had the look of someone who was grateful to know what was required of him, even if it was only making a coffee.

Finally, after an hour of impotent boredom whose only distraction had been the slow drying out of my jeans, Hentze arrived. He was carrying a plastic evidence bag with my possessions in it and as he handed it to me he gestured to the door. "Can you come with me?" he said. Seeing him in proper light for the first time that evening I realised he looked tired: worn down and weary.

We didn't go far. Three offices along the corridor he unlocked a room and led the way in. I saw immediately that details of Erla Sivertsen's murder were written up on whiteboards, along with photographs and a timeline. The photos jolted me for a moment. She'd been someone I knew, albeit briefly.

"What's happening?" I asked Hentze. "Is there any news about Annika?"

"Yeh, she's okay," he said with some relief. "She has some small burns but she will be all right. From what we can tell the girl she was chasing had a petrol bomb, but when it went off Annika was still far enough away for most of the fire to miss her."

"And the girl?"

He shook his head. "Not so good. She has second-degree burns on her face and neck. They also think she may have damaged her lungs."

"They were bombs for definite, then? I only got a brief look."

"Yeh. The security people are only saying 'improvised explosives' but, yeh, petrol mixed with diesel and oil is what we think."

He shifted then, as if he'd already stayed longer than he'd intended. "Do you need anything? I have to see someone, but then I'll come back."

"No, I'm okay. But just so I know, am I under arrest?"

He shook his head. "No, not so much. But upstairs would like to know where you are – until we know more. You may be a witness."

"Okay," I told him. "I won't go anywhere."

51

REMI SYDERBØ MET HENTZE AT THE STAIRWELL AND THEY WENT
up to the fifth floor.

"Uniform are missing two people," Remi said. "Karl Atli
Árting and Rosa Olsen. The GPS shows Karl Atli's car at
Runavík but he isn't responding to the radio."

Hentze shook his head. "I told him not to. They have the
woman from the Alliance house with them: Veerle Koning.
I wanted to keep her out of the way in case the Danes were
looking for her."

Remi frowned. "Why would they be?"

"Because she has information about Erla Sivertsen's
movements on Saturday evening. They weren't as we were
told. Veerle was being abused by her boyfriend – a man called
Drescher – and Erla found out. Now Veerle says she thinks
Erla may have confronted Drescher about the abuse."

"And that makes you think Drescher could have killed
Erla?"

"I don't know," Hentze said. "If nothing else, it gives us a new
line of enquiry – but only if we can get a statement from Veerle
and then interview Drescher without the Danes interfering. I

don't know where he is, but I think there's a good chance he may be one of the people the Danes are out looking for."

Along the fifth-floor corridor most of the office lights were on, despite a strange absence of people. It felt as if everyone had been summoned away, which of course they might have been, Hentze thought. Who knew how many briefings and meetings had been called because of what had happened tonight?

For the second time in two days Hentze and Remi entered Andrias Berg's office, but this time Remi Syderbø wasn't dismissed. Instead he and Hentze were waved to two chairs and it was Berg's turn to stand, leaning on his desk. In the same chair he'd occupied before the national security man, Munk, was examining his fingernails, as if the time this was taking was already wasted.

"This will be brief," Berg said, when Hentze and Remi were seated. "It's simply to apprise you of the current situation."

He looked to Munk, who now dismissed his nails and raised his eyes to the two seated officers.

"As you know, some members of the AWCA organisation have been arrested for terrorist offences in the last couple of hours," Munk said colourlessly. "These people are part of a radicalised splinter group who used the Alliance for cover. This group style themselves as *Defend '86*, or just *'86*, which is a reference to the date of the international ban on commercial whaling. As a group in their own right they've been on our radar for some time, but when it became known that they planned to infiltrate the Alliance protests in the Faroes we took a greater interest. To that end we've had a covert officer lodged with them for more than a year. He was able to get close to the ringleader and establish their intention, which was to destroy boats used in the whale drives, or simply any boats from the whaling locations."

"You say *he*," Remi said. "So this was not Erla Sivertsen?"

"No."

"But she *was* working for you."

Munk conceded to this with a small nod. "In an auxiliary capacity."

Hentze shifted. He hadn't been distracted by the side line. He said, "If you knew or suspected what the '86 group's targets would be, why did you wait until they were driving round the islands with petrol bombs before taking action? Why didn't you arrest them before?"

Munk considered this unhurriedly. "I'm not going to debate operational procedure with you," he said. "Our intelligence sources led us to think that Defend '86 might have had another agenda – another target – and access to other material. If so, the impact of their actions would have been much greater: politically, economically and environmentally. Therefore we waited until we could be sure of seizing all their materials and arresting everyone involved in one operation."

In his head Hentze ran through the list of places where there'd been reports of arrests and tried to think of possible targets that would have had the impact Munk was implying. The realisation came to him when he remembered there'd been an incident at Runavík.

"You thought they were after the oil rig," he said. "The *Titan* in Skálafjørður. Yes?"

Munk allowed that with a slight dip of his chin. "It was possible, yes."

"And this *other material* you thought they might have: was that explosives? Was that what you thought?"

Munk wouldn't be drawn. "We're satisfied now that the group only had improvised explosive devices," he said.

"*Now*, yes," Hentze said. "But did you know it *before* they set off round the islands?"

Munk was unmoved, beyond a slight pursing of his lips. "As I said, I'm not going to debate operational tactics. The fact is, we're facing a new kind of threat. Even for those who aren't motivated by religion, it's now become acceptable for radical groups such as Defend '86 to put the action before self. As long as they've made their statement for broadcast on the internet it doesn't matter whether they are caught or killed. Even if they fail, the fact that they've shown such a disregard for themselves is its own message."

Hentze remembered the video camera and white sheet set up in Gregersen's garage. He said, "Are you saying they *want* to be caught?"

"No," Munk shook his head. "I'm saying that the *true* radicals don't care. That's something they've learned from the jihadists. Of course, out here that may not worry you so much, but in Denmark, after the Copenhagen shootings, we take it seriously."

"We still take murder seriously," Hentze said flatly. "And in connection with that I believe one of the men from this Defend '86 group, Lukas Drescher, could be a suspect for the killing of Erla Sivertsen. Is he one of those you've detained?"

Munk nodded. "He is. Commander Berg has, or will be given, a full list of the detainees."

Hentze turned to Andrias Berg, but as if he suspected what Hentze might say, Remi cut in first. "I'd like to interview Drescher," he told the commander. "I'd also like to take a statement from Herre Munk's undercover officer for any corroborating information he has."

Berg inclined his large head. "Drescher can be interviewed in relation to the murder inquiry, of course. His terrorist activities are quite separate."

"And the undercover officer?"

Berg passed that to Munk with a look and the Dane made a studied and lazy show of thought before appearing to reach a decision.

"Yes, all right," he told Remi. "You may speak to the officer concerned, but only to provide clarification. It will not be recorded and any information he provides will not be admissible in court. You can have a few minutes, then he will have to go."

"Where?"

"To be with the other Defend '86 members," Munk said, as if it was obvious. "For the moment he is still working with them."

Remi and Hentze walked back along the deserted corridor in silence until they were in the stairwell again.

"He already knows what happened to Erla," Hentze said then.

"Munk?"

"Yeh. If he didn't he wouldn't have agreed to this."

"Well, let's not look a gift horse in the mouth, shall we?" Remi said. "You got what you wanted, which is more than I expected."

"You thought they'd close the whole thing down?"

"I thought they might try."

"You've caught Oddur's disease," Hentze said.

"Yeh, well, we'll see."

As a place near at hand, but one that would be unused at this hour, Hentze had walked the short distance down the road to the department gym. He was heartily sick of all this underhand nonsense, but if it meant they could just move things forward he was prepared to go along with it.

Now, in the recreation room at the back of the building, he paced and waited until Remi Syderbø opened the door, standing aside as he did so to usher in a man in his thirties. The man was bearded, dressed in black, with a spectacular bruise on his left cheekbone and another, or perhaps the same one, which reached up to his eye, half closing it. He was carrying a bottle of water and a blister pack of paracetamol.

"This is Peter Jessen of the security services," Remi said to Hentze, using Danish. He closed the door.

"Actually, I'm a police officer," Jessen corrected, but without any real feeling on the matter. He looked round the room with the same lack of interest, then moved to a chair and sat down heavily, as if he'd been on his feet for some time.

"Ah, okay. Sorry." Remi acknowledged the distinction,

then looked to Hentze. "We only have a few minutes, so you'd better go ahead."

Remi backed off a little to lean on the pool table while Hentze drew a plastic chair closer to Jessen and sat down.

"What can you tell us about Erla Sivertsen?" Hentze said. "Was she also national security?"

Jessen freed a couple of paracetamol from the blister pack and opened his water bottle. "No. She was only approached when it became clear that Defend '86 were going to infiltrate AWCA. She agreed to help because she thought it was the right thing to do."

"So what *was* her role?"

Jessen swallowed the tablets. "She was my link back to command," he said. "Lukas Drescher was paranoid about security – checking our phones and computers – so if there was information I needed to pass I gave it to Erla and she handed it on. Drescher didn't pay any attention to her, only those in the group."

"And Lukas Drescher is the leader of Defend '86?"

"This branch of it, yeh." Jessen nodded, then checked his watch. "Listen, what you really need to know is about Saturday, right? When Erla died."

"Yes," Hentze said.

"Okay. Well, I don't know all the story so you'll have to fill in the gaps, but the first thing I knew was a phone call from Lukas at just after ten thirty that night. He tells me I've got to come now to the house on Fjalsgøta: it's urgent, he says. I get there ten minutes later and Lukas lets me in. He's shaking – like he's wired – and he says there's been an accident and Erla is dead. When I ask where he takes me out on the back terrace and Erla is there, lying on the ground. Lukas has covered her with a piece of plastic sheet but I go and look and check that she's not still alive and then I ask him what happened."

Jessen paused to take another short sip from his water bottle, then refocused again. "What he tells me is that he came back to the house and found Erla looking in his room – the room he shares with Veerle. No one else is there and there was an argument, he says. They shouted at each other, some names were called, then Erla goes outside for a smoke. He told me then that he thought Erla could be an informer – a spy – but when he went to ask her about that there was another argument and she fell – tripped – and hit her head. Next thing she is dead."

"Did you believe him?" Hentze asked.

Jessen shook his head. "Some of it, maybe, but I know he's not telling the truth about Erla searching his room. She wouldn't have done that; there was no reason to. And I've seen how he looks at her, too – when he thinks she won't notice."

"You mean he might have had a sexual interest in her?"

"Sure, why not?" But as soon as he said it Jessen waved it away as if it was beside the point. "Listen, whatever had happened, Lukas knew he was deep in the shit. He says if he's questioned – if the others are questioned – the plans for direct action will be gone. So what can we do, he asks me. How do we fix it so the plan won't be ruined?"

"And what *did* you do?" Hentze asked.

"I helped him of course. I said I'd take her body away and

make it look as if someone else has done it. So we put her in the boot of her car and then I told Lukas to give me his coat and his jeans so there couldn't be any evidence of contact. After that I told him to go into town to find the others and make an alibi. He's to have some drinks, stay out late, and by the time he gets back it will all be fixed. Then I took the car and drove it away."

Hentze considered that for a moment. He knew what had happened then – or at least, he could guess – but for the sake of clarity, he said, "Did you take her body to Húsavík or did someone else arrange that?"

Jessen shook his head. "No, that wasn't me. I called my control for an emergency meeting. That was the procedure – do you know a lake beside route 12 to Gamlarætt?"

"Yes, Stóratjørn."

"Right. Well, there's a small shed there – a wooden hut. It was a prearranged place to go if something went wrong."

"Who did you meet? Was Munk your control?"

Jessen shook his head, to indicate that he wasn't going to give any names. He looked at his watch and then he stood up. "I have to go. Is there anything else?"

Hentze stayed seated. "Did you use Erla Sivertsen's murder to get closer to Lukas Drescher?" he asked.

"Sure, of course," Jessen said, as if it was self-evident. "He hadn't let me get very close until then, but that got me right in. That's why there was only one explosion tonight."

When Hentze made no response to that Jessen looked away. He gave Remi a nod, then made for the door. He had it partly open before he turned back to Hentze. "What was the name of that lake again, with the hut?"

"Stóratjørn."

"Okay," Jessen said with a nod. "And just so you know – it wasn't my idea, the way her body was left. I'm still a police officer and I liked her."

Then Jessen went out and Hentze caught a glimpse of someone waiting beyond the door before it closed. There was a brief sound of footsteps, then nothing else.

By the pool table Remi Syderbø shifted and frowned. "What was all that about the lake?"

"I don't know," Hentze said dispiritedly. "But if we believe what he says then there's no question about who killed Erla."

"*Should* we believe him, do you think?"

"What difference does it make?" Hentze said, standing up. "Even if it's true, we can't use him as a witness. So unless Drescher admits to the murder we're no better off."

Remi tried to remain positive. "The forensics may help, now that we know who to look at. And Drescher's going to be facing terrorism charges as well, so…"

"So the murder doesn't matter?" Hentze said bitterly, but immediately cancelled it with a gesture. "Sorry. You know what I mean."

"Yeh." Remi assessed him for a moment. "Listen, go home," he said. "You were out half of last night and there's nothing we can do till all the detainees have been processed and Munk's people have decided who's going to deal with them. We'll interview Drescher tomorrow and go from there. Okay?"

"Okay," Hentze acceded. He rubbed his eyes for a

moment. "Do you know if they've lifted the cordon at Skálatrøð yet?"

"I don't think so. Why?"

"My car's still there. It doesn't matter. I'll get a lift from someone."

52

"WHERE'S YOUR CAR?" HENTZE ASKED.

I'd told him before, but that had been a while ago. "By the east harbour," I said. "Why – need a lift?"

"*Ja*. If I drive myself I might fall asleep."

"The adrenalin's worn off."

"Yeh, or the coffee," he said. He held the door of the incident room open so we could leave.

Outside in the chilly, after-rain air Hentze struck up a brisk pace, as if exercise would revive him. "The security services or counter-terrorism have nine people in detention," he told me. "Five from the Alliance and four others who came to the islands in the last few days. They call themselves Defend '86. They're some sort of radical group using the Alliance as a disguise to plan direct action or... I don't know what. They all seem mad."

He shook his head, as if the whole thing was beyond his comprehension, which I knew wasn't the case, but he needed to get it out of his system. That's what I was for.

"Anyway," he went on after a moment, "they had arranged for detonators or timers to be smuggled here and then they planned to destroy fishing boats used in the *grind*.

Here and in Runavík and other places."

"And they're sure they've got everyone involved now?" I asked. "There aren't some they could have missed?"

"No, they seem sure. They have an undercover police officer with the group: he would know."

"So it wasn't Erla," I said.

"No, she was his messenger back to the controller for the security operation – a Dane called Munk."

"So why did they leave it so late before moving in? If they had someone on the inside they could have arrested everyone together before they split up."

"Yeh, you would think so," Hentze nodded. "But I think the Danes were afraid that the '86 group had real explosives hidden somewhere, not just homemade devices of petrol. I think they waited until the last moment so they could be sure that they'd get it all. It's hard to know the truth because they don't tell us everything, and what they do say I don't trust."

We reached my car and I unlocked it.

"So how does all that affect the murder investigation?" I said. "I can see why the Danes didn't want anyone asking questions around the Alliance if they had an operation in place, but now that's over does it open anything up?"

"You looked at the boards in the incident room?" Hentze asked.

"Yeah. Wasn't that why you put me in there?"

"*Ja*. I'm not so clever today," he said wearily. "I'll tell you on the way."

"Where are we going?"

"A place called Stóratjørn."

* * *

It should have been clear-cut. The way Hentze laid it out, whether Lukas Drescher had killed Erla Sivertsen because she'd told him to stop beating his girlfriend, or because she'd refused his sexual advances wasn't important. What mattered was that Hentze now had a witness who could link Erla's death directly to Drescher.

And then it fell down. His witness – Jessen – had already disappeared back into his murky covert role and couldn't or wouldn't stand up in court. Without him all Hentze had left was a circumstantial case against Drescher, open to argument and denial. If you wanted to look at it in the worst possible light it might not even put Finn Sólsker in the clear.

"So why are we going to this lake?" I asked when Hentze lapsed into silence. By now we were out of town on the road to Gamlarætt. A few cars had passed us, going the other way, but now there was nothing but darkness and wet tarmac.

"Because Jessen mentioned it twice, very specifically. He also wanted us to know he was *ein politistur*, not a spook."

"You think he was dropping you a hint?"

"I don't know. Perhaps. Or perhaps I'm just getting too old for all this. Here, this turn on the right. Do you see it?"

The turn was on to a track of loose gravel, but that gave out after twenty yards and then it was just overgrown cinders. Beyond the beams of the headlights there was a complete absence of light: the sort of darkness you only get when you're miles from the nearest streetlamp or building. After a couple of minutes, however, the headlights caught the side of a hut surrounded by long, coarse grass. "That's it," Hentze said.

I turned the car on a patch of flat, muddy ground so that its headlights shone on the hut. It was a roughly made thing, its wood greyed with age. Sheets of now-tatty plywood had been nailed on its sides, covering what might have been windows, and the tin roof was more rust than metal.

I left the headlights on when we got out of the car. Hentze had a small torch, which he used as we moved round the hut, looking for a door. We found it on the far side but it was blocked by a stack of wooden pallets, waist high. It was also padlocked. Clearly no one was intended to enter, at least not easily.

Hentze assessed this for a moment, then shifted the light of his torch to the base of the hut where the floor beams were slightly elevated on pillars of breezeblock.

"Do you know what you're looking for?" I asked.

"*Nei*," he said, concentrating on what he was doing. "But something."

It was pointless to follow him as he went round the hut, so I used the light on my phone and searched back in the direction we'd come, squatting periodically to shine the light under the building. Apart from a couple of beer bottles and a soggy newspaper there was nothing until I heard Hentze's call from the far end of the hut.

When I got there he was down on his hands and knees, reaching as far as he could under the floorboards. He grunted and muttered a curse in Faroese, then shifted position a little and finally withdrew. From underneath he brought out a white bin liner, tied at the neck. He was wearing surgical gloves, I noticed.

"You think that's your *something*?" I asked.

"Maybe. Let's look at the car."

When we got there Hentze put the bag on the bonnet, then handed me the torch while he undid the knot of plastic. He folded the bag back far enough that I could shine the light on its contents and from what I could see it was a coat of some sort: rough cotton and military green; army surplus, perhaps. It was folded or rolled, but the collar was visible, and the upper part of a zip.

"Okay," Hentze said flatly. "I think this is it." He made no attempt to take the coat out to examine it, just looked for a moment longer then started to re-tie the bag. "Jessen told us that he took Drescher's coat and jeans away after the murder, so – if we're lucky – this belongs to Lukas Drescher and it will have Erla Sivertsen's DNA on it – maybe even her blood."

"And Jessen left it here why?" I asked, half guessing the answer but waiting to see.

"I think it was his insurance, for us," Hentze said. "As a police officer he knows that if he can't go to court as a witness then our case against Drescher is weak. But if we have something else in his place then maybe we have what we need to prove that Drescher killed Erla."

"So you're banking on Jessen being a *good* police officer," I said.

Hentze pulled the knot tight on the bin bag. "There are some," he said flatly. "Even in Denmark."

53

Friday/fríggjadagur

THE TURF-ROOFED PRISON BUILDINGS AT MJØRKADALUR merged with the hillside on which they were set. Beyond them, where the land fell away, there was a dramatic view down the valley to the mountain-framed waters of Kaldbaksfjørður; steel-grey and sullen in the overcast morning light.

It was a view that would be well suited to the paying guests of an hotel, Remi Syderbø judged as he and Dánjal Michelsen crossed the car park. It seemed slightly inappropriate, therefore, that it was bestowed only on the handful of Faroese prisoners who were confined at the expense of the state. Remi could think of far worse views to look at for a few months.

Of course, things would be different for the nine suspects arrested last night. For them the increased levels of security would mean segregation and special attention, and Remi doubted that they'd get much of a view. There was already talk that they would soon be transferred to a high-security unit in Denmark. The Faroese weren't equipped to deal with terrorism suspects, nor did they want to. In fact, as far as

Remi was concerned, the sooner they were gone – terrorists, protesters, security services, the whole bloody lot – the better he'd like it. There was no place for any of them here.

Half an hour later, in a clean, cream-painted room in the eastern wing, Remi and Dánjal sat at an immovable table across from Lukas Drescher. The disposable white forensic suit Drescher was wearing made him look even more pallid, except for the sulky dark circles under his eyes.

"We have been told that you have refused to have a lawyer here," Remi said, speaking in English; the only language they had in common. "Also a translator. Do you wish to change your mind?"

Drescher shook his head. "No." He glanced at Dánjal's phone on the table, set to record the interview. "I do not deny anything," he said then. "This was a morally justified action we made. You kill the whales, therefore we destroy your boats."

"Except that you didn't," Dánjal said flatly. "You didn't succeed."

"Maybe not this time," Drescher said, matching his tone. "But when it is known what has happened here, there will be others. The world sees your barbarism, your murder of innocent animals. There will be others who come to stop you."

He sat back on the plastic chair and folded his arms resolutely. "You may bring charges however you like now. Terrorism or whatever: it makes no difference to me. I have nothing to say until I am in the court. Then I will make my statement. We all will."

Remi considered that for a moment. "I think you have not understood," he said then. "We are not here to ask questions about what happened last night. That is for others. We are here to question you about the death of Erla Sivertsen, for which we believe you are responsible."

A flicker of uncertainty shifted briefly across Drescher's face. He shook his head. "I know nothing about that. I have already told this to other officers who come to the house, therefore I have nothing to say."

"I understand," Remi said. "But now we have more evidence from your girlfriend, Veerle Koning. She has told us how you beat her. She has also told us that Erla Sivertsen knew this and that she was angry about it. Therefore we believe that you killed Erla when she told you to stop hurting Veerle. Isn't that true?"

"*Nein*. It is a lie."

"Is it?"

Remi's glance towards Dánjal was only slight, but enough. Dánjal reached down beside the table and brought up a large paper sack. From inside it he took out a clear plastic evidence bag holding an army surplus jacket.

"Do you know this jacket?" Remi asked as Dánjal held up the bag. Drescher looked but said nothing.

"Is it yours?" Remi said.

"No."

"Oh? You have been seen wearing it and Veerle says that it is."

Drescher's expression hardened. "She is a liar. I don't know it. Where is it from?"

"It was found in a hiding place," Remi allowed. "Not such a good one, which is bad luck for you. However, with DNA tests I think we can prove it is yours, and also that the blood we have seen on the sleeve comes from Erla Sivertsen. Do you have anything to say about that? Do you wish to deny it, or will you say, perhaps, that you killed Erla Sivertsen for your cause?"

For a couple of seconds Drescher seemed undecided, but then his stance hardened. "Fuck you, policeman. You think to talk about murder will weaken our fight against you? *Nein*. I will not talk to a whale killer – any of you."

Remi Syderbø was unmoved. "Very well, that is your right," he said. "And in that case we will leave you to the Danes – for the moment, at least."

He gestured to Dánjal, who stopped the audio recorder on his phone and put it away. Remi stood up and crossed the room to rap on the door.

"By the way," he said, turning back to Drescher. "We are not all whale killers here; just as not all of your organisation are woman killers either. Out of all of us only you, eh?"

I was eating breakfast when Tove Hald called the next morning.

"I think I can find an address for Rasmus Matzen," she said.

It took me a second to work out who she was talking about until I remembered the Colony commune. "A current address?" I asked.

"*Ja*, I hope so. Four years ago there was a TV documentary

454

made about the commune societies and a man called Rasmus Matzen was interviewed at his home in Denmark. The documentary doesn't give the address, but it says that he now lives near Nakskov on the island of Lolland, so I think it would not be too hard to find him. Would you like me to try to locate his address?"

"Sure," I said. "If it's not stopping you doing anything else. Where are you?"

"In Copenhagen."

"Don't you have better things to do, like studying?"

"Other things, sure, but not better. This is interesting to me. I will see what I can find from the local registrations and phonebook, then I will email you. And also with a link to YouTube so you can watch the documentary, although it's only in Danish."

"Okay," I said. "If you're sure."

"It will be the same rate of pay, yes?"

"Yes."

"Okay, then. *Bei*."

A little while later Hentze called. "I think you should come out to Múli," he said.

I drove down the rough track with the windscreen wipers intermittently flicking to clear the light, misty rain. There were swathes of sunshine in the distance, though, and for the last quarter-mile I could see the fire-ruined house on the higher side of the track. The stone gables still gave it the impression of wholeness until I got closer and saw that the rest of the structure was virtually gone.

There was a lonely-looking cop sitting in a patrol car beside the road, but apart from glancing up to see who I was, he did nothing. So I drove on, past the burned-out house, to stop behind Hentze's car and get out.

For a moment I couldn't locate him, but he must have been watching because there was a shrill, two-note whistle and I saw him with an arm raised a hundred yards away down the hill by the circular stone wall of a sheepfold. I waved back and started that way.

I followed the line of a shallow ditch down the slope, one of several that divided the areas of hay-cut grass into patches, and Hentze came a few paces up the hill to meet me. He looked less strained and better rested than he had yesterday: more the man of measure I'd come to expect.

"Hey," I said, coming to a halt. "I thought they'd have put you back on the murder case today."

He shook his head. "Not yet. Maybe later. Finn has been released this morning."

"He's in the clear?"

"Yeh, I think so. Veerle Koning confirms that the coat we found at Stóratjørn last night belongs to Lukas Drescher. It has blood on the sleeve so when we have it tested…"

I nodded. "Your man Jessen came through then."

"Not *my* man, but yeh, I would say so. Of course, it will still take some time to get everything in order, but I think we will manage it."

He seemed satisfied in his understated way: as close to pleased as he'd get, so I didn't push it any further.

"So what's going on here, then?" I asked.

"It's something I thought you should see because you're interested in this place," he said. "It's this way."

He gestured and turned to lead the way to the sheepfold, a dry stone enclosure of rough rocks, about chest-high and perhaps twelve feet across. There was a narrow entrance framed by two slabs of rock, which faced away from the sea.

"A man and his wife from Norðdepil came to look at the burned house this morning," Hentze said as we went. "To be curious. You know how it is. Then, when they have seen enough of the house, they take a walk and find this."

We'd come to a plastic sheet now, laid out on the ground a couple of yards from the sheepfold. Beside it there was an aluminium flight case – a forensic kit – and a camera, but that wasn't what Hentze was showing me. Laid out on top of the plastic there was a human skull and a long bone, plus several smaller bones, which could have been from a hand.

Hentze took a pair of surgical gloves from his pocket and handed them to me. "See what you think."

I put on the gloves, then squatted down to get a closer look at the skull. It was relatively light in my hands; adult-sized and missing its lower jaw. The bone was mottled with brown stains from age and exposure to damp earth, which still filled the eye sockets and nasal cavities, but there was less dirt on the cranium, as if it had been given a cursory clean. I turned it. There was no sign of trauma or fracture and after I'd looked for the nuchal crest at its base and then at the ridge above the eyes I said, "I think it's a female."

Hentze didn't reply so I upended it to look at the teeth.

They were all still in place and three at the back showed grey amalgam fillings.

"You've seen the fillings?" I asked.

"Yeh. So it's – she – is not ancient, not from hundreds of years."

"I wouldn't think so." I placed the skull back on the plastic and straightened up. "Where was it?" I asked. "Just out in the open?"

"No, over there, beside the sheep shelter." He gestured to the structure where a second plastic sheet was laid out, and now that I looked closer I could see that part of the encircling wall had either fallen or been pulled down.

"Have you got the rest of the body?"

"Yeh, I think so."

I followed his lead across to the wall, which had been disturbed down to the level of the muddy, dark earth. It was obvious that someone had set about dismantling the wall because its stones lay scattered down the slope of the land where they'd rolled to a halt.

Hentze moved forward and knelt on the plastic sheet by the base of the wall, then gestured me to come in beside him. I did so and he used a torch to illuminate a cavity under the remaining stones. Emerging from the earth I could see the end of another long bone – a humerus, given that there was also part of the scapula beside it – and perhaps part of a rib. Which meant that the body had been placed face down, probably in little more than a shallow trench.

"You've seen people buried like this before, in England?" Hentze asked.

I made a so-so gesture. "Similar, yeah."

"So can you say how long you think she has been here?"

I shook my head. "Probably not less than ten years, but after that I'd be guessing. You'll get a better idea if you can match her dental records."

"Yeh, if we can find them."

We extricated ourselves and stood up. If Hentze was disappointed he didn't show it. "It can't be a natural death," he said. "Not buried here, not face down in the earth. You agree, as a homicide expert?"

"Well it's suspicious at least."

He gave me a look, as if he thought I was being unnecessarily coy. "There is something else I found while I was waiting for you to get here," he said, then stepped back to his forensic kit and held up a plastic evidence bag. "I found this in the grass of the ditch. Also some cigarette butts thrown away."

Inside the bag was an empty vodka bottle with no cap. It didn't look as if it had been outside for very long.

"I'll send it for DNA and fingerprints," Hentze said. "But I think if we find any they will belong to Boas Justesen: not just because he owns the land, but because of what else happened here."

"You mean the suicide and the fire?"

He nodded. "Justesen knew he had only a short time to live and I think that changes a man: even one who drinks so much."

"So you think he dug up the body because he wanted to clear his conscience before he died?"

"Yeh, I think that could be why."

I made a moue. "You're making up stories," I told him. "You don't even know how long she's been here."

"No, I have some idea."

He reached into his pocket and handed me a small Ziploc bag. Inside, still dirty from the earth, there were half a dozen cube-shaped plastic beads of different colours, all about quarter of an inch square.

"They were in the earth by the bones," Hentze said. "I only saw them because the light made a reflection, but I think they may be part of a bracelet. Look at the yellow one."

I turned the bag and pressed on the plastic to get a clearer view of the beads. I could see that the only yellow one had been impressed with some sort of letter or sign and when I turned the bag again I saw what it was: the circle and upside-down Y of the peace symbol.

"Isn't that the sort of thing that a hippy would wear?" Hentze said.

"Maybe," I said, then handed it back. "But in the sixties and seventies wearing something like that was probably as common as having a charity band now. It doesn't mean she was from the commune, if that's what you're thinking."

Hentze knew that as well as I did, but even so he still wanted to make the link. "I think she was," he said. "Otherwise it's too messy: too many things together. But yeh, you are right. It's still a story. We'll see."

Without a forensic team there was nothing more we could do except cover the evidence, so I helped Hentze put a plastic sheet over the gravesite and secure it with stones. Then Hentze bagged up the skull and the bones.

"I'm going back to England on Monday," I told him. "After that I'm going to Denmark."

The last bit was something I'd only decided during the drive out here but I'd made up my mind.

"Yeh? To do what?" Hentze asked.

"Some research."

"About your mother?"

"Yeah."

"Good. I think you should."

He picked up his flight case, but before we started back up the hill he turned to look down the slope of the fields to the sea. The rain had blown over now and the sun caught the metallic waters of Hvannasund in occasional flashes of brightness on the roll of the swell.

"It's a good place to be, eh?" Hentze said.

I remembered Magnus saying much the same thing after they'd buried Signar. This time I said what I thought.

"Better if you're above ground, not below it."

Hentze nodded, just once, then cast a solemn glance back at the sheepfold. "Yeh, I think you are right. Above the ground is always best, I would say."

AUTHOR'S NOTE

BY AND LARGE THE GEOGRAPHY OF THE FAROES IS AS IT'S described in the book. However, I have used some licence with the descriptions of individual buildings and locations, some of which are transposed from other places. I should also point out that, as far as I know, there has never been a commune at Múli.

The Faroe Islands are a small, close-knit community so I would like to emphasise that this is a work of fiction and that none of the characters or incidents portrayed here are based on real people or events.

ACKNOWLEDGEMENTS

I CONTINUE TO BE INDEBTED TO THE OFFICERS AND STAFF OF the Faroe Islands Police Department for all their assistance and help. For this book I am also particularly grateful to Svend Aage Ellefsen for his knowledge of commercial fishing, Ben Arabo of Atlantic Petroleum, Per Skov Christensen for his forensic expertise, and Dr Nick Leather for his medical advice. Needless to say, all errors are mine.

As ever, I must also express my immense gratitude to Jens Jensen for his hospitality, endless patience and help with all these books, and this time for taking me on a "short walk" up the mountain to Stakkurin.

Finally, and shamefully late, I have to say *stora takk fyri* to Emma Herdman who should take at least some of the blame for all this.

ABOUT THE AUTHOR

CHRIS OULD IS THE AUTHOR OF *THE BLOOD STRAND*, THE FIRST book in the Faroes series – which *Booklist* declared "a winner for fans of both Scandinavian and British procedurals" – as well as two Young Adult crime novels. He is a BAFTA award-winning screenwriter who has worked on many TV shows including *The Bill*, *Soldier Soldier*, *Casualty* and *Hornblower*. He lives in Dorset.